Terence Strong was brought up in south London, after the Second World War. He has worked in advertising, journalism, publishing and many other professions. His bestselling novels (which have surpassed 1 million sales in the UK alone) include THE TICK TOCK MAN, WHITE VIPER and DEADWATER DEEP. He lives in the south-west of England.

You are welcome to visit the author's website at:
www.twbooks.co.uk/authors/tstrong.html

# Cold Monday

## Terence Strong

**POCKET
BOOKS**

LONDON · SYDNEY · NEW YORK · TORONTO

First published in Great Britain by Simon & Schuster UK Ltd, 2004
This edition first published by Pocket Books, 2004
An imprint of Simon and Schuster UK Ltd

A CBS COMPANY

1 3 5 7 9 10 8 6 4 2

Simon & Schuster UK Ltd
1st Floor
222 Gray's Inn Road
London WC1X 8HB

www.simonandschuster.co.uk

Simon & Schuster Australia
Sydney

A CIP catalogue record for this book as available from the British Library

ISBN: 978-1-84983-259-5

Typeset by Palimpsest Book Production Limited,
Polmont, Stirlingshire

Printed and bound in Great Britain by
Cox & Wyman Ltd, Reading, Berkshire

For Princess,
with love

And huge admiration for
your courage and fortitude
in such terrible adversity

# One

'He'll be armed and dangerous. And he's fast, so you'll have to make a clean kill.'

The previous night I'd listened to Morgan Dampier's words very carefully. My life would depend on them.

'What's he packing?' I'd asked.

'A Browning automatic. Spring-loaded holster on his belt. He cross-draws right to left. I'm sorry, Ed, we can't jark it.'

I'd understood. 'Jarking' is army slang for tampering with weapons. And a tampered-with weapon on a corpse would make the police ask too many questions. The wrong sort. I didn't want that either.

Now, in the cold light of day after a sleepless night, I found the man waiting for me. He didn't know it, of course. He would never know that he was sitting there, just waiting for me to kill him. Until it was too late.

I felt a grim sort of satisfaction at seeing him there, exactly as predicted, at one of the aluminium tables on the pavement outside the snack bar on the King's Road in Chelsea.

But, as I watched him from the opposite side of the street, that satisfaction did nothing to quell my growing sense of trepidation. He was tooled up and I knew just how dangerous he would be if I got it wrong. My heart was pumping so hard that I could hear the blood rushing in my temples and a slick of perspiration was gathering on my palms.

It just confirmed what I'd already begun to realize. I'd been out of this game too long.

Cool it, Coltrane, cool it. Take a deep breath. Long and slow . . . and again. As my lungs filled, my mind began to clear. Look and listen, I told myself. Observe. You can't afford to make a mess of this one.

Although the sun was bright in the clear December sky, there was a sharp chill in the air. My target's only concession to this was a long woollen scarf wrapped round his thick neck with the ends stuffed into the front of his dark suit jacket. No overcoat, of course, and no hat. No self-respecting Serb male of his ilk would ruin his macho image by making concessions to the cold. In the icy badlands of Bosnia's mountains or on the fashionable streets of London, the nature of the beast remained the same.

'Yeah, animal you are, Leonid,' I murmured to myself. 'And it's time to put you down. Once and for all time.'

It didn't do to be an animal of habit when you were wanted for war crimes, even if you thought you'd got away with it. Even if you'd been crafty or clever enough to end up working for those who'd issued the arrest warrant in the first place. Because people so devoid of moral principles would only make use of you for as long as it suited them. Then they'd throw you to the wolves.

And one day one of those wolves would come stalking you. Someone like me.

I smiled to myself at that, and gave a small growl beneath my breath.

So don't make it easy for them, Leonid. Never stay under the same roof for more than a day or two. Don't have your own transport and never use a telephone, e-mail or the post to contact friends or family or anyone else important to your survival. Vary your routes of travel and your weekly timetable, and always assume you're under surveillance – because you probably are. It's tough, but it's the only way you're going to make it.

I viewed my quarry through gaps in the never-ending

crawl of traffic before starting to cross to his side of the street.

So Leonid had got it all wrong. The smug, arrogant bastard was staying with his family at the unsafest place of all, a British intelligence 'safe house'. Most nights he gambled and whored with the money that our government paid him, then returned home drunk to slap his wife around before dragging her into the marital bed. No doubt she was long conditioned to his behaviour by now and thought it a small price to pay to enjoy her husband's wealth and protection.

It's never ceased to amaze me what the partners of thugs consider normal, and even come to respect, in their men.

But his puppet masters knew all this detail and it offended what passed even for their moral principles. And, of course, they handed the information on to me as part of the briefing.

But his personal conduct hardly came as a surprise to me. I knew Leonid Rusjivic. We'd never met, but what he'd done seven years ago had ensured that I'd never forget him.

And since then I'd been trying to find him – and the others – for five years, on and off. Okay, unsuccessfully, but I'd learned a lot more about the bastard before the trail had eventually run cold.

I reached his side of the street and sauntered along the pavement towards the snack bar. To give Leonid his due, he didn't take long to notice me. I sensed him taking in my leather jacket and brown cords, my Ray-Bans, the professional's camera around my neck and the aluminium photographic equipment case I carried.

But it was an idle curiosity and he'd lost interest by the time I took my seat at a table about fifteen feet away from him.

I deliberately faced the other way, with my back to him, and placed the aluminium case on the table before I examined the menu.

The combination of glass and the polished chrome

surround of the snack-bar window reflected my own face back at me. A useful sort of face, maybe more careworn than it should have been for my thirty-nine years. A face with no particularly memorable feature. A face that an impressionist comic would die for. A blank canvas that the simplest form of disguise could transform. The sort of face that a dozen people would describe in a dozen different ways. As I said, a useful sort of face to have in this business.

And, beyond that face in the window, I had a perfectly reflected picture of the man I was going to kill.

A bored-looking waitress, black skirt vacuum-packed to her hips, emerged from the snack-bar door. She hovered at Leonid's table, shivering and irritated at having to leave the warmth of the interior. 'Yes?'

She didn't have to wait long: I could have told her what he was going to have. The same thing that he had at this snack bar every Friday when he waited for his wife to finish her shopping.

'Nachos with hot chilli sauce,' he confirmed, smiling up at her so that the sun caught his gold tooth. 'And don't forget the sour cream on the side, sweetheart.'

Her smile in return was as sour as the cream he'd ordered. She moved past him and across to me.

'Just a black coffee, please.'

The waitress turned away and in the reflection I saw Leonid's eyes following the sway of her hips as she returned indoors. Only then did he take a folded copy of the *Daily Star* from his pocket and spread it open at the racing pages.

I still couldn't really think of him as Leonid Rusjivic. Not that it was an unpronounceable name to me, because I spoke very passable Serbo-Croat and had done several tours of duty in the Balkans. Nevertheless it was the absurd code name that our SAS team had given him that stuck in my head.

Leonid had always been 'Tex-Mex' to me and would be until the moment he died.

Seven years earlier, Tex-Mex had been one of President Slobodan Milosevic's bully boys, a Bosnian Serb secret policeman who ran a small fiefdom in the mountains north of Sarajevo enforced by a bunch of Chetnik irregulars. He'd strut his stuff in camo fatigues and a battered straw stetson, with a bandolier of machine-gun rounds draped across his chest. His unkempt *bandido* moustache and his penchant for nachos with hot chilli sauce had clinched our nickname for him. And it had stuck, officially adopted by the Int boys.

In those days he exercised total control of a mountain valley through which one of the crucial arteries to various besieged cities passed. It was Tex-Mex's roadblocks and drunken thugs that controlled access by the UN relief convoys and the peacekeeping troops. His men allowed or denied passage through his territory of any of the opposing sides – the militias of the Bosnian Serbs maintaining the siege or the ragtag Muslim army which was trying to break it.

That also meant he controlled all trade, including that in weapons and ammunition as well as contraband alcohol, tobacco and narcotics. As you might imagine, nothing passed through his domain unless a hefty private tax was paid to Tex-Mex and his merry men, who acted under the so-called regional 'command' of an evil scumbag of a Serb secret police chief, Brigadier Milo Domedzic.

Although run by President Milosevic's men in Belgrade – and therefore by definition supposedly backing the Bosnian Serbs – we soon learned that neither Tex-Mex nor his boss had any real political or military allegiance to anyone but themselves. Horse-trading was generally the name of the game. Sure, priority was given to the Serb military, but only at a price. That price just became even more extortionate when they were dealing with the opposing Muslims. And, of course, the Muslims were far more likely to be shafted or double-crossed, one way or another. So no one in Belgrade could accuse Brigadier Domedzic or Tex-Mex of being disloyal or unpatriotic.

It was impossible to establish such complete domination of territory in the middle of a bloody and chaotic civil war without an unhesitating resort to brute force. And Tex-Mex certainly showed no such hesitation. His power was as absolute as his corruption. He wallowed in his fearful reputation among the local population and even among the warring militias. Stories of massacres and other atrocities on his patch abounded and reached UN intelligence units almost every day. Many of these were confirmed, at the time or much later, but few details ever reached the TV news programmes in Europe or America. Even by the disgusting standards of the Bosnian war, some of the events were just too sickening to allow into the cosy living rooms of ordinary families.

It was just one such incident that had shattered and changed my life for ever.

I no longer talked about it. I'd like to say I didn't even allow myself to think about it, but the truth was that I'd never stopped doing so. It was there with me constantly. I reckon a man's exceptionally lucky if a woman like Astrid comes into his life at all, let alone if he has the chance to be married happily to her – for however short a time.

I'd been married before but, despite having a son from that relationship, a boy who was turning out to be a lovely kid, it had been a mess. Nothing like my later relationship with Astrid.

I'd wished to hell that I could lay her ghost to rest, but you don't ever forget someone like Astrid or the moments you shared together.

Yet just a month ago I'd been kidding myself I'd started to do just that. In the five years since I'd left 22 Special Air Service Regiment with the dizzy rank of Warrant Officer, I'd spent too much time and my lifetime's meagre savings returning to Bosnia–Herzegovina to search for Astrid's killers: Brigadier Domedzic who'd ordered her murder, Tex-Mex who had so willingly carried it out, and Zoran Mihac who'd gleefully recorded it.

Of course, in the aftermath of the conflict when they were wanted for war crimes by the International Court in the Hague, they'd all gone to ground. No one was talking and every door of inquiry was shut in my face. I'd pressed on with my quest until the wrong sort of people started to take notice of me and it just got too damned dangerous.

Then last year, at an SAS reunion party at an hotel in Hereford, I'd bumped into Dampier.

'Eddie?' I'd turned at the sound of the familiar voice. 'Eddie Coltrane, you old bastard, it *is* you!'

Morgan Dampier had emerged flush-faced from a scrum of heavily drinking ex-soldiers. He was as dapper as always, but his Guards tie was askew and his gait a little unsteady.

I'd grinned at him. You might not fully trust Dampier, but you just couldn't help liking him. 'Christ, Morgan, I haven't aged *that* much, have I?'

He'd slapped me vigorously on the back. 'No, Ed, old son, it's just that I haven't ever seen you at one of these shindigs before.'

'Not really my scene. I don't like looking back, never have. But Joe Monk persuaded me to give this bash a try. Said he expected a lot of old faces to turn up.'

Dampier nodded. 'Still wasn't expecting to find you here. Thought you spent all your time in Bosnia nowadays.'

That had brought me up short. My trips to Bosnia had been private and I certainly hadn't advertised them. In fact I'd told absolutely no one about them. But then, I shouldn't really have been surprised. I'd tried to sound cool. 'See you're still keeping the same company, then, Morgan.'

He hadn't actually answered, just given a twist of a smile. Dampier wasn't and never had been SAS, but I sometimes thought that he knew every soldier who'd ever been in the Regiment. Dampier was with the 'funnies', but you were never sure exactly which one at any given time. I'd first met him when I was running a training course for the top-secret army outfit that's become known as 14 Intelligence Company, or 'The Det'. The Regiment's expertise was used extensively in preparing recruits for their extremely dangerous close-reconnaissance role in Northern Ireland.

'You know how it is, Ed. Every now and again your name pops up on the computer. Ah, there's old Eddie Coltrane . . . sniffing round in Bosnia again.' His smile had faltered when he saw the look in my eyes. 'Er, sorry. I – er – I suppose it's all to do with Astrid?'

'You know damn well it is, Morgan.'

'Of course – sorry. No luck then?'

'You know that, too.'

He'd had the good grace to look truly embarrassed. 'Shit, Ed. I'm making a pig's ear of this. Too much booze mixing with my antibiotics.' He gave a nudge-nudge wink-wink sort of gesture meaning he was still the cad-about-town he'd always been. 'I didn't want to give the impression people are spying on you. It's just that—'

'I know. Save the explanations.'

'I can tell you something, Ed.' Dampier lowered his voice to a conspiratorial whisper. 'You could be wasting your time. For a start that Serb police chief – er – Brigadier Domedzic . . .'

'Yes?' Suddenly I'd been all ears.

'Dead.'

My heart had sunk. Stupid, really, if he was dead. It was just that *I* hadn't killed him. 'I hadn't heard that.'

Dampier had nodded. 'Fucked his own kind one time too many. Someone with a sense of humour booby-trapped his lavatory. Blew him inside out.'

'When was this?'

'Couple of months ago.' Dampier could hardly have missed my keen interest. 'And as for the others—'

'Others?'

He'd shrugged. 'Tex-Mex. Mihac and the other thugs . . . They've all disappeared. I doubt you'll ever find them. They might well be dead, too. Fed to pigs, buried in quicklime or chucked down a well somewhere. Chances are no one would ever know. They'd all made a lot of enemies.'

'I don't work on assumptions.'

'Sure, Ed. But I just hate to think of you wasting your life. You know, your time and money going down the pan while you're chasing shadows.'

'Been reading my bank statements, Morgan?'

His smile had returned. 'I don't have to, Ed. I can imagine.' He'd drained his glass and took mine from me. 'C'mon, let me fill 'em up.'

And so we'd gone on to get totally blitzed that night, with me waking up the next morning in my hotel bedroom with a splitting headache and a girl nearly young enough to have been my daughter asleep naked beside me. I didn't even remember who she was. Only while giving her coffee before she sneaked out of my room did I discover that she'd been working behind the bar downstairs the previous evening. Her goodbye kiss was small consolation for the real-ization of just how far out of it I must have been. I hadn't been drunk like that for years.

Brooding over another mug of coffee and a cigarette, I'd suddenly realized that Morgan Dampier was right. I'd been in serious danger of going over the edge. The madness had to stop. As he'd said, I was probably chasing shadows anyway. Domedzic was dead and so, possibly, were Tex-Mex and the others. That or else they'd made sure they would never be traced.

Just then I'd almost heard Astrid's voice in my ear, saying, *'Time to stop, my love. It's time to let me go.'*

Yes, Dampier was right. Astrid was right. It was time to end this idiocy and get myself a life.

Now I looked up as the snack-bar waitress came through the door, carrying a tray. She dumped Tex-Mex's nachos and sour cream unceremoniously in front of him and, ignoring his lascivious leer, put down my coffee before scurrying back inside.

I looked at my watch. Eight minutes to go. Somewhere in a nearby side street two vehicles would be parked – a van and an old Nissan saloon – engines running, their drivers anxiously studying their dashboard clocks and the ticking minutes.

So Morgan Dampier had been wrong and in many ways I was now wishing that he hadn't been. Because in the year following our chance encounter at the Hereford hotel, I really had tried to put my life in order.

I'd cancelled my next planned trip to Bosnia and put in a call to Rob D'Arcy at IAP, an outfit that hired a lot of ex-SAS and other British military personnel for above-board overseas contracts. But, as I might have guessed, at the time all he had was mine-clearing work . . . in Bosnia! I tried a few other similar companies, but with the armed forces going into meltdown under Blair's New Labour, there were too many people chasing too few jobs. Perhaps fate was telling me that it was time to take a proper crack at Civvy Street.

There the situation was reversed. Too many jobs that no one wanted because either the pay or the hours were lousy. So I took one of those, finally landing a warehouse under-manager's job on the strength of my army quartermastering skills. At least I was well used to long and unsociable hours and the salary wouldn't have been that bad if only I hadn't already run up so many debts and had creditors baying at my heels.

At least the job had helped me keep my head above water

and, just a month ago, I had been looking forward to a couple of weeks' holiday. That was when Morgan Dampier had turned up again.

He'd arrived one evening unannounced at my cheap rented flat on the top floor of a dilapidated Victorian semi in a run-down street in Southwark. Since getting home from work, I'd just had time to kick off my shoes, loosen my tie and pour a stiff whisky when I heard the doorbell ring. Few people knew where I lived, so I expected it to be one of the neighbours I'd yet to meet after three months or one of the endless number of people trying to sell burglar alarms. That or the Jehovah's Witnesses.

I'd thrown open the door with a less than welcoming expression on my face.

'Ah, *not* pleased to see me,' Dampier had observed with a laugh.

The hallway light was a feeble unshaded bulb. 'Morgan?' I'd peered at him. 'What the hell are you doing here? Didn't know you even had my address.'

Another chuckle. 'Well, I didn't, but I know a man who had. And I was in the area so I thought I'd just pop in on the off chance to say hello to an old mate.'

I stepped aside to let him in. 'No one just *happens* to be in this area, Morgan, you lying bastard. People avoid it like the plague unless they enjoy being mugged. Still, it's good to see you anyway.'

He'd been quick to notice the whisky bottle on the coffee table. 'Started without me, I see.'

I'd moved through to the adjoining kitchenette. 'No soda, I'm afraid. Will water do?'

'Splendid, Ed, thanks.' He looked slowly around the room, taking everything in. 'Nice place you've got here. Very – er – minimalist.'

'Very – er – diplomatic,' I'd mimicked back, handing him his drink.

In my case minimalism wasn't a fashion statement, it just meant I didn't have any money. And, without any female guidance, my knowledge of interior decor erred distinctly on the side of functional after a lifetime spent in the military. I'd made an effort, though. Instead of following my natural instinct for white paint, I'd allowed the shop assistant to talk me into pale beige for the walls. With my colour sense that suggested the cheapest brown nylon carpet I could find, which was so full of static that I got a shock every time I turned on an electrical appliance. Not that there were many of those. A cooker and fridge-freezer in the kitchenette and a second-hand TV and music centre in the lounge. The sofa, chairs and flip-down dining table suite had been a bargain range from the Argos catalogue. At least they were all in a matching beech and blue finish, which I'd read somewhere was all the rage. There wasn't a wall picture or ornament in sight.

Dampier had thrown his raincoat over the arm of the sofa and sat down beside it. 'No woman in your life, then?'

'Meaning?'

'No woman would put up with a pad as bare as this.'

I'd grinned. 'I'm sure you're right.'

'So what happened to that floozie at the hotel after our last meet?'

'Believe it or not, Morgan, we never kept in touch.'

'Not to be the love of your life, then?' He must have seen the shadow pass behind my eyes then and realized his mistake. 'Sorry, Ed. Still keeping the candle alight for Astrid, I suppose.'

I hadn't answered – I couldn't. If I'd tried to speak, I'd have just cracked up. Even after all this time, when you think you're over the worst, it'll suddenly come and hit you when you're least expecting it. A careless word, a familiar tune, a forgotten memory unexpectedly flooding back . . .

Morgan had seemed to sense it. He'd cradled the tumbler in his hands and appeared to study it. He chose his words carefully. 'I understand, Ed, really I do. Astrid was special. Everyone thought so. I only met her the once, but – well – she made quite an impression.'

I'd realized he was struggling to say what he'd come to say. I cleared my throat. 'Yeah, Astrid was special. So?'

'You haven't been back to Bosnia?'

'You've been watching?'

He'd shaken his head. 'But someone always is – as you know.'

I'd swallowed the last of the whisky in my glass. 'No, Morgan, I haven't been back since we last met. I took your advice, remember?'

His smile had been uneasy. 'And you've buried the ghost?'

Our gazes had met and seemed to lock together. 'What do you think?'

He'd averted his eyes suddenly and stood up, as if desperately in need of fresh air and some excerise. Striding to the window, he stared down at the back garden several floors below.

'Do you know who I'm with at the moment, Ed?' he'd asked after a moment.

I'd lit a cigarette, wondering just where the hell he was coming from. 'I never have known who you're with, Morgan, ever. It's part of your charm. I'd guess the Ministry of Defence or the Foreign Office – or somewhere in between.'

He'd turned back to face me. 'Somewhere in between, Ed, that's about right. Part of my job is to commission people, trusted people for various black ops in the national interest.'

'Oh, yes?' I'd responded non-committally. I'd never been totally convinced that Morgan Dampier wasn't at least a partial Walter Mitty. The world surrounding intelligence and special forces seems to attract more than its fair share.

'Various deniable jobs for various departments of government, shall we say. I've done it for a while now. Interesting work.' He'd sighed a little wistfully. 'But now it's time for me to move on.'

'Yes?'

It had hardly been the third degree, but it brought a response that I wasn't expecting. Perhaps he'd just felt the need to unburden himself on someone. Someone who didn't matter in the great scheme of things. Me.

'You know I was with the FRU, the Field Research Unit in Northern Ireland,' he'd confided. I didn't *know* any such thing, but I wasn't surprised. The somewhat notorious FRU called themselves 'Fishers of Men' and ran all army agents and informants in the province under the auspices of the army's Secret Intelligence Wing.

Anyway, Dampier had gone on as though I knew all about his involvement. 'Well, the politicians are setting the dogs loose on us. High-level police inquiry into everything we got up to, no stone unturned. As if Number Ten and Whitehall knew nothing about it, of course. Anything to appease PIRA and keep them in this bloody joke of a peace process.'

I'd read some snippets in the Sunday papers. 'It doesn't surprise me, Morgan, if you're being hung out to dry. There's no honour any more, no respect, no loyalty. You know that's why I left the army.'

His smile had been terse. 'I seem to remember you made it pretty clear at the time. Upset a few sensitive souls who didn't want to hear the truth . . . Anyway, I've decided it's time to make myself scarce. Pastures new. There's a job turned up in the European Commission that looks like it'll suit my talents. I'll bury myself away in Brussels and hide behind one of those million unmarked bureaucratic doors.' The smile had faded quickly. 'It'll also offer me powerful protection against any inquiries by the British police.'

'Sounds like the right place to be,' I'd agreed. 'But what's this to do with you coming to see me? I take it there *is* a connection?'

He'd held out his empty glass for a refill. 'Observant as ever, Ed.'

'It doesn't take a genius.'

'My last commissioning job for my current employers – whoever they might be. Your name's cropped up in fairly exalted circles, old friends who remember your work in the province and Bosnia.'

I'd been sceptical. 'Didn't think I had any friends left in exalted circles.'

'Oh, yes. Not the fair-weather ones, but old school.'

Some ex–SAS officers somewhere, I'd guessed. 'What sort of commission? Abroad? Close surveillance?'

'Here in the UK.' He'd hesitated. 'And, yes, some close-surveillance work – er – but that's not quite all.'

'Spill it, Morgan.'

'It's a wet job.'

I'd laughed so hard that I spilt the whisky I'd just topped up. 'I take it that *is* a joke?'

He'd leaned forward and fixed me with his stare. 'I'm deadly serious.'

My humour had drained away instantly, to be replaced by a swelling anger. 'I thought you were supposed to be a friend, Morgan. I'm not *that* hard up.'

Dampier had sat back, still looking intently at me. 'Not fifteen grand hard up? That's not what I heard.'

I'd become really riled then. 'And just what did you hear?'

He'd looked suitably abashed and had shrugged. 'That maybe fifteen grand would get you out of the shit and give you a fighting chance to sort your life out.' He must have seen my second's hesitation and had pounced like the true professional he was. 'I think you should know who the target is that they have in mind for you, Ed.'

'Not interested, Morgan. Forget it.'

But there had been no stopping him then. 'Remember I told you Brigadier Domedzic was dead, and probably the others were too ... Well, I was wrong about the others. One of them's over here.'

He'd got my attention then all right. 'Who the hell is the target, Morgan?'

Dampier had said quietly: 'Tex-Mex.'

The memory of the way he'd dropped the bombshell into my lap brought me back to the present with a jolt.

I'd allowed my concentration to flag. I was staring at the image of Tex-Mex in the reflection of the snack-bar window, but only seeing Astrid. Wide-eyed and close-up with her lips parted in that infectious smile that would stay with me for ever.

Damn it, Coltrane, get a grip.

I squeezed my eyes hard shut until the image faded from the inside of my eyelids. When they opened again, I was back at the pavement table on the King's Road. It must still have been cold, but I felt like I had a fever. My heart was pumping hard and I could feel sweat gathering in the small of my back.

I glanced at my watch. Six minutes to go.

Casually I reached into my pocket and extracted the thin clear filament of fibre-optic flex, pushing its small plug-end into the receptor-jack hole in the photographer's aluminium case that I'd placed on the table. The thin cross-hairs and red laser pinpoint appeared in the right-hand lens of my specially adapted Ray-Ban sunglasses.

I shifted the position of my chair, as if getting away from the glare of the sun, until I now had a direct view of Tex-Mex's back. Then I nudged around the aluminium case on the table, so that the concealed 9mm barrel and the laser light above it were directly aligned within the cross-hairs on the centre of the target's spine.

The version of the weapon inside was specially modified

for close-quarters work. Rapid fire if necessary, but no full auto. Anyway, I intended to fire only a single round. The silencer and baffled outer casing were remarkably efficient in a noisy urban environment, and a battery-operated motor would suck back in most of the gunsmoke before filtering, deodorizing and dispersing it away through two outer vents in the base of the case.

Five minutes and thirty seconds to go. All set. I felt calmer now, my heart rhythm slowing to steadier half-second beats. My head began to clear, my awareness and vision sharpening and the sensitivity of my hearing increasing as though someone had turned up the volume on a television. Sounds rushed in from all directions at once, each demanding attention and analysis. The rumble of a London bus, the squeal of a taxi's brakes, the impatient hoot of some chinless wonder in a Porsche, the conversation of two Dutch tourists at another table . . .

Then an all too familiar voice. Tex-Mex's.

'Hey, Zeta, you spent all my money already!'

I looked up. Oh, shit! It was his wife, a tall, mean-faced blonde wrapped in an expensive coat with an astrakhan collar and matching hat. She was loaded down with carrier-bags and had their two kids in tow.

She was half an hour too early. I really didn't want to believe this; she never *ever* joined her husband before one-thirty! I cursed myself for not having thought about the possibility. Of course! This was no longer the usual Friday shop, it was the start of the pre-Christmas trawl.

Zeta laughed without humour. 'I may have spent all the money, Leonid, but I'm only halfway through the present list!' She dumped some bags on the chair next to him and put others on the ground. 'The shops are so busy you can hardly move . . . and I still haven't found anything for your mother.'

Tex-Mex had a mother. Christ, that was something to

make you think. She was probably a harmless old crone living in a poky flat in Belgrade and doting on her son, his picture in pride of place on the mantelpiece.

'Give yourself a break, Zeta. Join me for some lunch.'

*NO!* I screamed silently. If she and the children sat down I'd have to abort. The risk of killing or injuring them would be too great.

She shook her head. 'I've too much to do. I thought I'd just dump some of these bags with you before my arms drop off.'

Tex-Mex shrugged. 'No problem. Leave the kids too, if you want.'

The boy looked to be about ten, the girl a year or so younger. They were both snuggling up to him in a way that suggested he was a soft touch compared to their mother. He grinned at them, ruffling each one's hair in turn in a show of genuine affection.

God, I didn't need this. Top of the list of rules – never get to know your target on a personal level. Never spare the wife or girlfriend a moment's thought. Forget he has a mother and father of his own, or anyone else who'll be eaten up with grief at his passing. And certainly never watch him playing with his kids.

Zeta shook her head and reached for her offspring. 'No, Leonid, I've got to get them both new shoes. I'll be back in about an hour. You okay waiting here?'

He waved his newspaper and chuckled contentedly. 'No rush – I've plenty to read. Take care.'

Thank God for that, I thought as I watched Zeta walk away with the two children skipping at her side.

And just momentarily I thought how the fair hair that peeked from beneath the astrakhan hat could have been Astrid's, and the kids could have been ours. *Should* have been.

My gaze went down to the watch on my wrist. Now just one minute and thirty seconds to go to the diversion – *if* my masters were as good as their word. Because in special forces we all knew from long and bitter experience that you could never trust politicians and civil servants or anyone in the intelligence business – as Morgan Dampier had reminded me only the last time we'd met.

Even as I recalled his words, I felt the chill on the back of my neck. 'You can trust me, Ed, but a word to the wise. I've learned that when doing a job, it's smart never to do it at a time and place pre-set by others. And whoever you have to trust, never trust your own. Especially your own.'

Well, despite all that, I did trust Morgan Dampier – just about – and I assured him that, anyway, there definitely weren't going to be any *other* jobs. This was my one and only.

He'd sort of smiled at that and said we also wouldn't be relying on 'our own' for the diversion. That would be provided by hard men from a professional East London gang who acted on contract for cash only with no questions asked. With a kill going down, there wouldn't be an MI5 or Special Branch operator anywhere, seen or unseen. Although Tex-Mex hadn't known it, he had been cut adrift to look after himself from the moment he and his family had stepped out of the 'safe house' that morning, his usefulness to Her Majesty's Government at an end.

They'd want none of their own around when the presumably Serb assassin unexpectedly wreaked revenge out of a clear blue sky. I'd obligingly left a deliberate trail for the police to pick up later. I'd spoken Serbo-Croat in a pub around the corner earlier where I knew there were bar staff from the Balkans. I'd also left a couple of answerphone messages that I knew they'd discover during the murder inquiry.

No one in government, Whitehall or the intelligence services would want their connection with Tex-Mex known.

As Morgan Dampier had told me when we'd sat in my flat at the beginning, the man had signed his own death-warrant the moment he'd agreed to help in return for avoiding arrest for war crimes. Even the 'safe house' was a fake – with no traceable links to the intelligence agencies.

I'd listened in amazement to Dampier's explanation of how the government had wanted to rid itself of some awkward customers in the ranks of Loyalist terrorist organizations in Northern Ireland who were holding up the peace process by insisting that the whole thing was a sell-out to the Provisional IRA. Knowing that these same outfits were actively seeking an arms deal in Serbia, undercover intelligence officers had introduced them to Tex-Mex, who was fortuitously in a position to supply absolutely *everything* they required. The Loyalist negotiators couldn't believe their luck. It had gone like clockwork.

Twenty seconds to go.

Even as I scanned left and right along the streaming lines of King's Road traffic, I knew that armed police and troops would be swooping on a container ship in Lurgan docks in Northern Ireland. They would seize the arms shipment arranged by Tex-Mex and arrest the troublesome Loyalists – so providing another propaganda coup for their enemies in the Provisional IRA and giving the peace process another prod along.

Tex-Mex's involvement was now a potential embarrassment, of course. But not for long.

Then it happened. There seemed to have been no real reason for it, because the nearside traffic flow on its way to Sloane Square was barely crawling. A plain white van stopped completely, just a short distance from the snack bar where we sat, but the ageing Nissan saloon behind it didn't. All heads turned at that distinctive sound of shattering glass and the crumpling of cheap metal.

A large bruiser of a man with shaven head and tattoos climbed down from the van to come face-to-face with the equally aggressive-looking car driver.

'Are you fuckin' blind . . . ?!' was the screamed opening gambit.

As Tex-Mex watched the furious pantomime and pedestrians gathered to gawp in morbid fascination, I reached into my pocket for my cellphone and pressed the pre-logged number.

This bit wasn't in the plan. No one knew about it, not even Morgan Dampier. This was personal and it broke every sodding rule in creation.

Tex-Mex was startled and looked mildly irritated at having his mobile phone go off while he was enjoying the angry debacle taking place just feet in front of him. He dragged it from his jacket pocket and as he did I glimpsed the leather holster on the left side of his belt.

'Is that Leonid Rusjivic?' I asked in Serbo-Croat.

He grunted. 'Who wants him?'

'Jesus,' I replied gently.

'What?' he snarled, suddenly aware that this wasn't right.

'Remember Astrid Kweiss?'

'Who?'

'Astrid Kweiss. The UN interpreter you murdered in Bosnia seven years ago.'

He was getting really angry now, and the anger was quickly changing into fear as he suddenly realized he didn't know what the hell was going on. I could see the sweat breaking out on his skin and it wasn't from the chilli sauce on his nachos. 'Who the fuck are you?'

I had to raise my voice to be heard above the yelling drivers. 'I am the avenging angel of Astrid Kweiss—'

I hung up but didn't bother watching as he stared in disbelief at the mobile in his hand.

At the moment it dawned on him that someone could be watching and he looked up, I pressed the handset button in my pocket.

The red laser spot marked the centre of Tex-Mex's back

where the single silenced 9mm dum dum round slammed home from the concealed firing port in the aluminium photographer's case on my table. He pitched forward. His belly hit the table rim and he rebounded against the chairback. For a second he rocked with the momentum, his head lolling sideways. As his mouth fell open, his right arm dropped down limply towards the pavement. His mobile phone detached itself from his grasp and clattered into the small but rapidly growing pool of blood.

It had been so quick and silent that no one had noticed. As I picked up the photographer's case from my table, turned and walked slowly away down King's Road towards Fulham, the two arguing motorists were finally calming down.

The last thing I heard was someone say: 'Is that bloke all right? Looks like he's had a heart attack.'

Then I crossed the main road, turned a corner and kept on walking, steadily and looking only straight ahead.

They say revenge is a dish best served cold.

Well, if this was the dish I didn't like the taste of it. I felt no joy, no sense of victory or even of righting an injustice. I didn't feel the welcome warm flush of relief or the cold hand of fear. I felt absolutely *nothing*.

Worse, I couldn't even conjure the image of Astrid's face in my mind's eye.

To all intents and purposes I felt about as dead as the corpse I'd just left on the King's Road under the cheerless December sun.

# Two

I'd never collected blood money before and I found the very thought strangely unsettling. A numbered account in an obscure bank in Liechtenstein. Passwords to be exchanged with complete strangers in dark rooms. It was a whole new world to me.

Yet the prospect was nowhere near as daunting as the past few days had been. After the killing, I'd dumped the laser-gun rig in a left-luggage locker at Waterloo for someone to collect. I'd changed my clothes in the toilets and removed the toupee. By the time I'd driven a hire car from London to Newcastle and taken the ferry as a foot-passenger to Bergen, my nerves had been in tatters. They'd still felt frayed as I travelled south through Norway by rail and took another ferry to Denmark.

Although everything had actually gone like clockwork, I'd been anticipating that the situation would go pear-shaped at any moment. It's what the SAS trains you to expect: 'the embuggerance factor'. The totally unexpected at the worst possible moment.

My particular dread had been that someone, somewhere had given the police or port authorities a tip-off of my whereabouts. It was one thing you could never really guard against . . . if, for whatever reason, your political masters decided they wanted a sacrificial lamb.

'Never trust your own.' Morgan Dampier's words kept beating a distant tattoo in my head throughout my travels. 'Especially your own.'

I had trusted Dampier, but you could not know when – or why – someone might betray him too.

Only when I drove the hired Merc convertible out of Copenhagen, with the hood down and the radio belting out Vivaldi, was I finally able to settle down, relax and take time to think on the long journey ahead, across Europe to Liechtenstein.

Did I say 'think'? A bad idea . . .

It came to me somewhere on the German autobahn running south. Like a bolt of lightning, unannounced and just as unwelcome.

I hadn't killed Tex-Mex for Astrid at all – I'd done it for me. Astrid would have been horrified to have seen the man's torn body bleeding into the gutter on the King's Road. And the anguish on his wife's and children's faces as they witnessed what had been done to the man they loved.

The stupid thing was that none of it could bring Astrid back into my life.

The feeling of regret at what I'd done was growing. Not remorse that Tex-Mex was dead. He was an evil little shit for whom death was too good. It was that I had killed him and in doing so I had lowered myself to his level. I had mistaken revenge for justice. Worse, I had somehow fooled myself into thinking that I was doing it for Astrid, when anyone who knew her would have realized it would have been the last thing she'd have wanted.

I'd killed before, but only ever in the heat of battle when it was a question of kill or be killed. A firefight against Iraqi troops during the Gulf War; in an ambush against the Provisional IRA on a filthy wet night in South Armagh; during the seizure of a wanted drugs baron in Colombia. And I'd never lost a minute's sleep over any of them.

But as I drove alone in the Merc, with my foot hard down on the gas, I was starting to wish that I hadn't been so easily tempted by Morgan Dampier. Killing Tex-Mex hadn't been self-defence. It had been murder. It was purely personal and it was criminal. In fact, just about as criminal as you can get.

The fact that it had been secretly sanctioned by Her Majesty's Government didn't make it any less so. Even worse, in a way. Because Tex-Mex should have been arrested by armed police and handed over to the International Court of Justice in The Hague. The only reason he hadn't been was because faceless mandarins in Whitehall wanted to protect themselves and their political masters from the scandal of their own skulduggery.

I'd allowed myself to be used – again. Allowed myself to be part of the deceit and hypocrisy of politicians that had driven me to leave the SAS in the first place.

I crossed the border into the snow-covered mountains of Liechtenstein in a more sober and reflective mood. I'd take the blood money – and run. I'd leave the whole sorry business behind me, give Astrid's memory a decent burial, and get on with my life.

It took me some time to locate the bank, an anonymous building identified only by a discreet brass plaque beside the studded oak door. I gave my name and password over the intercom before I was allowed to enter. I was then shown to a small wood-panelled office that smelled of beeswax and the metallic, inky odour of banknotes.

An expressionless clerk in late middle age, wearing a dark suit, looked up from the leather-topped desk. Somehow managing to avoid eye contact, he asked to see my passport. Having satisfied himself that I was who I said I was, he asked politely but stiffly what he could do for me.

I said: 'I understand a deposit has been made into my account?'

He nodded, consulting a ledger on his desk. 'A transfer two days ago, from Premier Asset Holdings and Investment in the Cayman Islands.'

Interesting, I thought: the Cayman Islands were where Britain's Secret Intelligence Service had run various banking scams to catch out international narcotics cartels. Obviously the boys from MI6 had found their own illegal uses for their quasi-legitimate financial institutions. And what was this man thinking? A sizeable sum paid into a new customer's account from a Caribbean company in the middle of the most active drugs-dealing areas of the world . . . And he didn't even blink.

It felt almost vulgar to talk amounts, but I thought I'd better. 'Fifteen thousand sterling?'

A small tic came to life at the side of his thin mouth. 'Ah, actually ten thousand, sir, according to the ledger.'

I frowned. 'I think there's a mistake . . .'

The tone of voice didn't alter. 'No mistake, sir, we double-verify all transactions as a matter of course. We attempt to eliminate any chance of error in our business. Premier Asset confirmed.'

I was winded. Morgan, the bastard! In the beginning I'd assumed they'd pay a percentage up front, but he'd said that when you're virtually dealing with Her Majesty's Government you did it their way. And they considered their word to be their guarantee. As safe as government bonds.

That was a laugh and a half. Now I'd been suckered and who the hell was I supposed to complain to? Still, at least ten grand would clear my debts. Well, almost.

The clerk regarded me without expression. 'What would you like to do, sir?'

There was nothing else for it. 'Withdraw the money,' I decided. 'In cash. Sterling.'

'And the interest, sir?'

'Interest already?'

'Oh, yes, sir. Or would you prefer to leave that in?'

I just wanted to get out of the place. I shook my head. 'No, I'll take it all and close the account.'

For the first time he showed a flicker of genuine emotion. To me it looked like personal hurt. 'You don't want to keep it open for further deposits?'

'There won't be any further deposits,' I said flatly.

Fifteen minutes later I left and began my drive back to France, the grip containing ten thousand plus sitting next to me in the passenger seat. It made a surprisingly unsatisfactory travelling companion.

I dropped the Merc off at the rental company's Rennes office in Brittany and took a taxi out to the chateau where I'd checked in ten days earlier. When I arrived my own car, a smart but ageing BMW saloon I'd picked up for three grand, was still parked where I'd left it on the gravel forecourt. The hotel owner enquired after the health of my ailing grandmother, which was the reason I'd given for the sudden interruption of my holiday. I looked suitably solemn as I told him the bad news and he commiserated by opening a bottle of his finest cognac and sharing it with me. The English often say that they hate the French — but then, maybe they just haven't met the right ones.

Having reassumed my own identity, I had three days left to complete my official holiday and I was determined to make the best of it. I set off to explore the windswept shores and coastal towns while over-indulging in vintage red wine and huge *degustations* of the world's finest seafood.

Before I knew it the fifteenth dawned and it was time for me to leave for Cherbourg to catch the ferry, which was heaving with boisterous weekenders on the seasonal fags-and-booze run.

Suddenly the anniversary of Astrid's death on Christmas Eve seven years earlier was racing towards me. And there was nothing I could do to avoid it.

I struggled up the stairs to the flat with my suitcase and

grip of blood money to the all too familiar thud of hip hop from the Rasta couple who lived in the basement, past the doors of the other neighbours I'd seen but never actually spoken to: a reclusive Russian woman who lived with at least a dozen cats; the single teenage mother with her ever-wailing brat; the gay male couple who always dressed in black and only ever went out at night; and, on the floor below mine, Southwark's oldest and ugliest prostitute.

And it was 'Cristobelle' – if you could believe the unlikely legend on the postcard pinned to her door – who was alerted by the creaking landing floorboard and who ambushed me mid-stride.

'Oh, there you are!' As her door was flung open, the shriek of recognition came from a vivid orange-lipsticked mouth set in a face that reminded me of congealed lard. The bright red hair could hardly be the same age as the heavy body decorously draped in a semi-transparent night-dress. Thankfully it had been hastily covered with a quilted dressing gown. Her blue eyes, the lashes laden with mascara, looked inquisitive and mildly flirtatious. 'It *is* Mr Coltrane, isn't it?'

Immediately I was on alert, as I'd never even spoken to the woman before. My acknowledgement was little more than a grunt.

Cristobelle gave a deep chuckle. 'Didn't *think* you was one of my punters.'

Did she mean that, at nearly forty, I was twenty years too young? I feigned innocence to be polite. 'Punters?'

'A little sideline of mine, Mr Coltrane. Hostessing.'

'I see.'

'Only there was this young lady come to see you.' Cristobelle indicated the fish-eye security lens in her front door. 'I see her a couple of times, then on her third visit she rings my bell. Asked if a Mr Coltrane lived on the top. Well,

I had one of your bills delivered to me by mistake while you was away, so I was fairly sure it must be you. That was about three days ago. Away on business, was you?'

I gave a tight smile. After serving years in the SAS you get a bit anally retentive about casual questions from strangers. 'Holiday.'

'Nice time?'

I ignored that. 'Did this lady have a name?'

Cristobelle's smile was more generous than mine, revealing nicotine-stained teeth and receding gums. 'Wouldn't say. Pretty lass, a bit buxom. Early to mid-thirties. Brown hair. Spoke with a London accent, not your BBC. Sound like an admirer of yours?'

'I wasn't aware I had any.'

She gave another of her little squeals of mirth. 'You quiet types never are. Blind to the blindingly obvious. We girls have to spell it out sometimes.'

This time my smile was a little more genuine. 'I'll remember that, Miss—?'

'Just Cristobelle, Mr Coltrane.' She stepped back inside her door and beyond I saw the glow of a red bulb in a bedside lamp. 'If I don't see you before, have a good Christmas.'

'And you.'

I trudged the last flight of stairs, deep in thought about the identity of my admirer, secret or otherwise. It was far more likely to be an investigator from a debt-collection agency than any wannabe lover. I just hoped to God it wasn't a plain-clothes cop on the Leonid Rusjivic murder inquiry.

Entering my flat was like walking into a fridge. Only it wasn't just cold, it also had a distinct smell of damp. There was a pile of envelopes on the mat, mostly brown, and junk mail addressed to the previous tenant. I dumped my bags, picked up the post and wandered into the lounge. The message indicator on the answer machine wasn't even blinking. Two weeks away and not a single message. How sad was that?

I plugged in the kettle for a coffee and sat at the table, leafing through the bills and final demands. There was one Christmas card – from my landlord, with a little note reminding me that I was now two months behind with the rent. He was a Pakistani and a real gent, doing his best to be diplomatic, which was more than I'd have been in his position.

The last envelope in the pile was lilac-coloured, unstamped and marked simply *E. Coltrane*. It smelled strangely floral as I prised it open and extracted the matching sheet of paper

> *Dear Ed*
> *Where the hell are you? Been looking for you everywhere.*
> *Please ring number below immediately you get this.*
> *Yours*
> *BEX*
> *PS. Sorry to disappoint. This isn't a love letter, had to borrow it off the bloke downstairs.*

Bloke? Cristobelle a man? surely not. But then, my neighbour had certainly never won a beauty contest and – hell – aren't women always better at spotting that sort of thing? Or was it just a typical Bex wind-up?

I'd known Rebecca Bunnet for around ten or eleven years. She and her best mate, a slightly younger girl called Jude, both from Essex, had been getting bored with life and deployment restrictions within the Women's Royal Army Corps. Miraculously, considering their penchant for practical jokes and bending every rule in the book, they'd both made the rank of corporal while still in their mid-twenties.

A switched-on officer had spotted their disillusion and

potential and suggested that they volunteer for the enig-
matic 'Project Alpha', teasingly described as involving 'special
duties' in Northern Ireland.

In fact Bex and Jude had unwittingly applied for one of
the most ferocious and gruelling selection courses that the
British Army could devise. In the unlikely event of them
passing – the failure rate was extraordinarily high – it would
lead them eventually to becoming operators within 14
Intelligence Company, the highly secretive covert intelligence
unit operating across the water.

At the time I had been on secondment from 22 Special
Air Service Regiment to 14 Int's Directing Staff at Camp
Alpha in Wales, training new recruits in the dangerous art
of close surveillance of terrorist groups in Ulster, both
Republican and Loyalist. Everything from mounting observation posts in both remote rural and heavily populated
urban areas, covert infil and exfil, trailing suspects, and
secret communications to armed and unarmed combat,
anti-interrogation methods and the unit's notorious driving
techniques.

It was one of the toughest courses imaginable and the
'Essex Girls', as Bex and Jude had inevitably become known,
almost sailed through it with their indefatigable sense of
humour and attitude to life, putting many of their male
counterparts to shame.

The first time I'd begun to get to know the girls had
been one winter's night on a bleak Welsh hillside where
their OP overlooked a farmhouse – which, for the purposes
of the exercise, was an IRA hideout. There was a thick
sheen of ice on the grass and snow was driving almost
horizontally under a bitter north wind. For once, my
stealth-approach technique – which usually resulted in a
severe bollocking for the lax recruits caught napping – let
me down. Instead, I was met with a pinched blue grin-
ning face – and the muzzle of a 9mm Browning auto-

matic pointing out from under the OP's lid of chicken wire and turf.

Then I felt another gun muzzle jammed in my back. The other recruit had somehow got behind me.

The first words that Bex ever said to me were: 'Tough luck, Staff. We're ordering you into our OP to warm us up as best you can.'

Absolutely furious at getting caught out, I muttered darkly: 'You're playing with fire, young female persons. From now on your lives aren't going to be worth fucking living.'

'Nah,' Jude said from inside the OP. 'You wouldn't do that, Staff. This is called using our initiative! That's what you DSs are always telling us to do.'

Her words had been immediately followed by the blinding flash of a compact camera – the cheeky minx had actually photographed me in the compromising position of having a recruit's pistol stuck in my back.

If it had been anyone else but these two, I'd have crucified them. For the rest of the course I and the other DSs would have beasted them like you would not believe until they'd bled and cried and begged for mercy.

As it was my revenge had been fast and sweet. In a split second I had Bex over my shoulder and thudding onto the ice-packed ground with a force that should have knocked her fillings out, the elbow of her gun arm snapping against the joint so that the pistol fell free.

'Oh shit,' Jude observed from the OP. Then she grinned and wrinkled her nose. 'Fancy coming in for a hot cuppa before we're charged, Staff?'

They had the charm of the very devil and it was bloody difficult not to be affected by it. With the wind screaming over the mountainside and my marriage pretty much in free fall at the time, for a split second I was sorely tempted to accept their invitation.

Instead I had petulantly demanded that Jude hand over

her camera for confiscation. 'Right, you've had your fun, girlies. Now you can stay in this OP for another two days without resupply.' I added with a typical DS sneer: 'Hope you think it was worth it.'

In truth, after the incident I had lived in dread of being the butt of my fellow DS instructors' jokes about how I had fallen victim to the Essex Girls, but to Bex and Jude's credit the true version of events never leaked out. Wise really, because it gave them a sort of unspoken hold over me for the rest of the course. Despite much resentment from the sexist and macho culture existing in 14 Int at the time, both Bex and Jude went on to be crack operators both in Northern Ireland and, later, with some limited work in Bosnia.

It was three years since I'd last seen either of them and I couldn't think why the hell they should want to contact me. They'd sent a Christmas card to my first address after leaving the army, but I hadn't reciprocated and never did get round to telling them my next address. Somewhat bemused, I poured a strong black coffee and made my way to the phone.

I lit a Gauloise and dialled the mobile number. The voice answered almost immediately, pure Estuary, husky from too much tobacco but with a slightly musical lilt to it. 'Ace Personal Protection. How can I help?'

There was a lot of background noise that sounded like a pub. 'Is that Bex?'

Her reaction was immediate. 'Ed! Holy smoke, at last! We thought you was dead!'

I smiled to myself; she always had that effect. 'Exaggerated rumours. I've just been away.'

'How you doin', Ed? It's been a while—'

'Fine, and what about you? What's this Ace Personal Protection?'

Her laugh was throaty. 'Well, it's not part of Army Int.

Jude and I got out about six months back. The province was getting boring and ... you know ... it felt like pissing against the wind.'

The expression suddenly reminded me; the two of them had learned to do that, too, standing up like men. A useful trick on operations sometimes. 'So you're running a protection racket, eh?'

'Funny man. We're trying to do VIP stuff, but mostly it's been nightclub bouncing. It's hard to break into. Ever heard of the girl band Femco?'

'No.'

'Yeah, well, not surprising. Nor had anyone else, so it didn't last long. Not much point bodyguarding someone no one's ever heard of. Jude reckoned their manager was planning an assassination attempt just to get them publicity, but it never happened – and neither did the band. Not surprising with a name like a sanitary towel. At least we've got a toehold in the entertainment scene.'

'But don't call us, we'll call you?' I guessed.

'A bit like that,' she admitted.

'So why the contact, Bex? Doesn't sound like you need extra staff.'

She came back quickly. 'Jude wants you to take a DNA test for paternity—' For a second she caught me out, except that I'd never had that sort of relationship with either of them. 'Only joshing, Ed! No, I need to have a chat about something.'

'Fine,' I said. 'Where you living nowadays?'

'Not a million miles from you. We've got an office over a chip shop in Barking and a couple of camp beds.'

'Come over for a meal one night,' I invited. 'If you don't fancy one of my home-made curries, I'll take you out for a steak.' I think the ten grand blood money had gone to my head already.

A serious note crept into her voice. 'Thanks, Ed, but not

a good idea. Listen, what's tomorrow . . . ? Saturday. You doing anything tomorrow?'

'Not now.'

'I'm playing in a local league tomorrow.' It was all coming back, how she was a keen amateur rugby fly-half. 'We can meet after I finish around lunch. You can come and cheer us on.'

I understood. Behind the banter Bex was saying that she wanted to meet on safe and neutral ground. 'Give me the location, I'll be there.' I jotted down the name of the municipal playing fields. 'And Bex, you're not in any kind of trouble, are you?'

'Me, boss? Never. I'm not that sort of girl.'

But I wondered if her answer wasn't just a bit too glib. Bex was just that type of girl. I said: 'Take care, young female person, I'll see you.'

'Hokey-smokey. Bye, lover.'

I hung up, feeling inexplicably unnerved. With some effort I pushed the uncalled-for worry aside, finished my coffee and poured a Scotch. I decided I'd have a quiet night in, ring for a pizza and spend the night in front of the TV.

I was looking forward to meeting a friendly face again. It really had been far, far too long.


I'd actually been fancying the idea of standing on the touchline, watching twenty-four strapping lasses in shorts knocking the hell out of each other. A pity I hadn't looked at the weather forecast first.

When I arrived at the playing fields in Essex at midday, it was more like midnight. The leaden sky seemed barely clear of the treetops and the rain was coming down like Niagara Falls. Typically, I found Bex's 'Essex Warblers' locked in mortal combat with the 'Dagenham Diehards' on the pitch farthest from the car park. By the time I'd trudged across the quagmire, my shoes were ruined and my raincoat had given up all pretence of being waterproof. It just surrendered big time.

There was only one other supporter on the touchline, one of the Diehards' rugby-mad fathers. After we'd exchanged a couple of words, it seemed unchivalrous to beat a retreat to my car, so I felt obliged to stay put until the mud-wrestling contest finally ended at fifteen minutes to one. Bex had played as well and as hard as I'd have expected and her legs looked better than I remembered. In fact I was sure she'd lost quite a bit of weight since we'd last met. The only minor compensation for the whole soggy mess was some of the girls exchanging shirts at the end of the match. But it would have taken a pretty desperate man to have been much aroused by the sight of all those mud-splattered heavy-duty sports bras.

Bex trudged across the mire towards me, her elfin grin glowing like a beacon amid the grime on her face. 'Hi, Ed. Enjoy the game?'

'I can't think of a better way to spend a winter morning.'

She landed a playful blow on my ribcage. 'You're going soft, lover.' She glanced up and down the touchline. 'Mind you, you're doing better than most. If we were blokes playing, all our girlfriends would have to be dutifully lined up and cheering us on. It's expected. So where's this lot's husbands and boyfriends?'

We fell into step with the straggling players making their way towards the pavilion and shower block. I said: 'I thought Jude usually did the cheer-leading honours?'

'Only when she's between relationships.'

'So there's a man in her life?'

'Well, there was when I saw her in the disco last night. Met this hunk of a fireman. This is *the* big one, she says. But you know Jude, it's probably all over by now.'

'And you?'

Her grin faded a fraction. 'You know me, Ed, I can't pull until I'm down to a size 14.'

'You're looking pretty good to me.'

'Allowing for your failing eyesight, I'll take that as a compliment. But it proves my point – I've just hit target. No more army-canteen scoff, see, and worrying about the business. Besides, I can't *afford* to eat any more.'

That hit a chord. 'I know the feeling.'

'So what you doing now?'

'Warehouse management. Very civilian.'

She glanced knowingly at me. 'And bored out your skull?'

'You get used to it. Life still has its moments.'

'Like your trips to Bosnia?'

I was annoyed that she should have known about that. 'Who's been telling tales, Bex? Bloody Morgan Dampier, I suppose?'

She looked abashed. 'Sorry, Ed, but it was common knowledge. Not just Morgan. All the lads were still keeping an eye out for you when you were snooping around out there. They're on your side.'

I shrugged. 'Anyway, I've left all that behind now. The trail had gone cold.'

She stopped abruptly and turned to face me. 'You haven't heard, have you? How long have you been away?'

'A couple of weeks.'

'It happened about ten days ago. Some Serb wanted for war crimes. Rusjivic, or something. Christ, with names like that those Serbs must be world champions at Scrabble. Anyway, this bloke was assassinated on the King's Road.'

I swear to God my heart stopped beating and momentarily I seemed to be struggling for breath.

'You okay, Ed? You've gone white as a sheet.'

I took a deep breath to refill my lungs. 'A bit of a shock, that's all.'

'So that *was* him. One of those involved in your wife's murder – I was *sure* that was the name. It was in all the papers. The police reckoned it was an assassin from the Serb underworld . . . Hope that makes you feel better?'

I nodded numbly, unable to think what the hell to say.

'You need a drink,' Bex decided. 'I'll just grab a quick shower—'

One of the other Essex Warblers called out: 'Who's your boyfriend, Bex?'

'Not me boyfriend, Sharon, he's me Dad.'

It was a welcome change of subject. 'Thanks for that, Bex,' I said.

The Warbler laughed. 'Looks all right for an old 'un to me. Ask 'im if 'e wants to join us in the hot tub.'

Bex wagged her finger at me. 'Bad idea, Pops. You and twenty-four Essex girls. They'd eat you alive.'

I grinned, starting to regain my composure. 'But hell, what a way to die.'

'In your dreams, lover. See you in a bit.'

She disappeared inside the pavilion and I parked myself on the steps, just clear of the rain, and lit a cigarette. After a while the girls reappeared in ones and twos, now showered and dressed and looking halfway human, heading for the cinder car park.

Suddenly I glimpsed Bex walking straight past me in a bright red tracksuit, that once familiar mane of bronzed curls flowing over her shoulders.

I sprang to my feet, ran a couple of steps and touched her sleeve. 'Can't shake me off that easy, Bex—'

She turned and I found myself staring into the face of the Essex Warbler called Sharon. 'Nice try, grandad,' she said, then winked and walked on.

Muttering my apologies, I returned to the shelter of the steps and looked back. As Sharon and a friend drove off, only my BMW was left in the car park.

'Pssst!'

I turned to see Bex waving from the pavilion door, indicating for me to join her.

She was dressed in jeans and a leather bomber top, her hair hidden under a Rasta-style woollen beret. 'You've met me body-double, then?'

Something was going on, but I couldn't fathom what. 'Sharon?' I asked, bemused.

'She's doing me a favour, taking my car home. Her hair's similar to mine and with my tracksuit on, we could be twins.'

'But why?' I asked.

Bex smiled a little uncomfortably as she looked over my shoulder and scanned the deserted, rainswept playing fields. She said quietly: 'Just a precaution, Ed . . . in case anyone followed me here. I'll explain over a pint. Okay if we use your car?'

There didn't seem to be an option. As we hunched against a fresh squall, I grumbled: 'If anyone is bothering to follow you in *this*, girl, you really are in trouble.'

I took the pint of bitter and long glass of Evian with a lemon twist across to the window table where Bex was sitting.

I thought how she no longer resembled the overweight tomboy I remembered. Her body had become noticeably more statuesque, stronger and athletic. And, as always, it had taken only a hint of mascara and lipstick to make the most of those beguiling blue eyes and the ever-ready smile.

I placed the Evian in front of her. 'Never thought I'd see the day, Bex.'

'Yeah, well, needs must.' She shrugged. 'I'll never be a stick insect, but I feel better like this. Amazonian is the best I can hope for. So it's a run every day and the gym twice a week and avoid the after match booze-up with the team.'

'So you're just using me?' I said.

'Just a smidge. You're this week's excuse to miss it. The Warblers think any player's a wimp who doesn't down eight pints after a game – and I'm desperately trying to keep my street cred.'

I raised my glass. 'To your street cred.'

Bex laughed, took a swig of mineral water and grimaced. 'Yuk! I'm not sure it's good luck to toast without alcohol. But hell, Ed, it's good to see you again anyway.'

I nodded. 'Likewise. But I'm still mystified as to *why* you've been to so much trouble to track me down. Then those silly games today. You said you weren't in any trouble . . . ?'

The smile faded from her lips. 'I'm not, Ed, but we've a mutual friend who is.' Then the smile was momentarily back. 'Well, that is, he *thinks* he is, which isn't necessarily the same thing.'

My patience was running dry. 'Come on, Bex.'

'Sorry, Ed. I'm talking about Marcus.'

I think I'd only ever known one Marcus in my life. 'Marcus Whitby?'

'Sir Marcus, actually. They knighted him somewhere along the line.'

'Good God,' I breathed. It was like a name from a previous life; it must have been nine years since I'd last met him. 'And he's looking for me?'

Bex nodded and sipped more of her water. 'Says you're the only one he feels he can trust.'

'Me?' I still couldn't believe it. 'I'm surprised he even *remembers* me . . .'

Although on reflection, perhaps it wasn't that surprising. It had been at a traumatic time of his life. He had been one of the few modern politicians at the time who'd once been a professional soldier, ending his distinguished military career as colonel of an infantry line regiment, and had entered the House of Commons late in life under the Major administration. As such he'd been snapped up as a junior defence minister.

Unfortunately for Sir Marcus, he'd assumed that Parliamentarians operated to the same traditional code of old-fashioned honour, honesty and plain speaking as was generally found in the armed forces. Big mistake. Temporarily popular with the media for his forthright approach he soon took enough rope to hang himself. Telling the world what a mess the administration had allowed the armed forces to get into with underfunding, poor equipment and overstretch was not exactly what the Prime Minister, the Defence Minister or the Whips' Office wanted to put across.

Whether he thought that by publicly exposing the short-falls of his own department the government would actually do something about it – or be shamed into it – God only knew. So whilst he quickly became regarded as a champion by almost every soldier, sailor and airman for speaking out so courageously, he was quickly handed the traditional poisoned chalice and reshuffled to junior Northern Ireland minister within a year.

That, of course, was where I met him. And at the time he was a very unhappy man. It was in the middle of the so-called 'peace process' and it was Sir Marcus's job to do some dirty dealing and horse-trading with some decidedly unsavoury types. He was capable of doing what had to be done, but he person-ally disapproved of much of what was going on.

However, he'd been read the riot act and had been left in no doubt that if he just once dared to speak his mind in public he would be fired. In consequence, much of my minder duties with him were more often spent avoiding media ambushes than would-be terrorist assassins.

Once we'd got to know each other, Marcus Whitby confided how uncomfortable he felt in the role he'd been given, especially having to be nice and polite to known Irish thugs who he knew had killed and maimed. But he'd been seduced by the promise of selection as a Tory Member of the European Parliament when he stood down at the next election – once his deep knowledge of Northern Ireland's military politics had been fully exploited.

The thought of being an MEP had been very appealing to him. Not only was Sir Marcus now sick to death of the British political circus but, as a genuine Francophile, he loved the concept of all those Europeans mucking in together – if only to put the Americans' noses out of joint. Sir Marcus was never big on Americans. Moreover, as an MEP he knew he'd be financially secure for the rest of his working life, which was important to him since his wife Jo suffered from multiple sclerosis and it was clear that she was going to need a lot of expensive care in future years. The last I'd heard of him was in a newspaper item about his resignation shortly before the 1997 election. I never did hear whether or not he had made it to Brussels.

'Oh, Marcus remembers you all right,' Bex said. 'Seems to think the sun shines out your jacksie ... I was so surprised when he contacted me. I had no idea he's an MEP now.'

'Nor did I,' I replied.

Bex giggled and shrugged. 'Does anyone know or care about Euro MPs?'

'Probably not. At least I know that's what *he* wanted.' I frowned. 'What sort of trouble can he be in?'

She made a face. 'Look, Marcus isn't *certain* he is in any kind of trouble. But he thinks he might be and wants your advice.'

'You sure he doesn't need a solicitor rather than me?'

'It's not that sort of trouble, Ed.'

'Stop talking in riddles, Bex.'

'Sorry, lover, but riddles is what it is. Marcus phones me up, out of the blue. Apparently he wangled my number through an old mate of his in Europol – and that must have taken some doing.'

I dug in my pocket for my pack of Gauloises. 'You two didn't keep in touch, then?'

She knew what I meant. Bex and Sir Marcus had made

an odd couple, and it had been taking 'close protection' above and beyond the line of duty.

It was one of the few times I'd ever seen the cold blue steel behind her eyes. 'It was strangers-in-the-night stuff, Ed, all over in a month. Things were difficult between Marcus and Jo with her condition – and I'd just broken with my ex. Marcus was sweet to me and I felt sorry for him. Like it *nearly* was once between you and me.'

'*Touché,*' I murmured and lit my Gauloise. Bex and I had once got close – but not quite close enough.

'Can I have one of those?' she asked. 'All part of my diet. I just don't buy my own.'

I handed her one and lit it for her. She grimaced as she inhaled the strong and pungent smoke. 'Anyway, when he finally found me, Marcus said he'd tried to get hold of you but failed. Thought I might know your whereabouts.'

I thought that was strange. If a pal in Europol could find Bex, then why not me? Any Europol officer trying to reach me would have been given Morgan Dampier's name sooner or later and he knew where I was. But then maybe Dampier didn't want anyone else to know. Given what had just gone down with Tex-Mex, I could have seen his point.

Bex continued: 'So I went through my own little black book, phoning all our mutual friends. Finally I hit pay dirt with Joe Monk, who'd just got back from a stint abroad. But he only had an obsolete mobile number for you and wasn't sure your address wasn't also out of date. And, of course, your landline came up ex-directory.' She paused to drag on her cigarette and I watched her lips with fascination as she blew a near-perfect smoke ring. 'As far as I can make out Marcus has got hold of some information about Europe – I don't know, something about malpractice in the Commission or something – and thinks his life's in danger as a result.'

I smiled at that. 'What's he think they're going to do?

Tie him up in red tape and throw him in the North Sea with all their dead fish? Malpractice in Brussels is hardly new.'

If I thought Bex would join in the joke, I was mistaken. 'Marcus isn't laughing, Ed. He's deadly serious.'

'I seem to remember Marcus was also prone to paranoia.'

Bex looked almost angry. 'He was entitled to when we worked with him in Northern Ireland. I seem to recall we escorted him to some pretty dodgy meetings. Deserted farmhouses on dark nights in the pissing rain. That might have meant nothing to you, Mr Super Cool, but I expect it scared the crap out of him. Marcus's background was line infantry, not special forces.' She stubbed her cigarette end out furiously in the ashtray. 'Maybe he just didn't have a death wish like you and me.'

Of course, she had a point. You can get a bit cocky when you serve in the SAS for a time, and it's as well to rein yourself in now and again. Besides, Marcus did have some gallantry gong to his credit, I seemed to recall. Some action in Aden, I think, when he was a young subaltern.

I raised my hands in surrender. 'Okay, Bex, his paranoia might be justified. Unlikely, but possible. What do you want me to do?'

She was starting to look exasperated. 'Just meet him, for God's sake, Ed. A few minutes of your time.'

I shrugged. 'Fine, no problem. Just set it up—'

My voice trailed off as at that moment the door swung open and a tall figure in wet-look leather motorcycle fatigues and dark-visored helmet strode in, looking left and right.

I'd been out of the business quite a while, but some habits die hard. Like always keeping your back to the wall in a room and facing the door. I could sense the eyes behind the visor focus on me and I felt the hairs on the back of my neck stand up like filings under a magnet.

The figure moved suddenly and decisively in our direction. Instantly my mind went into overdrive, looking to see what weapon he carried and deciding which way to push Bex clear and dive for cover myself.

# Three

The motorcyclist stopped a few feet from our table and, as his hands went up to take off his bone-dome, I realized two things simultaneously.

'He' was unarmed – and female.

Jude Sinclair shook her hair free. The grin on the once familiar cheeky urchin face seemed to run from one ear, laden with rings, to the other. 'Hello, big boy! Sorry if I gave you a turn. You've gone white as a sheet.'

Bex laughed and nudged me hard. 'Now who's paranoid?'

Jude leaned forward, eyes twinkling mischievously. 'Don't I get a kiss for old times' sake?'

I noticed the pierced ring in her left nostril. I would have thought it ugly and stupid on anyone else. But Jude, always a dedicated follower of fashion, carried it off with her usual panache. I said: 'Won't I get damaged by all that heavy metal?'

'I'll be gentle with you, Ed. Just keep your tongue out me throat.' And she gave me a kiss that was a fraction longer and heavier than it should have been – no doubt just to wind up Bex.

Her best mate grunted. 'Haven't you eaten today, Jude?'

Her friend made a deliberately loud sucking noise as our lips separated. 'Yep, I have now!' She sat astride her chair like she was riding a horse, with arms folded across its back, and regarded me closely. 'Well, is Ed coming – or is it just the way he's sitting?'

That was the thing about Jude. She was a couple of years

younger than Bex, whom she idolized, and had a slimmer build. She was also flashy and flirty with a sort of in-your-face good humour. You either loved her or hated her, and most eventually came round to loving her.

Certainly most men seemed to, but from what I knew of it, most found her too hot to handle. Her relationships had never seemed to last long, probably not helped by her ongoing adolescent rantings about Royal Marines, workmen's bums and the Chippendales. Despite her impetuous and fiery nature, I'd always found Jude the consummate professional on operations. No doubt due to the fact that Bex clearly served as her role model.

'Coming or going where?' I asked.

Bex intervened. 'To meet Marcus. Just in case his house was being watched, Jude smuggled him out this morning in a borrowed plumber's van and brought him down from Bedford.'

My eyes narrowed. 'I haven't agreed to anything.'

'But Bex knew you would,' Jude interrupted. 'If not, she said we'd just have to kidnap you.'

'So where is he?'

Jude said: 'He's waiting at a friend of mine's house a few miles away.'

'We thought we'd RV somewhere innocuous and private,' Bex added. 'There's a car-park stack I know that's hardly used at weekends.'

I groaned inwardly, accepting that I'd been quite ruthlessly stitched-up. But then, it would be good to see Marcus again. I put a brave face on it. 'Sounds good. Let's go.'

'Hold your horses, partner,' Jude cut in quickly. 'You haven't changed, Ed. Too mean to buy a girl a pint first, are we?'

The light was failing when we reached the car-park stack on the outskirts of Brentwood and the rain had started to ease. I took a ticket from the automatic barrier and drove in. The place mostly served a business area of town and, as Bex had predicted, there were few cars. By the time I reached the open concrete top deck, we had it all to ourselves. I killed the lights, then Bex and I got out, our eyes drawn beyond the graffiti-daubed parapet to the rash of fairy lights spun out across the misty shadows of the town.

I took out my cigarettes and offered Bex one. 'Like old times,' I said.

She cupped her hand around mine to shield the flame from the cold breeze. 'Waiting for some informer to turn up,' she agreed as she inhaled. 'And it was always bloody raining.'

I held my palm out; at least this was just an icy drizzle. 'This isn't Belfast rain.'

'I miss it, Ed. Those times.' She glanced sideways at me. 'Do you?'

'Sometimes,' I admitted. 'But those times have moved on. So we have to as well. You know what they say. Never go back.'

Bex said thoughtfully: 'Those times might come back of their own accord. They also say that what goes around comes around. The Provos have gone all political, so all their hard-core members have joined the Real IRA or Continuity. It's the same people. If talking doesn't get them what they want, it'll be back to bombs and bullets. Only this time all the main players have got a get-out-of-jail-free card.'

I drew deeply on my Gauloise. Irish politics were as sick as Balkan politics, and as always it was the innocent who did most of the suffering. 'Maybe peace will prove too popular.' I grinned at Bex in the gloom. 'I've always reckoned that living's got more going for it than dying.'

Stray light played on her even white teeth as she smiled. 'Meaning we should get on with the living bit, even if it is boring the pants off me and Jude?'

'Death's no bundle of laughs either, Bex. We were lucky, we got away with it. Maybe it's time we all settled down.'

'You're sounding like an old codger.'

'I'm nearly forty.'

She gave me a disapproving frown. 'Yeah, Ed, forty. Not frigging eighty.'

We both heard it then, the throaty twin exhausts of a motorcycle from deep in the depths of the stack, the noise echoed and magnified so that it sounded like the first early rumblings of an earthquake.

'Guess that's our Jude,' Bex said and tossed her cigarette butt into the oily puddle at her feet.

Moments later, the headlamp beam of the ascending motorcycle carved a swathe on the dark tunnel of the concrete ramp, followed by the machine itself driven at such high speed that it became momentarily airborne to the accompanying whine of a banshee, hit the deck and slewed towards us in a fast braking turn. It jerked to a halt just feet away, the white-faced pillion passenger in the camel coat clutching onto the rider for dear life.

Jude flipped up her lid. 'Hi, guys. All present and correct.'

She held the bike steady as Sir Marcus gingerly released his grasp on her leathered waist and dismounted. I swear to God he was visibly trembling as he unstrapped the old-fashioned helmet and brushed flat the shock of hair that was much too pure white to be natural at his age.

'Were you followed?' Bex asked Jude as her friend kicked down the prop-stand.

'No bloody way!' Sir Marcus intervened. 'I tell you it would've been damn *impossible* to have followed us! She's a madwoman. Even my guardian angel got left behind at a red traffic light.'

The MEP had that terse public-school way of talking through his lower teeth and each sentence was clipped short in the traditional Sandhurst manner. It was a voice that fitted the distinguished face, with its heavy shoeblacked eyebrows in marked contrast to the white hair of his head and skin that had the scrubbed, ruddy glow of a man who'd spent many years in the open air.

'Well?' Bex pressed.

Jude hooked her helmet on one of the handlebars. 'Can't be sure,' she replied, with an uncertain smile. 'You know what it's like when you're flying solo.'

I got the feeling that she didn't want to say more in front of Sir Marcus.

The politician grunted. 'With friends like young Jude here, I really don't think I have need of enemies. She'll do the job *for* them.'

Jude giggled. 'Be nice to me, kind sir. Remember you've got the return journey to make yet.'

He raised those black beetle brows to the heavy rain-clouds as he seemed to notice me for the first time. 'Eddie? Great to see you again. So glad they could find you.'

I stepped forward from the shadows and shook the offered hand. 'Sir Marcus,' I said. I'm a bit old-fashioned and formal like that – probably because I'd made good as the son of a working-class mother who respected everyone with influence and power whether they deserved it or not.

But this was one man who had never abused his rank or position, which was one reason we'd hit it off from the start. 'Just call me Marcus, Eddie. The knighthood was just a sop when the Party pushed me out into the cold.'

'I thought you jumped,' I said to make him feel better. 'Didn't you always want to be an MEP? Seem to remember you waxing lyrical about European nations acting together in the world. An economic force for the Yanks to reckon with.'

'Ah,' he said ruefully. 'Was I really that tedious?'

I smiled. 'You could get a bit heavy.'

Sir Marcus nodded. 'How little I knew then. But that was

the clever part, you see. They make you think you're jumping of your own free will, when in fact it *is* a push.'

'They?'

He shrugged. 'The modern political professionals – spin doctors and private advisers –they run all the main parties now as well as the civil service. Just as much in Westminster as in Brussels.'

I really didn't want Sir Marcus mounting one of his favourite hobby-horses – life was too short. So I said directly: 'Bex seems to think that you're in some kind of trouble.'

Bex cut in sharply: 'No, Ed. I said Marcus thinks he is, not me.'

The MEP smiled at that and said quietly to me: 'Mind if we take a stroll? Best this is for your ears only. Safer for them.'

Bex and Jude shrugged in unison, but it was clear that they didn't like it. I couldn't blame them either, but Sir Marcus was very much old-school military. He was of the era when it was unthinkable for women to be anywhere near the front line in combat. It was the prevailing sexist attitude that Bex and Jude had had to endure when they'd first worked as undercover troops with 14 Int in Northern Ireland. The two of them had proved their worth many times over, but I had to admit I still had very strong reservations about female combatants as general policy.

As we wandered out of earshot, Sir Marcus relaxed visibly. 'I don't want to seem ungrateful to them, Eddie, but I'd rather not get them involved.'

'I think they already are.'

'No, you don't understand.' He fished in the pocket of his camel coat and pulled out a small leather-bound hip flask. 'Fancy a snifter? Macallan. I'm afraid that ride really did unsettle me.'

I accepted the flask and swallowed, enjoying the bite and mellow aftertaste of peat.

Sir Marcus continued: 'Bex was the only route I could think of to reach you. I don't want her — or her friend — to be any more involved than that. It's much too dangerous.'

'But not for me?'

He took a swig of the malt himself before replying. 'I know you can handle yourself, Eddie. You've been around. You've got age and wisdom on your side. Besides - you're a feller.'

I was getting a little bit fed up with this. 'C'mon, Marcus, what the hell's going on? You've got something on corruption in Brussels and you think your life could be in danger — and now mine. Get real.'

The anger was back in his eyes. 'Don't patronize me, Eddie. I know I've been naive in my time, but I'm not a bloody fool. I'm sixty years old and alone—'

'Jo?' I interrupted, suddenly reminded of his charming wife who had always had a smile and a ready laugh even though she'd been suffering horribly from multiple sclerosis.

Sir Marcus said: 'Jo died last summer. She was going downhill and her hospital wasn't allowed to give her the beta-interferon drug that might have made her life a little more endurable. Deemed too costly. I'm afraid to say Jo took an overdose of sleeping pills.'

I was shocked. 'God, I'm sorry.'

He waved my words aside. 'Jo knew what I was doing, and would have wanted me to go on. Not retire into senility because it was too dangerous. She wanted me to fight on for the sake of our grandchildren and the nation's grandchildren. It was the last thing she said to me in the evening before she died.' Moisture was gathering in his eyes, and I don't think it was the chill breeze. "Cometh the hour, cometh the man," Jo said to me. "'And I know you, Marcus — you *are* that man."'

A bit melodramatic, but Sir Marcus sounded deadly serious. I was almost tempted to think that it wasn't all in his mind.

I said: 'I can only think you must be ruffling a few feathers with whatever you're doing.'

He nodded. 'I've been as discreet as I can with my research and my enquiries, but word still gets about. It filters up through the Brussels whisper system. And, indeed, it does seem to have ruffled some feathers, as you put it, Eddie. Feathers of some of the most powerful men in Europe.'

That, I realized, was the problem. The credibility gap. 'But, Marcus, most people in this country think of the European Union as a bad joke – if they think about it at all.'

He smiled faintly. 'Hardly menacing, eh? That's the sinister part. It already controls or affects almost every part of everyone's life and they don't even know. Or, it seems, care. But, believe me, they *will*.'

I wasn't aware of the breeze picking up, but as he spoke I felt a chill sensation on the back of my neck. 'What exactly do you mean, Marcus?'

He sighed. 'Let's just say the "European Project" has come a long way since the days of the Common Market – a trading block of European nations. It's now well on the way to becoming a United States of Europe.'

Even I understood that. 'You always used to say that it would rival the USA one day.'

'But what I didn't realize then was just how *different* a United States of Europe would be. With none of the democracy, justice or checks and balances. An unelected Commission deciding policies put together by bureaucrats and rubber-stamped by a European Parliament without powers. Change the names if you will, Eddie, and just ask yourself what we're *really* looking at. In effect, a centralized socialist dictatorship.'

I could see what he was getting at. Change 'Commission' to 'Politburo' and 'Council of Ministers' to 'Central Committee' . . . It was all sounding a bit Orwellian, like some demonic totalitarian state in the making. But, to me, none of that seemed to resemble daffy old Brussels with its wine lakes amid the lavender meadows and butter mountains.

I tried not to let him see my reaction and put on my best poker face. 'What exactly is it that you're investigating, Marcus?'

The man smiled and tapped the side of his nose. 'Need to know and all that. It's safer that way for all concerned. I'm preparing a detailed dossier.'

'So how can I help?'

'I'm being followed constantly, Eddie. In Brussels and over here. My office has been rifled twice to my knowledge and I'm sure that my phones are bugged. Then a couple of weeks ago there was a break-in at my home while I was out. No valuables taken and everything exactly as I'd left it, except for the forced window.'

I lit another cigarette. 'Not very professional.'

'It is – if they *wanted* me to know that my home had been broken into. Put the frighteners on me, so to speak.' He shook his head at the very memory of it. 'It was absolutely unnerving. That was when I decided I had to do something to safeguard my dossier.'

'Was your dossier in the house at the time of the break-in?'

'Thank God, no. I always keep it with me. Even sleep with it under my pillow.'

'I hope you don't want me to sleep with you for protection.'

It was a crass joke, but Marcus had the good grace to smile. 'Not exactly, Eddie. I've decided to make four copies of the dossier. I was hoping you might be able to find a safe place to hide three of them in case something happens to me or the original. At least until it's finished . . . I've still got to shine a torch in a few dark places.'

The request didn't sound too onerous. 'Sure, Marcus. That's no big thing.'

'It is to me. I need to know that this information is totally secure. You're one of the few people I've ever met who I feel I could trust with this.'

'Where are these copies?'

He turned towards Bex and Jude. The two of them were smoking and chatting together in low voices. 'They're on the motorcycle.'

As we began walking back across the dank concrete, Bex looked up and threw away her cigarette stub. 'Are we in business?'

Marcus nodded. 'Eddie's very kindly agreed to assist me.'

Jude reached into the panniers of her bike and extracted four large and weighty Jiffy bags. Each was wire-bound and sealed with solder. Bex and I took two each.

I said: 'You mentioned three, Marcus. What about this fourth one?'

'Ah, yes, I almost forgot. I wonder if you could give it to a friend of mine. She's an investigative journalist on French TV.' He rummaged in the inner pocket of his camel coat and extracted an envelope. 'Her contact details are in here. She's in London at the moment. Do some of your sneaky-beaky stuff, Eddie. What you call fieldcraft, I seem to recall.'

I couldn't resist a smile. 'I was a soldier, not a spy. But I get the point. I'll be discreet.'

'Do, Eddie, because no doubt they're watching her too.' Marcus indicated the envelope. 'There are also the names and addresses of my solicitor and my accountant. If anything happens to me, use my solicitor to help make sure that the dossier sees the light of day. The journalist will also be able to help with that. She can be trusted implicitly. The accountant will take care of all expenses and make sure that you are well rewarded.'

Bex leaned past me and put her face up close to Sir Marcus. 'Lighten up, sunshine, nothing's going to happen to you,' she said with a reassuring smile.

The man's lips twitched. 'No, of course, not. But, just in case . . .' He glanced at his wristwatch. 'Time I was going, I think.'

I said: 'It's been good to see you again.' And I meant it. It was just a shame that we couldn't crack a couple of beers and get him to unwind a little. I knew for a fact that after a drink he could be bloody good company.

Jude thrust her spare bone-dome at him. 'Let's mount up, cowboy.'

'Look, young lady,' he said, strapping it on. 'As there's no way anyone could have followed you here, perhaps we can slow down a bit on the return journey . . .'

But Jude wasn't listening. Her helmet was already on and she was swinging one leather-clad leg over the machine and kicking it into life.

As Sir Marcus climbed gingerly on, she flipped up her visor. 'Have a nice day, Ed.' She grinned broadly. 'Missing you already!'

Her passenger was about to offer me his hand, but he was too late as Jude throttled up and accelerated away so hard that she almost left him behind.

Bex and I watched the tail light disappear over the ramp to the next deck. 'That's my girl,' she murmured.

We began walking back to my car with our packages. The rain was picking up again and suddenly it seemed a colder and more lonely place on the roof of the deserted car-park stack. Why did I have this sudden and profound feeling of foreboding?

As I closed the door and threw the ignition, Bex said: 'You can drop me at the Tube, Ed. I'll make my own way home.'

'Playing Sir Marcus's game?' I goaded.

Her smile was hesitant. 'Playing safe. Jude wasn't sure, you know.'

We moved off and down the ramp. 'About being followed here?'

'She clocked a red Astra and a motorcycle more times than she should have.' Jude, of course, was well trained in recognition. 'But if she's right, she reckons they were good. Must have been running a 4-V box.'

A four-vehicle box is what MI5's watchers use. The idea is a vehicle – a car, taxi, white van or motorcycle – in front of the target and one behind, plus two others driving on a close parallel route. That way everything's covered without making it too obvious. Only the old KGB had the money and resources to run anything up to a 12-V box. It wasn't unknown for them to collide with each other, they were so mob-handed.

Bex added: 'That's when she decided to jump some red lights and drive down a pedestrian precinct.'

Momentarily I closed my eyes. 'Jesus, she must have been spooked.'

Bex chuckled. 'Enough to tell me that she really wished she'd been tooled up for the first time since Belfast. Says next time we help out Marcus, she'll pack her Dad's old starting pistol.'

Now that really wasn't a good idea. That sort of deterrent could get you killed by police marksmen. But then, I hardly had to tell the Essex Girls that. I just said: 'I hope Sir Marcus is paying you well.'

Bex's laugh was loud and genuine. 'Enough for us to pay the office rent for another month.'

That, as I knew from my own predicament, was a pretty good incentive.

I dropped Bex off outside Barking Tube station and continued on towards home on the south side of the river. Traffic was heavy with that frenzied pre-Christmas congestion as everyone poured onto the street to spend to their credit-card limit on overpriced gifts that most of the recipients neither needed nor wanted. Call me a Scrooge, but for years now I'd thought it a sad indictment of what society had become. Since Astrid had died, I tended to lock myself away in my flat over Christmas with some good paperbacks I'd always meant to read and a few bottles of whisky. A couple of carol services on the TV or radio would suffice to lighten my mood, but apart from that I'd just keep my head down until it was all over.

Stuck in yet another jam, my mind wandered over the events of the day. It had been good seeing the Essex Girls again. They'd certainly been well wound-up over Sir Marcus Whitby, but I really couldn't see it. Maybe his wife Jo's death had finally flipped him. That really had been sad news. Nevertheless, I was happy enough to do him such a small favour if it would keep him happy.

At last I pulled into the tatty Victorian street that, disturbingly, was beginning to feel like home. I found a parking space a few houses away, dug out a couple of huge Tesco carrier bags from the boot and filled them with Sir Marcus's packages before trudging up to the front steps.

Then I climbed the main stairway, the rap music from the basement fading away on the first floor where I was engulfed in the smell of red cabbage cooking and cats from the Russian woman's flat. Another flight up and I was assailed by the noise of the screaming baby to be followed by the uneasy silence of the gay nightclubbers' landing.

A burble of deep laughter came from within Cristobelle's flat as I passed and mounted the final flight. Halfway up, I stopped dead.

Light was coming from the gap beneath my front door. Someone was in there.

Involuntarily I took a step back down until my eye level dropped below that of the landing floor. What the hell . . . ?

Of course, I thought immediately of the police. Officers investigating the murder of Tex-Mex — there's nothing like a guilty conscience to get you going.

Then all of Sir Marcus's dark and unlikely warnings began rushing into my head. Although I'd instinctively dismissed it as nonsense, both Bex and Jude were less convinced that it was all in the politician's mind . . .

Suddenly I was aware of voices. Muffled and burbling. The television. Someone had my television set on. So the visitors were hardly likely to be cops. I tried to think rationally. Most probably it was a break-in by a couple of mindless druggies who had discovered my hoard of duty-free Scotch and decided to make an evening of it. Then I remembered the ten grand of blood money sitting behind the panel in the bathroom and panic set in.

I quickly retraced my footsteps to the landing below and rang Cristobelle's doorbell. It took an agonizingly long time before she answered it. Her face was decidedly flushed and she was still tying up the sash of a flimsy red robe that had white fake-fur trimming. Was this some Mistress Santa Claus fantasy or what?

'Oh, Mr Coltrane – sorry to keep you, I was a bit tied up.'

'And I'm sorry to interrupt,' I said quickly. 'But I seem to have an intruder in my flat. You didn't see anyone—?'

Cristobelle shook her head. 'No, I'm afraid not. D'you want to use my phone to call the Bill?'

Police? With ten thousand quid of blood money waiting to be found? I thought not.

I noticed the umbrella stand just inside the door. 'I suppose I couldn't borrow that walking stick?'

'What? Oh, of course. It was my late partner's.' As she handed it to me, I realized it was actually a weighty blackthorn shillelagh. Very useful. 'You will be careful, won't you?'

'There's probably a simple explanation,' I said, but I only wished I could think of one.

She indicated the two heavy Tesco bags at my feet. 'D'you want me to look after those for you?'

'Thanks.' I handed them over, adding: 'And please don't give them back to anyone except me, will you?'

It was out before I realized how stupid it must have sounded.

Cristobelle gave me the tight sort of smile people use when dealing with imbeciles. 'No, Mr Coltrane, of course not.'

As she closed the door, I stealthily climbed the last flight of stairs until I was on the landing outside my front door. Now I could see that it was slightly ajar. Very gently I eased it open with my left hand until I had a clear view across the small hallway to the living room. I could see the back of my armchair where someone sat watching the television. *Da-dum, da-dum, da da da da da-dum.* It was the inanely irritating theme tune of *Blind Date* that had blighted early Saturday-night televison since the beginning of time.

I took a step forward, throwing a glance towards the bedroom and bathroom doors on my right. Both were open and the lights were out. Confident that there would be no nasty surprises creeping up behind me, I ventured forward again with the shillelagh balanced lightly in my right fist.

I didn't make a sound, but the man in the armchair must have seen my reflection in the window glass. He was on his feet in an instant, turning to face me across the room.

As I'd been expecting to confront some spaced-out drug addict, the well-groomed thirty-something gent in the snappy Hugo Boss suit came as a bit of a surprise.

'Ah,' he said, ' you must be Edward!'

My initial shock gave way to anger. 'And who the hell are you?'

He smiled a patronizing little smile. 'Please forgive me, Edward. Didn't know when you'd turn up, so it was either sit in the cold outside or . . . Helped myself to a cup of tea. I was sure you wouldn't mind.'

Whoever he was, his arrogant assumption that he could just waltz into my private flat was bad enough, but calling me Edward was his biggest mistake. I'm not a bloody potato or a cigar – or a minor Royal, for that matter.

I said slowly: 'Well, sunshine, you got it seriously wrong. I mind a *very* great deal. How'd you get in?'

Of course, it was my own fault for not having got round to changing the locks. I saw his reply coming a mile off: 'You know the old credit-card routine, Edward. I'm a bit rusty – afraid I buggered up my gold card.' He took a step forward, offering a slim white hand. 'I'm Tony Tromain, taking over from Morgan Dampier for my sins.' He looked nervously at the shillelagh. 'Don't think there's any need for that, Edward.'

I left his hand clasping at thin air. 'That depends how fast you get out of my flat,' I replied. 'I've finished with Dampier and his people. He knew it and they knew it.'

Tony Tromain looked a trifle pained and withdrew his hand. 'You're forgetting the debrief, Edward. You know the score, always the debrief.'

'Stuff the debrief. Get out of my flat—' I hesitated, suddenly remembering something slightly important. 'Unless you've brought the five grand your lot short-changed me.'

Instantly I realized it was a mistake – we both did. I'd thrown myself on the hook before it was even baited. There was a slight note of triumph in Tromain's voice that he was unable or unwilling to disguise. '*After* the debrief, Edward. We'll talk about it then. Shall we sit down and discuss this like two adults? Just a few minutes of your time.'

To my shame, I'd allowed myself to be suckered. Five grand would make all the difference between floundering to keep my head above the stormy financial waters and a proper life-raft. I tossed the shillelagh on the sofa. 'You've got ten minutes, Tromain. Then I want you out of here.'

He watched as I went through to the adjoining kitchenette and poured myself a whisky. I didn't offer him one before propping myself against the breakfast bar and lighting a Gauloise.

Tromain turned off the television and returned to my armchair. I waited while he searched for his opening gambit. 'It seems that everything went smoothly, Edward. Very clean. The gentleman appears to have expired instantly, certainly by the time the ambulance arrived.'

Dampier's successor irritated me. His skin colour and texture reminded me of wallpaper paste, emphasizing the heavy eyebrows that knitted together over his nose and the fathomless dark eyes that I couldn't read. He took his time to talk, chewing on his words for several moments before finally spitting them out. And when he did they were pitched so low that you had to strain to hear. And everything he said, I noticed, had a practised politician's gloss that made the words, however outrageous, sound like sweet reason itself.

I found myself inclining my head to catch the rest of what he was saying: 'That tart of his and their kids were fast-tracked out of the country as illegal immigrants within twenty-four hours when it was found that their visas were forgeries. They were on a flight to Belgrade before they even had a chance to call a lawyer. And in Northern Ireland we managed to arrest five members of a Loyalist terrorist group when the arms shipment was intercepted.'

'Whoopee,' I said flatly.

Tromain's eyes narrowed a fraction. 'And how did it go for you?'

As if he didn't know, I thought. But I played along just to get it over with. Briefly I ran through the events of Tex-Mex's killing and the immediate aftermath, following with chapter and verse of my escape route in the UK and across the North Sea by ferry to Norway.

Tromain sat silently and watchfully until I had finished. Then he nodded: 'That's fine, Edward. All angles covered and all incriminating weaponry retrieved and suitably disposed of. Generally my people were pleased with the results.'

That pissed me off. '*Generally*?' I queried. 'One war criminal that *they* let get away neatly slotted and the police searching for a non-existent Serbian assassin. And they meanwhile pull off another dirty double-cross into the bargain. All neatly wrapped, with no comebacks. I should bloody well think *they* were pleased – *generally*, of course.'

Tromain stroked his cheek with one neatly manicured index finger. 'There was the question of the phone call.'

I didn't follow. 'What phone call?'

'Your call to Leonid Rusjivic on the point of his departure.'

Oh, shit, I'd forgotten that. I shrugged. 'A personal touch.'

Tromain dispensed with the veneer. 'A personal touch that could have – correction, could still get you into deep water, Edward. That did *not* please them. It won't happen again.'

I rounded on him. 'Two points, *Tony, old friend*. It was a pay-and-go phone bought with cash so no comebacks. And second, you're dead right it won't happen again.'

A supercilious grin spread across his face. 'Never say never, Edward.'

I ignored that and lit another cigarette. 'Right, you've had your debrief. We're all square. So what about the five-grand shortfall? Morgan Dampier made it quite clear that HM Government's word was its bond, as he put it.'

'But Dampier's not running the show now, Edward – I am. And I like a little insurance.'

Of course I'd met the likes of Tony Tromain before. New wave who liked nothing better than to reinvent the wheel. From privileged backgrounds, these university high-flyers were parachuted into top jobs with no practical experience of life and the real world. Their views were the only ones that counted, and they were the only ones entitled to respect and a decent living. Mostly I'd met the sort as short-commission officers in the army but now I'd seen enough of Civvy Street to know that nowadays the bastards were everywhere.

'Insurance against what?' I asked. 'I'm hardly likely to go running to the media or boast about it in the pub.'

He didn't answer me directly, but what happened next explained exactly what Tony Tromain meant by insurance. He wanted control and was stupid enough or inexperienced enough to think that withholding my money was the way to guarantee my cooperation.

The man reached into his inside jacket pocket and took out a buff envelope. 'Tell me if you recognize this man, Edward.'

I stepped forward from the breakfast bar, took the offered envelope and pulled out the glossy photographic print from inside. It was a very long-distance telephoto shot of a short, stocky man in a raincoat, peering furtively back over his shoulder. It was grainy and slightly blurred, but the flat Slav features of the face were unmistakable. And for me unforgettable.

'Zoran Mihac,' I breathed.

There was a distinct hint of smug self-confidence in Tromain's voice as he said quietly: 'I think this one's got your name on it, too, Edward.'

But I was only half listening. Mihac. Tex-Mex's number one gofer and yes-man. With his ugly squashed face, girlish giggle and teeth rotted by slivovitz, we'd named him the 'Poison Dwarf'. His sideline had been peddling pornography to which he made his own contribution with Polaroid photographs and with videos of the unsavoury activities of Tex-Mex's Chetniks. Rapes and murders were routinely and zealously recorded by Mihac like he'd been commissioned by the devil himself. Our SAS unit had long hoped that such careful cataloguing of his group's atrocities would eventually provide the evidence for their downfall. But it had never happened.

'Not dead?' I asked after several long moments spent studying the picture.

'Very much alive, Edward.' Then Tromain added: 'For the moment.'

I said: 'Only a year ago Dampier told me he thought both Tex-Mex and Mihac were probably dead like Brigadier Domedzic.'

'Dampier didn't know everything.'

Or was it, I wondered, because I was the only one in the world still looking for them and I'd been getting too close for comfort. But I just asked: 'Where is Mihac now?'

'In the UK and not a million miles away,' came Tromain's smooth reply.

I paused for thought a moment before asking: 'And working for you – like Leonid Rusjivic?'

Tromain's pasty cheeks suddenly showed a little colour. 'Not quite like Rusjivic. Separately and for the other side. Sorting an arms deal with the Croats for the Real IRA.'

'And was your ploy successful?' I wondered aloud.

The colour in Tromain's face deepened. 'Need to know, Edward. I've said too much already.'

Yes, I thought, he'd said quite enough. Enough to tell me that the Real IRA hadn't been as easy to dupe as the Loyalists. This time Tromain's mob had been dealing with the breakaway professional hard core of the old Provisionals and the expression on his face told me that it had all gone pear-shaped somewhere along the line. My guess would be a double bluff and a delivery switch, so that the Real IRA got their arms courtesy of Mihac while leaving the police attempting to arrest thin air. If so, now Mihac would be an even bigger embarrassment than Tex-Mex had been.

I said: 'Thanks, but no, thanks. I'm not interested.'

The darkness in Tromain's eyes deepened a fraction and he began chewing on his words again, ready to speak. 'But you're perfect for this, Edward. The mystery Serbian assassin

strikes again. Same modus operandi. A connection with
Leonid Rusjivic and the police left chasing the same shadow.'
He paused, chewing up another sentence. 'And I'm led to
understand Zoran Mihac is on your personal hitlist. With
Brigadier Domedzic dead and now Leonid Rusjivic, getting
rid of Mihac will complete the hat-trick.'

I thought about that for a second. But I'd killed Tex-Mex
and his death had made me feel no better – and Mihac,
unpleasant as he was, was just the organ-grinder's monkey.
The bloodletting had made me see sense. This tit-for-tat
mentality was what had made the Balkans such a bloody
mess in the first place. Besides, to kill again would be getting
in dangerously deep.

'Mihac is wanted for war crimes,' I said. 'Just arrest him.'

Tromain looked pained. 'You know we can't do that. We
both know what would come out in court.'

'I said I'm not interested.'

He ignored that. 'That five grand in your pocket immediately, Edward. Plus another fifteeen for the Mihac job.'
Then he added generously: 'Now we *know* we can trust you,
you'll get it *all* up front this time.'

'Are you deaf or something?' I asked.

His voice dropped again, almost to a whisper. 'I think you
owe it to your late wife. To Astrid.'

For a moment I was stunned. I could not believe what
he'd just said. I felt my eyes narrow and the veins bulge in
my neck. Tromain should have seen the signs, but he didn't.
And his reactions were too slow as I launched myself from
the breakfast bar, grabbed him by the lapels and with one
powerful heave lifted him out of the armchair like a rocket
taking off for Mars. I heard the Hugo Boss suit start popping
at the seams under his arms.

I held his face so close to mine that I could see the cracks
in the whites of his wide-open eyes and smell the spearmint
mouthwash on his breath. 'I don't care what you *think*, you

little scumbag,' I snarled. 'Don't play fucking games with me. And don't you ever mention Astrid's name again. Understood?'

He nodded dumbly before I threw him back into his armchair with all the power of the contempt that I felt for him. For a moment he was winded and started fiddling with his shirt collar, trying to get some air down to his neck.

'I've tried being reasonable, Coltrane, but that sort of behaviour won't help your case,' he muttered as he inspected the splits in his suit.

Coltrane, eh? At last we were getting somewhere. 'My *case*?' I asked through clenched teeth.

He scowled up at me with a hatred that I could feel. 'You need all the friends you can get. You need us. You need me.'

That was a very good joke. 'You think so?'

Tromain suddenly looked pleased and smug, as though he was about to say what he'd wanted to say all along. 'You're a murderer, Coltrane. You've just murdered a man on the streets of London and the police are looking for the person responsible. Given Leonid Rusjivic's background, the intelligence services have been routinely asked if they can cast any light on the matter. Do I have to spell it out?' I wanted to wipe the conceited smile off his face with my fist as he went on: 'As far as I'm concerned, Coltrane, you're either with us or you're against us.'

I pulled another Gauloise from the pack and lit it, much to Tromain's disdain. 'And if I'm *not* with you?' I goaded.

This time he didn't bother to chew his words first. '*Against* us is a life sentence of twenty years, minimum. And you'll go down because our involvement with Rusjivic was totally sanitized from start to finish. And you had your *own* motive – revenge for Astrid Kweiss's murder – nothing to do with us.

'At best for you it will be your word against that of Morgan Dampier, a senior civil servant, the intelligence services and Her Majesty's Government. And no classified documents will be available for your defence.' He paused to let that sink in, then added: 'On the other hand, *with* us means a total of thirty grand in the bank and our protection from any future police investigation.'

'Your protection,' I repeated and swallowed the last of the whisky in my glass. Suddenly it tasted like gripe water. 'Now there's a thought.'

The world seemed to be closing in around me, the shadows darkening.

Tromain was on his feet. 'I'll not waste any more of your time, Edward. Obviously I'm leaving you with a lot to think about.'

Oh, no, we were back to Edward. The bastard knew that he had the upper hand again. He didn't bother to offer a handshake as he moved towards the front door. 'Just a thought – when all's said and done – once Mihac is dead one thing is certain. He'll never be able to visit grief on anyone else ever again. That alone's got to make it worthwhile.'

It was a sop to his conscience or mine, but I couldn't say he didn't have a point. Or was I just fooling myself and starting to accept the unthinkable?

Tromain added quietly: 'I'll be in touch.'

'Don't bother,' I snarled at his back.

As the door shut my whisky tumbler shattered like a hand grenade on the timber just above where his head had been. I watched the glass shrapnel burst in the air and rain down all over the carpet.

I had no one to blame but myself. I had walked into this trap with my eyes wide open. And the damn thing was, I could see no way out.

# Four

The next morning dawned late.

It was almost ten when I came to on the sofa where I'd fallen asleep. I had a thick head, a crick in my neck and some kiddies' programme presenter was screaming manically at me from the television. On top of that someone was knocking on the front door.

I cranked open one eye and tried focusing on the whisky bottle that I'd emptied the night before as I'd been working out where the hell to go from here. With a huge effort I climbed to my feet and killed the television. In the blessed silence that followed, I orientated myself and staggered out of the room.

I threw open the door to be momentarily startled by Cristobelle's powdered white face and smudged scarlet lipstick. She was clutching my two Tesco bags. 'I think you forgot these, Mr Coltrane.'

'What?' I scratched my head. 'Oh yes, sorry.'

'I gather you *didn't* have burglars. I was listening in case of trouble . . . I heard raised voices, but it sounded like you knew each other?'

Cristobelle's eyes told me that she was itching for some gossip, so I said the first thing that came into my head: 'Never lend keys to friends, they just take liberties. Don't we ever learn?'

Her eyes suddenly sparkled as she put two and two together and made sixty-nine. 'A lovers' tiff, Mr Coltrane? I understand.'

A lovers' tiff? Me and Tony Tromain? Just what planet was Cristobelle living on, I wondered? I said: 'Sure, I told him to pack his dresses and sling his hook.' I reached forward and took the Tesco bags from her. 'Thanks for looking after these. Bye for now.'

Closing the door on my perplexed and perplexing neighbour, I took the bags through to the kitchenette. I dumped them on the table and put the kettle on. Since Tony Tromain's visit, helping out Sir Marcus Whitby by distributing his four precious packages suddenly seemed like a ridiculous chore I could really do without. This was the last Sunday before Christmas so I had a full schedule.

First I telephoned an emergency locksmith from *Yellow Pages*. Then, over black coffee and toast, I opened the envelope that Sir Marcus had given me and ran through its contents. As he'd said, it contained the names of both his solicitor and accountant, each with prestigious-sounding City addresses.

The third was the French investigative reporter. Mme Francoise Paquet. Against her name was the address of what sounded like a production company, *Televu-News Expresse*, her home address in Paris and a London contact number at the Moncrief Hotel in Bayswater.

I reached for the telephone, then hesitated. No! To call direct was hardly the *discreet* approach I'd promised Sir Marcus. After all, that was what he was trusting me to be. It was why he had gone to such great lengths to track me down. However much I might dismiss his concerns as pure paranoia, at least I owed him my word.

Then I reminded myself just how convinced Jude had been that the MEP really might have been under surveillance. Even Bex was far from sure, one way or the other . . .

I replaced the receiver, a plan forming rapidly in my head as the hangover began to subside. If I took the matter seriously, the first job had to be to get Sir Marcus's copied dossiers off my premises. As a temporary measure, I decided to combine the operation with my day's planned pre-Christmas visits, get the dossiers off my hands until I could arrange for somewhere more secure to squirrel them away.

At eleven the locksmith arrived and spent an hour fixing a couple of decent five-lever Chubbs to the front door. The next time I got an unannounced visit from Tromain he could damn well cool his heels in his car or on the landing. Besides, I wanted to be sure that no casual burglar could stumble across my blood money by accident. There was also the small matter of the Argentinian officer's automatic pistol, my treasured souvenir from the Falklands War – and totally illegal.

When the locksmith had finished, I took the Tesco bags and another filled with Christmas gifts down to my car and locked them in the boot before setting out for Clapham. Half an hour later I pulled up outside a tall Edwardian house just off the Common. The converted ground-floor flat was the home of the Kweiss family.

I really wasn't looking forward to this. I'd only met Astrid's parents once briefly before our marriage. The next time had been at Astrid's funeral. Afterwards it had been difficult to know what to do. I hardly knew them – but then, I couldn't just ignore them after Astrid's death. So I made a point of seeing them around each Christmas and made one or two rather strained hello-calls during the course of the year to see how they were. They, I noticed, never attempted to contact me.

Papa Kweiss was German and a retired clockmaker. Mira Kweiss was Serbian and had once worked at an antiques auctioneers in Belgrade where the two of them had first met. Once married they had lived in Austria for several years before moving to London. Astrid had come to them late in life when they'd both given up hope of ever having children. Not surprisingly, their beautiful and clever daughter had meant absolutely everything to them. Since her death they had both aged noticeably.

That fact came home to me yet again when Papa Kweiss opened the door, wearing his old brown cords and food-stained cardigan. He was hunched and wizened and seemed to have difficulty recognizing me as he peered over his pince-nez with watery, pale blue eyes. It was his colouring that Astrid had inherited.

I smiled. 'It's me – Eddie. Just popped round to wish you happy Christmas.'

'Ah, Eddie, of course!' His face lit up. 'Do come in.'

It was dark and sombre in the flat as he led me to the living room where thick velvet drapes protected the antique furniture from any vestiges of daylight. The place smelled of dust, mildew and cat litter.

'Look who's called, dear,' Papa Kweiss said.

Mira was sitting in an ancient club chair, crocheting by the light of a standard lamp. Eyes as black as anthracite looked up from beneath a head of greying hair that was swept severely back into a bun. She inclined her head in acknowledgement but the thin lips did not smile.

I held out my gift-wrapped peace-offering. The over-powering smell of hyacinths was a giveaway as to the contents. Mira put down her knitting and accepted the package with a barely audible 'Thank you.'

'Hope you're both well?' I said brightly.

Mira's smouldering stare was unsettling. We both knew exactly what she thought, although she had never actually said it.

Papa Kweiss broke the awkward silence. 'We're both fit enough, anno domini considered.'

Without a further word, Mira rose and left the room for the kitchen, closing the door silently behind her.

'She has to prepare the lunch,' Papa Kweiss said by way of explanation. 'Come, we just have time for a drink together.'

I followed him back down the dark corridor and into his den. It was filled with all sorts of clocks, all chiming discordantly at different rates. There were freestanding grandfather and grandmother models, lantern and skeleton and cuckoos, carriage and anniversary clocks. A large, hand-engraved brass face lay on his workbench, its mechanical innards laid out in neat rows.

'I'm repairing that for a local pub. A beauty – dated 1780,' he explained as he fetched a bottle of plum brandy from the cupboard. 'It hasn't worked for thirty years. There are no longer the people who can do this sort of work.'

He poured two small tumblers and handed me one. '*Salut!*'

'Happy Christmas,' I said. 'It's good to see you both again.'

There was suddenly moisture in the old man's eyes. 'Thank you, Eddie. But I doubt any Christmas will be happy ever again. Maybe I could try to put it behind me, but Mira will not let go.'

I noticed then that he was looking at a small framed picture of Astrid on his workbench. Quickly I averted my eyes. I'd just caught the halo of light in her fair hair and her smile, but it was enough. I wished I hadn't seen it, but it was too late. Purposely, I had thrown out all my own photographs of Astrid because I found the memories they evoked just too painful.

I said: 'Mira still holds me responsible, doesn't she?'

Papa Kweiss shrugged. 'If Astrid hadn't met you ... If you hadn't broken the army's rules and secretly married her ... Unfair, I know, but that is how Mira thinks. And she has the Slav capacity for unforgiveness.'

I wondered if the old man knew. I said: 'Did you and Mira hear about the Serb killed in London a couple of weeks ago? I think that was Astrid's murderer.'

He looked at me curiously, long and hard, and I couldn't quite read his thoughts. At last he said quietly: 'Eddie, forgive me, but I think perhaps it is better if you do not come again.

I know you mean well, but it just upsets Mira. Old memories are stirred. We probably do not have long together and I want to make our time as happy as possible. Do you understand? I am sorry.'

There was nothing I could say to that. I can't say it didn't hurt, because Papa and Mira Kweiss were my last link with Astrid. Maybe I, too, needed to cut the link. The noise of the ticking clocks seemed to swell to a cacophony in my skull until I wanted to scream.

Quickly I finished the brandy. 'Of course, I understand.' I just wanted to get out of there and in my haste to leave I almost forgot Sir Marcus's dossier. 'There's just one favour I have to ask.'

Papa Kweiss accepted the Tesco bag. 'This?'

'Could you keep it safe for me for a few days? We're always having break-ins where I live and they're valuable documents. Just until I can arrange something more permanent.'

The old man smiled. 'Of course. Ring me when you want to collect them and I'll bring them out to your car. No need for you and Mira to see each other.'

I thanked him and left Papa Kweiss with his bottle of malt in its Christmas wrapping.

The next leg of my journey across the suburbs of South London to Wimbledon passed in a sort of haze. I couldn't get out of my head how much Mira must have hated me. It's very unsettling to have the mother of your wife hold you responsible for her daughter's death. And, irritatingly, Tromain's words kept playing in my head like muzak on a continuous loop. *Just a thought – when all's said and done – once Mihac is dead one thing is certain. He'll never be able to visit grief on anyone else ever again. That alone's got to make it worthwhile.'*

Wendy's place was a smart three-bedroomed semi in a quiet residential neighbourhood. She'd done far better for herself than if she'd stayed married to me and I was genuinely pleased for her. Her husband Dick was honest and hard-working with a promising career in retail management.

If anyone had to be the substitute father for my son Timmy, then I couldn't have chosen better than Dick myself. And I knew he would never raise a fist to Wendy in anger as I had when I'd been younger. She hadn't had the independence of spirit to make a suitable army wife and her continual griping had got to me. Once or twice, too much booze had combined with the stress of some of my work with the SAS in Northern Ireland to make an explosive cocktail. That impetuous violence had cost me my marriage and my son.

It was Wendy who opened the door with a bright and welcoming smile. Each time we met she seemed slightly plumper and more content than the time before. And also a touch more flirtatious. I think she'd finally forgiven me and, just perhaps, still carried a small torch for me somewhere in her heart.

I handed over the gift-wrapped PlayStation 2 and the second Tesco bag. 'That's for Timmy and that's for safe-keeping, if you wouldn't mind.'

Wendy laughed. 'What are you up to, Eddie?'

'My place was broken into,' I explained. 'I thought next time the little scrotes might vandalize my legal papers for the hell of it.'

'Can't you move to a nicer area? I do worry about you sometimes.'

I winked at her. 'Only sometimes?'

'That's for me to know and you to guess,' she countered brightly.

Just then Timmy came down the stairs behind her, frantically pulling on his anorak. 'Hi, Dad, I didn't hear the door-bell ring.'

Wendy stood aside as he rushed past. 'Nose stuck in your computer, young man, that's why!'

Timmy grinned up at me. We didn't kiss or hug; you don't do that sort of stuff when you're a macho eleven-year-old. 'There's a movie on I'd like to see. *Gladiator*. You'll love it, Dad, honest. And no gunfights for you to pick holes in.'

'And a McDonald's first, I suppose?' I looked up at Wendy. 'Is that okay? Not too late?'

She shook her head. 'School's broken up. You just enjoy yourselves.'

At the local McDonald's Timmy met one of his schoolmates and I left them gossiping over their cheeseburgers and fries to use the public call box outside.

I dialled the number of the Bayswater hotel and asked for Francoise Paquet. The room extension rang for several minutes before it was answered.

''Allo, Room six.' The heavy Parisienne accent sounded husky with sleep.

'Madame Paquet?'

'Mademoiselle,' she corrected. 'Yes?'

'My name's Ed. We have a mutual friend who has asked me to deliver a package to you.'

There was a slight hesitation. 'And who is this mutual friend?'

'Best I don't say on an open line.'

There was a hint of a laugh in the voice. 'But I have many friends.'

'Are they all this cautious?' I countered.

The laugh deepened. 'Many, yes. Tell me, is this friend English?'

'Very. But he works in Brussels. He has warned me to be very discreet.'

Francoise said: 'That narrows it down a bit, Mr – er – Mr Ed, did you say? And you have something for me? When do you want to meet? I go back to France on Tuesday.'

I was due to start work the next day, but reckoned I could

get into London for a while around one. 'Could you make lunchtime tomorrow? Central London.'

The tone stiffened slightly. 'I do not do lunch with strangers, Mr Ed. I can see you at three. At my London office—'

That irked me somewhat. I hadn't exactly invited her out and, besides, it wasn't the sort of discreet contact that Sir Marcus was relying on me to provide. I said: 'No, I'm afraid not. I'll see you at five-thirty tomorrow evening. In the lobby of the Charing Cross Hotel.'

There was an unmistakable intake of breath at my suddenly assertive tone and I wondered if I detected a little more respect as she said: 'Very well, Mr Ed. I think I can make that.'

I added: 'I'll need to recognize you.'

'I have fair hair and will wear a beige raincoat.'

She disappointed me by not adding she'd be wearing a beret and smoking Disque Bleu. I said: 'Could you also carry a copy of *Le Figaro*?'

'Sure, if that will help.'

'And bring a large empty carrier bag with you.'

'Yes?' She sounded perplexed.

'Fill it out with some tissue paper and carry it, okay?'

There was a hint of amusement now. 'If it pleases you, Mr Ed.'

'Thank you, Mademoiselle Paquet. I look forward to our meeting.'

I replaced the receiver, a mental picture of Francoise Paquet already forming in my mind. Dammit, strange how women with foreign accents get us every time! It must be something to do with the quixotic and unknown. And, of course, it works the same for women. I'd heard it said by people in Int that if ever you want to recruit an agent, use a foreigner to seduce them into your honey trap. It's ten times more likely to succeed.

Having told myself that Ms Paquet was probably a sixteen-stone frump in woollen stockings who just happened to have a sexy French voice, I rejoined Timmy and set off for the cinema.

It was an absorbing and enjoyable film, although I couldn't help thinking I'd seen it all – and a better story – with Kirk Douglas starring in *Spartacus* years before. I avoided mentioning this to Timmy, or criticizing some of the combat sequences, and we returned to Wimbledon in good spirits. I even got a kiss under the mistletoe from Wendy that went on a little longer and deeper than was quite proper, given our new relationship. She looked happy and a little flushed as she wished me happy Christmas and pressed a small package into my palm as I left.

I drove home in a cheerful mood and actually didn't turn off the radio when carols started to be played. Somehow life seemed to be looking up.

After fiddling with my new double-locked security system, I entered the flat and had just put the kettle on when the telephone rang. Absently I wondered if it might be Wendy, perhaps inviting me to join her, Timmy and Dick for Christmas lunch. Well, you never knew . . .

'Hello, Edward,' the voice said.

My heart dropped. 'What the fuck do you want, Tromain?'

'Changed your locks, I see. Very wise in that neighbourhood.'

'What do you want?' I repeated.

I was aware of him masticating his words before he spoke. 'Wondered if you'd given my proposition any thought. We're anxious to get things moving.'

My anger flared. Despite the threats he'd made, I impulsively decided to call his bluff. 'Yes and no. Yes, I've thought about it . . . for two seconds. And the answer's the same and always will be. Now, piss off out of my life—' I slammed the receiver down.

After that my mind was in turmoil. For over an hour I

sat with a whisky, watching the phone and waiting for Tromain to ring again. He didn't. I eventually fell asleep on the sofa around two-thirty in the morning, a good day totally ruined.

I awoke with a start to the distant ringing of the alarm clock in my bedroom. It was seven and I felt like shit. Stripping off for a shower and shave, I cursed Tromain again. With work the next day, I'd normally never have had more than a nightcap — not half a bottle.

By seven-thirty I'd towelled down and dressed in my bargain-basement suit, white shirt and tie which I still couldn't get used to. I was just preparing a tomato juice and shot of Worcester sauce when there was a heavy knock at the front door. Immediately my heart skipped a beat: it was the loud and authoritative way the police tend to announce themselves, never bothering with doorbells in case they're not working.

As I crossed the hall I reminded myself that courier delivery men in a hurry often did the same. Vaguely wondering if it was a Christmas gift from someone, I threw open the door.

Immediately my initial fear was realized. The two men standing there in dark raincoats might as well have had the word 'police' stamped through them like a stick of seaside rock.

'Mr Edward Coltrane?' asked the smaller of the two men. He had thinning ginger hair and skin that looked like it hadn't seen daylight in months.

'Who's asking?' I answered cautiously, having to force myself not to glance towards the bathroom where my blood money and souvenir pistol were hidden.

He flashed his pass. 'Inspector Kingdom, Metropolitan Police Special Branch,' he said glibly, already looking over my shoulder at the interior of the flat. I noticed that he had a wall eye, and it was difficult to know exactly when he was looking at me. 'This is DS Cherry.'

The taller, gawky man with a slight stoop grinned at me with buck teeth that would have looked good on a rabbit.

'No need to be alarmed, sir,' Inspector Kingdom added. 'We'd just like to see if you can help us with our inquiries into the murder of a Serbian gentleman by the name of Leonid Rusjivic. Perhaps you heard about the incident?'

I was aware of the blood rushing to my face. 'Er, yes.' I turned away quickly. 'Do come in. I've just got some coffee on.'

'That's most welcome, sir,' Kingdom said as he followed me in, his eyes glancing seemingly everywhere and in two directions at once. The two of them sat on the settee and waited until I brought them two mugs.

'Excuse me a minute,' I said, reaching for the telephone on the breakfast bar.

'What are you doing, sir?' Kingdom demanded.

I had the receiver halfway to my ear. 'Phoning work. I'm going to be late.'

Kingdom shook his head. 'Not a good idea.'

'I'm due back off leave. They'll need to know.'

'I can't let you do that,' Kingdom insisted.

That angered me. 'Am I under arrest?'

'No, sir,' Kingdom answered evenly. 'But I *would* be fully justified in arresting you now on suspicion of murder until such time as we can eliminate you from the inquiry. And I'll have no hesitation in doing so if you do not cooperate with us fully. That includes not making calls to anyone outside this room.'

DS Cherry explained helpfully: 'The killer of Leonid Rusjivic almost certainly had accomplices whom he would wish to tip off about our investigation. That could be someone at his place of work. I'm sure you understand. Later we'll let your employer know you were helping us—' He showed me his teeth again. 'So they know you weren't just swinging the lead.'

I wasn't sure that was a bright idea, but I let it pass. I replaced the receiver. 'Okay, so what can I do to help?'

Kingdom sniffed at his coffee before taking a couple of noisy slurps. 'Special Branch is not part of the main murder inquiry. We're hoovering up around the fringes where the matter touches on areas of national security. As you are no doubt aware, Leonid Rusjivic was wanted for war crimes.'

It was a rhetorical question and I could tell that Kingdom already knew I knew. So I just nodded.

'The murder-case officers therefore asked us to check with – er – the intelligence agencies about the victim's background,' Kingdom explained. 'We've been told that among the long list of heinous crimes on which he was to face charges was the murder of Astrid Kweiss – who, I understand, was your wife for a short while before she was killed.'

Another rhetorical question. I wasn't sure which of Kingdom's eyes to focus on. 'That's true.'

He pulled an expression that was supposed to be understanding. 'I'm sorry if this is painful for you.' His lip-service to a one-day Hendon course on 'sympathetic policing' out of the way, he continued more aggressively: 'I also understand that since you left the army five years ago, you've spent time and money privately trying to hunt down Rusjivic and others you deem to be responsible for your wife's death. Is that so?'

I could hardly deny it. I took a deep breath. 'Up until last year. By then the trail had run cold. I decided I was wasting my time.'

Then DS Cherry chimed in. 'Do you speak Serbo-Croat, Mr Coltrane?'

'Yes.'

'Are you in the habit of wearing sunglasses?'

I shook my head. 'Can't stand them. It's an army thing. In the British Army we're trained to see the whites of the enemy's eyes.'

'This isn't a joking matter,' Kingdom scolded.

DS Cherry went on: 'Are you in the habit of dyeing your hair or wearing a wig?'

In my attempt to suppress a laugh, I almost blew a mouthful of coffee over the idiot. 'I thought you said this wasn't a joking matter. What sort of a fool question is that?'

Kingdom kept a straight face. 'Just answer it.'

'No – and neither am I in the habit of murdering people,' I retorted.

DS Cherry said: 'Why else would you have tried to hunt Rusjivic down?'

I smiled sweetly. 'So that I could report his whereabouts to the authorities so they could arrest him.' The lying words came out out with surprising ease.

However, DS Cherry was on a roll. 'But you did wish him dead, did you not?'

I stared back at him. 'At the moment, Detective Sergeant, I'm starting to wish *you* dead, but it doesn't mean I'm going to kill you.'

'That's quite enough,' Kingdom growled.

'Quite enough,' I agreed. 'To save you wasting my time with any more daft questions, can I just point out that I was on holiday abroad when Rusjivic was murdered. Perhaps your informers in intelligence weren't aware of that small fact?'

Inspector Kingdom looked as though he'd received a mild electric shock as DS Cherry glanced at him for some sort of lead.

I said: 'Let me show you.'

I went to the sideboard drawer and took out all the used tickets and travel documents covering my trip out and back by the Portsmouth-to-Cherbourg car ferry.

After scrutinizing these thoroughly, Kingdom asked: 'And where did you stay while you were there? Which towns and hotels?'

That question made me feel distinctly hot under the collar. 'All over northern France. I was touring. I don't remember exactly. I'd have to go back and try to remember the route.'

'How did you pay? Credit card?'

I smiled. 'Sorry, cash.'

'Convenient,' Kingdom said.

'I find it so,' I agreed.

After a long pause, Kingdom said: 'I'll have to take this documentation and check it out with Customs and Immigration.'

'Be my guest,' I replied as the two men rose to leave. By that point a couple of questions were floating around in my mind. Neither the Secret Intelligence Service nor the Security Service – repectively known as MI6 and MI5 – have powers of arrest. Their link to the regular police force is Special Branch, which in many respects does their bidding. In some situations, the three organizations dance down the street together, holding hands. And, as Kingdom had pointed out earlier, Special Branch was not at the centre of the Leonid Rusjivic murder inquiry. Which raised a question I knew they would not answer directly.

I said: 'Didn't the killing happen almost two weeks ago?'

Kingdom had reached the front door. 'That's correct, sir.'

'It's taken an awful long time for you to interview me,' I pointed out, not reminding him that they hadn't even known I had been out of the country.

DS Cherry was immediately on the defensive. 'We were only told about you last night, Mr Coltrane.' He added, with a hint of menace: 'Believe me, we don't let the grass grow.'

Kingdom scowled at him, then the two men turned and walked towards the stairs. As I closed the door behind them and fell back against it, I found that I was shaking.

Tromain, the bastard! When I'd hung up on him the previous evening, he must have picked up the phone and called Special Branch immediately. If this was a poker game, he'd just countered my bluff and raised the stakes. And I wasn't sure I could afford to stay in the game. Worse, I didn't know which department Tromain actually worked for or even have a telephone number for him. It seemed like he held all the cards.

I'd lost my appetite for breakfast and made do with a double dose of caffeine and nicotine as I tried to work out what the hell to do before the dynamic duo of Kingdom and Cherry contacted the French police or carted me off to retrace my supposed wanderings around Brittany and Normandy.

Finally I put in a call to the front desk of the Ministry of Defence and asked to speak to the 'security section'. When a Scotswoman of obviously mature years answered, I told her I was a former special-forces soldier who'd been contacted by someone in one of the intelligence services, but didn't know which.

She remained unfazed when I gave his name. 'Mr Tromain doesn't seem to be one of ours, Mr Coltrane. But leave it with me and I'll see what I can do.'

After an hour sitting by the phone waiting for her to call back, I gave up.

When I finally arrived at work it had gone eleven. The warehouse manager glared at me as I entered. 'I know why you're late, Coltrane. I've had the police on the phone and they've explained you're the subject of a murder inquiry.'

'Not exactly—' I began.

That was as far as I got. He cut in: 'Personnel want to see you straight away, if you please.'

Ten minutes later I was out of work with a three months' redundancy cheque. Apparently in future my work in the warehouse was to be done by a computer. The murder inquiry wasn't even mentioned. It was an unlikely reason for the dismissal, but it would have taken months of waiting and a tribunal to try and disprove. My only consolation was that the cheque for four grand almost made up the shortfall from the extermination of Tex-Mex.

I cleared my desk and arrived back at my flat at three, opening the door to the accompaniment of the telephone ringing. I picked up the handset before the answerphone kicked in.

'Hello, Edward. I gather you've been asking after me.'

I felt a reluctant surge of relief. 'Okay, Tromain, you win. Call off the dogs.'

There was a pause. 'It might not be that easy . . .'

He was playing games now. I said: 'Don't mess with me if you want the job done. Right?'

Tromain didn't chew his words, he spat them straight out. 'And you don't mess with me, Edward, is that clear? It's a done deal. I'll let SB know you were doing a courier job for us while on your jaunt to France. That'll explain your few days' disappearance if it ever comes to that.'

'And I've lost my job through this,' I added.

'We're not bloody Social Security, Edward. But anyway, you're not going to be able to do regular work for the moment. I need to see you tomorrow. Meet me at eleven opposite Platform Eight at Euston.'

The next day was Christmas Eve. I said: 'I'll have to check my diary.'

'Be there,' Tromain replied tersely and left me talking to the dial tone.

I wasted several minutes swearing at the receiver before stuffing the two remaining copies of Sir Marcus's dossier into a couple of Happy Shopper bags and setting out for the car. On my way to central London, I dropped into my solicitors' office and paid off an outstanding bill in cash before requesting that they keep one of the dossiers in their safe for me. Plucking an exorbitant handling fee out of thin air, they agreed and I drove off with the remaining copy in the boot of my BMW.

It took a while until I found a spare meter behind the Charing Cross Hotel. Leaving the dossier in the car, I made the rest of my way on foot and arrived at five o'clock with thirty minutes to spare. It gave me time to buy an *Evening Standard*, find an armchair in the lobby and view the scene. Apart from the hotel staff, there were the usual comings and goings of guests and people passing through, some apparently lingering as they waited for others to join them.

After fifteen minutes I was fairly sure that everyone was genuinely going about their ordinary business. Staff were another matter, of course. As is common practice with most governments and their intelligence agencies, in London the Security Service – still called MI5 in the media – has hotel personnel on its payroll. Usually it's the security manager who knows all about visiting guests, especially VIPs who may be visiting foreign nationals of interest, including governmental dignitaries and businessmen who run seemingly respectable fronts for arms or narcotics trading. Security managers can usually get MI5 rooms for meetings or surveillance purposes at a few minutes' notice, as well as access to guests' rooms, left luggage and CCTV footage. They can also facilitate bugging if the hotel runs a concierge car-parking system. Other staff are also on backhanders for low-grade information and assistance.

Of course, I had no way of telling if Sir Marcus's mythical shadowmen were working alone – with little blue flags with the circle of gold stars stuck in their hats – or with MI5 co-operation. Or if they existed at all.

Then, ten minutes before my rendezvous time with Francoise Paquet, I noticed a shortish man with dark features and wearing a grey overcoat stroll into the lobby and glance slowly but carefully around. He made no effort to hide the fact that he was looking for someone specific. Then he glanced at his watch, shook his head in an attitude of dismay and took a mobile phone from his pocket. He started talking.

I wondered why my attention was drawn to him as I peered over the top of my newspaper. After a few moments the penny dropped. He was *acting* his part. I knew from his body language that he'd arrived either late or on time and his contact wasn't there. That was his excuse to get on the phone and find out why.

The use of mobile phones en masse has made some intelligence 'watchers' sloppy. In the old days they smoked or chewed gum obviously to cover the fact that they were talking into a hidden mike. Now they just have to pull out a mobile like everyone else. Only it clearly wasn't a phone but a secure radio on an open channel. This grey little man with his dark Slav-like features had omitted to pretend to dial even a single number.

So I wasn't surprised when he pocketed the phone, pulled the furled newspaper from under his arm and leaned against a far wall to read it while he waited for his imaginary contact. I recognized the picture and headline on the front page; it was yesterday's news.

I'd barely shifted my attention from him when Francoise Paquet strode in through the main glass door. Instantly I just *knew* it was her. The copy of *Le Figaro* that she carried was unnecessary. She was tall and poised, her long beige raincoat in a soft material floating around her slim body like a cloak. There was a confidence, perhaps even arrogance, about her as high heels clacked on the hard floor surface before she halted and scanned the lobby to see if the 'Mr Ed' she did not know was obviously looking out for her. Her head turned briskly from side to side like a tango dancer's so that the fair hair, cut in a stylish no-nonsense bob, was tossed around her high cheekbones like a curtain in a breeze.

There was no doubt about it, the girl had presence. And the tasteful small drop earrings and Hermes scarf around her throat were unmistakable statements of Continental *chic*, as was the empty carrier bag I'd asked her to bring. Our exchange was going to be a case of Harvey Nichols meets the Happy Shopper.

Convinced that I was not yet there, she found herself a vacant sofa and parked herself on it with an elegant intertwining of her legs. Thank goodness she didn't enquire at the concierge's desk if a 'Mr Ed' had asked after her.

Not surprisingly the man reading yesterday's news was on the phone again. Then, just after Paquet had sat down, a second man entered the lobby from the street, also on the phone. It didn't take a genius to work out that they were probably talking to each other. Having arrived, the man I guessed had been following her suddenly didn't seem to know why he was there. He began to develop an unusually keen interest in wall panelling and soft furnishings.

These guys weren't MI5, the Security Service. They weren't that bad, but they weren't good. But they did seem to have professional resources. If Paquet hadn't blabbed to a third party, then they'd managed to bug her Bayswater hotel phone, because one of them had been waiting for her to arrive.

It was time for me to reposition. I folded my *Standard*, stood up and went to the gents. Five minutes later I returned and wandered across to where Francoise Paquet sat. There I paused and glanced at my watch, tapping the face with the index finger of my left hand.

Then I sat beside her. 'Excuse me, do you have the right time?'

'Pardon me?' The Parisienne accent was as delicious as cognac and cream.

'Do you have the correct time?'

Her eyes were grey, intelligent and beguiling. She looked distracted. 'Sorry, of course.'

I might have guessed. A gold Cartier clung to her slender wrist. 'Five thirty-five.'

I said: 'I thought so. I'm fast. Arrived too early.' I took a packet of Gauloises from my pocket. 'Smoke?'

She shook her head. 'I do, but not now thank you.'

I used the tiny book of paper hotel matches to give me the opportunity to make several convincing attempts to light up. Just long enough for me to whisper: 'Mademoiselle Paquet, I want you to wait ten minutes, then leave here and take a taxi immediately to John Lewis in Oxford Street. Go in the front entrance and straight through the store and out the rear exit. I'll be waiting for you in a gold BMW.'

Worry lines fractured the smooth skin of her forehead as one finely sculptured eyebrow was raised. 'Mr Ed?'

I finally got the cigarette burning. 'Who else? Thanks for the light.'

Then I was up and away. Once outside and round the corner, I broke into a trot. If Paquet's shadowmen thought I was anything other than a casual passer-by, they'd have to break their cover by running.

But no one had showed by the time I reached my parked BMW. I started it up and moved quickly into position on a double yellow outside Charing Cross Station, just in time to see Paquet join the taxi queue. As her black cab pulled away a few minutes later I watched a blue Peugeot sweep up outside the hotel entrance. Yesterday's news and the soft-furnishings expert piled in as it set off at speed to catch up with Paquet's taxi. I slid into gear and followed.

# Five

I kept the blue Peugeot in my sights all the way to Oxford Circus as it followed in hot pursuit of Francoise Paquet's taxi until it finally stopped opposite the John Lewis store in Oxford Street.

The moving lights of the traffic conspired with illuminated shop fronts and overhead Christmas decorations to create a confusing kaleidoscope of reflection and colour on the wet street. Squinting through the thrash of my car's wipers, I slowed for just long enough to see that the journalist was paying off the cabbie and that her two shadows were rapidly deploying onto the pavement from the Peugeot.

Then I swung right, across the oncoming traffic and down Holles Street, which ran alongside the store. Another left-hander and I drew up on a double yellow with a view of the John Lewis rear exit.

I was impatiently watching for what seemed an age before the glass doors opened and Paquet emerged. She halted at the pavement edge and glanced anxiously up and down the street. I gunned the BMW forward and pulled up in front of her, reaching over to throw open the passenger door. The moment she was in, I hit the gas and pulled into the passing stream of traffic to a protest of hooting motor horns.

'Very dramatic, Mr Ed,' she reproached me, trying to find her seat belt.

'Didn't you see them?' I asked.

'Who?'

In the rear-view I recognized the first of the two men as he appeared, staring hard in our direction. The last I saw he was talking frantically into his radio phone. I nearly hadn't bothered changing the number plates; now I was glad that I had. I said: 'Two men and a car. Blue Peugeot.'

'I wasn't aware of anyone.' She gave a chuckle, a pleasant musical sound. 'Now I am *certain* our mysterious mutual friend is Marcus.' No use of his title, I noticed.

I still had one eye on the mirror for any sign of the Peugeot. 'Just 'cos he's paranoid, it doesn't mean they're not out to get him.'

I was aware of her frowning at me. 'Is that an English joke?'

'Yes,' I answered. 'But you *were* followed. Low-priority, though – two men and a car is pretty miminal stuff. But then, they thought they knew where you were going.'

'Knew?'

A pizza-delivery motorcycle pulled out ahead of me. 'Did you tell anyone you were going to meet me?'

'No.'

'Not your husband, a boyfriend, anyone at the office?'

'I am divorced.' There was an edge of irritation in her voice. 'And, no, I told no one at the office. In London there is just our stringer and his part-time secretary. Besides, we journalists all guard our stories and little piles of information very jealously, you know.'

We'd hit a jam approaching Baker Street. I was stuck behind a white florist's van after the pizza bike turned off. I said: 'Then your hotel room or switchboard is wired. I used a public phone and yet someone knew you were going to meet me at the hotel.'

'That's not possible.'

'Someone was waiting for you and someone else was

following you,' I told her. 'And they tailed your taxi to John Lewis before we lost them. A smarter outfit would still be onto us.'

She pulled a face. 'Who would do this?'

'I know no details, but I gather Sir Marcus is investigating stuff that might upset the European Commission,' I suggested.

She shook her head. 'Marcus is always talking about spies and being watched and break-ins and telephone taps . . . But I have told him a hundred times before, the EU has no ability for this sort of thing. It is not a nation state. At best it has a little embryonic police unit of drafted officers called Europol. They just organize the exchange of information on terrorism, narcotics and international crime. Nothing more.'

I nodded my understanding. 'But that doesn't actually *stop* national security agencies like MI5 getting involved in EU concerns if they think it's also against their own country's national interest.'

She went quiet at that one. 'True, I suppose,' she conceded.

'Or maybe some angry Commissioner has hired his own private detectives,' I added.

'Put hands into their own pockets?' she laughed. 'That I very much doubt.' Then she went quiet for a moment. 'But it is worrying, if you are right about someone following me.'

'I *am* right,' I assured her. 'I used to do undercover work in Northern Ireland.'

'Ah,' she said. 'So that is how you came to know Marcus. He doesn't trust many people, you know.'

'I minded him for a while.'

'Minded?'

'Sort of bodyguard.' I always felt uncomfortable with the term. It assumed I was prepared to throw myself between the target and an assassin's bullet and I wasn't sure I was really up for that. Especially not to save a politician, even one as honest as Sir Marcus.

She gave a small shiver of apprehension. 'If Marcus and

you are right about this, I am starting to think *I* should be
having a bodyguard.'

At last we'd arrived at Baker Street. On impulse, I said:
'I fancy a drink after all that excitement. Care to join me?'

To my surprise she said: 'Thank you, Mr Ed, that would
be nice. I really am now feeling a little uneasy.'

'Just call me Ed.'

I drove to the fringes of Bayswater before parking outside
a quiet backstreet pub. I fetched the Happy Shopper bag
from the boot and showed Paquet into the saloon bar. There
were just a couple of regulars perched on bar stools and I
ordered a couple of brandies before we took a window seat
that was out of their earshot.

'How long have you known Sir Marcus?' I asked.

'Since he first came to Brussels in '97. I interviewed many
of the new MEPs.' She smiled as she recalled. 'He was such
a gentleman, so English. Well, that is English as they are
*supposed* to be. We became good friends. Sadly he thinks it
is not too wise for us to see much of each other at the
moment.'

'His investigation?'

She nodded. 'He doesn't want me to be under suspicion
as a – er – that awful word for the French, a collaborator
with him. Not until I have been able to research and substan-
tiate his findings for publication or broadcast. He is also
worried that I could be at some risk . . .'

'But you think he exaggerates?' I guessed.

'Maybe.' Another smile to melt an iceberg. 'Until today.'

I offered her a Gauloise, which she accepted.

'Not many English smoke these,' she observed, inhaling
deeply. 'I think maybe you are a closet Frenchman.'

I grinned at the thought. 'I just like tobacco with bite . . .
and French food – er – and wine – er and cognac. Yeah,
maybe you're right.' As she smiled at my answer, I took the
dossier from my Happy Shopper bag and placed it on the

table. 'This is what Sir Marcus has for you.'

She looked genuinely taken aback. '*Mon Dieu!* So much.'

'You know what he's been working on, don't you?'

'Of course. Widespread fraud and corruption,' she murmured, removing the tissue paper that filled her Harvey Nichols bag before sliding the dossier inside. 'And recently some other stuff – more disturbing . . .'

'Yes?' I was just beginning to get seriously intrigued by all of this. Or maybe I just liked the delicious sound of Francoise Paquet's voice.

'I am sorry – er, Ed, Eddie – I cannot say more.'

I felt mildly affronted by that. 'You don't trust me?'

She cocked her head to one side. 'I hardly know you. Besides, a lot of it I find hard to believe myself. Corroboration is crucial for a journalist. But now Marcus has found someone who has agreed to talk to me. Someone on the inside. Someone who can confirm his findings.'

'A whistle-blower?' I suggested.

She gave a little shrug. 'I cannot gossip about something this serious.'

Had I stumbled on the only journalist in the world who had a conscience? Whatever the reasons, it was clear that she wasn't happy with the direction the conversation was taking. She began examining her Cartier. 'I really must be going. I return to Paris tomorrow and have much to do. Thank you for the drink, I feel much better now.'

Just as I was considering dropping her off a short distance from her hotel, I instinctively glanced out of the window at my car. A movement across the street caught my eye. A pizza-delivery motorcycle was parked by the pavement and its rider stood hunched in a doorway talking on a mobile phone.

I realized then that I'd blown it. Big time. The blue Peugeot hadn't been acting in isolation after all. The surveillance team – whoever they were – had called for back-up or another element of their box and that pizza-delivery motorcycle had cut across my escape route halfway to Baker Street. I recalled the incident now and had thought nothing of it because he had positioned himself in *front* of me, not behind. One of the oldest tricks in the book. And, of course, when he turned off I'd thought no more about it. In fact, some other vehicle had taken over.

'They're back,' I announced quietly.

'Who?' Paquet asked.

I felt more than a bit foolish over my earlier misplaced confidence. 'Our friends. Don't look now, but someone's watching my car.'

She paled. 'What can we do? Will I be safe?'

I tried to sound reassuring. 'I'm sure you'll be safe, but I'm not sure about Sir Marcus's dossier.' However, in all honesty, I had no way of knowing what or who we were dealing with here.

Now she was turning things over in her mind. 'I could be burgled – or even mugged. I will not be safe until I get it back to our Paris office.'

I thought quickly. 'How are you travelling to Paris?'

'I have a flight booked from Heathrow late morning.'

'And do you really *have* to go back to your hotel tonight?'

'I have my luggage, clothes and toiletries . . .'

I said: 'They can be posted on to you in a couple of days.'

Her eyes were wide. 'What are you suggesting?'

'Go to a different hotel tonight,' I suggested. 'A good one that will be happy to supply emergency toiletries.'

She gave me a strange look. 'And a change of knickers? Contrary to some popular English myths, we French are very fastidious.'

Was she winding me up? 'Get some new ones on Waterloo station tomorrow morning—'

'I am going to Heathrow.'

I shook my head, my plan developing well. 'Not any more. Take the Eurostar. Sir Marcus has given me a fund to meet necessary expenses. He'll cover all these extra costs.' Well, I bloody well hoped he was as good as his word.

Her eyes blazed at me. Perhaps she was angry that I hadn't been as smart at evading her shadows as I'd made out. 'Aren't you forgetting one thing? They are watching your car outside.'

I said: 'I'll leave by myself in my car. Hopefully I can shake them off . . . And besides, I don't think they know me from Adam.'

She looked aghast. 'And I just stay here?'

'Of course not. But will you go with the rest of the plan?' I pressed.

Francoise Paquet was one very unhappy bunny. 'It will be a great inconvenience and I will be late for appointments and . . .' She shrugged, resigned. 'I suppose I have no option. That is, if I can escape from here.'

'Leave it to me,' I promised.

I strolled over to the bar and caught the manager's eye. 'Sorry to be a nuisance,' I said, 'but I'm in the middle of a messy divorce right now and I've just seen my wife's private eye loitering outside. Any chance my lady friend here could slip out the back way?'

The manager was fat and surly but clearly knew all about messy divorces. He viewed Francoise Paquet with an appreciative eye as he continued polishing a glass beer mug. 'I don't want no trouble.'

I shook my head. 'No trouble, friend. He's a private dick, not the jealous husband.' I slid a twenty across the bar. 'He must have been following my car, that's all.'

'Down the back, past the lavs,' he said, with a toss of his head to indicate the way. 'And don't antagonize me dog in the yard or he'll have your leg off.'

'What street does it come out on?'

'Poorman's Mews.'

I thanked him and moved to the payphone on the wall. It took just a couple of quick calls to find a minicab company that could promise to have a car waiting at the end of Poorman's Mews in five minutes.

'All set,' I told Paquet as I returned to finish my drink and explain what I had arranged.

Although the pub quite clearly didn't have a public rear exit, any decent surveillance team would cover any such unlikely escape route. I still didn't think we were dealing with people as good as MI5's watchers, so there was a chance we'd get away with it. In case not, I gave Paquet a crash course in anti-surveillance techniques as best I could. I advised her to take some time, get the minicab to drop her at a Tube station, switch trains a few times, use more cabs and finally approach the hotel of her choice on foot.

I said: 'When you get to your hotel, give me a call to let me know you're safe.' I jotted my number on the back of a beer mat.

She didn't look too impressed, but said nothing. In fact our conversation seemed to have dried up like the Kalahari. So much so that it was almost a relief to tell her that it was time to go.

As she picked up the weighty Harvey Nichols bag, she said: 'I'm just pleased that you obviously made a better job of things than this when you were looking after Marcus in Northern Ireland.' She didn't smile, kiss my cheek or even offer her hand. 'Thank you for the drink, Eddie. Goodbye.'

'*Au revoir*,' I ventured.

But that was it. She slipped behind the bar with the manager's stare still following the arrogant sway of her hips as she disappeared down the dingy corridor . . . God, but she was gorgeous!

A second later I heard a ferocious bark.

'Mean bitch,' muttered the manager.

I stared at him.

'But her bark's worse than her bite,' he added with a mirthless chuckle.

I'm not sure about that, I thought savagely, and left by the front door in a mood meaner than the pub dog's. I gave no indication that I'd spotted the pizza-delivery motorcyclist.

Now we were giving him a split target. Would he follow me or wait for Paquet to emerge? In the event, it was me he chose. No doubt someone else would take over outside the pub.

At least with the pizza man following me, I knew *who* my tail was. I drove off at a sedate pace, wondering how the hell I was going to shake him off. I didn't want to lead these bastards, whoever they were, back to my flat. And certainly not while I was involved with Tromain.

The trouble was I didn't know London well enough to lose the motorcycle or break up his box very easily. MI5's drivers actually complete the cabbies' 'knowledge' as part of their training, so if the motorcyclist *was* one of theirs I was at a severe disadvantage.

For a while I took it steady, trying to lull him into a false sense of security. Their prime target was Francoise Paquet and I hoped that I was very much of secondary interest. Therefore, if I played the innocent for a while, they wouldn't think I was worth extra resources. Or, even if I was of interest, I'd succeed in stretching those resources to breaking point.

After ten minutes, I thought it was paying off. The motorcyclist was still with me. He was good, I'll say that for him. He was always in one of my blind spots and, if I hadn't already been aware of his presence, I'd probably never have spotted him.

I worked my way south, over the River Thames to Battersea and then Clapham. It was an area that I knew quite well and a plan began to form piece by piece in my mind. I knew a stretch of road where there were three sets of traffic lights that ran in sequence. Catch the first and you caught the lot, and vice versa.

I approached the first set with caution. They had just turned to red with one car waiting. The area was well lit and the pavements around the junction had broad grass verges that offered a reasonably wide view of the crossroad approaches. The nearest vehicle coming in the opposite direction was a good two hundred yards away and slowing.

Changing down, I made my decision and hit the accelerator pedal. The BMW surged forward as I snicked the wheel right to overtake the car waiting at the lights. I had to rely on a quick flick of the head to allow my peripheral vision to check right and left as I jumped the red. Clear! Thank God!

Wrong! The sound of airhorns rent the air. The driver of the small sports car coming from the right must have had his foot on the floor to beat the green before it changed.

I sensed rather than saw him slither his way behind me as he tried to control his skid. A second later I had him in my rear-view, momentarily stationary and slewed at an angle across the juction. Then he sped off in an obvious temper, leaving the pursuing motorcycle to wait for a renewed stream of traffic to clear before he too could jump the red.

Then I lost him round a kink in the road. I jumped the next two lights in less spectacular fashion and kept my foot down until I dived right into a maze of residential side streets lined with Victorian terraced houses. Time and again I swung left and right, then right and left, almost confusing myself with my labyrinthine manoeuvres.

Finally I left the sprawling residential area and rejoined a main road heading back home, as confident as I could be that I'd shaken off the motorcyclist. On the way I pulled into a deserted industrial estate with wide verges that was an excellent place to spot any surveillance vehicles. For ten minutes I watched from the shadow of a cul-de-sac between two prefabricated factory units. A couple of cars used the estate's artery road as a short cut, and a learner driver used it to practise his three-point turns, but that was all.

At last I felt I could breathe again. I quickly changed my number plates back before completing the journey.

I entered my flat, poured a tumbler of whisky and fell onto the sofa in front of the electric fire, exhausted. It was nine o'clock and just three hours away from Christmas Eve. The anniversary of Astrid's death. Year seven and the pain, it seemed, was just as raw as ever. Wouldn't it ever go away?

I knew drink wasn't the answer, but it was the only one I had. Not for the first time I wished I hadn't thrown away all the photographs of her, although it had seemed a good idea at the time. Anyway, by the time I was on my second tumbler I didn't need a photograph. I just had to squint and I could see her sitting on the armchair, legs tucked under her and her hair dancing at her shoulders, blue eyes transfixing me seductively over the rim of her glass. That woman had been everything. A shrewd and intelligent professional as a translator for the UN, an absolute lady and witty conversationalist at social gatherings, a delightful companion – and, although you'd never have guessed it, an absolute whore in private behind closed doors.

I smiled at the memory of how she had broken down my typical British reserve and inhibitions and taught me things about myself and her that I doubt even the Kama Sutra could have told me. I'd never felt so relaxed or enjoyed sex so much with anyone before or since.

How on earth did you replace the irreplaceable? I felt my eyes begin to sting and the agonizing knot of emotion gathering in my throat . . . I couldn't bear the thought of the night that I knew lay ahead.

Then the phone rang.

'Hi, lover.' It was Bex.

I sniffed heavily, cleared my throat and found my voice. 'Hello, glamorous Size 14 person, how you doing?'

She laughed. 'Doing fine with compliments like that. Our mutual friend's been asking how you're getting on with his request. He's being quite a pain.'

I said: 'Mission accomplished – given a few hiccups.'

'Hiccups?'

'Not over the phone.'

'Sure.' There was a hesitation. 'You sound a bit – down?'

'Knackered, to be honest.'

'I know what tomorrow is, Ed. Jude and I were just talking about it. How you must be feeling.'

I was staggered that either of them had actually remembered it was the anniversary of Astrid's death, let alone given thought to how I was likely to be feeling. It's funny what a tide of emotion an unexpected kindness can release at times when you're at a low ebb like that. I forced myself to get the words out. 'Thanks. Not much anyone can do.'

'Maybe help you take you mind off it – well, a bit maybe.' She added quickly: 'Jude and I have got our glad rags on and we're going to a disco. Come and join us.'

'I don't think so—' I began.

'Please, grandpops. You know Jude, she'll be on the pull and frankly I'd be glad of your company.'

Suddenly it seemed like a good idea. Anything had to be better than an evening crying into my whisky, even a disco – if only I could find the strength. 'Okay, you talked me into it. Where're you going?'

'Great!' Bex sounded genuinely pleased. 'Get yourself a quick heart bypass and come to the IceCube.' She gave me the address in Romford.

'What time?'

'Things don't start warming up till eleven. Meet me outside because the bouncers will never let you in unless I can sweet-talk them.'

I hung up, feeling decidedly past my sell-by date, then phoned and arranged to be picked up later by a local minicab

firm. Then I had a shave and a long, hot shower. I don't do
fashion, so I settled more for anonymous with clothes that
bouncers didn't actually take exception to: dark slacks instead
of blue jeans and loafers instead of trainers, topped with a
slate-grey shirt and an old black jacket from the back of the
wardrobe that smelled faintly of mothballs.

I was hoping Paquet would call to let me know she was
okay before the minicab arrived to collect me, but she didn't.
Truly I can't say that I was surprised and equally I didn't
really think she'd be in any real physical danger. All those
watching her would know was that she'd had a rendezvous
with a total stranger. There was no reason to believe they
knew that she now had a copy of Sir Marcus's dossier. And
if they didn't know that, there was no likelihood that they'd
attempt to snatch it.

With that comforting thought I relaxed in the back of the
beat-up Cavalier for a white-knuckle ride to Essex in the
hands of a mad but very friendly West Indian in a woolly hat.

The pavement outside the IceCube was heaving with
hormonal youngsters queuing in shirtsleeves and minuscule
party dresses, oblivious to the cold damp night. A dull background thud emanated from the bowels of the club like a
volcano on the boil. I paid off the driver and looked around
for the girls.

Simultaneously I heard a tooting horn and the howl of
wolf whistles from the lads in the queue and turned to
witness the incongruous sight of Jude in a twinkly blue
micro-dress and a helmet, her long bare legs astride her
motorcycle as she steered into the kerb. Bex was on the
pillion and a little more sensibly attired, with her pink clubbing number half-hidden beneath a long camel coat.

'You're in luck,' Jude called out. 'It's half-price-for-
pensioners night.'

As she parked the machine beside the entrance, Bex walked
across and greeted me with a kiss to the cheek. 'Glad you

could make it, Ed. Nice to see you dressed up for the occasion.'

'Just be thankful I didn't wear my Marks and Sparks cardigan,' I returned coldly.

She delivered a playful but painful knuckle-punch to my bicep before she approached the bouncer and exchanged a few words that allowed the three of us to jump the queue and head down the stairs to the thumping epicentre of the earthquake.

'An ex of mine,' she explained as she led the way through the seething mass of gyrating and perspiring half-naked humanity. 'He knows better than to mix it with me.'

I fought my way through to the bar and after an age returned with three lagers. Jude was already out on the floor strutting her stuff with no less than three males who were dancing with their eyes on stalks and their tongues hanging out.

'She's on form tonight,' Bex observed with just a hint of envy. 'Stunning.'

I nodded and gave her a gentle nudge. 'Not looking so bad yourself.'

She liked that and gave me that delicious cheeky smile of hers. 'C'mon, let's find a quiet table – if that's not a contradiction in terms. I'm feeling middle-age coming on.'

We discovered an alcove seat and settled down, content to watch the floor show. 'So you got Marcus's packages out the way – what was this hiccup you mentioned?' Bex asked.

'Only when I went to meet his French journalist friend, Françoise Paquet. Someone had a couple of tails on her.'

'For sure?'

I nodded. 'No doubt. Stuck like glue. I thought we'd thrown them off, then we went to a pub for the handover. Low and behold, another one was waiting outside.' I explained how we'd split up and I'd been chased.

'And she didn't call?'

'No. Probably thinks I'm bad news, one way or another.'

Bex took two hard swallows of her lager and stared thoughtfully at the near-empty glass. She was back on her old form. 'Who do you think these people are, Ed?'

I'd been giving that some thought. 'As this is all to do with Sir Marcus, it rather depends what he's been up to. Perhaps these people have been hired by someone in the European Commission or by criminal elements protecting their own interests.'

'You don't think they're Box?' She meant MI5.

I shook my head. 'They're professional, but not quite slick enough to be A4's watchers.'

'Sounds like they have good comms and some sort of infrastructure,' she observed. Then she added: 'Marcus reckons a heavy lorry tried to run him off the road yesterday. Ended up in a ditch, but only his pride was hurt.'

I shouldn't have smiled, but I couldn't help it. Sir Marcus wasn't the best driver in the world and a bit of retaliatory road-rage hardly amounted to a badly bungled assassination attempt. 'Then it definitely isn't Box. Bumping off MEPs isn't their style.'

Bex gave me a strange look. And, of course, I realized why. We of all people knew that while peacetime counter-intelligence did not involve assassination or physical violence against targets, in serious scenarios like Northern Ireland MI5 was quite capable of playing with the big boys. It might not pull a trigger itself, but when push came to shove it always knew the people who would. After all, whoever they *actually* worked for, Morgan Dampier – and now Tony Tromain – were like electrical connecting cables between government agencies and someone like me. Whilst I didn't know who had decided that Tex-Mex and Zoran Mihac had to die, you could bet your last tuppence that both MI5 and SIS were somehow mixed up in the operations that had made it necessary.

'But I suppose putting an MEP like Marcus in the frame isn't very likely,' Bex conceded after a moment's reflection. Then suddenly her face brightened and she made a determined effort to uplift the mood. 'Bah, I'm not going to let that paranoid old git ruin the evening. It's Christmas! My shout.'

Then she was deftly on her toes and on her way to the bar with hips swinging beneath the sheer pink silk dress. I lit a cigarette as my gaze followed in unfettered and self-indulgent male appreciation of the female form.

The next hour was like travelling back in time. As the thudding beat drove remorselessly on and the graveyard of dead glasses grew and were joined by living ones – by the trayload now, to avoid the queuing – and our faces became flushed and voices animated and our laughter careless and loud, we could have been on army R-and-R in any bar anywhere in the world, letting off steam after the strain of dangerous operations.

Jude dropped by occasionally for a pit stop, always with a new hopeful in tow, to top up with Stella Artois to fuel her next circuit of the dance floor.

By around one Bex's voice had become a little slurred around the edges and we had mellowed, hunched over our beers as we began the inevitable amble down memory lane. Remember this and remember that? That night so-and-so threw a snowball at a redcap Land Rover just as the MP decided to stick his head out? Or when the OC of that armoured regiment actually buried a Challenger tank in the Saudi desert because somehow he had one too many when the MoD planned an inventory check?

Bex giggled. 'Did you know your nickname among the girls in the Det was Blowjob?'

'What?' With the music blasting I wasn't sure I was hearing right. I hoped not.

She nodded. 'You once told us if ever we got compromised in a mobile OP in Provo territory, we should get our head down in our partner's lap till the coast was clear.'

It was true. Whether advice based on experience, or just a gag devised by ever-hopeful lads on the Det, it had entered into 14 Int's training folklore, on the basis that Provo dickers were unlikely to think intelligence staff in a surveillance car would ever take their cover as a courting couple quite that far.

I said: 'I meant pretend.'

'Jude didn't realize that. No wonder they were all so keen to share a car with her.' Bex's laughter peeled out above the disco row.

'Still missing army life?' I asked.

She nodded. 'Desperately, if I'm honest. Just don't feel I belong anywhere any more. If Jude wasn't still with me, I'd be suicidal. It's that adrenalin buzz and being part of a team. I'd never get that again even if I joined the police – if they'd have me. Probably reckon I was a psychopath.'

'And what about your flying?'

In Northern Ireland on many of the ops in very high-risk areas like South Armagh, to their chagrin female Det members were frequently assigned to helicopter surveillance duties – a few thousand feet out of harm's way. Typical Bex, she set out to learn to fly the damn things herself and won her civilian pilot's wings in short order. She shrugged: 'Not the time or money nowadays, Ed.'

I pulled another full glass of lager from the rank in front of me on the table. 'I've said before, Bex, maybe it's time to settle down.'

Not to be outdone, she reached for another glass herself. 'Content like you, you mean?' she asked sarcastically. She sucked the froth off the beer and shook her head. 'I can't, Ed, I just can't. It's something in me. My mum died young when I was just fifteen. It was such a waste and I vowed then that I'd always live life to the full. That's why I joined the army.'

The alcohol seemed to be giving me wisdom. 'Do you mean living life to the full or challenging death?' I asked.

Bex blinked like she'd just been slapped. 'I'd never thought of that. Challenging death – to get my own back for mum? Very profound.' Then she grinned. 'Cor, lummy, mister, you a trick cyclist or summat?'

At last the DJ seemed to be running out of steam and put on a smoochie number, the smoky tones of Sade a sudden cue for all the lads in the bar to put their Dutch courage to the test and grab a girl in the anxious hope of a leg-over that night. I said: 'Wanna dance?'

'You askin'?'

'I'm askin'.'

'I'm dancin'.'

We shuffled without talking, her head on my shoulder and my hands feeling the sway of her hips beneath the thin stuff of her dress. The smell of her hair and perfume was mildly intoxicating and we drifted away in thoughts of our own as we danced. Being so close to Bex again brought back memories of when we had both teetered on the brink of an affair just before my divorce from Wendy. I remembered how easy and enjoyable I had always found her company . . . and yet we had both pulled back and I don't think either of us had ever really known why.

I glimpsed Jude from the back in a dark corner, snogging someone whose hands were pushing their luck with the hem of her microskirt. An inch too far, I mused, and we'd have a corpse on our hands.

Bex snuggled closer. 'You were supposed to hand in your gun when you left the Regiment,' she mumbled almost dreamily.

I pulled back as I suddenly realized what she meant.

Bex giggled and tightened her arms around my shoulders. 'No, it's okay, big boy, I like it.'

As the DJ faded the fourth Sade number into West Life,

I said: 'I've got an early start tomorrow. Would you mind if we left now before the crowd?'

Reluctantly she loosened her embrace. 'Sure. That was nice, Ed. Haven't had a good dance in months.'

I shook my head. 'Thank *you*, sweetheart. It was a great evening.'

Jude appeared from the throng, running her hands over her head to tidy up slightly askew hair. 'Hi, guys, time for the off?'

'You seemed to be having a good time,' I observed. 'Where is he?'

'Good time?' Jude retorted lightly. 'I was trying to tell him goodbye, but he wouldn't take his tongue out me throat. Fool t'myself – in the end I forgave him and offered him a lift home. You two okay?'

I said: 'I'll take a cab and drop Bex on the way.'

'Sure?'

'If Ed doesn't mind, that's fine,' Bex replied.

We got to the cloakroom for Bex's coat before the queue started building and walked towards the taxi rank around the corner. At least the rain had stopped and the air was cool and fresh after the hot and fetid atmosphere of the nightclub. And there were plenty of cabs.

As we settled back to watch the illuminated street scenes flash past, Bex said: 'I hope tonight helped. They say time's a great healer, but I reckon some wounds never heal. I still miss my mum after all these years. Think about her lots. Ask her advice, wonder if she'd approve of me doing this or that. I still feel cheated, how she was taken from me like that. You must feel the same about Astrid.'

I nodded. 'It gets a bit easier, but not much. Such a terrible waste of a life. Two, really – hers *and* mine. A million times you say stop feeling sorry for yourself, because now that's all it is. You can't undo history.' I paused as the inevitable flashback came. The smile and the laughing eyes. 'But she was special – to me at least.'

'I know that,' Bex said softly. 'I only met her a couple of times and everyone seemed to like her. I was as envious as hell.'

'Really?' I was surprised.

'I know we were never quite an item, Ed, but when Astrid came on the scene you only had eyes for her.' Bex gave a wry smile and turned her face towards the window. 'All that beauty – and brains as well. We Essex girls know when we're outclassed.'

I said: 'I'm sorry. I didn't realize.' What else could I say?

She shrugged. 'That's life, Ed.' Then she laughed. 'Anyway, I'm well over you now. In fact I'm thinking of giving up men altogether and getting a cat. Or a dog. Or a horse. Hell, maybe all three!'

Ten minutes later the taxi was cruising alongside a shopping arcade in a run-down neighbourhood. Bex leaned towards the driver. 'By the chip shop, please.'

'You spending Christmas here?' I asked.

'Yeah, me and Jude and maybe Tommy. He's the old Chinese guy who runs the chip shop. He's promised us free fries to go with the roast. Then Jude will go spend Boxing Day with her old man. Poor girl has to try and keep all us loners happy—'

She was ferreting in her handbag as the taxi pulled to a halt. 'Oh, sod, I've forgotten my keys. I'll have to call Jude on her mobile.'

That sounded ominous if Jude had her mind on other things. 'I hope she's got it switched on. I'll wait with you.'

'No need, Ed. I'll be fine.'

'I'd like to.'

The cab pulled away to leave us on the pavement with Bex tapping Jude's number into her cellphone keypad. 'Hi, Jude, it's Bex. Sorry if I'm interrupting anything, but I haven't got my key . . . Oh, would you? What a sweet child you are. *Ciao*.'

'All right?' I asked.

She stuffed the phone back into her bag. 'Says she'll fake a quick orgasm and come straight over. Doesn't want to hurt his feelings.'

It was starting to rain again.

Bex stared at the locked-up chip shop. 'I could kill for a bag of old Tommy's fish 'n' grease.' She then looked at the side doorway with the legend *Ace Personal Protection*, taken from a computer printout, covered in cellophane and pinned to the surface. Business presentation obviously wasn't the Essex girls' most obvious strength. She said: 'I suppose you could pick the lock for me, Ed. I always was crap at that.'

'Not without my box of tricks,' I told her.

She was just about to make some witty retort, when she seemed to notice something over my shoulder. 'Oh no, surely not . . .'

I turned and looked across the street. A row of park railings ran alongside the pavement and I saw the slightly hunched male figure in a raincoat walking towards us, half hidden in shadow beneath the overhanging branches. He glanced about furtively, then raised a hand, waving in our direction.

'Is it . . . ?' I began.

'Bloody Marcus,' Bex breathed. 'I really don't believe this. That man is really starting to be a bit of a pain.'

Now he was scurrying across the deserted street, slightly breathless. 'Thank God you're back, Bex. I've been hanging around for hours. And you, Eddie, my luck's changing at last.'

Bex planted her hands firmly on her hips. 'Marcus, what the hell are you rabbiting about? We're just back from a night out – do you realize what time it is?'

Sir Marcus Whitby looked a little sheepish. 'I suppose it must seem a bit crazy . . . But I'm in big trouble.'

As he turned his head, I caught sight of the bruising and

congealed blood on the side of his face. 'What happened to you? Looks like you've collided with a revolving door.'

'That's what I mean,' Marcus gasped. 'I left home this morning in my car. I'm spending Christmas in Paris and planned to stay over today and tonight in London before catching the Eurostar tomorrow morning. I've got a shoebox flat-cum-office in Pimlico and I had a lot of work to do before I go. My house is constantly being watched, I'm sure of it – there always seems to be an unmarked van parked nearby. I thought I'd feel more comfortable, at least, at the flat.' He took a deep breath. 'But I was barely ten miles on the way to London when this big landcruiser overtook me – and I wasn't hanging about. The driver suddenly cut right in on me and forced me off the road. I plunged down this huge embankment. Luckily I started glancing off trees like a pinball. That slowed the final impact when this big oak finally stopped me.' He rubbed his neck. 'I was out cold for a few minutes and got awful bloody whiplash.'

'Did the other driver stop?' Bex asked.

Sir Marcus stared at her as if she should know better than to ask. 'Did he hell! He was well gone by the time the police turned up. I was breathalysed and taken to the local hospital A-and-E. No bones broken. Thank God they build Volvos like tanks.'

I gave a sympathetic smile. 'What did you tell the police?'

'Not that it was another murder attempt, if that's what you mean,' he retorted. 'Not after that time a few days ago. They'd think I was a right nutter. Anyway, what would they do? Again there were no witnesses – at least, there was no one around afterwards who actually saw it happen. I said maybe I'd hit some diesel spill on the wet road.'

'Did they believe you?' I asked.

He gave a bitter laugh. 'I don't think they were convinced. They were obviously contemplating a charge of some sort, but decided against it. Anyway, I finished the journey by train and came here.' He noticed the look on Bex's face. 'Oh, don't worry, I made sure I wasn't followed. At least I learned a few tricks from you and Eddie here in the old days.'

Bex frowned. 'It may be a silly question, Marcus, but why come here at all?'

'You're the only friend I knew who won't think I'm going mad – or won't freak out if they actually believe me. Besides, you're one of the few people not in my regular loop of contacts.' He looked a little sheepish. 'Look, I know it's an awful cheek, but I wondered if you couldn't put me up for the night. On the sofa, floor, anything. Then I can head for Waterloo first thing. What you used to call a safe house.'

Bex shook her head slowly in dismay. 'Well, it's safe apart from the odd chip-pan fire once in a blue moon. But God, Marcus, you are in a state, aren't you?'

His eyes were pleading. 'So you will?'

She smiled and nodded. 'Yeah, sure – well, it is Christmas. That is assuming Jude turns up. Otherwise it'll be cardboard city tonight for all of us.'

Sir Marcus reached forward and kissed her cheek. 'Can't tell you how grateful I am. You are an angel . . .' His voice trailed off suddenly. 'What's that?'

The three of us were standing by the kerb on the wide pavement, Bex leaning against a pillar box. There was a builder's skip some forty feet to our right and plastic cones had been placed to allow room for a truck to come and pick it up. Through this gap in the parked vehicles we could see the headlights and dark shape that had crept around the corner.

'It's a car, Marcus,' Bex observed testily. 'Believe it or not, we get them around here sometimes.'

'What's it doing?' Marcus murmured.

At that second the headlamps were switched to full beam,

momentarily blinding us as the driver swung the wheel. We all heard the high-pitched revving of what sounded like a powerful V8 before we were fully aware that the vehicle was now accelerating fast towards us behind the dazzling orbs of light.

For a crucial split second too long we stood rooted to the spot like startled rabbits.

Oh shit, I thought, as the rising scream of the engine filled my head.

# Six

We were swallowed up in the brilliance of the auxiliary driving-lights as the black landcruiser burst through the line of plastic cones. Its steel cowfender sent them spinning in every direction. The huge cross-country tyres leapt over the kerb with contempt and headed straight for us.

Suddenly I was stone-cold sober.

Training kicked in. Bex and I acted as if with a single thought. It was a reflex reaction. But it was still almost too late as we grabbed Sir Marcus and hauled him back behind the pillar box for some protection.

I felt the slipstream of the vehicle as it caught the thing a glancing blow. A shower of sparks exploded as though from a welder's torch.

I stumbled and half-fell over the others' legs where they'd crouched for cover. As I climbed to my feet again I heard the screech of rubber on wet concrete as the driver executed a sharp and professional handbrake turn. The rear end slewed round, missing the shopfronts by inches, but sent the chip shop's free-standing A-sign clattering down the street like a demented bat.

The landcruiser shuddered to a halt in perfect alignment, ready for a return run. It was an eerie spectacle, as if the gleaming black monster had a mind of its own, no human face visible through its smoked-glass windscreen.

'Christ,' Sir Marcus breathed. 'What the hell do we do now?'

A growl came from the massive curved bonnet and a cloud of blue diesel smoke gushed across the pavement. The wheels were starting to turn.

Suddenly I knew this was no ordinary vehicle. Its front cowfender and maybe even chassis must be reinforced because, with total confidence, the driver was coming straight for the cast-iron pillar box behind which the three of us were trying to shelter.

The V8 screamed as it bore down on us.

'RUN!' I yelled as soon as the vehicle had reached the point of no return.

Bex was away first, sprinting back towards the builder's skip, with Marcus racing hard behind me in an effort to keep up. I glanced over my shoulder and just caught sight of the impact. The landcruiser shuddered to a halt, but not before the pillar box had been uprooted in its entirety from its concrete base and rolled heavily into the gutter under its own weight. A scratched and slightly dented fender was the only damage that the vehicle had to show for the encounter.

Sir Marcus caught up as I reached Bex. She'd ducked down behind the skip. 'Jesus, Ed,' he gasped, 'is that *another* of them?'

Up ahead a motorcycle was pulling in to the kerb. Well, if it was, now our escape was cut off. Completely.

The landcruiser inched forward again, the pavement clear now between us and it. Clearly, we had no choice but to run for it . . .

The vehicle suddenly stopped and the passenger door opened wide. I watched in dread fascination, my mouth suddenly parched, as a dark figure emerged. The street light glinted on something in the man's right hand. Gunmetal.

I grabbed Sir Marcus's sleeve and pushed him towards Bex. 'Quick, behind the skip!'

We'd barely taken cover when I was aware of the muffled

*phut-phut* of two silenced rounds and the metallic *ping* as they sparked off the steel rim above our heads.

Then we heard the revving of the motorcycle. I turned my head. Looking back, I was unable to see beyond the brightness of its headlight as it accelerated noisily across the street towards us. Before I was fully aware what was happening, the motorcycle had pulled in alongside the skip. The muzzle flashes were blinding and the hard crack of the rider's pistol rounds reverberated in my ears.

A woman's voice beside us was yelling: 'HALT! ARMED POLICE!'

I did a double take as Jude dropped the motorcycle at her feet and crouched over it, the automatic pistol held in a two-handed grip. She let rip half a dozen more well-aimed rounds at the landcruiser.

I don't know what the hell the gunman must have made of the armed female cop in her nighclub minidress and bone-dome. The sheer shock of it and the hail of shots persuaded him not to hang around to think about it. He'd barely leapt back inside the landcruiser than it reversed away fast across the pavement, passenger door flapping wildly. Then it turned in a tight semicircle, bounced back onto the road and accelerated away into the night.

Dogs had started barking and now lights were coming on in windows above the row of shops.

Bex, Sir Marcus and I looked at each other, bewildered, shaking and gasping for breath. Still in a state of shock, we turned to Jude. She had the visor of her helmet up. Her face was as white as wax and I could see her hand trembling as she lowered the smoking pistol. 'Oh, fuck, Bex, what have I done?'

Bex gulped. 'Saved our bloody lives, I think.'

Jude shook her head. 'Oh shit, really? Thank God for that. I couldn't believe what I was seeing . . . I just acted on instinct.'

'Where the hell did you get that thing?' Sir Marcus demanded suddenly. 'For God's sake, Jude, put it away before someone sees it and calls the police.'

Jude stared at him, quickly regaining her composure. 'There's thanks for you.' Then she tipped the pistol into her unfeasibly tiny sequinned shoulder bag.

'You didn't hit bugger-all, though,' Bex observed.

'That's a blessing,' Sir Marcus muttered.

Then I remembered. 'Your dad's starting pistol?'

Jude smiled. 'Yeah. Said I'd pack it just in case. Never reckoned I'd really need to use it. Still can't believe what I saw going on.' She stared at the demolished pillar box. 'You guys okay?'

'Fine,' I assured: 'Now stop gassing and let's get inside before the police turn up.'

The lights had come on in the chip shop and little Tommy Chan the Chinese owner was standing in the doorway in his singlet and striped pyjama bottoms. 'Hey, that you, Bexy? What all this commotion going on? What happen to postbox?'

'Just some drunken vandals in a big car,' Bex replied dismissively.

He looked sceptical. 'I think I hear gun shootings.'

'Just the car backfiring, Tommy. Nothing to worry about.'

He shook his head in disbelief and muttered: 'You go bed now. Not safe round here at night. I should have stay in Hong Kong.'

As he shut and locked his chip-shop door again, Jude produced her key and the four of us trudged up the uncarpeted wooden stairs to the offices of Ace Personal Protection.

The first room had bare magnolia walls and was filled with two matching and obviously second-hand sofas in brown corduroy and chrome and two Homebase-kit desks with one laptop between them. A Vettriano print of sinister men in trilby hats and a rubber plant dying silently in one corner

were the only concessions to decoration. A curtained-off
alcove hid the tiny kitchen area.

Through an open door I could see the second room with
two camp beds and a flap-down dining table. This area obviously served as the girls' living quarters.

'Loo and shower is that door on the landing,' Bex
announced. 'Not much but it's home. D'you mind sleeping
on the sofa, Marcus?'

The MEP just looked thankful to be alive. 'Anywhere,
Bex, anywhere will be fine.'

'And you, Ed. It's late – and after what we've just witnessed,
maybe there's safety in numbers.'

I said: 'Reckon you're safe with me, do you?'

But her playful mood had long gone and she missed the
irony. 'Yes. And certainly safer if those other buggers turn
up again.'

Sir Marcus looked mortified. 'Christ, d'you think they
will?'

Bex said: 'Unlikely. If they want to take you out, they'd
no doubt prefer to do it cleanly. No collateral damage, no
innocent bystanders.'

Then, just to unsettle us, Jude added thoughtfully: 'Unless
they decide to torch the place. Make it look like a race
attack against Tommy. There's been some of that around
here.'

'Got a hammer and nails?' I asked.

They hadn't, but Bex unearthed a toolbox with a Black
& Decker, a handful of screws and some timber offcuts. In
ten minutes I'd managed to secure the letter-box flap downstairs and the door itself for good measure.

I'd just finished when a police car pulled up outside and
two young-looking officers stood staring, baffled, at the
uprooted pillar box in the gutter. But no one was about
and they obviously decided that there were more pressing
claims on them at that time of night. They cordoned the

cast-iron cylinder with police tape and departed, no doubt leaving it for council or post-office workmen to sort out the next day.

When I returned upstairs, Jude had got a brew going and the three of them were sitting around lacing their mugs with generous helpings of cheap brandy.

Bex was saying: 'I think it's about time you let us in on what you're up to, Marcus. Things are getting well out of control.'

He looked uncomfortable. 'What you don't know can't hurt you. I don't want to get you any more involved.'

God, the man could be stubborn. I said: 'Listen, Marcus, no outsider can possibly *know* how much the three of us know. But they'll assume the worst – they have to. So we're involved now, like it or not. Whoever's trying to kill you will already be linking us with you, depending who's seen who and whether or not they know who the hell we are. Whoever these people are, they're professional.'

Bex added: 'Ed's right. You thought you'd shaken off any tail, but in fact you led them straight to us. Now even this place isn't safe – for any of us.'

Sir Marcus looked like he wanted the earth to swallow him up. 'I can't tell you how sorry I am . . .'

Bex waved that aside. 'Never mind all that, Marcus. We don't want to know all your murky secrets, just enough to judge who and what we're up against.'

That seemed to persuade him. 'You've got a point, Bex, I suppose I at least owe you all that.'

'So how did it all start?' I asked quickly, before he had time to change his mind again.

He sipped at his tea before speaking, giving himself a moment to gather his thoughts. 'A couple of years ago I was appointed to a committee of MEPs in Brussels to investigate corruption and fraud inside the European Union. Our remit was to establish the extent of it and to make various recommendations. Such committees have come and gone over the years, but nothing much has ever changed.'

He glanced at me. 'As you know, Ed, I've always felt pretty passionate about European unity. More than anything else, all this endemic crime and corruption served to undermine the entire project.'

'So did your committee fare any better than the ones before it?' Bex asked.

Sir Marcus shook his head sadly. 'I don't think most of the other members took it that seriously. MEPs don't feel that accountable, you see. Unlike national politicians, no one back home knows what they get up to – or even cares.'

I said: 'You make it sound like there's no one at the wheel.'

Sir Marcus smiled at that. 'That's the impression you can get. But there are people at the wheel all right – only not the people you'd expect to be there.' His eyes clouded. 'That's really the whole point of what I began to discover on the committee.'

Bex said: 'I thought you said the committee didn't get anywhere?'

'Not as such, no. Most of my fellow members were happy to soak up their special allowances visiting the various directorates of the Commission, wining and dining top individuals at the best restaurants, travelling first class supposedly to investigate this or that alleged fraud "on the ground". It was a joke.

'Only I and another MEP, a Danish Eurosceptic called Thor Engell, thought that we ought to take it a bit more seriously. I was an ex-soldier and he was an ex-policeman and so we hit it off rather well.' He smiled at the memory. 'Engell and I decided to handle it like an intelligence *operation*. My experience in the army in Cyprus, Aden and Kenya and his against drugs traffickers. I must say it worked rather well. Low-key stuff. We by passed the top EU officials guarding their own reputations – other committee members were doing all that – and spoke to knowledgeable outside experts, journalists and security advisers first. That was to give ourselves a better idea of where to *start* looking.

'Then we began investigating at lower grades in the Brussels apparatus. We targeted junior civil servants, clerks and secretaries. We contrived introductions at a social and recreational level – MEPs have a lot of spare time to fill. We befriended them, went drinking together . . . Well, some of the results were astounding. These people were the foot soldiers just carrying out orders. And many did not at all like what they thought was going on. But usually they kept their mouths firmly shut. They were on superb salaries and perks, with wives and families to support – and the EU is merciless when it comes to staff it regards as whistle-blowers. And it now has the full legal backing of the so-called European Court of Justice – you should be aware of that.'

'But these people still opened up to you?' Bex pressed.

Sir Marcus gave me a knowing wink. 'I used the old technique, Eddie. Told them a few of my secrets so they'd feel safe telling me some of theirs. Forget about small-time fraud by individual farmers, that sort of thing. I'm talking the *really* big stuff.

'Huge sums cross borders and individual countries resent central EU interference. As a result no one is really accountable and no one wants to rock the boat. Even by the EU's own Court of Auditors' admission, unaccounted losses have run into *billions* over the years. So much, in fact, that they say it isn't even possible to give a reliable *estimate*!

'The shock to me was not so much what was going on, but the size and organization of it. Old Italian and the new Eastern Bloc mafias have even been working together – all orchestrated from somewhere deep within Brussels.'

Bex pursed her lips and whistled softly. 'Isn't that what the European police – what's it called, Europol? – are supposed to be investigating?'

Sir Marcus shook his head. 'That's a popular misconception. Europol was conceived at Maastricht as an embryonic European FBI. But many countries were against a federalist agency that meant ceding control of their own national police forces. At the moment it retains a small department concentrating on cooperation on terrorism, drug trafficking and other major international crime. Internal EU matters are not generally part of its remit.'

I said: 'But surely what you've been talking about *is* international crime?'

'Europol officers have thought so too on occasions,' Sir Marcus laughed. 'We found that out. But I assure you that they got pretty short shrift and rapped knuckles whenever they went near people *inside* EU institutions.'

Jude had been listening carefully in silence until now, but was clearly getting impatient. 'Well, you must have found out something, Marcus, if these Eurothugs are trying to bump you off.'

'Actually, it wasn't me,' Sir Marcus replied. 'It was Thor Engell who got the real breakthrough. A mysterious phone call one night. From a German, someone well placed to have a good idea what was going on beneath the surface.'

'Who?' Bex asked.

Sir Marcus hesitated. 'I daren't tell you who he is or what his job is. Or else he too will be at risk. Anyway, he and Engell met secretly and he explained how, over the past twenty years, what began as ad hoc fraud has slowly and steadily been hijacked by organized crime. These people are professional and know the old maxim that every man has his price. They gradually set about building a network of agents – some witting, others unwitting – that reached throughout the EU apparatus like an octopus. It is they who have the real control and power – and they intend to keep it that way.'

Jude grunted. 'Hence our Eurothugs?'

'Where's Thor Engell now?' I asked.

Sir Marcus smiled awkwardly. 'In a cremation urn in Copenhagen.' He saw the expression of bewilderment on my face. 'He died in a gas explosion at his home last summer.'

'An accident?' Bex asked.

The MEP shrugged. 'Apparently. But what I can't get out of my mind is the fact that only a week earlier he had taken a report of some of his findings to a personal contact of his at Olaf – that's the EU's own fraud-investigation unit. However honest and upright that department may be – and that's the general impression – Engell's information would have been made immediately known to a wider audience. The public domain within the EU administration.'

'And a week later Thor Engell was dead,' Bex murmured.

'Three weeks later,' Sir Marcus added, 'so was Thor's friendly official at Olaf. Lost overboard while fishing alone on the Limfjorden. His body was never found.'

'No question of foul play?' I asked.

'It was never raised in either case, Eddie. But afterwards I told Engell's wife about his report and we searched high and low for a copy of it at his home and at his office. But to no avail. And when I approached Olaf, I was told that they had no official record of having received it.' Again he shrugged. 'That may well be true – or a policy statement to let sleeping dogs lie. Who knows?'

It certainly explained why Sir Marcus was so keen that the same fate didn't befall his own massive document. Suddenly copies at my solicitors, and at Wendy's and the Kweisses' family gaffs didn't seem such a bright idea. I resolved to make their safety a priority immediately after the Christmas break.

Jude said: 'So these Eurothugs –' she was quite clearly becoming attached to her new catchphrase '– are probably connected to organized crime? What, say, Italian, Sicilian or Russian mafias?'

I noticed the slight hesitation before Sir Marcus replied, and the tiny give-away pulse on his forehead. 'Sort of, most probably. But you should be aware that some of those involved – especially on matters of surveillance – could be national security agencies. These people are so well connected in Europe that official inter-government requests for help are very likely to be granted. People like me are increasingly seen as a subversive threat against the interests of individual states as well as the EU itself.'

I was getting tired – only half of what Sir Marcus was saying was sinking in. But I got the distinct impression that he was holding back on something. The question was, how important was it?

Bex, too, was ready to crash. As if reading my mind, she stood up, yawned pointedly and announced: 'I'm off to throw some zeds. I'm so knackered I couldn't care if Jude's Eurothugs blow us up in the middle of the night.'

For once Jude was looking serious, staring fiercely at the tea mug clasped between her hands. 'I'm going with you tomorrow, Marcus,' she announced suddenly. 'If you don't have a professional minder, you could end up in serious doo.'

The MEP shook his head vehemently. 'Oh, that's so kind, but I couldn't hear of it.'

Jude looked up and smiled sweetly. Very sweetly. 'Not kind, Marcus. It'll be both sensible and very expensive. But I've decided you're worth it. I know you can afford me, so please don't argue. When do we leave?'

'I'm putting my alarm on for six, but really—'

Bex laughed. 'Don't argue with a Challenger tank, Marcus. If Jude says she's going with you, she's going with you.'

'See you at six,' Jude called over her shoulder as the girls headed for their bedroom. That the nightclubbing dolly-bird with her skirt barely an inch below her knickers could be an effective minder for the MEP was hard to imagine. But in this case I knew that looks could be lethally deceptive. Jude's professional skills would allow her to pick up on any shadows, pinpoint trouble spots ahead and steer her charge safely to his destination, always keeping well clear of potential danger and staying safe in public places where an attack would be least likely.

'Just don't take that starting pistol with you!' I called out. But the bedroom door shut and I doubt she was even listening.

Then Sir Marcus and I wriggled into two threadbare green maggots – ex-army sleeping bags supplied by Bex – and took a sofa each. Within seconds of lights-out I could hear him snoring gently. Despite feeling utterly exhausted, I couldn't sleep. Events of the evening and the things that Sir Marcus had told us kept swirling round and round in my brain. But as the minutes ticked agonizingly by, I found I had more questions in response to the answers he'd given us.

A slow and chilling realization of the magnitude of the trouble that Sir Marcus had unearthed for himself was slowly dawning as I finally drifted away . . .

I awoke in a cold sweat to the sound of Bex clattering around in the kitchen area. A smell of eggs, bacon and coffee was in the air.

Unzipping the maggot, I swung round to place my feet on the floor and looked at my watch. It still felt like the middle of a stag to me, but it was nine o'clock.

'That's a sight for sore eyes,' Bex chuckled, viewing the unedifying spectacle of me in shirt and boxers. 'Could turn a young gel's head.'

She placed a tray of black coffee and a wholemeal bacon-and-egg wedge beside me. 'They left a couple of hours ago. Marcus asked me to thank you for distributing those dossiers. Apologized that he forgot to say thanks last night.'

I nodded. 'And what did you make of it all?'

Bex sat beside me with a tray of her own on her lap. 'Sort of believable and unbelievable at the same time. But definitely scary. I just hope Jude'll be okay.' She glanced sideways at me. 'You didn't feel moved to go with Jude – or instead of her? Marcus would have preferred that.'

Was that an implied criticism, I wondered? 'I'm afraid I've got some business of my own to attend to today. And I'm not in the close-protection business any more.'

Bex gave an uneasy little smile. ''Course not, Ed. I understand . . . but maybe I should have gone with her,' she added thoughtfully. 'Jude and I had planned to do the books and the bloody VAT returns today.'

I made light of it. 'That's obviously why she volunteered to go. I recall that Jude and paperwork don't mix. Don't fret, girlie, Jude'll be fine.'

'She'll be away until the New Year. So it'll just be me and Tommy Chan for Christmas dinner.' Her eyes widened suddenly. 'Unless you'd like to join us?'

I wasn't sure that this was going to be the most memorable occasion of my life, but then, it didn't look like Wendy was going to throw an invite my way this late in the game. 'Sure, Bex, it would be a pleasure.'

'Great,' she said. 'And what *is* this business you're doing today?'

Immediately I seemed to have that nasty taste back in my mouth. Tony Tromain. Euston Station at eleven. 'Just a man about a dog, Bex.'

She looked at me oddly, but took the hint and asked no more.

As it was, I misjudged the state of the traffic and the time it would take. When I paid off the cab it was ten past the hour.

When I'd crossed the concourse to Platform Eight I found Tromain stomping around irritably like a tiger in a cage. He'd dressed down in a tatty parka, jeans and trainers and was carrying a padded shoulder bag.

'What bloody time d'you call this, Edward?' he demanded. 'When I say eleven, I mean eleven.'

I scratched my unshaven chin. 'I've left the army, in case you hadn't noticed. Free market forces apply. If you don't like my timekeeping, get someone else.'

He leaned towards me, scowling, until I could smell his mouthwash. 'Don't fuck with me, Edward. Not unless you want DI Kingdom breathing down your neck again.' He drew back, his point made. 'Right, I've got the tickets. Let's go before the train leaves without us.'

It was an InterCity and we travelled Second Class as far as Leicester. Tromain insisted on a no-smoking carriage that was almost empty.

Once we were under way Tromain took an envelope from his pocket and pushed it across the table to me. 'That's what Zoran Mihac looks like nowadays. From now on we'll refer to him only as "Mr Black".'

I pulled a computer printout page and a photograph from the envelope. I confess I might not have recognized Mr Black if I'd seen him on the street. He'd lopped off his moustache, got himself a shave and had his hair professionally done in a sort of gelled brush-cut and clearly gone blond because he wanted more fun. His roots still showed, but I think that was a fashion thing. He'd finished off his new look with a snappy beige suit, wraparound Fly shades and a gold earring.

But the one thing even a plastic surgeon couldn't change was the bastard's ugly squashed face and short body with bow legs that had earned him our 'Poison Dwarf' nickname.

'We've had nothing to do with him since the summer,' Tromain murmured to the passing bleak winter landscape beyond the window. 'With the money he got for helping us and the nest egg he made in Bosnia, he's bought himself a smart detached house in the suburbs of Leicester. Runs an Audi coupé . . . Thinks now he's helped us he'll be left alone to get on with his life.'

Remembering the sudden appearance of Tex-Mex's wife and kids, I asked: 'Family?'

'Only distant relatives living in Mostar and Tuzla. Not married – hardly surprising. Anyway, he's more interested in playing Jack the lad now. He's got enough money and a scam to get him the sort of girls he wants.'

Tromain paused to lift the padded shoulder bag he'd been carrying from the seat beside him and dumped it on the table. 'Some toys for you to play with. A video camera and a Pentax with telephoto lens. All second-hand and untrace-able.' He gave me a sneery little grin. 'But I'll still want it back afterwards, so don't think you can do a runner with it . . . If you need any other kit, I'll see what I can do.'

I spent the rest of the journey trying to make any kind of sense of the Japanese instructions for the video camera, printed so small that reading them gave me a headache. By the time we were pulling into Leicester station I reckoned I'd mastered the fundamentals. Just to piss Tromain off I videoed him on zoom from the end of the carriage when I went out for a smoke.

At Leicester we alighted and picked up an expensive-looking hire car with smoked windows that was waiting for us in the car park. Tromain took the wheel and first picked up the ring road running north before exiting onto the A6. After a couple of miles he turned into a run-down district with lots of cheap-rent shops. He pulled across the street and into a space in the line of parked cars.

'Handy,' he muttered and switched off the engine, but left the electrics on so that he could wind my window down a fraction. 'That's chummy's place of work.'

The shopfront almost opposite had the words *Blue Diamond Agency: Photographic & Promotional Models* stencilled across the window in a garish typeface. I recalled the name from the printout I'd been given on the train. Beyond the glass I could see the second-hand 1980s office furniture and our man sitting in rolled-up shirtsleeves, dwarfed by his huge desk. Lots of gold was hanging from his neck and wrists and he was clearly trying to impress the skinny wan blonde girl sitting in front of him. An unsavoury-looking youth, unshaven and with a mop of wild dark hair, leaned against the far wall with a camera around his neck.

'A new potential mug,' Tromain observed. 'Will she, won't she? If she falls for it, he'll note all her family details and take her to the studio upstairs after she's handed him two hundred notes for her portfolio pictures. He'll ply her with wine and gradually during the session he'll persuade her to take her kit off. When she's nicely relaxed at the end he'll show her some soft-porn mags and try to get some shots of her with her legs open. Promising lots of easy money, of course.'

'Then?' I asked.

Tromain smirked as if he almost admired the man's audacity. 'Then he lands her a supposedly lucrative modelling contract with friends of his in Belgrade, Russia or the Ukraine. These guys are virtually running the European hard-core scene now. The girl will most likely disappear for a time. When she finally gets out of their clutches she'll probably be a junkie with HIV and have a prolapsed anus.'

So Zoran Mihac, who'd so lovingly filmed Astrid's last moments on this planet, was still up to his old tricks. He'd moved on from photographing the pornography of war to the general commercial kind, and no doubt the worst kind at that. No wonder Tromain's masters – whether it was MI5 or MI6 or some other outfit – wanted him slotted. Especially given his present occupation. No politician or civil servant would want such a man arrested for war crimes or anything else with the certain knowledge that he'd reveal in court how he'd been paid by the British Government to try and dupe the Real IRA into an entrapment deal involving serious weaponry.

At that point Mihac and the girl stood up, then walked slowly through a doorway at the back. The youth shuffled after them. Then Tromain and I waited patiently for some twenty minutes.

Suddenly the blonde appeared at the back of the office, her hair dishevelled and her dress partly unbuttoned. She scurried awkwardly to the front door in her high heels, struggling not to drop the overcoat and large shoulder bag that she carried. Then she was out on the street, gasping. Without a backward glance she disappeared into the stream of passing shoppers who failed even to notice her.

'Ah,' Tromain said. 'The one that got away.'

'Good girl,' I said and meant it.

Seconds later Mihac reappeared in the shop, unfazed and smoking a cheroot. I had a clear view of him chatting to his scruffy assistant and I lifted the video camera to the gap in my window to get my first shot of him on tape. After a moment or two he picked up an expensive-looking camel coat from the corner stand, hooked it over his shoulders like a cloak and headed towards the door.

'Going for lunch,' Tromain advised. 'I'll follow if you want to do some filming.'

'Why not?' I said.

Tromain started the car and eased out of the line of parked vehicles while I struggled to maintain the focus on the man who thought he was a debonair gift to all women but was rather let down by his bow-legged toddler's walk.

As Tromain had predicted it was a pub lunch at his local. There he held court with new-found friends who took advantage of the generous rounds of drinks he bought and then sniggered behind his back at his boastful war stories about Bosnia. In these he portrayed himself as some kind of hero fighting against the oppressive Muslims and Croats.

After three o'clock he paid a visit to the bookies and lost

two hundred pounds in half an hour before returning to the car he'd left outside his shop and driving home. It was almost dark when the automatic gates opened to allow his Audi coupé to enter the short gravel drive to a detached Regency folly that resembled a miniature Gothic castle. Not much change out of a million there, I'd have thought, as the gates closed in front of us.

Then Tromain headed back towards the railway station. As we left the car he pulled a package from the cargo pocket of his parka. 'Mr Black's house is clean now – we've pulled out all the probe cameras and microphones, but there's a house-plan and videotape in here with footage of the interior. Might be handy. Think about it over the holiday and we'll finalize a plan in the New Year.'

When we boarded the crowded InterCity back to London, we parted company. I left Tromain struggling through the crush of bodies, intent on evicting backpacking students from his First Class carriage. I headed towards the buffet for a Guinness and a Gauloise.

Christmas Day with Bex and Tommy Chan passed in an alcoholic haze. My lasting memory was of turkey, parsnips, sprouts and – Tommy's contribution – the biggest mountain of chips you've ever seen. That and an endless supply of gassy black-market Hong Kong beer from the Chinaman's second cousin.

Bex and I snuggled together on the sofa, watching the usual diabolical offerings on TV, any amorous possibilities rather inhibited by our snoring chaperone in the armchair opposite. By the time night came and Tommy finally returned to his own flat, Bex and I were decidedly the worse for wear.

She looked down at the sofa. 'That looks too uncomfortable, even for a rufty-tufty soldier boy,' she slurred and tried to wink, but her coordination wasn't too clever. 'Come with me, big boy, and I'll show you a – *boom-boom* – good time!'

Her Shirley Bassey impression wasn't too clever either. And neither was her following performance – or mine. The next thing we both knew we were waking together, huddled in each other's arms on her single bed, fully clothed, with daylight streaming in through the open curtains.

Bex propped herself onto one elbow, her hair a beautiful wild muddle, and winced at her headache. 'God, did you have your evil way with me, Ed?'

'Probably,' I said. 'But not necessarily.'

She shook her head. 'I don't remember a thing.'

I sat up and kissed her cheek. 'It's why so many SAS marriages fail. All that training to get in and out with no one noticing.'

The pillow hit me hard on the back as I stood up. I said: 'I'll put a brew on.'

Just before I left to drive back to my flat, Bex discovered an e-mail from Jude. She wandered in from the office in a cream satin dressing gown, and wearing a cute pair of gold pince-nez to read the printout. 'I think the girl had more fun than we did, Ed. Says: *Hi Bex, Having a great time in Gay Paree with Marcus. What a gent! Certainly knows how to look after a girl. Can see now why you had a fling with him. Might even ask him to be my sugar daddy. Nice bum for an old geezer too. Meanwhile all quiet on the western front. Leaving this super posh hotel tomorrow to visit some of Marcus's friends and contacts over next few days. How did your plan to seduce Ed go?—'* Bex peered over her spectacles. 'What a sense of humour that girl has ... She goes on to say *Have you finished the VAT yet? Don't wish you were here. Love, Jude.'*

I said: 'Sounds like they've been left alone. Thank God for that. Since that business on Christmas Eve, I've started to think that Marcus might have real cause to worry after all.'

Despite my own words, I still found it hard to believe that someone would actually do away with him. The worst I could bring myself to accept was that it was a heavy-handed attempt to frighten him off. To persuade him to stop his investigations.

'Maybe Jude is having a deterrent effect,' Bex suggested.

'Let's hope so,' I agreed. I didn't add that I wished she hadn't e-mailed us with Marcus's plan for the next few days. In security terms, she might just as well have broadcast it to the world.

At midday I arrived at Wendy's house to take Timmy out for a Boxing Day treat. In fact he wanted me to stay in and play tank commanders with him on his new Playstation 2. Apparently retail management hadn't given Dick the right sort of skills to knock seven bells out of an enemy and Timmy preferred tough opposition. If that made me feel just a little smug, I felt even smugger when Wendy said my son had asked if I could make my famous turkey hash curry for supper – *and* stay to eat it with them. Then a decidedly over-long and over-amorous smooch with Wendy under the mistletoe in the kitchen made it a perfect end to a perfect day.

On the doorstep as I left, she said: 'Thanks, Eddie. It was almost like old times.' She hesitated. 'You know I love Dick to bits . . . but sometimes—'

I put my forefinger to her lips. 'Some things are best left unsaid, eh?'

But her words left me wondering and feeling slightly haunted over the rest of the holiday break. Just how many mistakes must a man make in his life? I'd lost two women who'd loved me and couldn't say it hadn't been mostly my own stupid fault. If I hadn't taken to the bottle in those days and treated Wendy so badly . . . If I hadn't broken the rules and secretly married Astrid, then she wouldn't have become the unwitting means of Brigadier Domedzic's revenge. I was starting to question whether I'd ever want to risk another woman in my life. Mine was starting to look like the kiss of death in any relationship. Literally.

It was almost a relief to have something else on my mind when the next day I took myself off to Leicester with a small handgrip, plus my camera and camcorder. I'd dusted off the wig I'd worn for Tex-Mex's slotting and toured the streets surrounding Mihac's photographic shop and his house in search of any rooms for let. I found a couple, but neither was in a position suitable for mounting an observation post for either of Mihac's properties.

So I resorted to door-knocking, asking the residents if they knew of anywhere to let and saying I was willing to pay a hundred and fifty a week for my own room. I spent the whole of the second morning walking the surrounding streets before I got seriously lucky.

An elderly Polish woman took a shine to my Serbian accent and my impeccable manners and declared she had a spare room that she only used for storage. On the way up to the third floor she explained how she and her husband, a fighter pilot, had fled Poland in the Second World War and he had joined the RAF. She'd been widowed now for ten years and would be pleased of a little company from time to time. Maybe afternoon tea once a week? she suggested. Feeling like a heel I said that sounded excellent, but explained that I would be away quite a lot because I was looking for a job.

She opened the door onto the room that was filled to the brim with junk and cobwebs. But when I ran my hand over the window grime, I realized that I'd hit pay dirt. It wasn't an excellent view because the angle to Mihac's folly was too oblique. But someone, maybe Mihac himself, had built a large conservatory to hold what looked like a large tiled bath or jacuzzi that extended into the garden. And if

I was not mistaken at that distance, there was the actual squat figure of Mr Black himself, wrapped in a towel and with a young woman at his side.

I duly paid my new landlady six hundred for a month's advance rental and spent the rest of the day carting all the junk down to her garden shed. She provided a mop, bucket and vacuum cleaner and I set about turning the place into a home-from-home that would serve until my work there was finished.

From then until three days into the New Year I spent my time watching and sometimes filming Mihac – from my window, from my hire car, or on foot. Then I gathered together my tapes, photographs and notes and told my land-lady that I was off to London for a series of job interviews.

I got back to my flat early on Sunday evening. It was cold and unwelcoming, apart from an answerphone mess-sage from Bex. *'Hi, cowboy. It's me at midday Sunday. Where the hell are you? You've been gone for days. Got a secret lover some-where, you bum? Call me when you get in and invite me out for a tandoori – Oh, and by the way, Jude e-mailed to say she's still having a ball with Marcus and everything's as sweet as a nut. They're coming back later this week . . . I've a feeling those two are becoming an item. Love and kisses, you-know-who.'*

I grinned to myself. Sounded like Jude might be seriously going through one of her occasional 'older man' periods. Marcus really was a charmer when comfortable on his own turf and he certainly knew how to treat a lady. No doubt he'd shown Jude a bit of the sophisticated MEP's lifestyle she'd only ever read about in magazines. And that was a far cry from what the men she usually knocked around with had to offer.

I put a frozen pizza in the microwave and, after eating, settled down in front of the fire to run my videotapes on the television and start planning how to end the days of Zoran Mihac once and for all.

I awoke with a start around two-thirty in the morning.

I'd fallen asleep in the armchair with my surveillance note-book still on my lap.

Instantly and inexplicably I had the most awful sense of foreboding and couldn't for the life of me figure out why. I glanced around the room for some sort of explanation, because I'd learned in my soldiering days to trust my instincts implicitly.

My attention focused on the television. The last surveillance tape I'd been watching had finished and ejected and the video player had defaulted to *BBC News 24*. I could just determine the faint burble of words, but it was the visual image that jolted me. A long-shot over French police scene-of-crime tapes of something burning on a darkened street.

The camera panned to a medium-shot of the female reporter on the spot.

Her appearance was unexpectedly dishevelled for a television professional, the beige raincoat crumpled, the hair awry and what looked like dirt smudges on her face. It took several seconds for me to realize that it was Francoise Paquet.

Frantically I searched for the remote among the pile of my notes on the floor and thumbed the volume button.

With frustrating slowness the sound of her voice rose to an audible level: '. . . So far the Paris police will only confirm that it does indeed appear to have been a car bomb that has killed the British MEP Sir Marcus Whitby. They say that there have been no claims of responsibility by any terrorist organization. But, of course, it is known that Sir Marcus was once a junior Northern Ireland minister and as such would still be considered a target by various Republican splinter groups like the Real IRA.'

The live footage cut back to the news studio and I stared at the urbane and emotionless anchorman, barely able to absorb a word he said.

# Seven

Already *BBC News 24* was rolling on to its next story.

I sat there paralysed, still in a state of shock and not wanting to believe what I'd just heard.

Then, after a few moments, a million questions started tumbling through my mind. What the hell had actually happened? As Francoise Paquet had suggested to camera, had some of Sir Marcus's stalkers been Irish terrorists all along? Why hadn't that occurred to me before? Even so, had Jude failed to check Sir Marcus's car? Or had the bomb been detonated in a parked vehicle or a culvert by remote control?

And – oh, my God! – where in the hell *was* Jude? Was she okay?

And anyway, what the fuck was Francoise Paquet doing fronting the news item? She was a journalist and sometimes a feature presenter, not a news reporter. None of it made any kind of sense.

Then find out, I told myself savagely. You've got her telephone number. Frantically I pulled the personal notebook from my jacket and flicked through the pages. There were her numbers. I tried the Paris offices of *Televu-News Expresse*, but got the polite alien voice of an answerphone. Bloody things! Of course, it was a news-feature production house, not an around-the-clock live service. It wouldn't be opening until office hours.

I tried her cellphone next, not sure if it was a pan-European number. Anyway it was off and the voice of another alien told me to leave a message. I said: 'It's Ed Coltrane here – from London. Just heard the news about Sir Marcus. Please phone me urgently as soon as you can.' I left my number and then hung up.

I made a coffee and poured a whisky, not sure which I needed most. So I poured the whisky into the coffee and drank both together as I tried to decide what to do next. I had an overwhelming urge to phone Bex. But if I did, I couldn't tell her anything about Jude because I didn't know. Yet Bex might well have Jude's contact number in Paris . . .

Wait a bit, I told myself. No point in waking her in the early hours. By morning I might have been able to get hold of Francoise Paquet and then I'd know the score.

Impatiently I tried the French woman's cellphone again, and again, and again, every fifteen minutes as the next hour crawled by.

It had just turned three-thirty when my telephone rang, its unexpected and strident noise making me jump. I snatched up the handset. 'Coltrane.'

"Allo, Eddie. It's me, Francoise.' The cool French voice wasn't so cool this time. It seemed like she could hardly patch her words together into a sentence.

I said: 'I've seen the news on TV. Saw your report. I'm so sorry. What exactly happened?'

She was clearly devastated, still in shock. 'A bomb in the car, that's all I know. The police are saying absolutely nothing more.'

'And this thing about Irish terrorists?' I asked.

'Just speculation,' she replied tersely. 'A police inspector just said it was possible when I told him that Marcus was a former Northern Ireland minister. You have to say *something* when you report an incident on television – especially when no facts are known.'

That reminded me. 'And how come you reported it, Francoise? I couldn't understand that.'

'You didn't know why?'

'I missed the beginning.'

Paquet took a deep breath. 'I reported it because I was standing just fifty metres away when the car exploded. I personally saw the whole event. When the news crew arrived and found me there, they wanted me to give an eyewitness account.'

I was confused. Had I heard her right? Wasn't this just one hell of a coincidence that Francoise Paquet of all people should have been standing so close to Sir Marcus's car when it went up?

When I put it to her she replied: 'Oh, yes, Eddie, a very big coincidence.' Then she lowered her voice. I'm not sure if it was deliberate or if she was just breaking up with emotion. Maybe it was a bit of both. 'Marcus was coming to pick me up. He had his whistle-blower friend with him. The person who had made Marcus's investigation possible.'

'Did you tell the police that?'

'*Mon Dieu*, of course not.'

'Who was this person?' I asked.

'I really have no idea,' she breathed, suddenly sounding very weary. 'Until I spoke to the police at the scene, I did not even know if this person was a man or woman. Marcus was most protective of his sources. Tonight would have been the first time I would have known . . .' She paused. 'And now I will know anyway, after all – when the police release the name.'

I said: 'There is a friend of mine, Jude Sinclair. She is an assistant to Marcus. Do you know if she was in the car, too?'

'I do not know of this woman, Eddie. But I can tell you that there were definitely only two people in the car, both men. That at least the police inspector on the scene confirmed to me.'

Thank God for that, I thought.

'Look, Eddie, I am very tired. I must go now. I will telephone you tomorrow when I have more concrete information from the police.'

'Of course, Francoise. Thanks for getting back to me. Take care, now.'

I hung up and immediately phoned Bex. After several moments a sleepy voice gave her number.

'It's Ed. Sorry to trouble you—'

'Ed? It's friggin' four in the morning—'

'It's Marcus, Bex, he's been killed by a car bomb in Paris.'

A stunned silence. 'What? C'mon, Ed, is this a wind-up?'

'I wish it was. I caught it on the news.'

She gave a sudden gasp. 'Oh, God, Jude . . . ?'

'Apparently she wasn't in the car,' I reassured Bex quickly. 'I've spoken to Marcus's journalist friend, Francoise Paquet, who was at the scene. The police are certain that there was just one person with Marcus when he died. And he was male.'

'Sweet Lord. Poor Marcus.'

I answered a string of questions, mostly the same ones I'd asked Paquet. Then I asked: 'Have you got Jude's current number in Paris?'

'Yes. I'd better call her. I think she might have been getting it on with Marcus. You know, staying in his suite.'

'Then she's lucky to be alive.' It occurred to me then that Bex might have a problem on her hands. 'But if Marcus left her behind at the hotel when he went on this rendezvous, you might be breaking the news to her.'

'Oh, Ed, she'll be bloody devastated. And she'll blame herself . . . I'll call you back when I've spoken to her.'

'Okay,' I said. 'But wait till daylight. will you? I've got to crash. Good luck.'

'*Ciao*, Ed.'

With a mixture of deep sorrow over Sir Marcus's death

and relief that Jude hadn't shared his fate, I threw myself onto the bed fully clothed and went out like a light.

My sleep was deep and dreamless, so deep that when I started to come to it was like struggling to surface from underwater. I felt drugged and my eyelids were heavy as I stirred at the noise of the ringing bell that had penetrated into my subconscious.

It was still dark outside and the bedside clock confirmed that it was only six o'clock. The door chime began again. Thinking it was probably Bex, I swung my legs off the bed and stumbled through the living area and into the hallway. The door chimes were still echoing around my head like they were the bells of Notre Dame.

'Okay, okay! I'm coming!' I croaked and peered through the recently installed fish-eye spyhole. Outside Tony Tromain was standing, shifting impatiently from foot to foot. His hair was unbrushed and he looked in need of a shave.

I undid the locks and opened the door. 'Do you know—?' I began.

But he just shouldered past me. 'Yes, Edward, I do know what the time is.' He looked and sounded angry. 'I've got some bad news for you. Please shut the door.'

I shook my head, wondering why the hell Tromain should have known. Or why he should have connected me. As I closed the front door, I said: 'I know about Sir Marcus.'

He blinked. 'Do you?'

'The car bomb in Paris. I saw it on the news earlier.'

'And another friend of yours, Judith Sinclair?'

I said: 'No, she's okay.'

Tromain blinked again and raised one eyebrow a fraction. 'No, she isn't, Edward. She's dead too. She was travelling in the car with him.'

This was crazy! I shook my head. 'No. I've spoken to a reporter at the scene. There were just two men in the car.'

Tromain paused and gave me a tight, slightly patronizing

smile. 'You know all about bombings, Edward. Nasty stuff. A lot of confusion, police running round like headless chickens. Problem with identifying body parts.'

'But—' I began.

'Jude's dead, Edward. Believe me.'

I glared at him in furious silence, defying him to repeat his words. But he didn't even bother, because he had something else on his mind. 'I did not know you were mixed up with Marcus and that floozie. I just got a call at home from "Riverside".' He meant MI6, the Secret Intelligence Service. 'Apparently your name has cropped up in surveillance reports. Most embarrassing.'

'Embarrassing?' I repeated, hardly able to believe his callous and self-serving attitude. 'Well, pardon me if my friend's death has shown you and your department to be the incompetent tossers you so clearly are. Perhaps your vetting should have been a bit more thorough.'

Tromain rounded on me. 'Stow it, Coltrane. If we're to exchange accusations of incompetence, I'd ask you what the hell you thought you were doing getting involved with Marcus Whitby while you're working with me and doing the sort of work we're doing? Whitby was a high-profile political maverick and a troublemaker.'

That just made me livid. 'I thought he was an elected MEP and a knight of the realm.'

Tromain gave a snort of derision. 'That means nothing. He was a self-interested publicity-seeker, always sucking up to the media – and you know it. For you to have been anywhere near him ran the risk of the media starting to take an interest in you. You should've realized that.'

I took my cigarettes from the table. Before lighting one, I said: 'The press loved him because he was a rare commodity today – an honest politician who spoke his mind. That's what got him kicked out of the government and sent to Brussels.'

'Some people would call that irresponsibility,' Tromain

retorted. 'The truth is that he was a subversive and he was mixing with some pretty unpleasant types. Both intelligence services have files on him.'

I frowned. 'Hang on. Just who the hell are you saying was responsible for the bomb?'

That brought Tromain up short. For a moment he looked flustered, like an actor who'd forgotten his lines. Then he was smoothly back on track. 'The Real IRA, of course. Whitby was a known target . . . Too soon to confirm, but I don't think there's much doubt.'

He paused for breath then. Maybe he was starting to realize that his approach so far hadn't been the best way to win me over. 'Look, Edward, I do appreciate that Sir Marcus's death was unfortunate – sad, even – but men like him who crave the limelight set themselves up as targets. In that respect he really did bring it upon himself. And for that matter, so did your friend Jude. She always did break every rule in the book, I'm told, and continued to do so when she left 14 Int. With her history she should have kept well clear of a high-profile personality like him – just like you should have.' And just to spit on Jude's grave, he added: 'And she broke the rules one last time, didn't she? She obviously didn't check the car properly.'

It was pointless arguing with a man like Tony Tromain. Anyway, he had the whip hand with his threat to reintroduce the laughing policemen Kingdom and Cherry if I stepped out of line. My only objective now was to keep him sweet and steer him away from the subject of Sir Marcus and my involvement in his investigation. No doubt it was that which had made the MEP such a *dangerous subversive*.

Backing down to Tromain was like swallowing bile. I said: 'Yeah, I'm sure you're right. But I've just lost two friends – I'm a bit uptight right now . . . The fact is that my recent contact with Sir Marcus was fleeting, social and purely circumstantial – through Jude. She was a mutual friend.'

Tromain scowled at me in silence like he was trying to look inside my head, to see if I was winding him up or not. 'Well, in future keep away from the bright lights and stick to the shadows while you're working for me.'

I stubbed out my cigarette in the ashtray. 'Sure.'

For the first time he noticed the spread of photographs and street-layout sketches on the table and gave a half-smile. 'And how's the job on our Mr Black going?'

The Mihac job had completely gone from my mind. 'What? Er – oh, that's okay. I've put a final recommended plan together. Just needs a few refinements.'

'Good. I want it wrapped as soon as possible. Let's meet tomorrow and go over all the options.'

I really couldn't believe the insensitivity of this bastard. In one breath he tells me Jude's dead and in the next he's rabbiting on about killing someone else. I said: 'Give me a break, will you? This business with Jude . . . it's come as a hell of a shock. I can't even think straight just now.'

Tromain's eyes took on a catlike meanness. 'You've been chosen because you can be trusted and because you're a professional, Edward, not for schoolgirl emotions.' At least he didn't mention my pathetic desperation for the money or the fact that he'd virtually blackmailed me into cooperation. 'So sort yourself out today and we'll meet tomorrow. I'll get back to you with the exact time and place.'

It seemed like Tromain still held all the cards. Resisting the urge to throw him out physically, I agreed to the meeting before politely showing him the door. It was with a profound sense of relief that I saw the back of him. But even when he'd gone, the bad smell still lingered.

I slumped on the sofa, feeling absolutely wretched. My life had been rocked to its foundations. Overnight I had lost two people whom I'd known for a long time. Both had been close to me at some point and each in their own way had been a small but important part of my life.

When a vision of Jude's lithe young body cavorting at the IceCube disco just days before came into my mind unbeckoned, I nearly choked as I imagined the mess it must have ended up as in the bombed-out car. What a sick and tragic waste of such a beautiful and flamboyant creature who had brought fun and delight into so many lives . . .

Then I recalled the cheer that had gone up in the sergeants' mess in Hereford one evening years before when then junior defence minister Marcus Whitby had actually told the *Newsnight* television programme that his own government had got it wrong and introduced too many budget cuts. For weeks he had been the hero of every soldier, sailor and airman in the country – until the government had removed him from the post.

Moisture was welling in my eyes so that I could hardly see as I made a huge pot of strong black coffee. Sadly, I had no doubt Tromain was right in what he'd said and I wondered how the hell I was going to tell Bex about Jude.

But there was another sinister implication to Tromain's unannounced visit. It meant that - regardless of any Irish terrorist connection – the people who had been trailing Sir Marcus, Jude and even Francoise Paquet, now knew about me. And, of course, Bex.

Worse, one way or another I had now had it confirmed that those same people – whoever they were – had the connivance of Britain's own security agencies. Whether in part or in whole, there was no way of knowing and certainly no one was going to tell me. That was not so clever when I was in the middle of mounting a totally separate and secret assassination operation.

No wonder Tony Tromain had been spitting tacks when he discovered my connection. In his position, I'd have felt exactly the same.

I was only on my second mug of coffee when Bex arrived with the morning milk. Through the spyhole I saw her standing there, clutching the pint bottle she'd brought in from the doorstep.

Taking a deep breath, I opened the door. 'Come in, Bex. I'm afraid it's bad news.'

Her face paled. 'Jude?'

I grimaced. 'The initial report was wrong.'

She stepped past me as though in a trance and walked through to the kitchen bar. Very meticulously she went to the fridge and placed the bottle in the rack. If I hadn't been there, I've no doubt she'd have got out the vacuum cleaner. It's the strange sort of mundane thing people do when they're in deep shock.

'Give me one of those, please,' she said, indicating my cigarette pack. As I lit a Gauloise for her she said: 'I had a feeling. I couldn't get past the telephone receptionist at their hotel in Paris. My French isn't good, but I could tell she was being evasive. And somehow fraught.'

'I'm so sorry,' I said lamely.

She exhaled and placed a hand on my wrist. 'Yeah, Ed, I know . . . How did you find out? Was it on the news?'

I played a fairly straight bat. 'No, Tony Tromain came round.'

Bex frowned. 'Tromain? We called him T.T. One of the funny people.'

'The same. I'm doing a bit of freelancing for him.'

She frowned at that. 'Really?'

I smiled innocently. 'Just a bit of surveillance work.' I went on quickly. 'But he'd just been informed by MI6 about my connections with Sir Marcus and Jude.'

She gave a low whistle. 'And me, no doubt. I bet he was pleased.'

'I don't care about that,' I retorted. 'The point is, whoever was following Sir Marcus and Francoise Paquet, it rather confirms that Jude's Eurothugs, as she called them, really do have connections with both MI5 and MI6.'

Bex said: 'I put Sky News on while I was trying to phone Jude. They showed that clip of Francoise Paquet at the scene. There was mention of Irish terrorists—'

I shrugged. 'It's too early to know. In a way I hope it *was* the Real IRA.'

Her eyes clouded. 'What do you mean?'

'Because the alternative is too sinister – too terrifying to contemplate.' I indicated the TV set. 'Let's see the latest.'

She smiled sadly. 'Let me get a coffee first. And another cigarette.'

Bex joined me on the sofa just in time for the eight o'clock TV news. The Paris car bomb had already been relegated to the second story; MEPs, it seemed, didn't rate much in headline value, dead or alive. The original Paquet piece had been pulled and updated by the BBC's own Paris correspondent.

Detail was still sparse, but the speculation about it being the action of an Irish terrorist splinter group had already gained more emphasis.

Bex was scornful. 'Makes me laugh, all this splinter-group stuff, Ed. They're the same bombers who worked for the IRA. Are people really gullible enough to think they could still operate without the IRA's blessing?'

'Apparently,' I replied and then raised a hand to quieten her as the correspondent concluded his report.

The earnest voice was saying: *'The second victim has been described by police here as a security official from the European Commission in The Hague. We'll bring further details as soon as we have them. Back to John in the Studio—'*

Mystified, I turned to Bex. 'Still no mention of a third person.'

She opened her mouth and closed it again, speechless. Her eyes were filled with tears. I reached my arm around her shoulder and hugged her to me. Then she began to sob, her whole body trembling as the dam restraining the emotion she had been trying to hold back finally broke.

When she'd calmed down a bit, I poured her another coffee and added the last of my whisky stock. She was still blowing her nose and sniffing heavily as she asked: 'What the hell's going on, Ed? Either Jude was in the car or she wasn't. Call themselves journalists – why can't the bastards even get the basic sodding facts right?'

There was no answer to that, but the confirmation came at the half-hour update.

Standing beside the scene-of-crime tapes, the correspondent said: *'Police here in Paris have just released news about a third victim of the car bomb that killed the British MEP Sir Marcus Whitby and an as yet unnamed EU security official late last night. The third victim of this killing – which is possibly the work of an Irish terrorist splinter-group targeting the former junior Northern Ireland minister – has yet to be officially identified, but it is believed she was a young woman in her thirties . . .'*

Bex bit her lip and said nothing. She stared at the scene blankly, unseeing.

Just then the telephone rang and I crossed quickly to the kitchen bar to pick it up. It was Francoise Paquet.

'How are you?' I asked.

She sounded weary. 'I got some hours in bed, but I couldn't sleep. A police friend just phoned me with the latest on the second victim.'

I said: 'I just heard. Some EU security official.'

'Sure, a security official,' she said with an unmistakable edge of sarcasm to her voice. 'A man called Helmut Frauss.'

But I wasn't too interested in that. 'What about my friend Jude? They're talking about a third victim on the news here. A woman.'

'Yes, I know, Eddie . . . Obviously there was confusion at first . . .' She sounded hesitant. 'But I don't think it is your friend. My police contact is saying here that it was some call-girl Marcus picked up earlier.'

I frowned. 'Are they certain? Sir Marcus didn't mess with prostitutes.' I didn't add that he didn't exactly have to as women were naturally drawn to him. Once Bex, now Jude and, of course, Paquet herself.

'I know that,' the journalist answered sharply. 'I am just telling you what the police have said.' Before I could respond, she added quickly: 'Look, Eddie, I need to get away from here, I cannot breathe. I need to come back to London and speak with you.'

There was no mistaking the desperation in her voice. 'When?' I asked.

'As soon as I can arrange accommodation. The flat I usually stay in isn't available for a few days—'

I cut in: 'I've a spare room, if that's any good.'

'That would be wonderful.' The relief in her voice was clear. 'Just until—'

'Whatever,' I replied. 'When can you get here?'

'If I can get a spare seat on the Eurostar, I'll be there this afternoon.'

I said: 'This whole thing has the stink of rotten fish.'

It was already dark as Bex and I approached Waterloo International in my BMW, but even the weather was not as gloomy and brooding as the two of us had been since my conversation with Francoise Paquet earlier in the day.

'Even given her dress sense, the police surely can't have confused Jude with a Paris hooker, for God's sake!' Bex agreed vehemently. 'She had a British passport and the hotel staff would have known that she couldn't speak a word of the lingo. Plus the French police have obviously been in touch with British intelligence. So what's going on? Is Jude dead or alive?'

Rain began streaking the window, causing the oncoming headlights to dazzle. I said gently: 'Tromain was adamant, Bex. I wish we could, but I don't think we should hold out too much hope.'

She hunched angrily in the passenger seat, arms resolutely folded across her chest as she stared fixedly and unseeingly ahead. Not another word was spoken until we reached the railway terminal.

There I left her looking after the car on a yellow line while I went in and across the concourse to the Eurostar gates. A few minutes later I picked out Francoise Paquet striding through the teeming mass of disembarking passengers, her beige raincoat flowing behind her as she tugged along a small suitcase on wheels.

I'd obviously made a great impression at our earlier meeting because she walked straight past without recognizing me.

'Francoise!'

She turned abruptly, then smiled. 'Oh, Eddie, I'm sorry . . . My head was in the clouds.' Then, to my great surprise, she leaned forward and kissed me on both cheeks. 'It is so good to see you. And so good to be away from Paris.'

Her eyes were dark-rimmed, I noticed. Lack of sleep and too many tears. 'Let me take your case. The car's waiting.'

We had to scurry to avoid getting drenched. I opened the BMW's rear door, threw in her case and allowed Paquet to follow.

I scrambled into the driver's seat and shook the rain from my hair. 'Francoise, this is Bex, a trusted friend. Bex, meet Francoise Paquet.'

Their two hands reached across the seat backs. Bex smiled and I noticed her eyes flicker sideways in my direction. I wasn't exactly sure what their expression meant.

'I need to talk,' Paquet said earnestly. 'Somewhere safe.'

'Sure,' I replied. 'We can relax and talk at my place.'

She leaned forward. 'Forgive me, Eddie. But even your car may not be safe. Or your home.'

Although I wasn't blind to the possibility that either my car or flat could be bugged – now that Tromain had confirmed that 'Riverside' knew about my involvement with Sir Marcus – hearing Paquet suggest it so blatantly caused the small hairs on my neck to bristle.

Bex said: 'Ed and I haven't eaten all day – didn't feel like it. You hungry, Francoise?'

The journalist smiled bleakly. 'Like you, I imagine, I could not hold anything down earlier. Yes, to eat would be good.'

'Like English cuisine?' Bex asked. There was a glint in her eye.

Paquet hesitated as though wondering whether to give an honest answer. 'But of course.'

Bex nodded. 'Then I know just the place.'

I started the car and she gave directions, taking us over the river and along the Embankment towards Poplar. Roddy O'Halloran's was an off-the-beaten-track watering hole that was popular with City types wanting to slum it in style. It was a green-tile and sawdust-floor bar and restaurant which specialized in such delicacies as jellied eels, pie and mash and a range of bottled beers.

As we entered, Paquet's face was a picture. But I really don't think she realized this was Bex's idea of a wind-up and a put-down rolled into one.

Still not over-hungry, I went for a dozen oysters while Bex – just to make a point, I suspect – ordered eels. Paquet took refuge in the safest thing she could find and tried the beef-in-Guinness pie. She followed our lead with Fuller's London Pride, one of the few beers that tasted good out of a bottle.

As the waitress, dressed in striped apron and a cute straw boater, scurried away with our order, Paquet lit a cigarette.

She inhaled deeply before saying: 'Please, Eddie, I do not want to be rude, but can I talk in front of your friend Bex here?'

'I'd trust Bex with my life,' I replied. 'In fact, Bex was a closer friend of Sir Marcus than I was. And she was helping him *before* I was.'

Paquet nodded at Bex with an acknowledging smile. She took another deep drag before continuing with the words: 'I am afraid, Eddie, that I have a confession to make.'

That sounded a bit melodramatic. And ominous. 'Oh, yes?'

'I was spying on Marcus.'

Bex glanced at me, not sure that she'd heard right.

Paquet hurried on. 'It is true. Marcus and I had dined a few times and were getting close, but we had not yet then become – er . . . ?'

'Lovers?' Bex suggested softly. She leaned forward on her elbows, clearly intrigued.

The journalist just nodded. 'I was approached by an old contact of mine. An officer in the DST—'

'Is that an intelligence department?' I asked.

She nodded. 'The *Direction de la Surveillance du Territoire* – a mouthful, I know, but it is like your MI5. Internal security and counter-intelligence. Anyway, this man had once been a close friend of my late father, so I trusted him. He told me that Marcus was a dangerous and subversive person, working against the French national interest. He was trying to undermine the European Union and had links with various Fascist and criminal elements.'

'And you believed him?'

She shrugged. 'I had no reason not to. At the time I hardly knew Marcus and Marcus had not then involved me in what he was doing. I said I'd think about it and my DST contact promised that there would be no pressure, it was up to me.' She sampled her beer and pulled a face. 'Nothing happened for months and gradually Marcus and I became close – very close after his wife died. Because of what my contact had said and my own curiosity as a journalist, I slowly persuaded Marcus to take me into his confidence. I wasn't sure what to make of it. Although he was always careful not to say too much, he seemed utterly convinced that his was the work of a true European patriot.'

'You can't have been that convinced,' I suggested.

Paquet looked uncomfortable. 'I would not have gone back to my contact in the DST if he hadn't come to me. At the time I'd just landed my current job at *Televu-News Expresse*. It was the big breakthrough of my career. When I hesitated to continue cooperating with him, this man flew into a rage. He went over all the damage that he said Marcus was trying to do to the institution of the EU and to France. He was very convincing. And as I wondered about it, he asked what I thought my new employers would think if they knew about my collaboration with a man like Marcus.'

Bex grunted. 'In effect, they threatened to lose you your job?'

The journalist nodded. 'So, to my shame, I agreed to continue to spy. But, in truth, I remained undecided about what Marcus was doing. It was a blesssing that Marcus was so secretive, because all I could pass on to the DST was gossip and hearsay without names. And I told them as little as possible, because I was still not sure. The more deeply I came to love Marcus, the more vehement were the accusations that my contact in the DST laid against him. He demanded I try harder to obtain more details. He claimed that my father would turn in his grave at my lack of cooperation, my lack of patriotism.'

'So much for no pressure,' I observed.

Paquet killed her cigarette in the tin ashtray. 'So I told Marcus that I'd like to help him. If I knew more, I could help make the issues public through my work in the media. That delighted him, I remember. I think he was feeling very alone, very isolated. Having me on side was quite a relief to him. For a while he told me many things. Too many, perhaps. So it was actually almost a relief when, one day, Marcus said that we should not see each other for a while. Not because our relationship had cooled, but because he feared for my safety — even more than he did for his own.'

'Did you believe he was in danger?' I asked.

She shook her head. 'Journalists are cynical people. Despite what he'd told me, I didn't think he was in danger from people within the EU. That was until I met you in London, just before Christmas. I was shocked to find I was being followed. It really frightened me.'

I said: 'So what did you do with your copy of Marcus's dossier?'

'I was spending Christmas and New Year with relatives at Rambouillet. It is always very hectic and I knew I'd have no time to myself, let alone to study the dossier. So I had it put in the company safe at *Televu-News Expresse*. That's where we keep all sensitive investigative reports, videotapes and sound recordings.'

Suddenly I guessed what was coming next and a sensation like a cold hand crawled up my spine as she continued: 'After I did that news report at the bomb scene yesterday, I was still in shock. I still *wanted* to think that it was an Irish terrorist attack on Marcus. Something told me to go immediately to the *Televu-News Expresse* office. A voice in my head — Marcus's, I think. The night porter let me in and I went straight to the safe. The dossier had gone.'

My voice was low and hoarse. 'Jesus.'

Paquet added: 'No one at the office knew what had happened to it. Then I *knew* that the bombers were not Irish terrorists.'

'Did your contact in the DST know you had it?' Bex asked.

'I hadn't thought so. He hadn't phoned or called for months. There'd been nothing.'

'But now you think he did know?' I suggested.

'I'm sure of it. I must have been kept under surveillance the whole time. It was *you* who proved that to me, Eddie.'

Was that actually a compliment from the ice maiden? I said: 'And exactly who was this man who was with Marcus in the car? Some EU security official, they said. Presumably he was the whistle-blower?'

'I imagine so,' Paquet answered. 'But Helmut Frauss is — sorry, was — no ordinary civil servant. He was a police inspector on secondment to Europol from Germany. A senior specialist detective in the field of corporate fraud.' She paused and gave a wry smile. 'Marcus once told me that this man — at the time he never told me his name - was not very popular among his colleagues at Europol head-quarters in The Hague.'

'Why?' Bex asked.

'Because this man — obviously Frauss — believed that he'd found evidence of fraud and a diversion of funds to a secret Bermuda bank account run by people in Europol's own data-collection office. In the EU's own police service, can you believe?'

She shook her head as though still not able to accept it herself. Her hair, I noticed, fell perfectly back into place as she went on: 'These are the same people trusted with investigating such dangerously ill-defined offences as corruption, environmental crime, racism, money-laundering and xeno-phobia. No doubt Marcus would have been found guilty of that last one because of his work against the EU.'

Paquet gave a snort of derision. 'Helmut Frauss trusted his own colleagues *so much* that he actually contacted the Dutch police direct — to prevent any chance of a cover-up.'

'So what happened?' Bex asked.

Paquet shrugged. 'I think the investigation is ongoing. But with Frauss now out of the way, perhaps it will not be for much longer . . .'

'Why was Marcus arranging for you to meet Frauss?' I asked.

'If I was to make a programme exposing the information

in the dossier, I had to have separate verification from at least two people willing to go public. It is very important, especially in a story like this that could attract huge libel actions. I am sure that Frauss was the main source of information for Marcus, so he could verify the overall story. This would then be backed up by willing individuals for each small part of the picture.'

'And what *was* the overall picture?' Bex pressed.

Paquet regarded her coolly for a moment as she lit another Disque Bleu. 'The EU Commissioners were unhappy that despite their best efforts, including the work of Europol's own anti-fraud department, billions of dollars were still going missing each year. It was so much that the auditors couldn't even *estimate* the total! So Helmut Frauss was brought in as a sort of overseer, an anti-fraud tsar, as the media dubbed him. But he was resented from the start – even by Europol colleagues themselves. But Frauss was good, very good. First he discovered that another EU agency had actually sold sensitive computer data on border controls to organized crime. That, I believe, set him on the trail.'

'Trail to what?' I asked.

'To discover that, over the past twenty years, somehow, organized crime has inveigled itself into the very *fabrique* of the EU organization. To the extent that it is almost running it – not politically, of course, but financially, for its own profit. So much so, as Marcus liked to put it, that now the poachers have officially become the gamekeepers.'

'Officially?' I wanted to be sure that I'd got this right.

Paquet nodded as she inhaled on her cigarette. 'Yes, Marcus was adamant about that. But exactly how, he was very careful that I should not know. Just to have such information could be dangerous.'

Well, given the Paris car bomb, we could hardly argue with that.

During the brief and thoughtful silence that followed, the

jolly lass in her boater served up our meal. But I think we'd all suddenly lost any semblance of appetite that might have returned. I doused my oysters in lemon juice for that wonderful sensation of sea and ozone, but pushed my plate away after swallowing only three. Bex chomped on a few mouthfuls of eel, but clearly wasn't enjoying it. Paquet pushed a piece of beef pie around the plate with her fork.

'Sorry,' Bex admitted. 'Maybe this wasn't such a great idea.'

Paquet smiled. 'I think we are all still in too much grief to enjoy this strange food.'

'I still can't get the thoughts of Jude out of my head,' Bex said. 'I just see her all the time. I can't believe the police didn't realize that there were three people in the car from the start.'

'That is odd,' Paquet agreed. 'At the time they were adamant that there were just the two bodies. Only later was this story about a prostitute— I am, sorry, you are still convinced it was your friend Jude?'

I said: 'It's been confirmed by a contact of mine in British intelligence. He was certain.'

Paquet's beautiful and candid eyes stared into mine. 'Then I can only think that someone is hiding something.'

Well, at least the three of us were agreed on that. And during the drive back to my flat our discussion went round and round in circles discussing the possibilities and, of course, could come to no conclusion that made any kind of sense. I felt the tension and anger rising in the car like the build-up of electricity before a storm. There was no doubt in my mind that Bex shared my sense of rage and helplessness – a dangerous cocktail that could only serve to fray tempers.

I carted Paquet's Louis Vuitton bag up the flights of stairs to my flat and dumped it in my bedroom. The two women talked together while I changed the sheets and then put on some coffee.

'It's very kind of you to give up your bed,' Paquet said. 'But your sofa would be fine.'

I was aware of Bex studying me carefully as I shrugged and said: 'I wouldn't hear of it.'

Paquet left her coffee half finished. 'Then forgive me if I take advantage. I am so tired that I could sleep for a week.'

Having pondered what the hell to do about Jude's death during the journey back from O'Halloran's, I suddenly reached a decision. 'I need to go out for a while, Francoise. Help yourself to anything you want. I'll try not to disturb you when I come back.'

She was the picture of elegance as she paused and turned by the bedroom door, the clinging grey jersey material of her dress emphasizing the slender curve of her hips. 'Really?' She sounded surprised.

'Something I have to do,' I replied without elaboration.

She shrugged and nodded. 'Then I'll see you in the morning, Eddie. Thank you again . . . And goodnight, Bex.'

'One cool dame,' Bex muttered as the door closed. 'So what *are* you up to?'

I turned to face her. 'Have you got Jude's address?'

'Sure, why?'

I didn't honestly know the answer to that one. 'Because something's wrong about all this, Bex. We both know it. I mean, we can't even be *sure* she's dead, dammit.'

She looked uneasy. 'You don't think we'll find her at home knitting, do you?'

My heart sank. 'I wish – but no, of course not. Would it be wrong to break in, look around . . . ?'

'You won't have to break in. I've got a spare key.' Bex sighed. 'I'll come with you. To be honest, I'd like to sit quietly in her place for awhile. You know, sort of feel her presence again. Try and make peace with her. Accept that she's gone without saying goodbye—' She sniffed back the tears.

Reaching forward, I kissed her on the cheek. 'C'mon, tough guy, let's go.'

I followed Bex's car in my BMW and it had just turned

ten o'clock when we pulled up outside one of a row of dilapidated late-Victorian terraced houses fronting the street in Wanstead.

'Jude kept her motorcycle in a lock-up round the corner,' Bex said as we met up on the pavement. 'I put it back there for her after she went to Paris. Mustn't forget that when we clear up her effects.'

She led the way through the iron gate and down a steep flight of concrete steps to the basement door. It creaked open into a short passage that ran through to a scullery at the back of the house.

'Just the two rooms,' Bex explained. 'Living room at the back and the bedroom here.'

She stopped at the first door and turned the handle. As the light popped on, I took in the Ikea pine bed and two portable clothes rails filled to bursting with colourful clubbing frocks and more mundane everyday wear. While Bex sat silently on a corner of the bed, I began to look slowly around the room, taking everything in. There were pictures of male pop stars on the nondescript walls and a Chippendales calendar. Shelf-space was filled with a few neat piles of books, mostly on astrology and aromatherapy, a selection of candleholders and quite a few soft toys.

Absently I slid open the drawer of the little bedside cabinet with an old-fashioned, wind-up Mickey Mouse alarm clock placed on the top. Inside I registered the electric vibrator, pack of condoms and the headache pills . . . I closed it quickly again.

'Maybe this isn't such a good idea,' I said. 'I feel like an intruder.'

But Bex didn't seem to be listening. 'This isn't right, Ed. This is very apple-pie. Very un-Jude. Usually the place was a mess. There was always a pile of used knickers in the corner. She hated going to the launderette and so was always buying new ones. There were CDs and magazines all over the place.' Suddenly she sprang to her feet. 'And this shelf here. That's where she had all her mementoes from the army and all the photographs. I was in a lot of them. They've all gone.'

'Maybe she put them away—' I began, but Bex was already heading for the passage.

I followed her into the scullery. It was pristine.

Bex threw open the fridge door and scanned the contents. 'All perishables removed. It should be full of half-eaten convenience meals, gone-off milk and cheese past its use-by date.'

I checked the rubbish bin. 'Empty.'

Bex turned to me. 'The place has been sanitized, Ed, I'm sure of it. Bless her cotton socks, there's no way Jude would have left the place spotless like this.'

I recalled how she'd decided on impulse to go with Sir Marcus to Paris. She'd just packed a few clothes that she kept at the office and she certainly hadn't gone home before leaving with him.

A feeling of dread anticipation started to gather in my chest and I felt the adrenalin rush as I followed Bex into Jude's living room.

Again it was tidy and ordered. I caught sight of the answerphone on the sideboard and walked across to it. 'It's been switched off,' I said.

Bex was at my side. 'Try 1471.'

I dialled and listened for the disembodied BT voice. *'You were called today at six-thirty p.m. To return the call, press three.'*

I hit the button and waited for the ringing tone.

'Ralph Sinclair,' a rather tetchy voice announced.

Sinclair was Jude's surname.

'Sorry to trouble you,' I said quickly. 'Are you related to Judith Sinclair?'

'I'm her father.' He sounded impatient. 'Who is that?'

Oh, shit, I thought. How the hell was I going to handle

this? 'I'm a friend of hers. I'm so sorry to call you like this, but I don't know if you've heard about the accident?'

'Accident? What accident? She didn't mention anything about an accident.'

'I'm afraid it only happened last night.'

'Her and that stupid motorcycle of hers, I suppose. Anyway, she still didn't mention it when I spoke to her.'

That sounded odd. Had one of us got it wrong? 'When was that?'

'This morning.'

# Eight

I was stunned and for a moment I couldn't think how to respond.

'Look, whoever you are,' Jude's father said testily, 'I was just on my way to bed . . .'

That gave me the chance to change tack. 'I'm sorry, I just wanted to speak to her.'

'She hasn't lived with me for years. Can't think why she gave you this number.'

I thought quickly. 'She mentioned that she was visiting you over Christmas. Obviously I misunderstood. But I need to contact her urgently. Did she leave a number when she called you?'

'No, young man. Judith never leaves me numbers or tells me where she's calling from. Something to do with her work. Have you tried her home number?'

'Yes,' I said, 'but she's not answering.'

Ralph Sinclair grunted. 'Right – I called her back a short while ago and got no reply. In that case, I'm afraid you might be too late.'

'Too late for what?'

'She told me that she was thinking of taking a few days' vacation.'

'Do you know where?'

Her father sighed. 'You *are* a persistent young man, aren't you? No, she didn't say. Now I really must go. I've had a very tiring day and my heart is not as good as it was . . .'

'Sorry to have been a nuisance, Mr Sinclair. Thank you for your help.'

Bex stared at me hard as I hung up. 'Did I get half of that right, Ed?'

'Jude's dad,' I confirmed and took out my cigarettes, offering one to Bex. 'Says she called him this morning and told him she was taking a few days' holiday. Didn't say where.'

Both our hands were trembling as I gave her a light. 'This is scarey, Ed. She must be alive after all – please, God.'

I inhaled deeply to steady my nerves. 'Tony Tromain's the only one who's said Jude's dead,' I said with sudden realization. 'Perhaps his people have got their wires crossed somewhere. But if she's alive, why the hell hasn't she contacted us?'

Bex grabbed at straws. 'Perhaps she was shaken up by the news. Maybe heard about it in Marcus's Paris apartment and decided to hightail it out as fast as she could.'

It made a sort of sense. I added to the imagined scenario. 'Got back to the UK, phoned her dad, then slipped out of the country pronto.'

'Didn't contact us because we're possibly under surveillance,' Bex concluded, 'which I suppose is quite likely.'

I didn't see that mattered much. With Sir Marcus dead, I'd have hoped Bex and I were now considered somewhat irrelevant. Hopefully these mysterious thugs would lose interest in us. And it really didn't matter who knew we were visiting Jude's flat; there was certainly no law against it. I said: 'Perhaps we should expect her to make contact with us. Discreetly, and in her own time.'

Bex gave an uncertain smile. 'Does that mean we can celebrate?'

'Let's hope so. But if you're right about this flat . . .'

'Maybe the place was searched and then MI5's bin men cleaned up the mess,' she suggested.

It was possible, but it was also clear that there were going to be no conclusive answers to the puzzle – for a while, at least.

After inviting Bex to join me and Francoise Paquet the following evening for one of my infamous curries, the two of us went our separate ways.

When I arrived back at my flat, I found the message light blinking on my own answerphone machine. It was Tromain with the time and place for our meeting the next day to discuss the Mr Black case.

Suddenly I just couldn't wait. Because now I wanted some hard answers about Jude from the bastard.

It was disconcerting, having Sunday breakfast with Paquet. I didn't understand how anyone could get straight out of bed looking so damn good. Her hair seemed to fall immediately back into perfect shape when she took her head off the pillow and her make-up looked like it had just been applied. She sat down in a long satin dressing gown the colour of champagne, gave a little yawn and stretched her arms above her head with all the poise of a prima ballerina. And the glimpse of lightly tanned flesh as she languidly crossed her legs was almost enough to make me choke on my cornflakes.

'You have a very comfortable bed, Eddie. I slept like a baby.'

I smiled and offered her Marmite for her toast. She declined and opted for apricot jam which I don't think she liked very much. Or maybe it was the stale bread I'd used.

'I'll get some *croissants* for tomorrow,' I promised.

'That would be nice.'

'What are you doing today?'

'Take it easy, maybe go for a walk. And maybe sleep some more.' Her eyes were wide over the rim of her coffee mug. 'And you?'

I said: 'There seems to be more doubt over whether or not it was actually our friend Jude in the car. I hope to find out more.'

'Your contact in British intelligence?' When I nodded, she added: 'Then I hope it is good news.'

But I'm afraid it wasn't.

I met Tony Tromain in the lobby of the London Marriott Hotel off Grosvenor Square; spooks like meeting in hotel lobbies where a rendezvous is more likely to pass unnoticed. We just exchanged grudging pleasantries before going straight outside to hail a cab. I guess we both knew civil conversation wouldn't extend for the entire journey and we couldn't discuss confidential matters in a taxi, so we sat in stony silence, staring out of our separate windows at the London streets.

Eventually we pulled up in a pretty residential street in Holland Park. As soon as he'd paid off the cab, Tromain said: 'It's just a couple of blocks. A compromised safe house that we're about to sell off.' He started walking.

I fell in beside him. 'What the hell was all that bullshit you gave me about Jude?'

He continued staring straight ahead with a stern expression of indifference, but I thought I detected a tic of irritation tug at the corner of his mouth. 'What d'you mean?'

'She's not dead,' I said flatly.

This time he spared me a withering sideways glance. 'She's dead all right, Edward. Sorry about it and all that, but you've just got to accept the fact.'

I stopped dead, grabbed his sleeve and spun him round. 'Then how come Jude spoke to her father yesterday morning?'

Tromain glared at me, then cast a glance up and down the deserted street. 'That wasn't her. It was an old friend of hers from her army days. The girl was a bit of a mimic, used the sort of expressions that Sinclair used. They just put some fake static on the line to resemble a cellphone signal breaking up. It wasn't difficult – the old man's hearing isn't that clever.'

For a moment I was speechless with fury and disbelief. When I finally found my voice, it sounded like someone else speaking. '*Why*, for Christ's sake?'

Tromain took a deep breath, like he was a teacher explaining something to a dense child. 'Look, Edward, Sinclair died in the bomb blast. I'm afraid there wasn't much left of her, so the presence of a third victim wasn't realized at first. By the time it was, our people in Paris were on the scene. As soon as Sinclair's former connections with army and British intelligence were unearthed, it was obvious that her presence in the car with Sir Marcus could have been damaging and embarrassing if the media got hold of it.'

'So they said she was a French hooker?' I challenged him with disgust.

He was unapologetic. 'It was best for everyone – not least the girl's father. It happened over a weekend and our people will need a few days to set up another cause and place of death. Gentler and more acceptable. Lost at sea while on holiday in Cyprus.'

'That'll be the official story?' I asked in disbelief.

'Yes, probably by the end of the week. It solves all the problems for us and will make it easier for grieving relatives.'

He began to walk on and I followed, deep in thought. The whole thing filled me with disgust, but I could see it probably all made some sort of sick sense to politicians and their spooks. Admitting that Jude, a former British intelligence operative, was another victim of the car bomb could open an unwelcome can of speculation if the media got hold of it. Presumably on the lines that Jude's presence could indicate unofficial British government protection and thereby tacit blessing of Sir Marcus's activities . . . And Whitehall wouldn't want to be seen condoning the MEP's anti-EU investigation.

When I put that to Tromain, he smiled blandly. 'Got it in one, Edward. If the media got on the trail, it could unearth some of Sir Marcus's subversive work against the Commission. That in turn could lead to some spurious but very damaging speculation as to who carried out the bombing. Most unhelpful at a time when HMG is trying to persuade the great British public to throw its lot in with the euro – especially as it's pretty well established now that the Real IRA were behind the bomb.'

'Oh yes?'

He nodded. 'Fragments of the TPU have been found. They match standard Republican terrorist patterns.'

Not difficult to replicate, I thought. Even I had some squirreled-away plans for constructing IRA-model timing-and-power units, and British explosives experts were always making authentic copies for training purposes. But I let it drop.

'We're here now,' Tromain announced suddenly.

It was a smart Regency terrace of cream stucco with half-moon windows and Juliette balconies in wrought iron. After fiddling with the complex entry system, Tromain stepped into the hall. Various rooms led off from it and through the open doors I could see that all the furniture had been covered in dust sheets. I followed him into the rear living room where French windows overlooked a stone patio and a long narrow garden given over to a small lawn and ever-green shrubs.

Tromain seemed more relaxed now, knowing it was safe to speak freely. I got the feeling that he was making a real effort to be friendly. 'Look, Edward, I realize you and I got off on the wrong foot. Maybe there's a bit of a personality clash here . . . But we are both on the same side. The two of us know what happened in Northern Ireland and in

Bosnia. They were both the result of politicians with no balls failing to do what needed to be done. So in the end it was all fudge, injustice and compromise, which left a lot of mess.'

'And someone has to clean up the shit?' I suggested.

'Shit like Mihac,' he agreed. 'And you and I have had to do our share of the dirty work over the years.'

I was tempted to ask when *he* had last got his hands dirty, but decided to accept the offered olive branch. 'Any chance of a coffee?' I asked.

Tromain hunted in the near-empty kitchen cupboards and in the end we had to settle for a pot of tea made with the last two bags in the packet and no milk. We sat down at the table where I'd spread out street maps, sketches and photographs.

'So what have you got for me, Edward?' he asked.

'It couldn't be simpler,' I replied. 'I've got a rented room using my Serbian cover. All cash and no comebacks. Top-storey bedroom which overlooks the extension to Mihac's house. I can get a clean ninety-metre shot as he sits in his jacuzzi.'

Tromain winced and smiled. 'Painful. When did you have in mind?'

'He likes to take a soak most evenings before he eats or goes out on the razz. Usually sometime between six and seven-thirty.'

'Collateral damage?'

I shook my head. 'Not if I pick my moment. Sometimes he gets a girl in with him. Usually it's the one who plays house with him, but on occasion he persuades one of his new models. Either way, the only danger they'd face would be a few glass splinters, but the round should make a clean hole through the window anyway. Richochet damage can never be ruled out, but it's highly unlikely.'

He nodded thoughtfully. 'Simple, as you say.'

'I'm straight down the stairs, out the front door and away.

It would be hours before the police could work it out and pinpoint the source of fire.'

'I could have a car waiting.'

I shrugged. 'Whatever.'

'And what would you need?'

'A reliable sniper rifle with a collapsing stock and a good sight,' I replied.

Tromain scratched his chin. 'A Russian Dragunov, then. Plenty of them in service with the Serbs, and it's no problem for my supplier.' He smiled at me and for once it seemed as if he meant it. 'Well done, Edward. I like it.'

For another hour we went over the fine details and he made jottings in his notebook. At last he snapped it closed. 'I'd like to go for this coming Friday week. That gives us twelve days. You can leave the country on the Wednesday before and slip back on the Thursday ready for the operation. Same formula as last time. Sound okay?'

I nodded. 'Fine.'

'Get yourself a few pay-as-you-go cellphones and pay cash,' he added. 'Use them only for relevant communications. But no last-minute person-to-person calls to Mihac, eh?'

I'd learned my lesson. 'Of course not.'

Now I didn't want to rock the boat, but Tromain still hadn't mentioned the money again. I put it as subtly as I could. 'And the *other* side to our deal?'

Immediately he knew what I meant. His expression didn't change one iota. 'I'll see to it. Telephone the Liechtenstein bank tomorrow. I'll have your account reopened and they'll be able to confirm your new balance. You'll be able to pick it up in person as soon as you like.'

It all sounded a bit too pat, but I didn't have much option but to accept Tromain's assurance.

He shoved a piece of paper across the table with a telephone number on it. 'This man will supply your sniper rifle.

A Jew who calls himself Alfie Rabinovitch. You can trust him, he's done a lot of work for us. I know he's got a couple of clean Dragunovs in stock. I'll tell him to expect your call.'

And that was it.

I left Tromain in the flat to make some calls and stepped out alone into the street. The clouds had lifted for the first time in days and the sunshine felt almost springlike despite the chill breeze coming down from the north.

Strangely, although I'd had Jude's death confirmed, resolving the uncertainty of it all was something of an emotional relief. At least now Bex could get on with the grieving for her friend that had so far been denied her.

Making me slightly happier was the fact that now I also had a simple but excellent plan to eliminate that bastard Zoran Mihac from the face of the planet. At last I could lay my own ghost to rest and in the process accumulate a total of some thirty thousand sterling. A good start to sorting my life out.

I was even feeling a little more charitable towards Tony Tromain.

My mood continued to improve all day as I took my time purchasing three pay-as-you-go cellphones for cash from three different outlets. As soon as the first one was activated, I made a snap decision and telephoned a 24-hour travel agent to book a seat on a Swissair flight to Geneva the next day. This was mostly because I still did not trust Tromain not to play tricks again like he had after the assignment against Tex-Mex.

At last feeling that I was ahead of the game, I returned home to prepare my favourite Thai curry dish for Bex and Paquet that evening.

The French journalist was already there, her presence announced by two bottles of Château Rayas standing on the kitchen bar and the hiss of hot shower water from the bathroom. I emptied my shopping bag of ingredients and started work on the chicken and vegetables.

I was just about through when Bex arrived. I opened the door to her just as Paquet emerged from the bathroom in her champagne satin number, towelling her hair.

Bex's words of greeting rather faded away and I saw the smile falter on her lips. 'Hi, lover . . . Er, how are you guys . . . ?'

'A much-needed day of rest,' Paquet said. 'I'll be ready in a few minutes.'

As she sauntered off towards my bedroom, Bex dumped a six-pack of beer beside the wine. 'It's getting cosy here, Ed. Nice to see she's settling in.'

'I haven't seen her all day,' I said, aware that I sounded more defensive than I should have done.

Bex's eyes twinkled, but whether with mischief or frost it was hard to tell. 'Doesn't matter to me, soldier boy. I know these sophisticated French birds like their sugar daddies. Want a hand with the veg?'

'Thanks, but all done.' I decided to plunge straight in. 'I saw Tromain today. I'm afraid he confirmed that Jude died in the car bomb.'

Bex looked more concerned than surprised. Like me, I think she'd already accepted the worst scenario. 'But her dad?'

I repeated the explanation I'd been given. As I was talking, Paquet emerged from the bedroom; she'd changed into snug brown trousers and a floppy-necked angora sweater. Even without the diamond drop earrings, she looked good enough to eat.

She said: 'I heard what you are saying. Isn't that crazy?'

I shrugged. 'Maybe not from the British government's point of view. A holiday accident would cause no interest. Whereas if our press learned there was a young English girl killed in the Paris car bomb, the tabloids would make it their job to dig out her history. And when they discovered her former army and intelligence connections, they'd soon start asking awkward questions. Not least *why* did Sir Marcus think he needed her personal protection skills?'

'Perhaps that's why all the army mementoes were taken from her flat?' Bex suggested.

I nodded. 'Seems likely. If the media got really interested and started looking up all Sir Marcus's friends, they'd soon find out that he thought he was under surveillance. And that there'd been various attempts on his life. Then they'd want to know the reason why.'

'That is *exactly* it,' Paquet said flatly. 'It would lead to the media questioning if the bombers were really Irish after all. And if not, who?'

Bex and I looked at each other. It all made a chilling sort of sense.

The mood was a little pensive after that as the girls sat and made small talk over their drinks while I hit the wok for twenty minutes' worth of steamy, fast and furious cooking.

At least the meal seemed to go down well. I found myself watching Paquet for any sign of disapproval but she demolished it readily enough in that poised unhurried manner of hers. More than once Bex caught me watching her and I thought I read a look of sadness in her eyes. Did she really think something was going on between Paquet and me – or did she just recognize something I didn't?

After the beer, we followed on with Paquet's wine to go with my cheat's pudding from the freezer.

'So who is this Tromain person you mentioned?' Paquet asked. 'You say he is in British intelligence?'

'He's connected somehow,' I replied. 'Bex came across him in Northern Ireland some time ago. But nowadays I think he works in a *semi*-official capacity. Maybe a freelancer.'

'But *you* are working for him now?'

It may have been the curry and the alcohol, but her question brought a flood of colour to my face. I tried to make light of it. 'Just some freelance surveillance work. An extension of stuff I did with the SAS in Bosnia for the UN. Tracking down people indicted for war crimes. That's all.'

Paquet picked up that I didn't want to elaborate, but Bex wore a concerned expression on her face as she listened to me. I felt her eyes boring into mine and for a moment I could believe that she was reading my mind. 'Don't go getting yourself into any sort of mess you can't get out of.'

That was a joke. Was Bex clairvoyant or something? 'Course not,' I said lightly and reached for more wine.

It was gone eleven when I saw Bex to the door. 'When will I see you again? Are you free this weekend?'

She glanced over my shoulder to where Paquet had made herself at home on the sofa, flicking idly through a magazine. 'I'm going to be a bit busy, Ed. Jude left the office paperwork in a bit of a mess – and I guess I'll have to be looking after the funeral arrangements with her dad. As soon as her death becomes official, that is.'

I found myself smiling uneasily. It sounded like excuses to me. 'Of course. And any problems, you call me, right?'

'Hokey smokey, lover. See you around. *Ciao*.'

As I closed the door and turned back into the room, I found Paquet peering at me over the top of her magazine. 'I don't think Bex is happy with me being here.'

I made light of it. 'Why shouldn't she be?'

'Because I'm with you.'

'Bex is fine.'

She raised one eyebrow. 'You do not have an – er – relationship?'

I sat down beside her. 'Not that sort, not really.'

'No? She is obviously very fond of you.'

I took out my cigarettes and offered her one. 'And I'm very fond of Bex. We've been friends for a long time.'

Paquet accepted the Gauloise and my light. After a moment

she exhaled and said: 'Loving friends, as we say in France. Sometimes that is the most enduring love of all. It is very precious. Anyway, by the end of the week I should be able to use my usual flat.'

'You can stay here for as long as you want.' I hesitated before adding: 'I enjoy your company.'

She leaned forward and kissed my cheek. 'You are too kind. I feel I am safe with you.'

'Don't be so sure,' I quipped.

'I didn't mean that,' she replied. 'No woman wants to feel *that* safe with a man. I meant that I know you would protect me from the people who were after Marcus – except . . .'

'Except?' I echoed.

'This man you call Tromain. I do not like the sound of him. He is obviously mixed up in your intelligence circles and has been told about your friend Jude. That no doubt means he knows about me. And perhaps about Marcus's document.'

I shook my head. 'Not necessarily. He's certainly never mentioned it. Different departments and different agendas – and in my experience these sorts of people are as secretive between themselves as with outsiders.'

'Do you have to work for him?'

'Only for a short while. It'll soon be finished. Then my contact with him will be over. For good.'

She picked up on the way I said it. 'So you do not like this man? Then why work for him?'

Suddenly I felt irritated by Paquet's probing questions, her insight. I said tersely: 'It's something that has to be done, that's all. And I need the money.'

She smiled that smile that could melt an icecap. 'I am sorry, Eddie. That is the trouble when you are a journalist. Sometimes you must know when to stop.' She touched my hand softly. 'I will stop now.'

Eager to keep her away from the subject, I asked: 'Have

you decided what to do about Sir Marcus's stolen dossier?'

Paquet yawned and stretched. 'I have spent all day doing nothing else. I can hardly phone my contact in the DST and demand its return. He'd either deny any involvement in its theft or castigate me for having kept it from him. Instead I have been trying to think of people to interview who are not afraid to tell the truth . . . if *only* I'd had time to read that dossier before it was taken.'

I said: 'No worry on that score. I can retrieve one of the spare copies I've had put away for safe keeping.'

Her eyes widened. 'You have other copies? I never knew that. It would be wonderful − and so, so helpful.'

It was like I'd just offered her a free round-the-world holiday. She reached forward and kissed me again, this time on the lips. And this time it lingered a fraction too long to be just a gesture of thanks.

'And where are these copies, Eddie?'

Something made me close up; that old SAS wariness, I suppose. I tapped the side of my nose with my forefinger. 'Need to know, Fran, need to know.'

I left in my car for Heathrow the next morning before Paquet was up. I wrote her a note saying that I'd been called away unexpectedly for a couple of days, but would be returning by suppertime on Tuesday evening.

By noon I'd landed at Geneva. I took a hire car to Liechtenstein and the same anonymous bank building with its discreet little brass plaque. The same procedure with the same password and the same expressionless little clerk who avoided eye contact in the same small office. If anything it felt more confining and claustrophobic than before and I couldn't wait to get out.

'And I'd like to close the account,' I said, snapping the combination lock of my briefcase on twenty thousand in sterling notes.

He nearly looked at me. 'That's what you said last time, sir.'

'This time I mean it.'

Outside I gulped thankfully at the fresh alpine air before driving to the airport in time to catch a late-afternoon flight back to Heathrow. I'd taken a small suitcase for the purpose of easily disguising and getting the stash through Customs without being interrogated for hours as a suspected drug smuggler.

By early evening I was in a very comfortable room at the airport Marriott and used one of my new cellphones to call the number Tromain had given me for the supplier of the sniper rifle.

'Mr Rabinovitch? A mutual friend – Mr Redfern – suggested I should contact you about a rare antique display cabinet,' I said, using the open code as I'd been instructed.

There was just a moment's hesitation. 'Oh, yes, he mentioned that. Not so rare, actually, but I think it'll suit your purpose.' The voice was strongly East London with an odd Yiddish inflection at the end of each sentence. 'When did you want to have a look at it, Mr . . . er?'

God, we were all playing these somewhat silly if necessary games. I gave the first name that came into my head. 'Marriott. John Marriott. As soon as possible.'

'Tomorrow afternoon suit? Could you get to Suffolk for around one o'clock?'

'I'm sure I could. I'll come by car.'

Rabinovitch said: 'Good. Take the A12, past Ipswich and Woodbridge, then turn off right for Middleton. Stop in the car park of the Minsmere bird sanctuary. Make sure you've got an Ordnance Survey map with you. One to fifty thou' will do. Now, give me your mobile number.'

I told him and he cut off without a further word.

The next morning, I checked out after breakfast and headed north in the BMW.

The weather was better than it had been of late and by the time I'd cleared Colchester, where I stopped off to buy a map, the sky had become almost cloudless. But as I approached the coast and turned off for Middleton it had deteriorated again and a thin mist was rolling in over the landscape from the sea.

There were no other vehicles in the car park as I rolled in over the gravel and stopped. I'd barely switched off the engine when my mobile rang. It was Alfie Rabinovitch, who dispensed with pleasantries and gave me a map reference. 'My personal woodland, Mr Marriott. It'll take you about twenty minutes.'

I'd barely been going three minutes when I noticed that a car had fallen in behind me. As I'd anticipated, it stayed with me all the way until I pulled into the gated entrance of the woodland enclosure. A sign had been hammered to a nearby tree: *PRIVATE – Keep Out – Danger – Licensed Hunting*. Nice touch, I thought: getting shot was a better deterrent than a charge of trespass.

The car that had been following pulled alongside. A large bearded man in his fifties was in the Mercedes passenger seat and lowered his electric window. 'Just making sure you weren't followed, Mr Marriott. I'm Alfie. Just follow us in.'

His driver, a burly man with a head shaven and polished like a bullet, had climbed out to open the locked gate and reversed the process after both cars had driven through. I followed the Merc for a quarter-mile down a muddy track between the trees until it opened out into a small glade where an old-fashioned green caravan had been parked.

I left the car and joined Rabinovitch who stood hands on hips, breathing deeply and looking up admiringly at the trees all around. Without looking at me, he said: 'Best thing I ever did, buying this wood. Three years ago. Twenty acres for just fifteen grand. Can't build on it, but you can have a shed or caravan as a forester's hut – as long as you don't sleep in it for more than twenty-eight days every year. The kids love it.' He then turned his head towards me. 'And, of course, it's ideal for my purposes. You can test-fire here without any worries.'

'Seems ideal,' I agreed.

'How's Mr Redfern? Well, his reincarnation, anyway.'

Of course he was referring to the intelligence tradition of not changing cover names when the personnel changed. 'Fine,' I replied.

'Known this one for about eighteen months. Can't say I've taken to the feller. Heard a few bad rumours about him.' A snaggle-toothed smile emerged from within the beard. 'So I'm sure you'll understand if my driver checks you over. Make sure you're not tooled-up or wired-up.'

I understood and raised my arms to allow a quick but thorough frisk by the untalkative driver.

Rabinovitch regarded me carefully. 'Army, aren't you?'

'Was. That obvious?'

A shrug. 'You know, the bearing, the manner. Marks us for life. I was Parachute Regiment. Did my bit in Malaya.'

'I was Two Para,' I confirmed.

He nodded sagely as though I'd just confirmed something. 'And spent a bit of time in Hereford if I'm not mistaken. I did eight years.'

Of course he meant the SAS. I said: 'I got to see a lot of places.' I was keen to push on. 'Have you got the goods?'

Rabinovitch acknowledged my disinclination to discuss my service history and turned to his driver. 'Get the Dragunov out for Mr Marriott, will you?'

As soon as the weapon was removed from the boot, we crossed to the caravan and went inside. There were a few ancient armchairs with their stuffing hanging out and a trestle table on which Rabinovitch broke down the sniper rifle with professional ease and speed before reassembling it so I could see it was in good working order. He then led the way through the trees to a defile in the landscape that offered a natural shooting-gallery some hundred yards long. A wall of sandbags had been erected at the far end behind a plywood screen which was used for pinning up paper targets.

I took thirty minutes getting used to the Dragunov and zeroing-in the sight until I was satisfied. Then we began to trudge back through the thick carpet of dead leaves towards the caravan.

'All paid for and settled,' Rabinovitch said unnecessarily. 'Serb Army-issue, straight out of the wrapping. Redfern's lot have got to trust me over the years. Useful to have a tame but unconnected supplier. Good coastline for importing along here, too. I've been used in more ways than one, if you get my drift.'

I knew what he meant. Not only would he have been used to supply the hardware for straightforward missions like mine, but no doubt criminals and terrorists had been funnelled his way for police and intelligence operations and stings over the years.

I said: 'Why are you telling me this? Don't you find life dangerous enough?'

He smiled at that. 'It's interesting, true enough. But I just want you to know that these people don't own me. I'm happy to help bring some scumbag down for them – if I'm paid and there are no comebacks. I have my own standards and morals – and I'm more than happy to help out the individual client, too. If the big boys ever turn against you, you may want to remember that. Weapons, passport, money . . . mine's a broad church.'

Now I thought I knew where he was coming from. The words of Morgan Dampier came back to me again, his warning before the Tex-Mex killing. *Never trust your own, especially your own.* I said: 'This is about Redfern, isn't it?'

'Possibly. Like I said earlier, I've heard talk. It's a small world that we move in. I was stitched-up once by someone like Redfern – a long, long time ago. It's not pleasant and it's not something you forget.' We'd reached the clearing now and he halted beside the cars. 'You're part of the brotherhood, Mr Marriott, and we look after our own.'

I accepted the huge offered hand. 'I'll remember that, Mr Rabinovitch.'

'I hope you won't need to. But if ever you do, just remember your friend Alfie.'

The encounter left me feeling strangely unnerved on the journey back. Rabinovitch seemed straight enough, but you could never tell. His warning about Tony Tromain did, however, reinforce the natural antipathy I had felt for the man ever since we had first met.

I arrived back at four to find my flat empty and a note from Paquet saying she'd be spending the day at her London office, but not to cook anything because she would prepare the supper later. Very civilized, I thought.

Then the telephone rang. 'Edward, I need to meet you urgently. Right away.'

'What's up?' I asked.

Tromain was decidedly tetchy. 'Not over the phone. Do you know Durrants Hotel in the West End?'

'Sure, but I was about to wash my hair—'

He wasn't in the mood for playing games or appreciating my sarcasm at his supposed God-given right to make me jump whenever he pulled the string. 'Be there in an hour. Bring all the stuff you've got on Mr Black.'

I added my twenty grand and the Dragunov to the rest of my secret stash in the bathroom then deliberately took my time driving to the West End, arriving half an hour adrift.

Tromain had clearly been busy wearing a hole in the carpet and stopped pacing the lobby the moment I appeared.

I made the limpest apology I could think of: 'Sorry, the traffic was hell.'

But he wasn't interested. 'Let's get on. I'm going to be late for a dinner party tonight.' He stalked off into the heart of the sprawling hotel, leaving me to follow like his pet spaniel through a labyrinth of corridors until he found the bedroom he was looking for. Inside it was smallish and dark, even with the lights on.

'So what's wrong?' I asked.

He parked himself on the edge of the bed and looked up at me. 'Two things. Firstly Operations say they need to bring things forward by a week. Do it this Friday.'

'Why?' I demanded.

'No doubt they have their reasons – and they don't share them with the likes of us.'

Charming, I thought. Then something more important occurred to me. 'Today's Tuesday. It doesn't give me much time to leave the country, return under my other identity and be *in situ* in Leicester for crack of dawn Friday.'

Tromain gave me one of his dark looks. 'Don't make heavy weather of this, Edward. I've got you open air tickets here for Frankfurt. Fly out tomorrow and back in on Thursday. New passport, credit cards, the lot.'

I had the distinct feeling of being boxed in. 'So what else didn't Operations like?'

He said the next sentence so quickly that I almost didn't catch it; maybe that was the idea. 'They've looked over your plan and they don't like it.'

'Tough,' I replied. 'They don't have to carry it out. Anyway, what're their objections?'

'Too much to go wrong. You're not a qualified sniper, for a start.'

'That's no argument,' I snapped back. Tromain must have known that the regular British Army had only recently reintroduced two annual courses to train thirty-eight NCOs a year. So "qualified" snipers in the UK were pretty thin on the ground, let alone any willing to commit murder for the state. 'I trained when the SAS was the only outfit that still had the expertise.'

'Operations think the chance of missing the target is too great.'

'And they *are* qualified as snipers, I take it?'

Tromain ignored that. 'And they're worried about you hitting some innocent party.'

'Well, the Regiment didn't issue me with a health-and-safety certificate but I know how to achieve a clean kill with no collateral injury. I've already told you that. And the set-up from my firing position couldn't be better.'

'If Operations don't like it, Edward, it doesn't happen,' Tromain replied wearily. 'We've just got to accept it. I'll contact Rabinovitch and cancel the Dragunov.'

Just to be cussed, I didn't bother to tell him that I'd already picked it up. 'So what *do* Operations want?' I asked with a sigh.

'They've looked over the options and prefer your Plan D.'

I shook my head in disbelief. 'I rejected that.'

But he wasn't taking any prisoners today. 'Then I suggest we think again.'

I liked the *we*. It was me taking the risk of life imprisonment or being shot down by armed police if the mission went pear-shaped. I opened my briefcase and tossed the relevant folder on the bedspread. Tromain grabbed it and spread out the contents. Photographs of a greasy-spoon café that had gone Continental with a few plastic tables and chairs outside under a striped awning. It was where Mihac liked to breakfast on a bacon-and-egg sandwich most mornings, almost regardless of the weather. It was obviously a reminder of the habits and street-cafe life of his home in the former Yugoslavia.

Tromain forestalled my first objection. 'If we bring it forward to this Friday, we know that it'll be dry and fairly mild for the time of year. He'll be able to eat outside. It'll be almost a rerun of the King's Road job.'

But it wasn't, of course. The King's Road was a busy London street, and this café was on a quiet backstreet in the suburbs of Leicester. There was a world of difference.

I said: 'The gun in the photographic case won't work here. If there's anyone around, I'll be spotted immediately. The case would be a hindrance. And if I had to ditch it, it would be a hostage to fortune. Possible forensic evidence and it'll raise a lot of questions with the police that you'd rather not have asked.'

Tromain could see that. 'So what do you suggest?'

'That I go pillion on a motorcycle. We pull up in front of him, a double tap with a silenced weapon fired from the kerb, and then away.' It was a classic formula.

But Tromain was having none of it. 'We can't supply a motorcyclist. Operations won't hear of more than one suspect in the frame.' Stating the blindingly obvious, he added: 'It increases the chances of detection by a hundred per cent.'

'There's almost nil chance with the sniper approach,' I reminded him testily.

Tromain shot me a dark look and pulled out a sketch map of the surrounding roadside layout. 'Look, you approach, shoot at point-blank range, then leg it fifty metres to this pedestrian walkway. No vehicle could follow you. Just thirty metres long and there'll be a stolen car waiting for you at the other end. In fact, I'll be your back-up driver myself.'

I looked at him. 'Is that supposed to fill me with confidence?'

He allowed himself a smile. 'It shows I have confidence in both you and the plan.' With that, he reached into his attaché case and extracted a solid-looking parcel wrapped in oilskin. 'Nine-millimetre Heckler and Koch USP with attached silencer. Issued to specialist Serb units.'

It seemed like all the decisions had been made for me. And I didn't like it one little bit.

# Nine

I left Tromain in the lobby of Durrants. We were both in a bad mood; he was anxious about being late for his damned dinner party and I was fretting that short cuts on the up-coming job could lead to me spending twenty years at Her Majesty's pleasure.

I made my way to the nearest pub and ordered some brain food in the shape of a glass of Guinness and nursed it for half an hour while I went over everything in my head, time and time again.

It was now Wednesday and Tromain had brought the date forward a week to this coming Friday. I was having a plan forced on me that I'd earlier rejected. Yet Tromain himself was going to nursemaid me there and back after the killing. In short I'd have semi-official protection virtually throughout – apart from the actual moments of the assassination – and you could hardly ask for greater reassurance than that. The trouble was, it seemed just too good to be true. That sort of thing just didn't happen.

For two pins I'd have pulled out. But I now had thirty grand stashed in my hideaway and I desperately wanted to keep it. Call it greed if you will, but I was nearing forty years old and so far had nothing to show for my life. That money was a tidy deposit for a small home of my own somewhere. No, much as I mistrusted Tromain, there was no way I could bring myself to pull out now.

Instead I resolved to review Plan D until I was completely

happy with it. I decided then that I'd do things slightly differently. Having just done the Geneva trip in a day, I thought that I'd also use the Frankfurt tickets out and back on the same day, Thursday. But only if I was thoroughly satisfied with the set-up.

So I'd take a leisurely drive up to Leicester through the night in time to watch Mihac go for his regular breakfast at the café tomorrow morning. I'd go over everything with a fine-tooth comb, iron out any wrinkles and make sure that there was absolutely nothing I'd overlooked.

Then I remembered Paquet's promise of supper and wondered optimistically if she had anything in mind for afters? And that thought reminded me of my promise to retrieve one of the copies of Sir Marcus's dossier.

I left the pub and phoned my flat from a call box rather than use one of my safe new mobiles. I left a message telling her I'd be back by nine.

I returned to my car, by now fairly paranoid on two counts that someone might be watching me. Someone connected with Brussels might be still interested in my connections with Sir Marcus or someone else from Tromain's side might want to make sure that I didn't do a runner with their money.

But after a few backtracks and doubles I was confident that I had a free run. It was then I decided to call in on Astrid's parents on my way home and collect a copy dossier for Francoise Paquet.

I remembered just in time my promise to Papa Kweiss to telephone him first, so that he could slip out without telling his wife Mira he was meeting me. I pulled in and phoned from a call box on Lavender Hill.

'Eddie?' He sounded rather subdued. 'Yes, of course I can see you. In fact, Mira's taking a nap right now and I'm due to take Sasha for a walk.'

'Sasha?' I asked.

'A little terrier bitch, our new acquisition. Rescue dog from the Battersea Home.'

'I see. Okay, I'll be outside in about ten minutes.'

'No,' he said sharply. 'Not outside. There's a little pub down the road. I'll see you there.'

I frowned as I made a note of the name; there was something distinctly odd about Papa Kweiss's manner. Not unfriendly, more cautious than anything.

I parked up in a side street and walked back to the little Victorian pub with its finely etched windows and wood panelling and the faint smell of cats that you get in all Young's houses. Apart from a couple of locals playing dominoes, Papa Kweiss and Sasha were the only others in the place. He was sitting at an alcove seat with a plum brandy; Sasha was at his feet, lapping a saucer of beer slops. The pretty bewhiskered face, topped with a tartan bow, looked up as I approached.

The old man stood and shook hands and indicated the pint jug on the table. 'Pint of best, Eddie, is that right?'

I smiled at him and sat down. 'Nice to see you again. I like your girlfriend.'

A chuckle. 'Not girlfriend, Eddie. I think Sasha is our new daughter. It was Mira's idea. Didn't actually say, but I think that's at the back of her mind. Hence the ribbon in her hair . . . Mira makes a big fuss.'

'I hope she makes you both happy.'

For a moment I recognized the pain in his eyes as he nodded and rubbed roughly at his nose. As if to distract himself, he reached for the Tesco bag he'd kept beside him on the bench seat. 'These are your documents. Not just your insurance policies, I think.'

'What?' He was driving at something.

'It wasn't a break-in by vandals that you feared, Eddie, was it? These aren't just personal papers − certainly not if they're sealed in wire. These are documents that the government wants . . . Are they stolen?'

Papa Kweiss was far more perceptive than I'd given him credit for. 'They're not stolen. And no one wants them.'

He peered at me over the top of his pince-nez. 'You have never lied to me before, Eddie. Please don't start now. Yesterday we are visited by two men. One a policeman from Special Branch, the other – well, I don't know.'

I nearly choked on my beer. 'What did they want?'

'The Special Branch officer asked if we'd seen you recently. I'd have said yes, but Mira thinks of them as secret police, and says no. Serbians hate secret police. I didn't contradict her. He repeated the question and asked if you'd left anything with us. This time *I* said no.'

'And?'

'They went away. But the other man, not the policeman, gives a dark warning about the difficulties that people of foreign nationalities like us can face if crimes are committed. Especially crimes against the state.'

I was disgusted. 'He threatened you?'

Papa Kweiss shrugged. 'Not as such. A veiled warning, but that was not the point. He spoke to us in perfect Serbian. In fact, I have no doubt that the man *was* Serbian. It was enough to put the fear of God into a sick old lady like Mira.'

I found that very puzzling and could well imagine how it must have shaken them both badly. Yet I couldn't see that the intelligence services, let alone Special Branch, could muster many – if any – Serbo-Croat linguists.

I did my best to make light of it, saying: 'Thank you both, anyway. You did the right thing. Believe me, these documents *are* mine, and no one else's.'

He regarded me carefully, and not a little sadly. 'Finish your beer, Eddie. It will be the last drink that we have together.'

When I arrived back at my flat and opened the door I was

engulfed in wafts of garlic and a heady mix of other cooking herbs that I couldn't begin to identify.

I found Paquet in the kitchen area, deftly managing like a professional restaurant chef, with an array of saucepans and something sizzling under the grill. Except that chefs tend not to wear high heels and little silky black wrapround evening dresses that are sash-tied at the waist.

'Ah, *cherie*, you are home! I think it is time I do something to pull my weight. Maybe show you a little Parisian cooking for a change. Another half-hour, I think.'

Why was it that I had the distinct feeling she'd endured one too many of my curries? She already had a Côtes du Rhône open on the kitchen bar where I dumped the carrier bag before pouring myself a glass.

I said: 'I've got a spare copy of Sir Marcus's dossier for you.'

'Oh, wonderful! It can be an excuse for a celebration.'

Her good mood was infectious and only when I related Papa Kweiss's story did the laughing eyes cloud a little. 'Then we cannot afford to drop our guard, Eddie. Where did you say you left the other copies?'

'One with my solicitors. And the other with my ex-wife.'

Paquet's jaw dropped abruptly. 'Her name isn't Wendy?'

I nodded, suddenly alarmed.

'Oh, God, Eddie, I completely forgot. A lady called Wendy phoned earlier and asked for you to ring back.' Paquet looked embarrassed. 'I thought she sounded a little – I don't know – agitated, I suppose. But I didn't think too much of it at the time.'

I immediately went to the telephone. It was Dick who answered, but it was not the polite and mild-mannered retail manager I'd grudgingly grown to like. 'What the fuck are you up to, Eddie? We had the police around today – they took that package you left with Wendy. She's been in a terrible state all afternoon. Gone to bed now – with a couple of Prozac.'

'Listen, Dick, it's all a harmless mix-up,' I assured him. 'I'll explain next time I see you both. But it really is nothing that will involve you or give you or Wendy anything to worry about.'

Dick grunted. 'Didn't sound that way. Said we could be charged with aiding and abetting some felony. Warned us not to say anything to you. Of course, Wendy wouldn't listen and called you—'

This didn't sound too good. 'Look, Dick, they're just huffing and puffing. Some cops are like that, it's just a power game for inadequates. Trust me.'

Another grunt from Dick. 'Wendy might, but I'm not at all sure that I do.'

'I'd never do anything to endanger Tim or Wendy,' I promised him.

'Maybe not deliberately, Eddie, but you've always been a bit of a wild card.' He paused. 'Just keep away from us, eh? At least until we see if there are going to be any repercussions.'

I could hardly disagree, and hung up feeling upset and angry. When I explained it to Paquet she put a consoling arm around my shoulder. 'I'm sorry, Eddie. I thought that with Marcus dead things would go quiet.'

'So did I,' I replied. 'But we were both wrong.'

She fixed me with that clear and candid stare of hers. 'So what do we do?'

It was too late in the day to try my solicitors, but if Special Branch had been trawling around everyone I knew to see if I'd left the documents with them, I couldn't believe that they'd overlooked somewhere as obvious as my lawyers. That meant that the only copy left was the one in front of me. Thank God for the stubbornness of Ma Kweiss. I said: 'If the police have gone all around trying to hoover up spare copies without alerting us, there's only one obvious last port of call to close the net.'

Paquet was no fool. 'Here?'

I walked through to the bedroom and pulled back the curtain. As usual there were rows of parked cars gleaming after a recent shower, some lit in pools of street light but most in shadow.

I smelled Paquet's perfume as she tiptoed up behind me. 'Can you see anyone?'

'No, but it's impossible from this height.' Even at street level it would be difficult. There were so many places: in cars, on foot, or in any room that overlooked us. Rooms were coming up for let every day. I let the curtain fall back and turned to her, aware of the luminous whites of those gorgeous wide eyes caught in the stray light from the kitchen. I tried to think logically. 'One of two things will happen, Fran. Either we'll get pounced on as soon as we leave here, or else there'll be a dawn raid at some point.'

'So what can we do?' she asked again.

It was a good question. If only I had an answer. And it wasn't just Sir Marcus's confounded document that I was worried about – my thirty thousand stash, a Dragunov sniper rifle and my illegally held Argentinian pistol were also sitting behind a panel in the bathroom. I certainly didn't want to have to try and explain all that away to some bozo from Special Branch . . . Then it struck me.

'Cristobelle,' I announced.

'Who?'

'The woman— er, the person who lives downstairs.'

Recognition dawned on Paquet's face. 'That old transvestite?'

God, was it just me? 'I could leave it there.'

'Could someone like that be trusted, Eddie?'

I was sure that Cristobelle was on the game – or some sort of game. And my guess was that she – or he – wouldn't regard the police with any particular warmth and affection.

And so it proved when Cristobelle answered the door ten minutes later. 'Hello, deary!' she greeted me like a long-lost friend. 'You really have been keeping yourself to yourself. Every time I call in to borrow a cup of sugar, you're always out and some new and *delicious* young lady answers the door.' One huge false eyelash fluttered in a knowing wink. 'I can see I'm going to have some stiff competition for your affections! Do come in for a cuppa – I've not a lot on.'

I ignored the Mae West bit. 'Love to, Cristobelle, but I'm afraid I'm still busy as hell. And I've got to go away for a bit . . . Wondered if I could possibly ask a favour?'

She looked at the large cardboard box at my feet. 'This?'

'Would you mind very much? Just for safe keeping. Nothing valuable, but of great sentimental value.'

Cristobelle looked slightly disappointed but forced her scarlet lips into a smile. 'Of course not, deary. That's what neighbours are for.'

'Just one thing.' I was taking a gamble here, but could see no other way. 'It's just possible that the police might come asking questions.'

Interest reignited in her eyes. 'Really? Oh dear, these aren't hot, are they?'

I smiled. 'Nothing's stolen and everything's mine. But if they were found I could be asked some very awkward questions.'

'What a secretive, mysterious man you are, Mr Coltrane!' She giggled and shrugged her shoulders. 'We really *must* chat one day . . . But don't worry, as far as nosy Mr Plod is concerned, I know absolutely nothing.'

As I returned up the one flight of stairs, I felt sure I'd made the best decision. When I entered the room Paquet was serving up a gourmet meal that really put my culinary efforts firmly in the shade.

While we ate, I explained to her that I had to go away

later that night and would return tomorrow, after which I'd be going abroad for a few weeks.

'On holiday?' she asked. I felt chuffed to note the disappointment in her voice.

'Mostly business. The job I'm working on.'

'To do with this sinister friend of yours, this Tromain? Or TT, as Bex calls him?'

'It's sort of connected.'

She reached across the table and put her hand on mine. 'Then I hope it is not illegal or dangerous.'

'Of course not,' I assured her, changing tack quickly. 'And, of course, you can stay here for as long as you like.'

She tilted her head to one side. 'While expecting a dawn raid every morning? I don't think so, Eddie.'

Her hand was still over mine, I noticed. Her skin felt soft and warm, very warm. It seemed to be burning into me like a branding iron. The words caught in my throat as I tried to speak: 'So what d'you want to do?'

Her pupils dilated as her eyes looked closely into mine. They were so dark now, almost impenetrable. 'If you are going tonight, then I will pack my few things and move to an hotel. In a day or two I will be able to stay at my friend's flat again.'

Quite unreasonably, I cursed Tromain for forcing my hand and so allowing this gorgeous creature to fly the nest. I wondered if I'd ever get her back. I said: 'I can drop you wherever you want to go on my way.'

Her teeth glistened in an amused smile that set my pulse racing. 'So chivalrous, so English, Eddie. I see now what Marcus liked about you . . . You know, in many ways you are so like him.'

That was an odd one. 'Marcus and I were chalk and cheese.'

Her mouth was so close now. 'You mean your backgrounds. English aristocracy and working-class boy made good.'

I smiled at that. 'Maybe not so good, Fran.'

'You both fight for what you believe in, in your different ways.'

Suddenly I wasn't sure where this was going. 'When d'you want to—?'

'Go?' That smile filled my vision. 'We haven't had the lemon sorbet yet.'

What is it that throws the switch? What is it that tells you it's going to happen? A key phrase or just the tone of voice? A touch? I think it was all three. Because I instinctively turned the hand she was holding, so that our palms touched. It was like electricity.

By now our lips were so close that they seemed drawn together by a magnet. The few inches between us just disappeared and I was suddenly lost in the velvet moisture of her mouth.

Without knowing exactly how it happened, we were standing, embracing with a fervour and moving towards the sofa in a kind of dance. My hands found the knotted sash of her dress and it fell open. Underneath it she was wearing only high-cut black tanga pants. Her flesh was alabaster white, her breasts incredibly firm and moulded tightly to her torso like those of an *art deco* statuette. I felt her nipples hardening beneath my hands.

Then she was pressing down on my shoulders, pushing me back against the sofa. The sheer intensity of her kisses sent an urgent shock wave of high-voltage sparks flying through to my nerve ends. I was aware of my instant and involuntary response. Aware of her kicking the pants free from her legs, aware of her climbing astride me, her hand searching and finding and guiding me to where she wanted me to be.

And for one moment in my mind, this wasn't Francoise Paquet – this could have been Astrid.

No, this *was* Astrid.

There were long minutes of madness, of both wanting

and not wanting at the same time. This was making love to Astrid again. Impetuous, inventive, driven. Yet this wasn't Astrid, this was an impostor. The body and the movements, the skills were Astrid. The passion, the sheer physical need *was* Astrid.

My brain might have been protesting but my body wasn't; my confused emotions and thoughts were eventually shattered into oblivion by the exquisitely painful explosion in my groin that followed.

For a long time neither of us spoke. She lay down beside me, her face against mine and we stayed there in silence until the perspiration dried slowly on our skin.

At last she murmured: 'I hope that was okay.'

'Beautiful,' I said.

'I didn't think I liked you at first.'

'I think I realised that . . . And now?'

'I was wrong. You looked after me, like Marcus always did, and I was ungrateful. I'm sorry. Then suddenly I seemed to realize how like him you are.'

I moved up onto an elbow. 'I'm not Marcus, Fran.'

She looked hurt. 'I know that. I like you and I'm grateful. I needed to show it.'

'Needed?'

She looked a shade embarrassed. 'Sorry, *wanted* to. Please don't be so bloody English, Eddie. I needed to fuck you, to be fucked by you. There, I'm being honest. Is that so shocking? Is that too French for you?'

I kissed her forehead. 'You make it sound like I've been given the *Légion d'Honneur*. I'm flattered.'

It was a clumsy and slightly patronizing response that I'm sure left her feeling as uncertain as I felt.

And unsettled certainly was how I felt. Physically I'd wanted Francoise Paquet since the moment I'd set eyes on her, as any red-blooded male would. But suddenly I didn't trust her motives or my own. I had this crazy notion that she thought I was Marcus and I thought she was Astrid.

It was as though we'd both been making wild and abandoned love to two totally different people and we hadn't even realized it.

But now reality *had* to intrude. Time was getting on and I had a long journey to make.

I kissed her one last time. I'd intended it to be quick, but we both lingered, savouring the moment and finding it difficult to pull apart. At last she smiled and nodded: 'I know. It is getting late.'

While I made some strong coffee, Paquet started phoning to find a suitably expensive hotel for *Televu-News Expresse* to pay for.

We left my flat at just gone eleven and I think we both expected plain-clothes police to emerge from the shadows before we reached my BMW. But nothing happened. Apart from the distant sound of fighting cats, the street was as quiet as a cemetery.

Paquet sounded quite angry as I started the engine. 'We *should* have brought the dossier with us after all. I could have made more copies of it. This is crazy, Eddie – how can I work on what it was all about when all the time I'm afraid it'll get snatched from my possession!'

But, as we headed towards the bright lights, I had other things on my mind. Once the Mihac job was out the way and the dust had settled, I'd be able to concentrate on Sir Marcus's dossier and what to do about it. In the meantime, having to worry about it had become just a bloody nuisance.

As I dropped Paquet off outside the Kensington Park Hotel, her kiss was pleasantly lingering. 'Whatever it is you're doing, Eddie, please take care. *Au revoir.*'

'I'll call you in a few days,' I promised.

Her perfume still filled the car as I settled in for the long, steady drive north to Leicester. I put a Pavarotti CD on and turned the volume up, trying to push the hundred and one thoughts vying for attention from my mind. After a few miles it began to work and I actually felt quite relaxed when I arrived close to Mihac's neighbourhood at three-thirty in the morning. I parked in the deserted car park of a playing field, let the seat back down and catnapped until nearly seven. It was one of the more useful tricks that army life teaches you – the art of snatching sleep at any time wherever you are.

I sluiced my face in a handbasin at the nearby public convenience, then took a half-hour stroll to Mihac's patch. Just as the sun was rising I reached the local café frequented by breakfasting lorry drivers and building workers. The sky was clear and there was little wind.

I went in, ordered at the counter, then took a seat by the steamed-up window. It offered a perfect view of the three tables and chairs on the pavement just outside, where Mihac liked to eat, drink coffee and pore over his newsapaper. I charged up on a pot of strong tea and an egg-and-bacon wedge.

While I ate, I wiped away an arc of condensation and appeared to idly watch the street scene outside. Not so idly, in fact. I wanted to absorb completely this favourite haunt of Mihac. To check that I'd missed absolutely nothing that could cause a problem or put my mission in jeopardy.

The adjoining shops on each side of the café couldn't have been better. One was an outlet repairing and selling second-hand electrical goods and the other was used as the front office for an insurance broker. Neither were likely to attract a large influx of customer traffic. A tobacconist or sweet shop or a grocer's drawing in mothers and prams and kids on their way to school would have made it a complete no-no.

My gaze moved along the street. From left to right. A blank brick wall on which a shabby-looking Indian was fly-

posting with a brush and a bucket of paste – some forthcoming wrestling match in some local assembly rooms . . .
An alleyway and then the shopfront of a foam-upholstery
merchant, followed by a second-hand furniture store. Next
to that was a shop being refitted in which a couple of electricians were having a tea break. Outside the adjoining
bookie's a man was hunched under the bonnet of a car to
make some repair.

I leaned closer to the glass, extending my view farther
up the street to where the arcade of shops gave way to a
row of tightly packed Victorian terraced houses. A street
cleaner swept debris from the gutter towards his hand cart
without much enthusiasm.

Meanwhile the second hand of my watch edged towards
nine o'clock. Any time now and Zoran Mihac should show.
I beckoned the waitress to bring another pot of tea, lit a
cigarette and opened the copy of the *Sun* that I'd found
abandoned on the table.

It seemed that the main news event in the world was a
soap star caught in bed with someone else's wife. I flicked
through to the sports section.

The fresh pot of tea arrived at the same time as Mihac's
Audi coupé. He reversed it awkwardly into a gap in the cars
parked opposite and nearly ran over the feet of the man
trying to repair his engine. But when Mihac emerged, he
seemed oblivious to the near-accident. He wore a camel
coat over the shoulders of his powder-blue suit and sauntered across the road like he was the star of some Italian B-
movie. Only his squat build and waddling gait let him down.

He took his seat at an outside table and the waitress scurried out immediately. It seemed most likely that Mihac was
a generous tipper. He grinned and she smiled as she jotted
down his order on a pad and she didn't even flinch when
he blatantly patted her backside. Separated by the misty glass,
the accomplice to Astrid's murder was seated no more than

four feet from me. He was so close that I could see the pores in his swarthy skin and the dark bristles that had escaped his razor. I could see the dark roots and the gel glistening on his short, peroxide-blond haircut.

As Mihac unfolded his copy of the *Racing Times*, his gaze actually met and held mine for a fraction of a second through the beads of condensation. His irises were dark and fathomless, almost as dark as the pupils themselves; they showed no emotion, no humanity. It was unsettling being this close to someone who clearly had no regard for anyone's life – except, no doubt, his own.

The veins in my temples began to throb as I felt my heart rate surge and my mouth go dry . . . Then the moment had passed and he returned his attention to the racing form, marking his choice of runners with an expensive gold propelling pencil.

I edged back in my seat, suddenly aware that I'd all but stopped breathing. My hands trembled slightly as I lit a fresh cigarette and forced myself to concentrate on my plan for the following day.

I'd use the narrow alleyway opposite between two shops to loiter, reading a newspaper, until I was confident that everything was in place and no stray pedestrians were in the way. Then I'd simply cross the road in six or seven strides, slot Mihac with a double tap to the centre of the chest and turn abruptly to the right.

Then I'd walk away briskly unless the exact moment was witnessed by others. If a hue-and-cry went up, I'd run like the devil. Just a hundred yards up the street I would turn left along a pedestrian walk-through. This ran for some sixty yards behind back-to-back gardens and led to an adjoining cul-de-sac.

There Tony Tromain would be waiting with our sanitized getaway car. He'd have a secluded spot fixed where we would torch the vehicle and transfer to different transport.

It was all far from foolproof and this review just reinforced why I'd orginally rejected this plan for the alternative of a sniper shot into Mihac's jacuzzi extension from my
rented room. Not least was the angle of my approach. If I
got it wrong, I could end up shooting anyone sitting in the
seat I was occupying now.

Mihac was glancing frequently at his gold Rolex, I noticed.
I wondered who he was waiting for? Was it one of the list of
characters I'd noted over my days of observation previously?

Suddenly he raised his hand at someone approaching down
the street. I leaned my cheek against the window pane to
see, but the angle was too tight to get a view far along the
pavement. I couldn't actually see who it was until the figure
appeared in front of Mihac's table.

I didn't recognize him at first. He was a tall man, straight-
shouldered in an immaculately cut and pressed suit. The face
was thin, his cheeks pinched almost to the point of being
gaunt. A long, slightly hooked nose gave him the look of a
bird of prey, that impression emphasized by the alert and
searching eyes. Those eyes, a delicate pale blue. Eyes that I'd
seen before. But where?

It seemed like an age before the penny dropped, but it
was probably only seconds as the man took his seat opposite Mihac and reached across the table to shake his hand.

Yes, I *did* know those eyes. But I hadn't recognized them
immediately for two reasons. Firstly, they belonged to the
wrong face. It had been fatter then and the lower half had
been decorated with a trim dark moustache and an elegant
goatee beard.

And secondly, because the face belonged to a man who
was dead.

The man sitting right in front of me, on the other side
of the glass, was Brigadier Milo Domedzic of the Serbian
secret police. The man who had ordered Astrid's murder.

*             *             *

I drove south to London in a daze.

My head was full of confused thoughts and emotions. Was the man who'd met Mihac on the Leicester backstreet really Domedzic? Had I got it wrong? Did the man just have similar features? Like any other ethnic group, many unrelated Slavs shared certain physical traits, bone structure, mouth or nose shape . . . although the blue eyes were definitely unusual in a Serb. But the truth was, if I dug in my memory, I'd come across half a dozen men in the Balkans who'd otherwise vaguely resembled Domedzic.

After all, why the hell should Morgan Dampier have lied to me and told me the man was dead if it wasn't true? There was absolutely no sense in that at all.

The more I thought about it, the more intensely the pressure seemed to grow inside my skull like a brewing thunderstorm until I expected it to explode. At last I started passing signs indicating the outskirts of North London and realized that I'd been driving blind the whole way. I could remember virtually nothing of the journey: I'd been on autopilot and oblivious to other traffic.

That in itself was quite a shock and I forced myself to slow down, to take notice of what the hell I was doing. Despite the effort, it didn't quite work, but at least I managed to weave through the capital's heavy traffic and got back home in one piece.

As I opened the door of my flat, I was suddenly thankful that Paquet had gone and that I had the place to myself. Although it was only just past midday, I felt suddenly and utterly exhausted. I'd had a hell of a hectic week anyway and the shock of seeing the ghost of Domedzic had just about finished me off. I poured a stiff straight whisky and drank it in three gulps. Then I went into the bedroom and threw myself down on the duvet, just vaguely and pleasantly aware of the lingering smell of Paquet's perfume in my nostrils as I crashed into welcome oblivion.

That oblivion lasted for several hours, but when I came to at seven I still felt dreadful. I hadn't eaten since early that morning and now I felt hunger pangs – yet the very thought of eating made me want to throw up. I found some stale bread in the fridge and enlivened it with some Marmite; I managed to hold it down, but only just.

I poured some more whisky into a tumbler, my hands trembling slightly as I asked myself time and time again if it had really been Domedzic I'd seen that very morning. Or was my memory playing tricks?

In an attempt to break my depressed mood, I put on an Alex Mayer CD and turned up the volume. But the blue soul music was a bad choice and did nothing to stop me thinking about Domedzic's ghost . . . Then I suddenly realized that I probably had the solution, right here in my flat.

I had to steel myself to go to the bathroom and remove the panel where I'd previously kept my money stash and the Argentinian pistol. Reaching far into the hole my fingers finally located the cardboard case of the videotape wedged between some pipes. I extracted it and rubbed away the cobwebs and dead woodlice. I looked down at the smudged label with something resembling dread – almost as if the damn thing was contaminated. I had only ever watched it once, seven long years ago. But even that wasn't strictly true, because I had had to turn away before the end.

My mouth had become quite parched with anxiety in just the time it took to return to the living room. I shoved the tape into the mouth of the video player, sat back on the sofa and lit a cigarette, trying to summon the courage to press the button.

I took another swallow of whisky. Fuck this, you stupid bastard, go for it!

A moment's flicker of interference pattern on the screen gave way to the white card showing the laurel-leafed crest of the Intelligence Corps, and the scrawled reference numbers and titling in hand written magic marker: *Bosnia-Herzegovina – Sector 84 Blue – Covert Surveillance (by X Delta Bravo): 24 December 1994?*

The caption card gave way to shaky landscape footage of a snow-smeared mountain road taken from the rear of a moving vehicle. I braced myself . . . From the CD player the throaty voice of Alex Mayer seemed to suddenly swell and smother me . . . *I'm locked in a prison and someone's taken the key, I'm trapped alone in here with me, Just me* . . . Then I was suddenly aware that the doorbell was ringing above the sound of the music.

It was almost a relief to have an excuse to pause the tape, to have a breathing space. Perversely cursing the interruption, I made my way to the front door. I was about to answer it when it occurred to me that this could be the police raid I'd been half-expecting – Special Branch hunting for copies of Sir Marcus's dossier.

'They'd have frozen off by now,' Bex accused brightly, '*if* I had any. I've been ringing for ages and it's *perishin'* out here!'

I stepped aside to let her in. 'Sorry, I had music on.'

She laughed. 'So I hear. You must have deaf neighbours, Eddie. It sounds like a bloody rock concert.'

I closed the door after her. 'To what do I owe the pleasure?'

She was looking around, almost sniffing the air like an antelope in search of danger. 'No Francoise?'

'Found herself a hotel,' I replied, turning down the music.

'Oh,' was the rather ambivalent response. 'Well, anyway, I thought you should be the first to know. I was just packing up for the day at my office when I had an unexpected visitor. Well, two, actually. Tweedledee and Tweedledum. An oily little creep from Special Branch called Godsave. Inspector Godsave. God-help-us, more like. And some other bloke – from Box, I imagine.' She meant MI5. 'He didn't want to give his name. In fact he didn't say much at all. Godsave did all the talking. Demanded to know if I was in possession of any property of the late Sir Marcus Whitby.'

'The dossier,' I said unnecessarily.

'Well, I think the expression "restricted official documents" passed his lips more than once. Did I have them, know where they were, or know of anyone else who had them? Anyway, I said I knew nuthin' about nuthin'. Then he asked me if I knew you.'

'And what did you say to that?'

'I said of course I did, we were lovers.'

I smiled at that.

'It was bloody obvious that he knew I knew you, Ed. Anyway, he looked a bit embarrassed about that and asked whether you had these documents, blah, blah. When he got nowhere fast, he insisted on searching the office—'

'He had a warrant?'

'No, Ed, but there was no point in objecting. I had nothing to hide. When he found zilch he got really irritated and went into verbal meltdown. Threatened to have my business investigated by the police, invoked the Official Secrets Act . . . I think the terms Tower of London and gallows might have been mentioned, but I forget. All that I can remember was the threat of punishment if I breathed a word to you or anyone else about the visit.'

I raised an eyebrow. 'But you're here.'

'I told him to go far away and propagate himself.' She sat down on the sofa and took a swig from my whisky bottle. 'I said the person to have asked was Jude – oops, but now he couldn't, could he? Not now that someone in the British government or the EU had had her blown up with Sir Marcus.'

I winced. 'What did he say to that?'

She wiped her mouth on the back of her hand. 'He just looked at me as though I was bonkers. I honestly don't think he knew what I was talking about. Basically he went all anally retentive on me and left.'

'And the other one, the spook, he said nothing?'

'Very little. Mostly just watched. Creepy dark eyes, I thought.'

'Did he have an accent?'

Bex frowned. 'I think he did, actually, now you ask. Sort of European - south European.'

'Like Yugoslav?'

She did a double take then. 'I think you're right. How—'

I said: 'Those two clowns have already visited Astrid's parents and Wendy – and, no doubt, my solicitor – picking up the spare dossiers.'

Her eyes clouded. 'So I'm too late to warn you? I'm sorry.'

'It's okay.' I smiled. 'Astrid's parents weren't intimidated by them. I got a copy back.'

Now Bex looked alarmed. 'God, Ed, don't keep it here.'

I shook my head. 'I haven't. It's safe somewhere—'

She raised her hand. 'Don't tell me. The less I know the better.' But then a thought occurred to her. 'Francoise hasn't got it?'

'Not yet.'

Bex seemed to have difficulty deciding how to phrase her next sentence. 'Do you really trust her, Ed?'

I shrugged. 'I think so. But the truth is, she's the only one who's likely to be able to make any sense of it.'

She nodded and stared blankly at the flickering image on the television. 'True enough, Ed . . .' Suddenly it seemed to register what she was looking at. 'What's this, holiday videos . . . ? Hang on, that looks a bit like the Snake Pass. Sector 84 . . .'

'It is.'

She looked up at me, frowning. 'Should you have this? Isn't this MoD footage?'

'Yes. I managed to get a spare copy from a pal in Int after Astrid's death.'

'Are you all right, Ed? I thought how pale you looked when I came in. Look like you've seen a ghost.'

I said: 'I think I have . . .' But my voice quavered. I turned away so that she wouldn't see the moisture welling in my eyes, and lit a cigarette.

'Is this covert footage from the laundry van?' she asked.

I nodded, finding my voice with difficulty. 'Yes, the day Astrid died.'

'Why are you looking at it?'

'Someone I saw today. Or thought I saw. I need to check it out on the tape.'

I tried to avoid eye contact with her, yet felt myself drawn to look at her. Those blue eyes were wide with awareness and concern. That girl was perceptive, all right. 'Let me watch it with you, Ed.'

'Believe me, you don't want to see it.'

'I'm a big girl, Ed. I've been around.' Her smile of comfort was sincere, but obviously came with effort. She patted the sofa. 'Sit here, Ed. We'll look at it together.'

As I sat beside her I felt like a child needing a mother's comfort. She topped up my glass with whisky and handed it to me. Then she picked up the remote. 'Shall I?'

I nodded and watched with a numb sort of dread as the still picture jerked back into motion.

The covert camera had been secreted at the back of the van's rear wheel arch, its wide-angle lens just peeking through the shattered tail-light fitting. Laundry vans have a more colourful history than most people realize, because they can be seen anywhere and everywhere without raising suspicions as they criss-cross a neighbourhood. The Mafia used them in America for narcotics distribution, and army intelligence deployed them in the early days of the Ulster conflict.

At the time, we'd adopted the idea as a means of secret

surveillance in Bosnia. Despite the war, people still had to sleep and there were enough small hotels and guest houses being used by officers from both sides to justify the ruse. Well, just. It wasn't long before we were tumbled.

But at this time we were using the beaten-up old van to recce Sector 84, a remote but strategic mountain pass between two towns, which had been under vicious Serbian paramilitary control for several months and was proving to be a real nuisance to the aid distributors. With stories of atrocities committed under Tex-Mex's command increasing daily, something had to be done. Intelligence believed that Tex-Mex was in fact receiving orders direct from President Milosevic in Belgrade, rather than the local Bosnian Serb leadership in Pale. And the prime suspect in the area was a Serbian secret policeman called Brigadier Milo Domedzic.

Int's idea was to identify him on film and then present the *prima facie* evidence to Milosevic in Belgrade and so embarrass him into releasing the stranglehold on Sector 84 thus ending Tex-Mex's reign of terror.

That was our intent as three other SAS troopers and I, with grubby blue overalls covering our camo fatigues, sat in the van as it laboured up the steep, twisting incline into the mountains.

This was a dangerous game: I remembered the nervous jokes we exchanged and that our sweat of fear by itself had built up a fug of condensation on the windows in the unheated van. I recalled repeatedly checking that the Heckler & Koch was in its place under my seat and that I could reach the Browning pistol on my belt through the unbuttoned overalls. If things went pear-shaped at one of the roadblocks, we'd have to shoot our way out — hopefully with our precious photographic evidence intact.

But we hoped it wouldn't come to that. We were laden with bottles of hooch and cigarettes to bribe our way through and, as it was Christmas Eve, we thought that seasonal good-will might for once even extend to Tex-Mex's thugs.

The video footage didn't record our nervous banter, just engine and road noise and the rattle of the exhaust as we bumped over the rough icy track. Pine trees powdered with snow fell away steeply to the valley below.

Ahead, there was a hamlet. It was situated where the road ran down to the high pass and performed a tight U-turn before climbing back up the other side of the pass and to the first of Tex-Mex's roadblocks. Half a dozen war-damaged cottages were clustered around the bend next to the road-side café that was reputed to be the local Bosnian Serb head-quarters. Certainly there was never any shortage of armed militiamen at the tables and chairs on the pavement, smoking and knocking back *slivovitz* as they laughed and played cards.

I remember our lanky Glaswegian driver – known as Toothbrush, because he always managed to carry half the kit that most of us did – leaning forward to get a better view through the windscreen. 'Something am occurring, boss.'

I wiped some of the condensation from my side of the glass and lifted the pocket binos to my eyes. The jumpy image that presented itself was puzzling for a moment. A group of some fifty heavily armed militia were assembled to one side on a rocky slope, clearly an audience to some event about to happen.

What appeared to be half a dozen terrified local villagers were lined up on the veranda of the café under an armed militia escort. In front of them were three other civilians who had been bound by rope to white plastic chairs.

Tex-Mex himself was strutting back and forth with a lot to say for himself as he gestured extravagantly with his left hand. His right held a pulsating chainsaw that was emitting energetic puffs of petrol exhaust.

The combined body language of the members of the ever-nearing tableau was all too clear, despite the distance.

'Oh, shit.' I said. 'I think chummy's about to give a lesson in obedience.'

I was aware that Tomkins and Kelly in the back were leaning forward to try and see what was going on.

It happened so quickly and yet so slowly. Tex-Mex was standing in front of the three tied and seated captives, but with his back to them. Then in one movement he lifted the chainsaw with both hands and, with a twisting pirouette, swung round towards them in a wide sweep until the blade was level with the neck of the first man.

He didn't hesitate. In a series of four fast strides he totally decapitated all three men like swinging a scythe through grass. Blood under pressure burst skyward in a trio of scarlet geysers as the heads fell heavily to the patio and rolled around like discarded footballs. As the group of locals who had been forced to witness this horror gasped and tried to turn their faces away, a roar of approval went up from the audience of Tex-Mex's drunken militia. That poison dwarf Mihac was dancing around the growing pool of blood with his video camera, trying to get close-ups of the corpses.

'Jesus!' Toothbrush muttered, his foot automatically hitting the brake.

I overruled him – a decision I would regret for the rest of my life. 'Keep going. It's over now and there are too many of them.'

'Yeah, boss,' came the response in reluctant agreement. 'Guess you're right . . . Bloody bastards.'

One or two militamen were now glancing towards the noisy approach of our laundry van. But most had shifted their attention to follow Tex-Mex as he strode to the left of the café, where something quite large was hanging from a tree. I just caught sight of dark material fluttering in the stiff mountain breeze before low scrub on the bend blocked our view.

As we re-emerged, right on the bend, the scene at the

café veranda was passing by in a blur. I tried to make out what was happening at the tree. What was hanging from the rope and why was Tex-Mex brandishing his chainsaw again? My brain was stunned, unable to make sense of a scene that turned the world on its head. It took for ever to work out that the strange, fluttering object was in fact a woman hanging from the tree by ropes fixed to her ankles. She was unidentifiable behind the material of her skirt that had fallen down to hide her torso and head. There was a lasting image of white pants and the desperate flexing of her stomach muscles as she struggled to get free . . .

I never saw what happened, because the laundry van was now scrambling up the far side of the pass as fast as the pounding engine could turn the wheels to get out of range of the firepower of over fifty Serbian militia.

But the covert video camera had recorded it all. Bex squeezed my hand and gave a low gasp of horror as Tex-Mex brought the whirring blade down on the hapless woman and carved her in half like a carcass in an abattoir.

And there was Mihac and his camera again, laughing and prancing around like a court jester as he ducked in under the two swinging halves of the woman's body to get a better close-up.

I cursed aloud. I hadn't meant to watch this far. I'd always avoided it; knowing what had happened had been quite enough. I certainly didn't need to see it. I brushed aside Bex's hand as she put it over mine in a gesture of reassurance. Then I hit the rewind button until I had the shot of the man standing behind Tex-Mex.

As I froze the picture, Bex said: 'Dear, Ed. I'm so sorry. You could have had no idea that it was Astrid.'

I was barely aware of my own voice talking. It sounded disembodied, belonging to someone else. 'Not until we reached the checkpoint on the far side of the pass. Her abandoned car was there.'

'Why, for God's sake?'

'To set an example. It was rule by terror. She was a trans-lator for us, and she'd even married me, a Brit soldier.'

'But she wasn't technically a Serb.'

I didn't answer, couldn't. But Bex would have worked it out for herself. Astrid spoke Serbian, appeared to be Serbian, and that was good enough for the militia scum. Good enough to make an example of her as a traitor for helping the UN.

In situations like that technicalities and niceties counted for nothing.

I focused on the man on the screen. He was tall and gaunt, with a neat dark goatee beard and cropped grey hair, standing with his arms crossed arrogantly in front of him as he watched. There was no expression in those distant blue eyes.

Now I had no doubt.

'Who's that?' Bex asked.

I couldn't tell her that it was Brigadier Milo Domedzic, who had ordered the execution. I couldn't tell her that I had been told he was dead and that he was the ghost I had seen on a street in Leicester.

I couldn't tell her because seven years of suppressed grief and guilt had risen up inside me like a volcanic explosion and I broke down in a sobbing flood of tears that was totally unstoppable.

# Ten

Bex was aghast. 'Mihac? You're going to kill Mihac? God, Ed, are you mad?'

When the tears had finally dried it was gone midnight and time to talk. And I needed to talk, desperately. I had needed to for seven long years, but there had been no one to talk to. Now there was Bex and I guess there could never have been a better choice.

'Mad?' I repeated. 'Probably. But it's got tacit support from HMG.'

She looked horrified. 'You mean Tromain, don't you? He's set you up to do this.' When I didn't respond, she looked at me thoughtfully. 'And that *was* you who assassinated Tex-Mex . . .' It wasn't a question.

'Morgan Dampier set that one up, before he changed jobs.'

'Oh, the bastard, how could he?' Bex shook her head. 'I thought at least he could be trusted.'

I was starting to get irritated by her questioning my judgement. 'Look, Bex, there was a job to be done and I was the best one to do it. I speak fluent Serbo-Croat, so we could throw the police off the scent. I was willing and able – and I could be trusted.'

She looked scathing. 'You didn't mention money.'

That brought me up short. 'Yeah, well, that did help to tip the balance . . . But I'd have done it for nothing. Morgan was straight with me.'

'Not that straight, Ed. Not if he told you Brigadier Domedzic was dead.'

I lit my last Gauloise from the pack and tossed the wrappings in the bin. 'I don't know why he told me that. Orders, I suppose. But I'll get to the bottom of it with Tromain on Friday.'

She shook her head as she nailed me with her stare. 'So you're still going ahead?'

'Yes.' Defiant.

'However much those bastards deserve it, it's still murder, you know.' Bex wasn't giving up on me that easily. 'If it goes wrong, the government won't be able to help you. They'll throw you to the wolves, you know that?'

'I'll make sure it doesn't go wrong.'

'Please do, Ed, because I don't want to spend the next twenty years having to take you food parcels in prison. And if money's still a problem – well, with Jude gone, I'm short of a partner.'

That was touching. 'Thanks for the offer, Bex. I'll bear it in mind.'


I smiled to myself as I remembered the conversation later that day during my drive to Heathrow. I left the BMW in a residential backstreet in Slough and took a cab to the airport. My conversation with Bex into the early hours had left me in good spirits, despite feeling shattered after so little sleep. I caught up an hour's worth on the flight to Rome, where I moved into my rented self-catering holiday apartment.

I moved out again two hours later, taking just an overnight bag and picking up my hire car for the journey to Milan airport. Again, I left the car parked in a nearby street rather than an official car park. I donned my Serb-assassin wig and assembled the false passport and papers provided by Tromain before hailing a taxi for the terminal.

That evening I was again passing back through Heathrow before picking up a nondescript Astra saloon from a car-rental office on the concourse and setting off for Leicester. By nine I'd booked in at a hideously overpriced chain motel on the outskirts of the city. After a meal and bath, I was more than ready to hit the pillow by eleven.

At seven the next morning I had no appetite for breakfast and made do with black coffee and a Gauloise before setting out to meet Tromain as planned. This particular public car park had been selected because it hadn't yet succumbed to CCTV.

Tromain threw open the passenger door of his Volvo saloon as I approached.

'You can put that out,' were his words of welcome. I tossed the cigarette butt through the open window as he handed me the Heckler & Koch USP automatic pistol and silencer: 'This will do the business, Edward. Clean Serbian Army issue, only ever been test-fired by our people.'

I weighed it in my hand for a moment before checking it over, removing and replacing the magazine.

'Soft-nosed rounds,' Tromain said unnecessarily. He seemed unusually edgy. Perhaps he'd been too long out of the front line. 'Your usual double tap, I imagine. Mr Black won't be back for breakfast tomorrow.'

I was in no mood for Tromain's puerile wit as I pocketed the weapon and faced him directly. 'Morgan Dampier told me that Brigadier Domedzic was dead.'

The flicker of alarm in Tromain's eyes was unmistakable. 'Who?'

'Domedzic – Tex-Mex and Mihac's boss. He's dead, isn't he?'

Relief showed suddenly in the man's expression. 'Domedzic – er, yes. He's dead all right.'

'That's what I thought.' I had him now. 'So how come I saw him on Wednesday?'

'Wednesday?' he echoed.

'I decided to do another recce. I saw him talking to Mihac at the café.'

Tromain gave one of his patronizing little smiles. 'Think you were mistaken there, old son.'

'Fuck you,' I snarled. 'Cut the bullshit, Tromain. Tell the truth for once in your life, or I'll turn this bloody gun on you.'

For a moment he hesitated, his mouth going through that chewing motion of his, before he decided which way to play it. Finally he said: 'I'm sorry, Edward. I know how that must make you feel, but Morgan was under orders – just like me.'

I shook my head in anger and disbelief. 'So Domedzic's helping your lot, too – just like Tex-Mex and Mihac?'

Tromain shrugged apologetically. 'But unlike them, Domedzic's work with us is still current.'

'But why the deliberate lie?' I persisted.

This time Tromain didn't bother with the kid gloves. 'Look at yourself, Edward. You'd never accept that it was politically expedient to keep him alive. He's helped the UN and NATO intelligence – and now the European Commission. In the Balkans they need every and *any* friend they can get. To sort out the aftermath of the war. To establish a permanent and ongoing peace. And, believe me, Domedzic knows his way around over there.'

'He's also a fuckin' murderer,' I reminded him. 'The worst kind – a war criminal guilty of genocide, rape and torture against unarmed civilians.'

The light in Tromain's eyes darkened. 'You don't know all the answers, Edward, far from it. Domedzic was largely responsible for landing us President Milosevic himself to stand trial in The Hague. And he'll be helping the prosecution with inside information. He's the blue-eyed boy in Brussels.'

The implication of that was stunning. I paused and lit another Gauloise. This time Tromain didn't complain. I thought aloud: 'So, unlike Tex-Mex and Mihac, Brigadier Domedzic walks. He's bought his ticket, hasn't he? That's why I was told he was dead. New identity and relocation and all that?'

'You know better than to ask, Edward. I don't like it much either, but I'm a realist. And I have to obey my orders.'

I exhaled in his face. 'You could always resign.'

He gave me a pained look that said big mortgage and school fees now, and handsome pension later on. But he left his personal problems out of it: 'Like it or not, Edward, things take on a European dimension nowadays. In security, like everything else. Intelligence agencies listen to Brussels and whatever Brussels wants – as often as not – it gets. And Brussels wants Domedzic left alone.'

I'd heard enough and couldn't stomach any more. There was a dangerous job to do and I needed all my powers of concentration and survival for that. Once this was over, there'd be plenty of time to curse and cry in my beer. I reminded myself that I'd already sworn to walk away from my recent past, to leave Astrid's memory in peace.

I said: 'Okay, thanks for the pep talk. Now, let's get on and into position.'

Tromain looked relieved that he wasn't going to have to contend with any more tantrums. 'See you later,' were his parting words. 'Good luck.'

I returned to my hire car and watched as he drove off in his Volvo. As I waited five minutes, I thought it a strange farewell. It's the one thing in common with actors and soldiers. You never wish them good luck. It's tantamount to a curse. Tony Tromain should have known that.

I pushed the thought from my mind and set off for the Leicester suburb that was Mihac's patch. Ten minutes later I parked up three roads away from Mihac's café in a tree-lined avenue of middle-class semi-detached houses and left on foot. I made a point of approaching the arcade in which the café was situated by the same route I intended to leave by after the killing. One purpose was to check for any unexpected problems on the way – roadworks, parked cop cars – anything, really. The other was to make sure that Tromain was actually sitting there in our getaway Volvo.

He was and he scowled at me over the top of the newspaper he was pretending to read as I passed him. I turned off down the pedestrian walkway that led to the arcade.

I slowed down now, breathing deliberately and steadily as if doing yoga exercises. I shoved my hands deep into the pockets of my leather bomber jacket and adopted a shuffling walk. The same walk unconsciously used by so many of the local low-life, out-of-work chancers whose lives revolved around the pub, the betting office and the next petty crime or benefits scam.

The watery sun and chill northerly breeze hadn't enticed anyone to sit at the three tables outside the café and Mihac had not yet made his appearance. I crossed the street to the mouth of the alleyway opposite that offered a shaded waiting position.

As I stepped between the parked cars on the other kerb, I came face to face with the man I was about to kill. Because of his short stature, he'd been hidden from my view by the vehicles.

Now he was standing still right in front of me. For a moment dark, emotionless eyes stared from the acne-pitted face, silently challenging me to stand aside and let him through. His arrogance and sense of self-importance were unmistakable as he stood there in his snazzy suit, coat draped over his shoulders like a cloak. There was no way he was going to give ground. A condescending sneer played at his lips as I took a backward step to let him pass.

The sickly smell of cologne lingered in my nostrils and

it was all I could do to stop myself from throwing up before I reached the shadow of the alleyway. It took a few moments for my racing heart to recover from the unexpected encounter. Breathing erratically, I propped myself against the brick wall and pulled out a folded newspaper from my inside pocket.

Forcing myself to concentrate, I surveyed the street scene, checking that all was well. Checking that there was nothing new I had to take into account when I went for the kill.

Opposite, Mihac was now at his favoured table, giving his breakfast order to the waitress, sharing some lewd joke with her. To my right an Indian in old clothes was fly-posting with a brush and a bucket of paste. Some forthcoming wrestling match ... To my left the foam-upholstery merchant's, the second-hand furniture store, the shop being refitted and the electricians having a tea break. Outside the bookie's, a man with his head under the bonnet of his car was doing some repair. The street cleaner was working his way down the street with his handcart.

All quiet, all set. No stray pedestrians, no young mums pushing prams. A clear field of fire ... The waitress disappearing into the café with Mihac's order and the target himself sitting alone, absorbed in his racing paper. No one next to him. So I could approach to the right, hit him sideways on and avoid any ricochet into the café window. It was perfect. Time to move.

Quickly I stuffed the newspaper into my pocket and reached inside my jacket for the reassuringly firm grip of the silenced pistol ...

I really don't know what took me so long. Even then I might have missed all the signs, had it not been for that siren voice in my ears. But whose voice? It was Astrid's that I heard, but the words were Morgan Dampier's.

*Never trust anyone, even your own. Especially your own.*

Something was unsettling me, but for a few seconds I still

wasn't sure what . . . Then, it came at me in a rush, a premonition.

I could see myself crossing the street, drawing the silenced automatic from my jacket as I stepped onto the kerb. Saw Mihac casually look up from his *Racing Times*, his expression changing from one of mild curiosity to sheer terror as it dawned on him what I was and what I was about to do. I saw him rock backwards under the impact, the blood splattering down his smart suit as the double tap slammed home.

But even as I turned to walk away, I could see the Indian fly-poster and the road sweeper draw their concealed weapons, the man repairing his car and probably the electricians in their fixed OP all converging on me.

'GO! GO! GO!' I could hear their shrill cries in this silent street scene as they closed in on me.

I knew then. And the fact that I'd missed it all scared the shit out of me. Five years ago, still in the SAS, I'd have smelled this rat at a hundred paces. Now I was so rusty that I was dangerous – to myself.

The Indian fly-poster was reposting what I'd seen him posting two days ago on my recce. It was the same wrestling match. The electricians in the refitted shop were *still* standing around with mugs of tea, and, although the man and broken-down car were different, the set-up was the same.

Now I was looking for it, I thought I could see the almost imperceptible movement of lips talking to throat mikes, see the tell-tale drag of clothing around what I was now certain were holsters.

This was a trap. And this wasn't just about Mihac, it was about me. Me and Sir Marcus and the people who had killed him and Jude. About the visits to Astrid's parents, Wendy and Bex by Special Branch . . .

With sudden and amazing clarity I could see the whole picture, the whole plan. Mihac gunned down in a Leicester street as undercover security men wait to arrest him – and a Serbian assassin, who has already murdered in London, is fortuitously caught red-handed and shot dead. Or, better still, the sad case of a former British soldier who lost his mind and then his life in the attempt to take revenge on his dead wife's killers. The tabloids would lap it up.

One stone, two embarrassing birds dead. Nice one, Tromain.

I left the cover of the alley, turned right and started walking briskly. So brisk, in fact, that it was nearly a run. Was it my imagination, or did I notice the road sweeper look up, the electricians put down their tea and the Indian turn as I brushed past him? I don't know – I just kept going without a backwards glance.

It seemed an age before I reached the pedestrian walkway and turned down it towards the cul-de-sac beyond which Tromain should still be parked.

I was almost surprised to see the car there. As I got closer I could see Tromain was on his cellphone, looking anxiously in my direction as I approached. I grabbed the passenger door, flung it open and dropped into the seat beside him.

He looked bewildered, almost frightened. 'What the hell's going on . . . ?'

I indicated his mobile. 'You fucking well know already, don't you? I'm aborting.'

'Why, for Christ's sake?'

I glared at him. 'Because I don't like the set-up, never have. It stinks.'

'You can't just pull out—'

'Watch me.'

His face was turning almost purple with anger. 'We've got a deal . . . You'll have to return the money . . . You'll be sorry.'

'We had a deal, Tromain, but not any more. The money's no good to a dead man.'

'What do you mean . . . ? You're talking rubbish.'

I was in no mood for this. The longer I stayed there the more danger I was in. At any moment someone could change the game plan. And even as the thought entered my head, the Indian fly-poster emerged from the end of the pedestrian walkway. Suddenly he didn't look so tired and middle-aged. He looked fit and sharp after his sprint and was looking in our direction.

I turned to Tromain. 'Get out of the car!'

'Don't be stupid—' he protested.

I didn't have time to piss around now. I jerked out the pistol and stuffed the end of the silencer under his chin. 'Get out of the fucking car!'

The message got home at last and he started to shift, throwing open his door. 'You're making a big mistake, Edward,' he blustered.

'Fine,' I replied, sliding across into the driver's seat. 'But it's my decision to abort. Now get out of my life and keep out!'

I slammed the door, keyed the ignition and threw the wheel for a tight turn. As the panorama of the residential cul-de-sac spun past I glimpsed the Indian running towards Tromain, the road sweeper now close on his heels. The front wheel bumped over the grass verge and back onto the road. I hit the gas. A final glimpse in the mirror showed the three men talking frantically together, two of them gesticulating as Tromain punched numbers into his cellphone.

I swung left out of the T-junction into a street busy with traffic and sighed with relief.

But that relief was short-lived as I tried to focus on my options. It didn't help that I didn't really know what Tromain and his masters were trying to achieve or why. Perhaps their plan wasn't to kill me at all – the surveillance team was just that, with the idea of giving me back-up if I needed it. Was my paranoia just getting the better of me?

There was no way of knowing. So I decided to assume

the worst and concentrate instead on what I *did* know – and on *my* priorities.

There was no doubt they wanted Sir Marcus's dossier. It was my priority, too, along with my money.

Getting back home would be a race against time. If Tromain and his masters had really decided I was Public Enemy Number One, my flat would be the first place they'd look. Yet my aborting the mission would have thrown them into panic. It might take hours, even a day or more for Tromain and his masters to decide what to do about me. I reasoned that my best bet was to get home and grab what I needed before they could decide on a course of action.

I headed south, forcing myself to keep within the speed limits, until I hooked up with the M1. As both the car I'd hired and the one I'd snatched from Tromain were known to the intelligence services, it came as no great surprise when, just outside Toddington services, I found a white police squad car sitting on my tail. Subtle he was not. Even when I turned east onto the M25 London orbital at Epping he was sticking to me like glue, although he did drop back a couple of car lengths.

But I'd already worked out a plan. It was less than fool-proof, but better than nothing. I called Bex at her office on one of my new mobiles, but just got the answerphone. Then I tried her cellphone and caught her coming out of Tesco's with the weekend shopping in a trolley.

'Hi, Ed, this is a surprise!' There was a fleeting pause as the penny dropped that I'd hardly be likely to call her in the middle of an assassination mission. 'Is everything okay?'

'Everything's pear-shaped,' I said. 'I aborted and need some back-up.'

The hesitation was minimal. 'I'm yer girl, Ed, you know that.'

'Remember playing the Dagenham Diehards in the rain?'

A chuckle. 'I'll never forget the pneumonia afterwards.'

'Meet me there at . . .' I glanced at my wristwatch. 'Say, fourteen hundred hours.'

'Roger, boss.'

I felt a surge of relief, no longer alone. 'Remember, calls may be monitored for training purposes . . .'

'I'll watch my ass.'

I smiled for the first time that day. 'Leave that to me.'

It was starting to dawn on me exactly how difficult it was to go on the run in modern times. There was little doubt that Bex's mobile number was already known to the intelligence services. By phoning her, I'd given them one of my new numbers. Once they knew a number, they could use global-positioning satellite technology to pinpoint the whereabouts of both callers. I lowered the window of my car and tossed the mobile into the next traffic lane.

I was anxious to throw off my tail while they were still using regular police. Once I hit London, they'd no doubt be replaced by seasoned MI5 'watchers' and things would get a lot more tricky.

So I turned towards Rainham and pulled up on a single yellow outside a takeaway kebab shop. I walked inside and glanced back out of the window to see the squad car pull into a line of illegally parked cars thirty yards behind my Volvo. The officers seemed content to sit and observe until I came out again with my lunch.

I thrust a tenner at the bewildered Greek owner. 'Sorry, mate, but I need to go out your back entrance. I've got an angry husband after me.'

Before he could protest or agree, I pushed past him and into a corridor that ran through to the rear yard. I scaled the rickety fence and dropped down onto the pavement on the next street. Then a quarter-mile sprint took me to the nearest taxi rank. I fell into the back seat and gave the cabbie directions.

Twenty minutes later he dropped me off at the pavilion car park of the playing fields. Bex was standing by an unfamiliar blue Fiat Uno.

'Not yours?'

She shook her head. 'It's likely my car registration's been clocked – so I borrowed this off a friendly neighbour.'

'Smart thinking.'

Bex looked deeply concerned. 'What's gone wrong, Ed? I've been worrying myself silly.'

'I'll explain on the way.'

'On the way to where?'

'I need safe transport. You said Jude kept her motorcycle in a lock-up – d' you know where?'

'Sure, around the corner from her flat.'

'Then let's go.'

On the way I explained what had happened and my reason for aborting the mission to kill Mihac. Bex didn't interrupt, but drove with an expression of grim concentration on her face. At last she said: 'Forgive me for saying, Ed, but you should never have got involved. I understand why, but—'

With hindsight, I could hardly disagree. 'Well, I'm out of it now.'

'What will you do about the money?'

'Give it back, I suppose,' I replied without enthusiasm. 'I can't *prove* what I think they were going to do, and Tromain would only deny it. I'll just deduct some to cover my exes on the recce.'

She took her eyes off the road for a moment. 'Do you really think they'll let it rest at that? If you're right, they might want you out of the way now more than ever.'

'Maybe we can compromise.' I grinned at her. 'Maybe they'll pay me to go and live on a remote Caribbean island.'

'In your dreams,' she replied. 'Anyway, to be practical – what's your next move?'

I hadn't managed to plan too far ahead. 'Grab my money and Sir Marcus's dossier – then lie low for a while and sort my life out.'

Bex nodded her understanding, before saying: 'We're nearly there, Ed.'

We were entering a small private housing estate that had been built without garages in the 1950s. Bex pulled up outside a row of tatty lock-ups that had been added as an afterthought.

She produced a ring of keys. 'These are Jude's. She asked me to put her Harley back after she decided to go off with Marcus at Christmas.' Freeing the padlock, she threw open the up-and-over door. The big Harley Davidson sat there gleaming in the dim light, like a thoroughbred eager for a run.

There was a small selection of helmets on the workbench and I found one that was just about large enough for me. I hadn't ridden a motorcycle for many years so, after we mounted up with Bex as pillion, I set off somewhat tentatively towards the Thames and my flat on the South Bank.

Slowly we crossed the top of my street; there were no flashing lights and no obvious signs of unusual activity. Satisfied, I continued for thirty yards before turning left along the next street that ran parallel behind my own. I pulled in outside a house halfway down.

'What now?' Bex asked.

'This is the fence to the back garden,' I replied as we dismounted and crossed the grass verge.

We'd done all this sort of stuff before in Northern Ireland and hardly needed to discuss it. She stooped over beside the larchlap panelling and cupped her hands to form a stirrup for my foot. I used it to spring up, onto her shoulder and over the top. I'd picked the point where the gardener had his wooden composter and I used it as a raised anchor point to hoist Bex up after me.

'You've definitely shed a few pounds,' I commented.

'You lovely man.' She grinned in my face. 'Take me —
I'm yours!'

'Later,' I said, jumping down to the grass and starting up
the overgrown path to the rear of the house. As always the
back door was unlocked and we saw no one as we climbed
the stairs to Cristobelle's flat.

'Ah, dear Mr Coltrane!' she exclaimed. 'I was expecting
you.'

'You were?'

'Heard you upstairs earlier. Moving furniture or something.'

I frowned. 'When was that?'

Cristobelle shook her head. 'Naughty man, as if you didn't
know! Seven in the morning — disturbed my beauty sleep.'

I forced a smile. 'I'm sorry about that.'

'You've come for the box?'

'If you wouldn't mind.'

'I'll get it for you,' she said and pushed the door to.

'Who's been in your flat?' Bex wondered aloud.

'Maybe Fran came back for something. She's got a key.
I'll just have a quick look before we go, and I'd like to check
the answerphone.'

Bex looked dubious, but said nothing as Cristobelle
returned with the cardboard box containing my money,
Marcus's dossier and the snap-down sniper rifle.

'Thanks,' I said. 'And if the police come round, you still
haven't seen me, okay?'

'Mum's the word, Mr Coltrane.' Her curiosity got the
better of her. 'Off on your travels again?'

'For a little while,' I confirmed noncommittally and started
for the staircase that led up to my flat.

Bex looked on apprehensively as I quietly turned the key
and let the door drift slowly open under its own weight.
The wintry afternoon light was beginning to fade, but there

was still enough to see clearly across the hall and into the living room beyond. It was totally, almost eerily quiet. No furniture appeared to have been moved, nothing had changed. Moreover, the air smelled musty and just a little damp. Nothing new there, then.

I stepped inside. 'Don't touch the lights, Bex. I'll just check the answerphone.'

She was close behind me. 'Okay if I use your loo? Must be all this excitement.'

'Be my guest,' I muttered as I crossed to the breakfast bar to where the light on the answerphone was blinking.

There was just one message, recorded barely twenty minutes earlier. It was Francoise Paquet's voice. She sounded distraught and was gabbling so quickly that it was difficult at times to make out exactly what she was saying. *'Eddie, I know you're not due back, but maybe you do a remote check . . . ? You should know as soon as possible. I am very worried for you, Eddie. I have had a visit from your police at my office. It is very unpleasant, very aggressive. They say this is a missing-persons inquiry for the friend of you and Bex – Jude Sinclair. They ask me where you are. Do you have an affair with Jude – then ask if you have one with me or Bex? Then does Jude have an affair with Marcus? And are you a jealous type of person? Then, of course, do I know about information stolen by Marcus from the European Commission . . . ?! Of course, I say no to all of this. But I am worried, Eddie. They are with me for over an hour and they seem very, very serious. I am trembling when they go . . . I have two stiff cognacs even before I call you . . . Please speak to me as soon as you can. Take care, cherie—'*

I heard the chain pull in the bathroom and Bex emerge behind me. 'God, Ed, why on earth did you leave that carpet in there? There's no room for a girl to swing her handbag—' She stopped, seeing the expression on my face.

'What?' I sprinted towards the bathroom door. The bundle on the floor looked like the underside of a rolled-up Persian rug covered in polythene and held together with string. It was about five and a half feet in length and quite bulky.

Somehow I just knew. Instinctively I reached down, grabbed one end and pulled it through the doorway into the hall. It was much too heavy for a rug.

Bex had taken a step back, a hand to her mouth. 'Oh, Christ, Ed, I thought something seemed strange . . . The penny just didn't drop. Sweet God, I was just sitting there looking at it—'

I opened the Swiss Army knife I always carried on my keyring. 'Give me a hand,' I snapped.

Bex forced herself out of shock and came forward, helping to peel back the tough polythene. 'I'm not sure this is a clever idea—'

But I wasn't listening. I had to know, and yet somehow I already did.

I hacked frantically at the tough carpet backing, Bex's fingers helping to prise it apart. It seemed to take for ever. And then we were through the several rolled layers. A curl of hair fell out. I gave one final, ferocious downward rip of the blade.

Bex gasped and fell back. The beautiful face seemed to burst out of its wrapping of polythene and carpet. I stared down at the open eyes staring blankly back at me.

I whispered just one word: 'Jude.'

But I don't think the sound came out.

# Eleven

'You're crazy, Ed!' Bex yelled. 'This is some sort of set-up. For God's sake, let's get out of here!'

But I wasn't listening. I was much too intent on hacking away at the carpeting, slicing open the cocoon. It came as something of a shock to find that Jude's corpse was completely naked. So robust in life, she now looked like a broken porcelain doll, her skin a translucent white with a marbling of blue. The little tattoo of a bluebird just above her pubic hair was pathetic to see now. And she looked very, very cold.

I said: 'No marks, Bex. Maybe some light bruising around her neck and shoulders. She's either been suffocated or poisoned, I'd guess.'

'For God's sake cover her up.'

We both heard the squeal of brakes from outside on the street. Bex looked at me. It wasn't often that I'd seen her look so so alarmed. Even as I closed the ripped covering back over Jude's body, Bex was running to the front bedroom.

'Jesus, Ed,' she breathed as I joined her by the window. 'Armed police.'

There must have been five squad cars as well as the white van. It was supposed to have been a silent approach, no sirens and no flashing lights. Already in the twilight I could see crouching dark figures fanning out, seeking out shadows as they approached the house.

None of this was making any kind of sense. But sense or not, there was no doubt about one thing where Bex was spot on. This was some kind of set-up – and I was firmly in the frame. And if I hesitated for a minute longer than necessary, I'd end up in custody. Or perhaps even dead.

I glanced at Bex. 'You don't have to come, it's not you they're after.'

She stared back at me as though I was mad. 'We don't know that, Ed. Maybe I'm next on their list.'

I wasn't going to argue. 'Lock and bolt the front door, will you?'

As she ran back across the hall, I considered the cardboard box I'd retrieved from Cristobelle. It was starting to split at the seams; I wasn't going to get far with that. I sprinted back to the bedroom and hauled my old army bergen from the top of the wardrobe. Breaking open the box, I transferred the entire contents before hauling the strap over one shoulder and rejoining Bex in the hall. She'd already realized my plan and was staring up at the loft hatch.

'Down, girl,' I said, dumping the bergen beside her.

As she dropped to all fours, I stepped onto her shoulders and pushed the hatch cover aside with my palms. Using her shoulders as a springboard, I vaulted up and into the void, hooking my elbows over the frame. It took a couple of seconds to scramble up, reposition myself and grab the bergen that Bex thrust up at me.

We could hear heavy footfalls on the landing below as I hauled her up after me and replaced the cover. I fumbled in the side pockets of the bergen, which I'd always kept stocked with personal survival kit. I'd been on the reserve for several years and thankfully old habits died hard. The torch batteries were on their last legs but there was enough dwindling energy left to light the way across the rafters to the roof maintenance hatch.

Suddenly the entire building seemed to tremble as a heavy metal battering-ram was used to force the hinges on the front door of my flat below. It gave way with an almighty crash and was immediately followed by the aggressive shout of voices. 'ARMED POLICE! DON'T MOVE! ARMED POLICE . . . !'

The maintenance hatch resisted momentarily, then opened up to show the dying remnants of a spectacular purple and yellow sunset beyond the rooftops in the next street. I scrambled out and slid a few feet down the slates to the narrow brick parapet. The bergen came out next, followed by Bex. When she'd joined me, I began edging along the parapet to the corner of the house.

I had in mind for us to lower ourselves down the drainpipe to the garden. But as I peered over the parapet and quickly drew back, I realized that was no longer an option.

'What is it?' Bex whispered.

'Armed cops are round the back too.' Of course, I told myself, they would be.

'Maybe we can wait here until they go,' Bex suggested.

I realized that was wishful thinking. 'It doesn't matter who put Jude's body here – as far as the police are concerned, this is a murder scene. We'd be in for a long wait.'

She nodded, conceding the point. 'Then we're somewhat stuck. The expression up "a gum tree" springs to mind.'

I hunkered down against the tiles and looked around. Street lamps were coming on and the lights had already been switched on in many of the surrounding windows. The details of the houses were fading into inky outlines. My gaze moved along the parapet to the adjoining identical building.

Nudging Bex, I began edging along for a closer look. I stopped at the corner and considered the gap between us and the house next door. Enough for the fence, two pathways and narrow flower borders below that separated the buildings. Around fifteen feet – too far to jump.

Just as I'd resigned myself to the fact that there was no way out of this, it occurred to me that perhaps the answer was already on my back. I unshouldered the bergen and laid it on the sloping tiles. I hadn't used it in over five years; before that it had always been kept filled and ready for instant use whenever I was on leave from the Regiment. I could just grab it and go without thinking. And, as I'd been on the reserve, it had stayed that way on the top of the wardrobe. I unzipped one of the two large side pouches which could be detached and clipped together to form a day-sack. I fumbled around in the darkness until my fingers found what I had prayed was still there – a length of climbing rope.

Bex peered over my shoulder. 'Christ, Ed, what're you up to?'

'This just might do it,' I muttered, and glanced back at the gap. It was hard to tell in the poor light, but it looked as though the soffits and guttering on the roof opposite had been well maintained. And a short drainpipe stack matched the one by my feet. I began working one end of the rope into a bowline knot to create a small lasso.

A nervous edge had crept into Bex's voice. 'I hope you're not thinking what I think you're thinking.'

'A single-rope crossing,' I confirmed. 'You've done it enough times on the assault course.'

She looked horrified. 'You mean I've fallen *off* enough times on the assault course. Jesus, Ed, I never could get the hang of that.'

I glanced at her. 'You don't have to come, Bex.'

'We've been through all that.' she snapped back. 'So . . . hell, just get on with it.'

I tried to sound reassuring. 'Don't worry, I'll talk you through it.'

With the loop now complete, I carefully coiled and tossed the rope towards the drainpipe stack opposite. It missed. I tried again. And again. The edge of the loop teetered momentarily on the edge of the stack, then dropped neatly down to gutter level, allowing me to draw it tight. I tugged a couple of times, hard. The stack remained rock solid; solid enough, I hoped, to take my body weight. Bex looked on apprehensively as I lashed the other end of the rope to the stack next to me.

I'd also found a second length of thinner cord. 'Let me rope you to this. It'll be safer if you go first. I'll talk you across.'

Bex stared at me with a look of horror and disbelief. 'I'm not sure, Ed . . .'

'Trust me,' I said and began to thread the rope between her legs and around her waist to make a rope harness. When I'd completed it, I tossed the free end up around the chimney before picking it up. 'I'll belay you. If you slip, you won't go anywhere . . .' I grinned at her. 'But you will have to do it all over again.'

She tried but couldn't quite manage the returning smile. 'That's incentive enough.'

Reluctantly she crouched down at the edge of the single-strand rope bridge. It wasn't the easiest way to launch off, because she was at right angles. To her credit, she didn't hesitate, but dropped right down flat with the gutter and wormed her way forward, running her hands out along the rope that stretched across the forty-foot drop.

'Edge out, sweetheart,' I urged. 'Nice and steady. Nice and slow. Make sure the rope's running between your boobs—'

'Fuck you, Ed!'

I ignored that. 'I'll make sure your left foot's properly hooked over the rope. Use that to push yourself along. Nice 'n' gentle. Up and back, up and back.'

I swear I could feel the heat of fear coming off her. I knew that her heart would be thudding and her mouth would be as parched as the bottom of a parrot's cage. My own heart went out to her as she tentatively stretched her hands along the taut ropes, twisting and uncurling to inch out over the drop.

'You're doing great, girl,' I breathed. 'Nice and steady . . . that's the way.'

I just caught the response under her breath. 'Piss off, Ed.'

Bex's body began to sway, very gently, as she inched away from the safety of the parapet and became airborne. I checked that she had a good locking curl with her left instep around the rope and gradually fed out the belay cord as she moved farther out over the gap. Below, in the light cast from a downstairs window, I could see the two armed police chatting together as they had a smoke.

Fifteen feet doesn't sound far, unless you're clinging like a spider to a thin length of rope above a forty-foot drop. Now her hands had reached the ten-foot mark and she was past the point of no return. I prayed that she wouldn't freeze. Because this was one of those rare moments in adult life when you cry for your mother to help you – and mean it, whilst knowing that neither she nor anyone else on God's Earth can save you. It's all down to you alone. It had only really happened a couple of times to me during my time in the Regiment, and it wasn't an experience to cherish.

Bex's right hand stretched out gingerly again, followed by her left. She was gripping so tight that I could see the whiteness of her knuckles. Then she drew her left leg up towards her body, bending at the knee. Cautiously she tested the hook of her instep around the rope, feeling the purchase of her shoelace on the fibres, before she straightened her leg to push herself forward again. Yet just that slow, desperately careful momentum was enough to set the rope bridge's pendulum motion going. And while it did, I knew she wouldn't be breathing.

Five more times she repeated the process, edging forward a foot at a time. Only then I knew she'd make it and realized that I'd even stopped breathing myself. It was all I could do not to cheer as her right hand finally curled over the guttering opposite and she was able to give a last final haul.

That enabled her to get her grip on the parapet and drag herself clear. She turned and beamed at me with the smile you can only smile when you know that you've just cheated death.

I was more than pleased because, despite my assurances to her, I wasn't at all sure that the belay would have held if she'd fallen. The chimney brickwork had looked in dire need of attention and the cord that I'd been forced to use might not have been up to the job. Even if Bex was down to her twelve stone fighting weight.

Quickly she untied her temporary harness and tossed the belay rope back to me across the gap. This time I secured one end to my bergen, and looped that to the end of the rope bridge before tying the loose end to my waist.

Now it was my turn. I scrambled over the bergen and slid out along the rope in one fluid movement . . . and at that moment, as I swayed from side to side on my precarious perch, my confidence deserted me. It was years since I'd done this stuff, and the bravado of my youth had long gone. What I felt was sheer mind-numbing fear. It took a great effort of will to concentrate and force myself to loosen up. Terror automatically creates muscular tension and, of course, rigidity is the enemy of balance.

I looked up, away from the concrete paving far below, hummed a tuneless tune beneath my breath and decided to go for it. Long and easy contractions and expansions of the legs, feeding the taut rope through my fingers. After half a dozen shuffles I'd actually got quite a good rhythm going. I knew it must have looked professional, but by the time my hands thankfully grabbed the far parapet, my shirt was literally dripping in sweat.

Bex helped me up. 'See you haven't lost your touch, Ed.'

'Like riding a bike,' I replied as casually as I could, whilst trying not to let her see that my hands were trembling as I undid the cord tied to my belt.

I tugged the cord gently so that the bergen rolled over the gutter of the house we'd just left and slid down into the middle of the bridging rope, held on by its loop. It had made a bit of a scraping noise and one of the drainpipe stacks had started to pull away from its mounting. But below us the two armed cops were sharing a joke and their laughter hid the faint sounds.

Carefully I reeled in the bergen, inching it up the incline until I could reach out and pull it over the parapet. Finally I cut our end of the bridging rope and let it fall away against the wall of the house opposite where it might well hang unnoticed in daylight for some time.

Next we inspected our options to get down to the garden. Again I silently thanked the owner of this house who, unlike my own landlord, didn't mind spending money on building maintenance. Both downpipes at the rear were solid cast iron, freshly painted, and had recently had their mountings reset and rescrewed.

I chose the one in the corner farthest away from the cops, shouldered the bergen, and began my descent. Five minutes later, with just scuffed shoes and scraped skin on my hands, knees and shins, I was standing in the garden watching Bex follow me down.

Moments later we were over the fence and approaching Jude's Harley which was exactly where I'd left it.

'Where to now?' Bex asked. 'My place is no longer an option.'

I handed over her helmet. 'Somehow Tromain's lot knew we were in my flat. Maybe just good timing for them. Or maybe a hidden camera or radio bug.' I'd had little time to think since we'd found Jude's body, so I had to do as best I could on the hoof. 'They'll be out looking for us, but they won't know about our transport. That gives us a short-term advantage, but we need to go to ground as soon as possible for the night.'

Bex agreed as she took over the bergen and hoisted it onto her shoulders. 'Less chance of being caught in a road-block.'

We mounted up and I started the engine. It had been barely thirty-five minutes since we'd discovered Jude's body and as we drove out of the avenue behind my flat officers from a police patrol were beginning to seal off the end of the road with scene-of-crime tape.

One of them stepped out into the headlamp beam, starting to flag me down. Immediately I throttled up and felt Bex's grip tighten around my waist. Cocooned inside the crash helmet, I barely heard the cop's raised voice or registered the surprise on his face as I shot through the pulsing light of blue strobes.

I zigzagged to avoid other officers running towards me, then accelerated away into the maze of back-doubles. Thankfully, this was my own backyard and there was no chance that they could mount an immediate and effective chase. Bex gave me a congratulary pat on the shoulder as we slowed along the succession of residential streets.

Unnerving as it was, the incident had told me quite a lot. Surrounding streets are normally sealed off *before* armed police units go in. So this had been a very rushed job. No doubt because, after my aborting Mihac's assassination, Tromain's people were having to make it up as they went along.

This would explain their botched communications and liaison with New Scotland Yard. It also meant we'd escaped the net by the skin of our teeth, which made it our exceedingly lucky day.

It is said that when playing chess, at vital points in the game, you should do the exact opposite of what your opponent expects – even if it doesn't gain you obvious and immediate strategic advantage. Tromain's people and the police would no doubt cover Bex's place and any other possible ports of call, they would actually *expect* us to get as far away from the crime scene as possible.

No doubt the police had already issued an all-cars alert around the M25 orbital motorway and all major arterial roads out of London. Maybe they'd mount some random vehicle checks, maybe not. But the fact was, while we were on the road at night with an ever-decreasing amount of traffic, the more at risk we were. But tomorrow morning, the last place they'd expect us to be would be right under their noses just a few miles from the scene of crime.

When we reached Lambeth, I noticed the B&B sign outside a dilapidated high street pub. Slowing up, I turned round and rode through the old coaching-inn archway to the rear car park. I stopped behind a large wheelie bin outside the kitchen, where the motorcycle wouldn't be readily seen by other patrons or anyone giving the place a cursory once-over.

Bex removed her bone-dome and shook her hair free. 'Going to ground for the night?' she asked.

'I think it's best.'

'I agree, Ed. D'you think those cops got our reg number?'

I shrugged. 'No idea, but we should assume they have.'

'Then maybe we shouldn't walk in here in motorcycle kit.'

It was a good point, so we left the crash helmets on the machine before entering the pub's tatty interior. The lounge bar, with its vandalized leatherette seats and threadbare carpet, was deserted, so we had to wander into the busy pool room to find the manager.

'We're looking for a room for the night,' I said.

The bored expression on the unshaven face said that he wished we'd looked somewhere else and given them the unwanted hassle. 'Forty-five pounds and a full English at eight o' clock. All right?'

'Splendid,' Bex answered with a smile.

'Cash up front,' he added. 'And we don't take plastic.'

'Suits me,' I answered truthfully.

He glanced at the bergen I'd unchivalrously left Bex to carry. 'Backpackers?'

I pulled out some notes from my wallet. 'Sightseeing on a budget.'

He grunted. 'Not many sights to see round here.'

I think it was a joke – just like the room his equally taciturn wife showed us to. It was dusty and there were cobwebs in the corners, but it was warm and at least the sheets on the double bed looked clean. It was functional enough and neither Bex nor I were going to complain. We had other more important things to think about.

Bex filled the electric kettle and boiled up water for some tea. We were both deep in our own thoughts and neither of us spoke until she handed me one of the cups. 'I can't believe what's happened, Ed.'

I took a thankful gulp of the hot liquid. 'At least we know for certain Jude didn't die in the car bomb. No obvious sign of how she died. Very professional.'

'God.' Bex turned her head away and stared at some fixed point on the far wall. 'Why, for Christ's sake? I can't believe Tromain's people – our people – would do such a thing.'

I had to agree with her there. Whoever Tromain's people were – MI5, MI6 or even some other 'funny' intelligence outfit – it wasn't the sort of thing any British agency would be sanctioned to do, unless under really exceptional circumstances. True, they'd pushed the boundaries a bit in the fight against terrorism in Northern Ireland. But, dammit, this just seemed to be about Marcus's bloody document. And getting rid of me, of course.

Bex had already made that connection. 'I also can't believe they'd try to set you up for Jude's murder just because you aborted the Mihac job.'

I shook my head. 'It wasn't because of the abort. My

neighbour, Cristobelle, heard people in my flat *before* I decided to abort. It was all pre-planned.'

The blood drained from her face. 'The bastards ... God, Ed, you must have really upset some nasty and powerful people.'

'I'm obviously a serious embarrassment to someone,' I agreed. And I could think of two reasons. 'I know about government involvement in what would have been the killing of two indicted Serb war criminals ... And I'm somehow thought to be involved in Sir Marcus's anti-Brussels exposé. To some people, that could be reason enough.'

'But are the two things connected?'

It was a question I'd been asking myself. 'Do they have to be? We've no way of knowing who's running this agenda, how or exactly why – but we have to accept one thing. They want me – and now probably you – out of the way. And they can bring powerful influence to bear.'

Bex grimaced at the empty cup in her hands. 'Like the whole bloody Metropolitan Police.' She looked up at me. 'What the hell are we going to do now, Ed?'

There seemed to be only one answer to that. 'Go to ground.'

She nodded. 'But we can't run for ever.'

That was a salutory thought. 'We don't have an option – unless we can get to the bottom of this.'

'How can you do that without talking to Tromain?'

I considered for a moment. 'Then that's what I'll have to do.'

'How?'

'I'll think about it.' I lit a cigarette. 'And there's someone else's help we need. In fact, she might even need *our* help now.'

'Francoise?' Bex was bemused. 'The *last* thing she needs is help from us, Ed! Seeing how one or both of us seems to be wanted for Jude's murder.'

'She's in big trouble herself, Bex. There was a message on

my answerphone back at the flat. The police have been leaning on her heavily, too. Suggesting some bloody *ménage à trois* between her, Jude and me. If we're not careful it could look like Francoise and I conspired to get rid of Jude. Some sort of love-triangle feud.'

Bex stared at me, frowning as she mentally pieced together the way the story could be made to look in a court of law. 'This is getting nastier by the minute, Ed.'

I added: 'And if we're to work out exactly what Sir Marcus had uncovered – and why we're being hunted as a result – then we'll need Francoise's expertise. For a start we need to reunite her with a copy of the dossier.'

Bex looked at the bergen in the corner. 'I see your point.'

I took a deep breath, feeling utterly shattered by the day's events. 'Anyway, let's try and relax for tonight, recharge our batteries.'

She grinned. 'Good idea. I don't know what I need most – sleep, food, or drink.'

'Let's try all three,' I replied, 'but not necessarily in that order.'

We had a couple of pints in the bar, then walked down the road to the local curry house. During the evening we thrashed around all the courses of action open to us and what we should do the next day.

Finally we decided on our priorities. First was transport, in case the Harley was already compromised; second was to make contact with Francoise and give her our spare copy of Sir Marcus's dossier so that she could get to work on it. Only then could I think about the trickiest prospect of all – trying to make contact with Tony Tromain, find out what the hell was going on and, just maybe, come to some sort of deal with him to call off his dogs.

I had one other priority: some unfinished business in Leicester. But I didn't mention that to Bex.

By the time we returned to the pub, we'd both well and

truly unwound. After the traumas of the day, the drink had soon worked its effect. Bex bought a bottle of Scotch at the bar and, once upstairs, began lacing two cups of strong coffee with the stuff.

'Another fine mess you've got me into,' she said, handing me one of them.

'Sorry about that. And thanks for sticking with it today.'

She pulled the pin from her hair and let it tumble to her shoulders. 'Not sure I really had an option.' She smiled. 'Anyway, how long d'you think you'd last without me to look after you?'

I lit a cigarette. 'This is all getting a bit like old times.'

She sat beside me on the bed, reached over and took another Gauloise from the pack. 'Feels strange, though – having your own side against you. Weird, and very scary.'

That had to be the understatement of the year. 'We'll find a way through,' I reassured her, sounding far more confident than I felt.

She nodded, looked over her shoulder at the bed, and then back at me. 'Life seems to keep on throwing us together. Maybe fate's trying to tell us something . . .' She chuckled. 'Last time we shared a bed, if you remember, we both fell asleep. D'you think that's being ungrateful to the gods?'

I saw the light in her eyes. 'Probably.' I stubbed out my cigarette end in the ashtray. 'Is it what you want, Bex?'

She stood up and looked down at me, her expression suddenly quite serious. 'I want, Ed . . . If you do .. ?'

At that moment I could think of nothing I wanted more. As I'd learned in the past, the closer you live to the edge of death, the keener your appetite for life. I stood up and drew her to me.

'I smell of beer, whisky and cigarettes . . .' she began to protest mildly. 'Let me take a shower and clean my teeth . . .'

But I wanted her just how she was, not smelling like a boudoir. I wanted her then, that moment. I had again fallen in love with her courage and her humour that day. And I wanted to take her while she still had the raw fragrance of that day on her, clothes crumpled and limp, a sheen of perspiration on her skin. It was a primeval urge, an animal thing.

I ran my hands through her hair, wrapped it in my fists and arched her head back, exposing her throat.

'You bastard,' she murmured, but we both knew that she didn't mean it.

I'm not sure I'd ever seriously wondered what it would be like, making love to Bex. But I'm sure I'd never imagined it would have been as good as it was. It was something to do with the rapport between us. Not just conversationally, but physically. It was as if we had an innate knowledge of what we both wanted, being forceful and playful in turns. Advancing and retreating, aggressive and tender, laughing and snarling. And at the height of it all, we hit a wild and explosive oblivion so powerful that it almost hurt. As if we'd drawn up and absorbed each other's pain and fear. And, as the tide began to gently ebb away, we were suddenly becalmed.

We didn't even share a cigarette afterwards; we just fell silently asleep in each other's arms.


'Oh shit!'

The consternation in Bex's voice permeated my disturbing dream. I cranked open an eye and lifted myself up onto one elbow. She was sitting on the bottom edge of the bed in her bra and pants, fiddling with the remote control of the television. It must have been early because it was still dark outside.

'What is it, Bex?'

Her eyes remained fixed on the screen. 'I couldn't sleep. We were on the bulletin - I just caught the tail end. I'm trying to see if there's anything on ITV.'

This was not good news. I threw off the sheet, reached for a Gauloise and padded across to where she sat. 'What they say?'

'Here we are— '

It was the local London news segment. The female presenter was staring solemnly at the camera. *'Police have issued a warrant for the arrest of a couple they wish to interview about the murder yesterday of a young Essex woman, Judith Sinclair. They are Edward Coltrane, a former soldier, and his common-law wife, Rebecca Bunnet, both of whom are believed to have known the victim whose body was discovered at Coltrane's South London flat.'*

The fuzzy black and white photograph of me looked fairly recent. I guessed it had been blown up from a surveillance photograph. Bex's picture was a mug shot from her army days which had her staring at the camera with the fixed expression of a madwoman.

*'They are believed to be travelling on Judith Sinclair's distinctive Harley Davidson motorcycle. Police are anxious to learn of their whereabouts but warn members of the public not to approach the couple as they could be armed and may be dangerous. Anyone believed to have sighted the couple should dial 999 or their local police station with any information . . . Next, this morning's weather—'*

That was it. 'Makes us sound like Bonnie and Clyde,' murmured Bex. 'And I've been promoted to common-law wife.'

'They've got it all wrapped up,' I observed. 'Open-and-shut case. I think we'd better make a move, pronto.'

Bex agreed. 'I'll make a quick cuppa.'

Fifteen minutes later, we slipped out of the side door. In the back yard I saw the surly manager standing by the wheelie bin. He was bending over to examine the rear number plate of the Harley.

We jumped on the first bus to pass down the high street

heading west and, thirty minutes later, alighted in Clapham. 'What next?' Bex asked.

'Transport, I think.'

'How's your hot-wiring technique?'

I shook my head. 'I don't want anything stolen. I've got the cash, so let's go legit.'

There were plenty of car showrooms in the area, and at the third one we settled for an ageing two-litre Mondeo with fuel-injection. The paintwork was past its first bloom, but it had been well maintained with one listed owner. I handed over two and a half grand in cash and it was mine.

'Where to next?' Bex asked as we swung off the forecourt.

'We need to talk to Francoise.'

'As I said last night, Ed, that's going to be risky.'

'Yeah, I've been thinking about it.'

'When was that – between drinking and bonking?'

'Let's say it came to me in a dream. I've got a plan.'

She sighed. 'I thought you might have.'

We drove into central London and parked in the Paddington Street stack just off Baker Street. With a clean car, the capital was in some respects the safest place to be.

From there we walked down to Oxford Street. I went to Marks & Sparks to get some replacement clothes – underwear and a couple of pairs of trousers, shirts and a short winter lumber jacket – while Bex went off on her own shopping spree. Everything, of course, had to be bought cash. An hour later we met up for coffee and bacon rolls.

I did a double take. 'How much?'

'Fran won't wear rubbish, Ed,' she said, holding up the stylish fake-fur Tilly hat and designer-label coat. 'And if we pull her off the street, she'll need clothes. Does she wear thongs? They're all the rage.'

'How the hell would I know?'

She smiled at that; clearly a good answer. 'Anyway, I got

a mix of underwear for both of us ... And the two wigs didn't come cheap.'

I waved it aside. 'Okay, now we'd better make a move before lunch.'

We returned to the car and got to Francoise Paquet's office off Kensington High Street at just gone twelve-thirty. By now Bex had gone peroxide blonde with a ponytail and I'd donned Ray-Ban shades and a country gent's flat cap in becoming green felt.

Luckily we found a meter space that just gave us a view of the entrance to the block in which *Televu-News Expresse* had their small suite of rooms. A direct approach would be exceedingly dangerous because it was a cast-iron certainty that she was under surveillance. Possibly by the police, but more likely by someone connected with Tromain – even by MI5.

My hunch paid off. One thing you could guarantee about the French is their love of lunch and they didn't come more French than Paquet. At thirty seconds past one she emerged from the vestibule, as smart as ever in her trenchcoat and Hermes headscarf, and began walking along the pavement.

'Good luck,' I said as Bex threw open the door and walked after her on the opposite side of the street. Bex's simple make-over had transformed her. Long black skirt, denim jacket and swinging ponytail was a million miles away from the fearsome vision of her on the early TV news that day. She clutched a large Selfridges bag in one hand and one of my new untraceable mobile phones in the other. We had perfect secure comms for what was to follow.

Soon Bex's voice was in my ear. *'Hi, common-law husband. Our mutual friend is going into a sort of bistro. Looks like a cranky health-food joint, all apple and cottage cheese – urgh! I can't spot an obvious tail, but I'm following in anyway.'*

She closed down then, leaving me to sweat it out for another twenty minutes before she hit the redial button and came back on the line. It was crisp and to the point. *'We're leaving.'*

I knew exactly what had happened. Paquet had gone to the powder-room and Bex would have followed. Behind closed doors, she would have confronted her and insisted that Paquet should swap her scarf and raincoat for the contents of Bex's shopping bag – and leave the café immediately. Even if the switch worked we'd only have minutes before any watchers tumbled what had happened.

I started the engine and released the central locking in case they had to jump into the car in a hurry. Squinting to see through the throng of pedestrians, I picked up the woman in the fake-fur Tilley hat. Bex must have given her lessons, because Francoise had shortened her usual long, swaying stride and hunched her shoulders slightly. And she didn't do justice to the designer-label coat that had cost me a small fortune.

I couldn't discern anyone deliberately following her, but then MI5 watchers are probably the most professional in the world. It didn't help that every other person on the street seemed to be talking into a mobile phone, making it impossible to detect anyone who might be trying to talk surreptitiously into a radio mike.

As Paquet crossed over to my side of the street, I threw open the passenger door. She did a double take and peered in. 'Eddie? It *is* you! Oh, thank God.'

'Quick, get in,' I ordered.

Bex was gaining on us fast and, even as she opened the rear door, I was edging the Mondeo out into the traffic flow.

'I am so frightened, Eddie,' Francoise was almost babbling with relief. 'I didn't know what to do. The police were on the phone again, just before lunch. They want me to go to the police station for a formal interview. They are very – er – severe, very serious. When I laugh and say should I bring my solicitor they have a straight face – and say maybe that would be a good idea. They think I have murdered your friend Jude with you, I am sure of it—' She turned around in her seat to face Bex. 'I am so shocked and so pleased to see you in the toilet. The police say you are on the run, that Jude's body was found in your apartment – it was even on the radio news. How can that be?'

I concentrated on the traffic and on the bistro that we were now just passing. There was a woman standing outside, glancing up and down the busy street with an anxious expression on her face. She looked like any ordinary adolescent office girl – God, they were recruiting them young now – or was I just getting old?

I said: 'The police are jumping to what look like obvious conclusions. They've been set up just like us. Someone put Jude's body in my flat. When Bex and I found it, it was very cold. Like it had been kept in a fridge.'

Paquet paled and shook her head. 'That is horrible. I don't understand who would do such a thing.'

There was only one conclusion. 'The same people who killed Sir Marcus – and Jude – and who and want the three of us out of the way. Dead or locked up for a crime that we didn't commit. I doubt they're fussy which.'

'But I am not so sure running away is the right thing to do,' Francoise said slowly. 'Perhaps it is best that we give ourselves up to the police and explain everything that has happened.'

Bex leaned forward from the back seat. 'This isn't fairy-land, Francoise, this is real life. Through no fault of our own, we've made powerful enemies in high places. We've been set up by some sort of state-security apparatus. And the evidence against us will look pretty compelling, you can bet your life on that. I know this type of people and the way they work. Once they set their minds to something, they will be ruthlessly efficient.'

'But the British justice system—' Paquet protested.

I shook my head. 'Is open to political abuse. In cases where the state has an interest to protect, certain judges with certain views have an uncanny knack of cropping up to sit on key cases.'

'But the police—' Paquet began.

'They're open to pressure, too,' Bex came in quickly. 'If the intelligence services tell the police something in confidence – like that night is day – they're predisposed to believe them. They're all part of the same Establishment.'

But Paquet wasn't giving in. 'In court we can fight with the *facts*.'

'That's part of the trouble, Francoise. We don't *know* the bloody facts.'

Her journalistic pride pushed itself to the fore. 'But we can find them out, Ed! That's what we *have* to do. It's the only way to prove what's been going on.'

'I agree with you. But we won't be able to do that once we're in prison awaiting trial. It's not like in the movies.'

'Besides,' Bex chimed in. 'One, two or all three of us are going to be involved in a murder or conspiracy-to-murder charge – that much is blatantly obvious. Common law. Did any one of us kill Jude? Yes or no, as simple as that. Any other evidence – like it was all to do with some deep European conspiracy – will simply be thrown out as irrelevant. It would be a separate issue, if it was an issue at all.' She met Paquet's gaze. 'And it would only be an issue if the police were willing or able to pick it up and run with it. And as far as I can see, they've got bugger-all to go on.'

Paquet turned her head away from Bex and stared dead ahead as we cruised out of London on the A4 towards the west. There was a forlorn expression on her face. 'Then what *can* we do?'

I said: 'Run. And keep running.'

There was a desperation in Paquet's voice. 'We cannot run for ever, Eddie.'

That was starting to sound uncomfortably familiar.

'Not for ever,' I agreed. 'But for long enough for us to find out and get proof of what all this is about. And *proof* of our innocence in Jude's murder.'

'It's the only way,' Bex agreed. 'Ed and I have talked about nothing else. And when we've got what we need, only then we do approach the authorities.'

Paquet thought about that for a moment. 'I see . . . yes, I see your reasoning . . . but how do we set about doing this?' She didn't expect an answer and she didn't get one. But she was rapidly thinking things through, and came up with one of her own. 'I need to spend time on Marcus's dossier. To go through it in great detail . . .'

I glanced sideways at her as her voice trailed away. 'Are you okay?'

Her face had a crumpled, little-girl-lost look about it. 'What the hell am I going to do, Eddie? In fact, what are *we* going to do? We are all in such serious trouble.'

'Then it's best that we all work together,' I said.

'What do you mean?'

'Bex and I have already discussed what we're going to do. But we stand a better chance with you along.' I hesitated. 'The question is, are you going to throw in your lot with us – or do something else?'

'You mean go on the run?' she asked uneasily.

'In hiding,' I replied. 'A subtle difference. If you don't join us, how long do you think it would be before you're arrested?'

Paquet didn't answer; she didn't have to. She stared blindly out at the traffic for the next two or three minutes, before coming to her decision. 'Of course, Eddie, you are right. I am not sure this isn't the biggest mistake of my life, but yes, I will join you. Three minds are better than one to fight this conspiracy.'

I glanced at Bex in the rear-view mirror and saw the

look of relief on her face. 'I'm sure you've made the right decision, love,' she said.

'So what *are* we going to do?' Paquet asked.

'First we have to disappear,' I said. 'London has too much media coverage – we need to get away and into hiding.'

'Where would you do this?'

Bex interjected. 'Bedsit land. Thousands of rooms to let. We're thinking maybe somewhere like Bristol. There we split up. Ed's got some virgin cellphones so we can keep in touch and arrange a safe place to rendezvous. Maybe we should divide up Marcus's dossier and each study a section, then get together to compare notes.'

Paquet thought about that for a moment. 'There will be many queries and questions to be answered. I will need Internet access . . . Unfortunately, my laptop is sitting back in my office.'

Grudgingly I said: 'We'll sort something out.' It made perfect sense, of course, but I was the only one with an untraceable supply of cash. And at this rate my nest egg of blood money was dwindling fast.

We lapsed into thoughtful silence as we made steady progress out of London towards the M4 heading west.

'News time,' Bex advised.

It was only three o'clock but a new weather front was rolling in from the Atlantic and the sky was prematurely dark. I switched on the car lights along with the radio. It was tuned to one of the London stations and the signal was beginning to break up as we increased our distance from the capital. The first story was about troop deployments to Afghanistan, followed by items about NHS hospitals fiddling their waiting lists to meet government targets, and then the latest saga in the sale of the Millennium Dome.

I think we'd all been lulled into a false sense of security, when the announcer concluded: *'Finally, the police manhunt has intensified for former soldier Edward Coltrane and his common-*

*law wife Rebecca Bunnet, wanted for questioning about the murder
of their friend Judith Sinclair in South London yesterday. A statement from New Scotland Yard said police were now in no doubt
that the couple were deliberately on the run. A car salesman has
come forward to say that a couple answering the description of the
wanted couple bought a blue G-registration Mondeo from him this
morning for cash. Anyone thinking they have sighted the vehicle
or its occupants are advised to inform police as it is likely to be
dangerous to approach the couple, who may be armed. The registration number . . .'*

The signal finally gave out as we crossed the county
border into Oxfordshire. I thumped the steering wheel in
anger and frustration. 'Oh, for Christ's sake! Give us a break!'

Paquet glanced sideways at me and put her hand on my
leg. 'Maybe it will be all right, *cherie*. We are away from
London now and it is nearly dark—'

'I don't think so!' Bex interjected suddenly. 'Either there's
about to be an alien abduction or that's a police helicopter
coming up behind us!'

I glanced in the rear-view mirror. A mile back along the
road a bright light was hovering low over the motorway,
steadily closing the distance on us as its on-board surveillance camera checked out each registration number in turn.

I couldn't see any way out of this one.

# Twelve

I scoured the motorway ahead, praying to God that a turn-off would appear somewhere in the gathering gloom.

For a split second my hopes were raised as I saw the inky distant outline of a bridge spanning across the six lanes. But there was no sign of an approaching slip road and I quickly realized that the crossover bridge offered no escape.

Meanwhile the bright searchlight of the closing police helicopter was dazzling in the rear-view mirror as it continued its relentless checking of all vehicles heading west.

Then, suddenly, the idea came to me. Almost too late, but not quite. The span of concrete bridging was almost on top of us when I simultaneously hit the brakes and switched off our lights. Paquet gasped as the seat-belt snapped tight around her. I swerved violently to the left, the locking wheels burning over the surface of the carriageway as we slewed into the slow lane, onto the hard shoulder and into the shadow of the bridge.

The first driver behind us screamed past, blasting out his anger on the horn. I glanced over my shoulder, seeing Bex crouched on the back seat for a better view of the helicopter that was now closer than half a mile behind us.

The atmosphere in the car was tense and claustrophobic as we all waited for the helicopter's searchlight to illuminate us – and for the end to come. The aurora intensified, blinding in its brilliance, the noise of the aero engine swelling to a deafening crescendo. Bex glanced at me and shook her head.

This was it. Our hearts thudded in tempo with the rotor throbbing overhead.

And then it had passed. The heavy tom-tom beat of the helicopter began to recede. We could see the bright beam of its searchlight up ahead as it followed over the lines of traffic streaming off into the distance. The search was slow, methodical and in deadly earnest. But, in the darkness and dazzle of refracting lights, the helicopter had missed us as we hid beneath the bridge.

'Christ, Ed, I don't believe it,' Bex said hoarsely. 'We've actually got away with it.'

But I wasn't optimistic. 'They've got more squad cars than helicopters – either way we're not going to get much farther. And we certainly can't stay here.'

Paquet had recovered some of her composure. 'So what do we do now?'

'Abandon ship,' I said, glancing up. 'There's a road passing overhead. Let's get up there for starters.'

I switched the hazard lights on, got out and opened the bonnet to remove the rotor-arm from the distributor before collecting my bergen from the boot. When our car was inevitably found by a police road patrol – probably sooner rather than later – I wanted them to assume that the car had broken down and that the occupants were somewhere on the hard shoulder looking for an emergency phone. It could buy us vital minutes.

Bex had no trouble scrambling up the embankment in her trainers, but Paquet had to abandon her high heels and was struggling on the slippery wet grass in stockinged feet. I grabbed her hand and helped as best I could, but it was hard work getting to the top. Gasping for breath we made it to the side of the bridge and stepped over the crash rail. The road was lit only by the ambient light from the motorway traffic below. It was fairly quiet with vehicles passing over the bridge only every few minutes.

I said: 'We need to flag someone down.'

'Let Fran do it,' Bex suggested. 'She looks the most respectable. A perfect maiden in distress.'

Paquet gave us a pained look and indicated her mud-splattered coat and dishevelled hair. 'You think so? I don't!'

'You're the best we've got,' Bex returned quickly. 'Ed and I will get out the way. Just wave someone down.'

'Anyone?'

'Anyone who'll stop,' I said. 'Speed's the thing.'

'What do I say?'

I looked at the state of her. 'Say you crashed in a ditch up the road. You want a lift to the nearest town. By the time you've said that, we'll have taken over.'

She frowned. 'What do you mean?'

'We don't have time to explain,' Bex cut in. 'Look, there's something coming now. Ed an' me will make ourselves scarce.'

We left Paquet gaping after us with a bemused expression on her face and scurried into the darkness. The first vehicle picked up the forlorn-looking Frenchwoman at the roadside in its headlights, but ignored her. It was the pattern for the next five minutes, during which time I remembered where I kept a set of plasticuffs in a pocket of my bergen. These are like jumbo freezer-ties, which snap over someone's wrists and are jerked tight to become excellent and reasonably comfortable handcuffs.

Then Paquet got lucky. Perhaps not surprisingly it was a commercial vehicle that was the first to pull over, an artic hauling frozen meat products towards Grimsby. I smiled at first – it would provide far better cover than a family saloon. The smile vanished as I crept closer and saw the size of the driver who climbed out. There must have been sixteen stone of muscular bulk beneath that shaven bullet head and his bare arms were covered in tattoos.

But his mild manner belied his appearance. 'What's yer

problem, doll?' he asked amiably as he rounded the side of the rig.

Paquet shrugged helplessly. 'I am afraid my car comes off the road. I need a lift to the next town.'

'French, eh?' The man clearly couldn't believe his luck. 'Let me have a look, sweet'eart – maybe we can get it mobile for you.'

'I don't think so—'

I was now standing right behind him. 'Freeze, chum! And turn round real slow.'

The trucker stiffened momentarily, before obeying to find himself staring at the pistol that was to have dispatched Mihac. He looked disdainful. 'What the fuck is this – I ain't haulin' fags or booze, you know.'

I ignored that. 'Shut it. Put your hands behind your back.'

'Bastards,' he muttered beneath his breath as Bex moved swiftly in behind him, slipped the plasticuffs over his wrists and snapped them into a tight lock.

I hauled the man onto the verge and down a short slope, out of view from the road. Meanwhile Bex located the old army sleeping bag from my bergen. It had seen better days and was threadbare in places, but it would prevent the trucker getting hypothermia until he was rescued. I supported him while he stepped into it and Bex pulled it up to his waist.

'Down on the ground,' I ordered, 'and get as comfortable as you can. We'll call the police and have you found in a couple of hours. Got a mobile?'

'In me cab.'

'Fine, we'll use that.'

His fear and anger had been replaced by an expression of bemusement. Clearly this was a strange sort of hijack. He looked at the two women and then at me. 'Are you them people the cops are looking for?'

'The cops are always looking for lots of people,' I replied unhelpfully and peeled five hundred in notes from my roll.

Then I thought better of it, and put three hundred of them back. 'This is for your trouble.' I stuffed it in the pocket of his shirt.

'Fuckin' mad,' he muttered.

Bex and I moved away towards the lorry. Paquet lingered for a moment and mumbled an embarrassed apology to the man before joining us up in the cab.

I shoved the gearshift into first, gathering up the gas underfoot until the cab began to tremble and the artic moved smoothly off the hard shoulder, heading north. Bex had a map out and was shining her torch on it. 'What say we continue on this road north to Oxford . . .' she suggested. 'Maybe dump this truck there . . . ?'

Within ten minutes we'd agreed our plan. Just over two hours later we located a industrial estate on the edge of Oxford that had closed down for the night and parked up in a lay-by where the artic would not look out of place. Immediately we set off on foot towards the station.

Once there I put a call through to the Samaritans, giving them a message for the police as to where they could find one very pissed-off hijacked lorry driver. It was a trick I'd picked up from Irish terrorists, whose bombers used that method because the Samaritans made a point of not recording or monitoring incoming traffic from their stressed and often suicidal callers.

It was now seven-thirty and, having checked the timetable, we took it in turns to go to the booking office and pay cash for seats on the next train to Birmingham. By nine-fifteen we were all meeting up for a coffee on New Street station.

'Now we go to ground,' I said, handing out five hundred pounds each to Bex and Paquet. 'Take cabs separately and disappear into bedsit land. Pay for your advance room rental and everything else in cash.' I added: 'Remember, it's *my* money you're spending. But whatever you do, don't use plastic. That's all traceable.'

'How will we communicate?' Paquet asked.

I dumped the last three pay-as-you-go cellphones on the table. All virgins. 'Use only these and don't phone anyone from your previous life. No mums, dads, friends or lovers. No one who the police or authorities may know. We'll arrange an RV in a public place. A restaurant or pub.'

'RV?' Paquet asked.

'Sorry, rendezvous. We'll divide Marcus's dossier between us and meet up later to compare notes. See what we've come up with.'

Paquet nodded her agreement. 'Internet access will be helpful, Eddie.'

I just knew she wanted to spend more of my money. 'Then I suppose you'd better buy a laptop.'

She gave an awkward smile. 'I am afraid that will be another thousand, Eddie.'

I got the painful business out of the way as quickly as possible, then divided up Marcus's dossier into three roughly equal segments and put them into spare carrier bags.

Bex and I watched while Paquet set off first for the taxi rank. 'Have you given any more thought as to how to contact Tromain?' Bex asked. 'Find out what the hell they're playing at?'

I shook my head. 'Rather had other things on my mind today. I don't even know which government department he works for. Anyway, I expect he's a freelance on some sort of cash retainer. I haven't even got a number for him. Part of the deal – he always contacted me.'

'So it won't be easy.'

'It may be downright impossible,' I rejoined. But in truth I did have a glimmer of an idea – although it wasn't one of which Bex was going to approve.

She stood up. 'Time to go. I'll ring you when I've found a place to stay.'

I watched her walk out and couldn't help wondering how

the hell I'd have managed this far without her. It seemed safer to space out our departures, so all three of us weren't standing in the taxi rank at the same time. I ordered another black coffee, sat down and lit a Gauloise, trying to marshal my thoughts into some order.

But I was only halfway through smoking my cigarette when I noticed the group of police officers striding across the concourse. A senior figure in a peaked cap was leading half a dozen constables towards one of the platform gates. The platform at which our train had stopped.

Clearly it was time to go. I left my coffee, shouldered my bergen and slipped out of the nearest exit. Outside it was starting to rain and the taxi queue was lengthening as cabs quickly came to be in short supply. I saw that Bex was no longer there. Just as well, because a police officer in a fluorescent yellow jacket was patrolling the line.

I turned away and started walking. I didn't look back.

Of course it could have been paranoia, but in my mind I had no doubt that they were looking for us. That in itself was chilling. It was barely a couple of hours since I'd phoned the Samaritans with the location of the bound lorry driver.

In that time someone had drawn a compass circle around the point and decided that Oxford would have provided us with a quick link-up with public transport. Either they had then actually found the abandoned truck and spoken to the station ticket office. Or they had jumped that stage altogether and made an assumption – then covered Birmingham as the next most likely port of call.

Either way, someone was expending a lot of time and energy and not a little professional skill on trying to locate us. I now had no doubt that we had a professional manhunt team on our trail. That prospect was quite horrifying.

But as I disappeared into the dark rain-lashed streets, I knew that we still had the edge. For the time being, at least. In the bedsit land of a vast city like Birmingham, landlords were more interested in cash in their back pockets than in some vague notion of the greater public good. Unless there was a bigger monetary incentive involved, they'd much prefer to see and hear no evil, let alone speak of it to the police. Anything for an easy life.

In the end I caught a bus that dropped me on the edge of a fairly run-down and seedy area, where I began walking the quiet streets in search of vacancy signs. In a shadowed archway, I pulled on my Serbian wig and donned my glasses with the plain lenses before knocking on the first door.

It was answered by a small, white-haired Bangledeshi woman who looked at me suspiciously before I poured on the charm, apologizing for disturbing her at such a late hour.

She showed me to a clean but poky upstairs room. It only had space for a single bed, a small desk table and a minuscule wardrobe. The kitchenette, as she described it, was a sink, a three-foot work surface and a gas ring in an alcove behind a plastic curtain. The shared bathroom ran off the landing.

'Wonderful,' I said as though I meant it and that seemed to please her. The month's advance rental in notes pleased her even more.

But, in truth, it was good enough for me. And I shut and bolted the door behind the woman with a great sense of relief. Over the years I'd got used to army billets like this. There was something comforting in the confined space – perhaps it was akin to returning to the womb. A place to feel safe and secure from the madness of the world outside.

The previous tenant had left a few tea bags and packet of broken biscuits, so I got a brew going while I hung up my few clothes in the wardrobe. Everything else I kept in the bergen, in case I had to leave in a hurry – more old army habits that came in handy from time to time.

Then I settled down on the bed with a mug of hot tea

and opened up Sir Marcus's dossier for the first time. I seemed to have given myself the first section and I thought I'd read for twenty minutes before going out to grab a pint and a bar snack locally. I really was not looking forward to the task of ploughing through all this turgid prose on the European Union in the probably vain hope of finding something that could explain our current predicament.

But, unexpectedly, Sir Marcus managed to grab my attention from the very first page. It was clearly marked "*DRAFT – Not for publication*" and entitled *THE DARK HEART OF EUROPE – an independent investigation into corruption within the politics, finances and security of the European Union* by Sir Marcus Whitby DSO, MEP and Thor Engell MEP.

I quickly flicked over to Sir Marcus's introduction.

My late Danish colleague, Thor Engell MEP, and I were delighted when, two years ago, the European Parliament first asked us to join a Parliamentary Committee to investigate the continual allegations of corruption and fraud in the EU. The Committee was billed as being 'independent and far-reaching', but within days both Thor and I realized that this description was a sham.

So little independence did it have, in fact, that we were immediately bombarded with strict 'guidelines'. Not from the European Parliament, whose Committee we were, but from civil servants and members of the Commission. These guidelines even dictated the way the Committee was to be structured and run.

There was to be a triumvirate consisting of a chairman, a French hardline federalist MEP; a long-serving Italian MEP, who'd been questioned by the police about political corruption in his own country, and a supposedly 'independent' EU bureaucrat to act as legal adviser to the other two.

This trio would ultimately decide what was, and what was not, included in the Committee's findings when they were finally presented to the European Parliament. Thus all we other Committee members were mere window dressing.

Other 'guidelines' included a detailed restriction on whose evidence was admissible and whose was not. Since this largely limited inquiries to those within the monolithic EU structure itself, and its many dependent agencies, the Inquiry was crippled from the start.

Thor and I were soon drawn together as we found ourselves increasingly in fundamental disagreement with the other MEP members on the Committee, whose backgrounds did not cause them to question the control being exercised by the very people it was supposed to be investigating.

So, while the other members rushed off to meetings and had expenses-paid lunches and dinners with heads of directorates and senior bureaucrats, Thor and I pursued an independent line. Someone had to!

Pooling our combined professional expertise – Thor's as a police detective and mine with military intelligence activities – we spent a lot of time discussing how to proceed, becoming firm friends in the process.

We decided to use the credentials and authority derived from membership of the Committee to conduct our own *truly* independent investigation, using our own professional methods.

If the European Parliament – and the Commission – didn't like the results, then we'd publish our own separate report to the world at large.

Making full use of our official status, Thor and I took a completely different route from the rest of the Committee. Instead of interviewing 'insiders', we went outside the charmed EU circle. Instead of starting with 'knew best'. And I readily confess that Thor and I had previously been carried along on that same wave of self-delusion.

No one had the courage to suggest that, just maybe, the king wasn't wearing any clothes.

This inability to face reality or learn any lessons from history, combined with self-satisfaction, meant that the eurocrats saw no need to provide proper safeguards against corruption and malpractice, or to build in administrative checks. So corruption flourished.

Decades of unchecked and ineffectively policed acts, involving billions of pounds of expenditure, had allowed organized criminal groups to infiltrate the very heart of what later became the European Union.

So Thor and I turned our attention to the EU's policing and security operations and in doing so uncovered startling evidence that the 'mafias' infiltrated these operations too. Thus in many cases the mafias were the puppet masters pulling the strings inside the EU and especially inside the security organs – such as they were – set up to combat criminal activity.

In short the poachers had been put in charge of the gamekeepers.

This has been achieved by the secret formation of a specialist department inside the EU, whose very existence is barely acknowledged and which is not subject to normal police controls and is unaccountable to any representative body.

Here the paragraph was circled in pen with a notation, presumably in Sir Marcus's handwriting: *More info pending meeting with X.*

I then scanned the last couple of paragraphs of the introduction.

Needless to say, the official report of the Committee was published before we had finished our much more exhaustive inquiries, but after the tragic accident that took Thor Engell's life. I insisted on my official disagreement with the Committee's methods and findings being included and called the report – in more diplomatic language – a whitewash. As a result its publication was delayed until the summer recess and, thus, it went unnoticed by Europe's media.

As a result of our work I have completely reversed my opinion about the EU. I now strongly doubt the wisdom of Britain tying its future to a corrupt federal superstate, for that is what it will inevitably become. It is my firm belief that Britain should consider withdrawal and negotiate trading terms as a free and sovereign nation state.

That last sentence fairly took my breath away. Was that really Sir Marcus's conclusion by the time he'd completed his draft report? I could scarely believe it. Things must have been bad for him to have had such a complete reversal of his original fervent enthusiasm.

I looked again at the reference to a secret department, the paragraph with his notation in the margin. That seemed very important to him. Was this the key? And who was X? Could this possibly be a reference to his fateful meeting in Paris with the whistle-blower, Helmut Frauss, the police inspector with Europol?

Before I could give it any further thought, my mobile began chiming its irritating little call tune.

It was Paquet. 'Hi, Eddie, just to let you know I have found a place.'

'Good. Is it comfortable?'

She didn't sound too happy. 'It is clean, that is all. Do you want the address?'

people well disposed towards Brussels, we began with those opposed to it. We took informal soundings from hostile journalists and anti-EU political organizations in various countries. We did what few MEPs or national politicians have ever done – we actually listened to them.

That was something Thor and I came to realize we should have done long before – listened to these remarkably well-informed people and taken their warnings seriously.

After finishing our external inquiries, we turned our attention to the EU's own bureaucrats. We did not devote much time to senior civil servants, directorate-general heads or politicians. All these were primarily interested in protecting their reputations and their own backs – not to mention their large salaries, pensions and expenses. Instead we talked to lower-paid, middle-ranking executives and secretaries.

In fact we conducted our inquiries on the lines of a professional intelligence operation. And, eventually, the results we achieved were not only highly successful, but also shocking.

Our general conclusion was that the EU had tolerated deceit from the very start and that this deception was now deeply ingrained. Those at the centre of what could be seen as a huge political conspiracy were determined that the general public of the individual member nations should never learn what was being planned for them.

That determination – allied to there being no way that any actions could be called to political account – bred a pervasive culture of secrecy and arrogance in successive generations of well-paid eurocrats.

That arrogance stemmed from a quite genuine – though deluded – conviction that those in Brussels

'No, no,' I said quickly, 'not on an open line. Give it to me when we meet.'

'I understand – I have to get used to thinking like this. To always be careful. I am practising hard with my Spanish.'

I laughed at that. In readiness for any police description of a wanted Frenchwoman and the fact that it's near-impossible to hide that accent, we'd decided that Paquet should revive her rusty schoolgirl Spanish and pass herself off as a businesswoman from Madrid.

'So you got away with it?'

'I think so – just a funny look. As long as I don't meet someone who really speaks Spanish . . .'

'We'll talk again tomorrow.'

'In the morning I will go out and get a laptop.' I could sense her smiling. 'I promise one not *too* expensive . . . *À bientôt.*'

I turned back to Sir Marcus's report and flicked over the pages. After the introduction there was a list of contents, apparently running through a few chapters on the political and financial history of the EU, then others on fraud and crime and, finally, a section entitled *Superstate Security* with the intriguing description: *'Every aspiring nation state must make provision to protect itself and its people from hostile forces.'*

Disappointingly there was a scribbled marginal note in the contents listing saying *'In preparation'*, suggesting that this was another last part of the jigsaw Sir Marcus was working on just before he died. That section was with Paquet, so she would be the first to know just how much he'd been able to complete before getting caught up in the Paris bombing.

I'd intended only to glance at the first chapter, but I found myself sucked into the detailed revelations going back to the early days of the Common Market before it metamorphosed into the 'European Economic Community', then the more specific 'European Community' and eventually the blatant 'European Union'.

Under the heading *'Foundations of Deceit'* Sir Marcus began by concentrating on the speeches and private papers of Jean Monnet, an influential French politician considered to be the founding father of the EU.

According to this, from the very outset Monnet and his fellow politicians knew where they wanted to take the independent countries of Europe and how they were going to get them there. Mostly, as far as I could gather, by deliberately not telling their populations - and sometimes their national politicians – where they were ultimately headed.

By the early 1950s long-term public-relations programmes had already been put in place to lull easily bored populations, their career politicians and increasingly lazy media into a false sense of security. All the time there were to be constant reassurances that there was no question of countries ever surrendering their national sovereignty or monetary independence. And all the time it was known by those in power to be a downright lie.

And here was sir Marcus confirming it. How Monnet had claimed to have quite openly informed Prime Minister Edward Heath in 1970 how the process had worked from the start, step by step, gradually to create the Common Market and how he was convinced that it should continue in the same stealthy manner.

The message seemed to have been taken on board. When it came to signing the Treaty of Accession in 1972, Heath was backed into a corner and, reckoning that Britain's small fishing community could never pose a future electoral threat, he agreed to grant other member states equal access to the United Kingdom's territorial waters – which contained eighty per cent of European fish stocks – as the price of entry.

But the relevant paragraph of the treaty was conveniently 'not published' before MPs had debated and voted in favour. The devil – as usual with the EU, according to Sir Marcus – was in the small print that was revealed afterwards.

Later in 1975, millions had happily voted in a referendum to stay in the Common Market on the sole basis – as the government sold it to us – that it would give British business a home market the size of the USA. Other more important concerns about national independence, democracy and sovereignty were glibly dismissed as nonsense or scaremongering.

Yet over the following years I had myself witnessed the steady and endless flow of power and decision-making to Brussels – if I could ever be bothered to think about it. But like most people I didn't. I was too busy getting on with life in the army.

And so, according to Sir Marcus, the blatant trickery and duping went on, most seriously at the signing of the Maastricht Treaty when an English-language version was deliberately not published until afterwards.

A sentence appeared in italic at this point: *It was here that the Genk Protocol was also secretly signed by heads of state in the nearby Belgian town of the same name. (See 'Superstate Security', page 97).*

For some reason I felt a strange prickling sensation at the back of my neck. I had a feeling that this line was deeply significant. But that was it; nothing else to go on. Page 97 was in the section that Paquet had.

I glanced at my watch. I couldn't believe that it was nearly ten o' clock already. I'd missed the chance of grabbing a pub meal.

My mobile rang as I was in mid-curse. 'Hi, lover, how you doing?'

'Hungry – and it's too late for a pub snack.'

'Poor you,' Bex said.

'Got too engrossed in that document.'

'I did some shopping *first*,' she came back smugly. 'Nice omelette.'

'Smart-ass.'

'Fancy meeting for a drink? I could bring you a pork pie.'

'Sold,' I said. On the walk to my digs I'd noted the sites of several pubs that weren't too close. I gave her the name and location of one. 'I'll see you outside in about fifteen minutes.'

I left the bedsit straight away, flagged down a taxi and arrived at the rendezvous in just over ten minutes. I waited opposite, sheltering from the rain in a doorway, until Bex arrived. I called across the street to her and we walked for five minutes until we found another pub. This was just a routine precaution in the unlikely event that our conversation had been intercepted.

It was a bit of a dump with yellowing walls and a threadbare, beer-stained carpet. The barman and a couple of locals were watching a football match on the wall-mounted television, the sound somewhat overwhelmed by the noisy enthusiasm of some Indian and Sikh lads playing pool in the far corner.

I bought a couple of pints of bitter and some crisps and Bex put the pork pie on the bench seat between us so that I could eat it surreptitiously without offending the landlord's sensibilities.

'I got a very nice little flat,' Bex said. 'A very picky owner – I think she was over the moon to have a respectable female applicant.'

I smiled at that, having already demolished the pie. 'If only she knew.'

'So you found Marcus's document pretty engrossing?'

'I was surprised,' I told her. 'I thought it would be a very dull read. But it opened my eyes to a hell of a lot of things – and it explained many others as well.'

'Like what?'

I thought for a moment. 'Like the sudden enthusiasm for Welsh and Scottish devolution. Not to mention a mayor and elected assembly for London.'

She frowned. 'So?'

'According to Marcus it's in readiness for the break-up of Britain into regions under Brussels. Westminster – the national Parliament – becomes redundant. If it isn't already. The juggernaut of the European superstate rolls on – as do the political denials.'

Bex nodded slowly as she accepted one of my Gauloises. 'I've been reading something on those lines in my section. Seems now that all those countries adopting the euro have suddenly realized price differences won't harmonize until all countries in the Eurozone have the same tax system. And now it's too late for them to turn back.' She exhaled a long, steady stream of smoke into the dismal bar area. 'But most of the stuff I've been reading has been on crime. Scary stuff.'

I was intrigued. 'Tell me.'

Suddenly the barman and his customers let out a loud cheer. Apparently the recorded match being watched on TV was a local derby and someone had scored. The lads had finished their game of pool and had come in to watch. The barman turned the sound up.

Bex leaned closer to me so that she didn't have to shout. 'How about the systematic theft of duplicated printing plates for the new euro banknotes? Possibly the biggest counterfeit fraud in history – made easier because each country's notes are different.'

She sighed. 'Criminal activity seems to run through the entire EU structure. It touches virtually everything. Subsidies and compensation, construction grants, defence and civil contracts, overseas aid ... According to Marcus, as soon as any new project or programme is planned, there are criminal elements in on the ground floor. They actually manage to build the fraud potential in at the beginning.'

That seemed a sweeping generalization, even for the newly converted Marcus Whitby. 'If that's true, how the hell can they get away with it?'

'Marcus says it's the ethos from the top down. No one's really accountable and no one wants to admit the whole EU structure is fundamentally flawed. The Commission is fond of shooting the messengers who bring bad news. He cites the cases of several whistle-blowers. They feel the full wrath and indignation of the top politicos. So they lose their jobs or have legal action taken against them for breach of confidentiality. And the real culprits get away with it. Or get mildly reprimanded – or resign only to be reappointed.'

'So the whole thing goes unchecked?'

'Not completely, but almost,' Bex replied. 'Sure, they have investigations and committees like the one Marcus was on, but things rarely get done as a result. That's enabled organized crime to get deeply embedded in the whole political and bureaucratic infrastructure over the past twenty years. Marcus says that various Mafia families found their way in with the help of bent Italian politicians. Then the new Eastern Bloc criminals found their way in through their German connections after the USSR collapsed. The two groups pretty much carve things up between them.'

'But did Marcus give any clues, name any names?'

This time a gasp of exasperation went up from the audience gathered around the TV set. An equalizer in the last few minutes.

Bex shook her head. 'Marcus gives quite a lot of detail of the methods these people use to recruit EU politicians and civil servants. According to him, it's run like a very professional and very subtle intelligence operation. Victims are drawn in without realizing what they're doing or who they're doing it for.

'It might result from an approach by someone senior in your own department or another one. It might come from outside. It's always made to seem innocent, using false reasons for the action if necessary. When you cooperate, you get well rewarded with promotions and perks in the job, a holiday here, a night out there.

'It's rather like you've joined a very privileged but invisible Masonic lodge. Suddenly your career takes off, you start meeting influential people, you're given good private investment tips by your new friends, doors that were closed to you suddenly open.'

'And what happens to people who don't cooperate?' I asked.

Bex shrugged. 'That doesn't often happen because of the way the approaches are dressed up. If anyone realizes they've been drawn into illegal activities, it's too late. They themselves are already implicated and have too much to lose. Marcus says such people are most likely to face a brick wall in their careers. He says sometimes smear and whisper campaigns are mounted and other pressures come from outside. Like getting black listed in the jobs market, bank loans inexplicably called in . . . That sort of thing.'

'Nothing else?' I asked, thinking what had happened to the three of us, Sir Marcus himself and Jude.

She knew what I meant. 'Accidents or disappearances?' She shook her head. 'Right until the end I don't think Marcus *wanted* to believe such extreme measures were ever used.'

'And of course this was intended as a public document,' I reasoned aloud. 'If he'd made allegations like that without serious evidence, he just wouldn't have been taken seriously.'

She leaned sideways towards me, lowering her voice to a whisper. 'I think that's what stopped him from naming names. But he did refer to three lead players, all senior politicians or civil servants. A Frenchman, an Italian and a German. But they're only refered to as X, Y and Z. And there are no personal details to go on.'

'Shame,' I said. 'He must have known who they actually were.'

Bex stared thoughtfully at her beer. 'Maybe that's what his meeting with Helmut Frauss in Paris was all about. To collect some compelling evidence. We do know that he went there for something big, something vital for his investigation.'

'Where did Frauss live?' I asked, an idea suddenly occurring to me.

She shook her head. 'No idea. Why?'

'Maybe he kept files at home, information on his PC, copies on floppy disks – anything like that.'

'Yes, yes,' Bex agreed impatiently. 'But there's not much we can do about it, is there, Ed? We're not exactly free agents – we're on the bloody run! Unless you can somehow make contact with Tony Tromain and get him to call off the dogs.'

'I can't see why he'd do that, not now.'

'Not if we handed back Sir Marcus's dossier? We'll have gone through it ourselves shortly, found out as much as we need to know.'

'You think he won't realize that?'

'Yes, but if we say it was all a terrible mistake . . . After all, each of us got involved by accident rather than by design. Maybe if we can persuade him to think of us as allies rather than enemies . . .'

I thought that Bex was being naive and told her so. 'They're *committed* now, don't you see? Someone made a decision to dump Jude's corpse on us – and then went public, pulling the police in on their side.'

But she was having none of it. 'We've *got* to try, Ed. Tromain has got to be made to change his mind. Or else *one* of us – most likely you – or all of us are going to spend the next twenty years behind bars. Then our only hope would be some twerp on a *Rough Justice* TV doco fighting to get us out of the shite. It'll be a long wait.' She fixed me with an accusing stare. 'Please don't lie to me, Ed. Don't you have *any* idea how to contact Tromain?'

I sighed and lit another cigarette. 'There's only one way I can think of that will *guarantee* he crawls out of the wood-work. But I don't like it and nor will you.'

'Try me.'

'I finish the job. I kill Mihac.'

Bex stared at me. 'I didn't hear you say that, did I?'

'I know where Mihac is, I've still got the rifle and paid-up digs that provide an ideal lying-up position. If Mihac is suddenly assassinated, Tromain will show. After that it'll be down to us.'

'You want to involve me? That would make me an accom-plice to murder.'

The TV match at the bar had ended in a disappointing draw and the customers began to disperse, their faces sullen.

I said: 'I told you that you wouldn't like it. And neither do I.' I'd smoked half the cigarette already like some psychotic in a lunatic asylum. 'But it's the only way to be certain when and where he'll show up. Then we'd have to decide what to do.'

She blew out her cheeks. 'Wow, you sure know how to surprise a girl.'

'*Here is a newsflash,*' said the TV announcer.

Instinctively Bex and I turned towards the set at the bar, anticipating some international disaster. Then I realized it was the local Midlands news.

'*Police are hunting three people wanted for questioning in connec-tion with a murder in London yesterday. They are . . .*'

The picture cut to a grainy overhead shot of a cafeteria table, two women and a man. It was CCTV footage taken from Birmingham New Street station earlier that evening. I recognized myself placing my bergen beside the table and looking around.

I looked real mean, and shifty.

# Thirteen

'Jesus Christ!' Bex gasped as we paused for breath after legging it out of the pub and half a mile into the dark, wet streets. We never did know if the locals had recognized us and put two and two together because we scuttled out of there before the TV announcement had finished.

I heaved in a lungful of air, realizing that I was well out of condition. 'This is getting beyond a joke,' I agreed. 'They're putting one hell of a big effort into finding us, huge resources.' Bex started walking again. 'D'you know where we are?'

'Roughly. I think my digs are a couple of streets along.'

There was little traffic here and few pedestrians braved the new front of chilly rain sweeping in from the north-west. A grocery shop marked the corner of the street that we were looking for and there Bex froze.

I drew alongside with a sudden sinking sensation in my stomach. The blue strobes of police cars were pulsing around the dank brickwork of the terraced houses.

We pulled back into the shadow of the shop doorway. 'Your place?' I asked.

Her ashen face gave me the answer I already knew. 'All my kit's there. And the middle section of Marcus's report . . . I wonder if the landlord saw that newsflash? God, Ed, what do we do now?'

I looked around at the drifts of squalling rain that seemed to be settling in for the night. 'Let's get back to my place and hope the landlady took an early night.'

It was with some trepidation that we approached the house where I had my own rented room. But, in marked contrast to the scene at Bex's place, there was absolutely nothing and no one on the rain-lashed street except for the rows of tightly packed cars. The curtains were drawn at the house and only the bulb in the hall showed enough light for me to use the key that I'd been given. I eased open the door. The air smelled faintly of curry and coconut; the living-room door was ajar, through which I could glimpse the younger members of the household watching a loud and garish Bollywood video. I turned and waved for Bex to follow me in and quietly shut the door behind her. Then we tiptoed up the stairs to my room.

I turned the key and shoved the bolt home.

Bex was wringing the rainwater from her hair as she looked around. 'Couldn't have found somewhere smaller, could you?'

'It's cosy.'

'You sound like an estate agent.' She glanced at my kitchen. 'No food, I know. Any coffee?'

'Tea.'

'This milk's off.'

'Black tea,' I replied, slipping off my sodden jacket and sitting on the edge of the bed. 'I'll try Francoise. Keep your fingers crossed.'

It was a long while before anyone answered and I was starting to sweat by the time I heard her sleepy voice. 'Oh, Eddie, I think I'd just dozed off. I've been reading for hours. It is frightening stuff that Marcus has.'

I said: 'Bex's place has been compromised.'

'Compromised?' She sounded confused about the expression.

'Bex and I met up and when we went back to her place the police were already there. She's come back with me. There was a news story about us on TV. With video footage from the rail station cameras.'

There was a moment's anxious hesitation. 'There has been no trouble here. What should we do?'

Rain was rattling like gravel against the window pane. 'Stay put for tonight,' I said. 'But we'll need to move on tomorrow. Bex and I will discuss it and I'll call you first thing.'

I closed down the cellphone and took the offered mug of tea from Bex. 'I suppose we should be thankful for small mercies,' she said.

'She's not happy. And I think she still doesn't believe that we're making the wisest decisions.'

'She doesn't have an option, Ed. Any more than we do.'

'Oh, yes, she does. She can walk into any police station and hand herself over, blaming everything on us. For all I know that would be her best option in the end.' I lit a cigarette to go with the tea. 'But we can't afford for that to happen. We need her expertise.'

'So what are you suggesting?'

'Get away from here first thing tomorrow, out of the area. Travel separately but then meet up somewhere safe. Reassure her. She's not used to danger in her life. Then we discuss what we've learned from the document and try and work out a strategy of action.'

Bex sipped thoughtfully at her tea for a moment. 'If we think she might go wobbly on us, I think you should travel with her. If she's on her own and scared, she might decide to throw in the towel.'

It was a good point. 'Mind you, we've got to work out how the hell we manage to go *anywhere*. We were on the TV news and no doubt the radio too. The police will have the train station covered. They'll no doubt have alerted used-car dealers – we've already had a bad experience with that – and besides, I can't keep on throwing away money on cars we have to abandon after a day.'

'Go by bus,' Bex suggested. 'National Express.'

I wasn't keen. 'Do you really think they won't have the bus terminals covered?'

She gave me an exasperated look. 'Maybe, maybe not. We could at least take a look-see. I know you don't want to use stolen cars, but we're fast running out of options. Unless you want to walk.'

I looked at the serious expression on her face and had to see the funny side. 'Walk to *where*, exactly? Anywhere except here?'

But she didn't smile back. 'You talked about completing the Mihac job – the only way to get hold of Tromain. Where does Mihac live?'

'Leicester.'

Box raised her eyebrows. 'Really? Leicester can't be more than thirty miles from here.'

I said: 'I don't want you involved in murder.'

'I don't have to be. But when you've done it, you'll need back-up if you're going after Tromain.'

I wasn't happy. 'That would still make you an accessory.'

She was persistent. 'Even if we both deny I knew anything about it?'

'That would be down to a jury, Bex.'

She folded her arms stubbornly across her chest. 'That's assuming it ever comes to that, Ed. Look what happened to Jude and Marcus. I'm not at all sure that if we're cornered we're just going to be politely arrested. The police have already been primed that we're dangerous criminals and putting either of us on trial is likely to prove a major embarrassment to Whitehall and Brussels.'

I held her gaze for a long moment. 'Your final word?'

She inclined her head. 'I saw that video, Ed. I'd like that bastard Mihac dead, almost as much as you. And I think we *have* to try and speak to Tromain.'

I smiled without much humour. 'So Leicester it is then.'

It was a cramped and listless night spent together on the single bed. Neither of us could have snatched more than the odd few minutes' sleep, but for all the wrong reasons. It was hot and airless in the bedsit and the rain battered noisily and continuously at the window.

By the time seven o' clock came it was a relief to get up, wash and dress. While Bex made more black tea, I dialled up Paquet to tell her of our changes of plan and to set a rendezvous with us for eleven. That would give enough time for her to get to a computer store to buy a new laptop and for Bex to replace the clothes she'd left behind at her digs.

I'd planned to slip quietly out of my flatlet, but Bex and I were confronted at the bottom of the stairs by the Bangledeshi landlady.

We instantly thought that she had recognized us from a police warning on TV, but that apparently wasn't her concern. 'How dare you do this! Sneak in a woman to your room! What do you think this place is? What sort of people do you think we are? That we run a bawdy house? You will ruin the reputation of my family! Please, what will our neighbours think? And I believe you are a very respectable gentleman . . . !'

I'd have been laughing except that the last thing I wanted to do was draw attention to ourselves. 'I'm so sorry, you misunderstand. This is an old friend of mine. I met her yesterday evening and she missed her last bus – it was raining and . . .'

My defence petered out lamely as the landlady looked Bex up and down. Clearly she didn't believe a word of it. 'And how do I know that she is not a lady of the night?'

'Madam!' Bex looked most indignant. 'I can assure you that I am not!'

I cut in quickly: 'I'm taking her home now. We can talk about it later.'

The landlady shifted ground grudgingly. 'Very well . . . But it must not happen again.'

I smiled demurely. 'I can assure you that it won't.'

Then we were out of the door and onto the street. The rain had cleared and a wintry sun had even ventured out. I was aware of the landlady standing at the top of her steps, watching us until we turned the corner.

'Blimey,' Bex said with unconvincing innocence. 'Do I really look that much of a tart?'

'Couldn't possibly comment,' I replied. 'C'mon, happy hooker, we've got things to do.'

Bex made short work of her shopping. I restricted her budget so it was down to a cheap rucksack, shirts and jeans from a camping shop and a handful of underwear from a discount store.

We got to the branch of McDonald's with ten minutes to spare and had just picked up a brunch of cheeseburgers and coffee when Paquet arrived. She was carrying her hand-grip and a brand new laptop case. I'd told her to dress down, hoping that she'd blend less conspicuously with her surroundings. But even in stonewashed jeans and a crumpled jogging top, she managed to look stunning. I think she'd have turned heads if she'd been dressed in a black bin-bag.

She took one look at what we were eating and decided to make do with a milk-shake.

'I am beginning to really understand what Marcus was up against, Eddie.' she said. 'From what I am reading last night, I think we have got ourselves into a very dangerous situation.'

She looked tired and uneasy, even when Bex placed a reassuring hand on her wrist. 'Don't worry, hon, we'll get us out of this. We've been in stickier situations.'

Paquet smiled in appreciation of the kind words, but I thought she still seemed doubtful.

Shortly afterwards we left and made our way to the bus station. Bex, looking deliberately scruffy and carrying a rucksack to give the impression of perhaps being a student tourist, approached alone.

Paquet and I huddled together like lovers as we walked, talking to each other, gazing into each others' eyes, apparently oblivious to the world. We stopped at the edge of the terminal and embraced, so I could position her to allow me a good view of the buses and queues of travellers over her shoulder.

At first glance it was a normal day, with the usual slightly frenetic activity of mud-sprayed coaches and their passengers, some of the people late and panicking, others impatient with waiting. Yet others anxiously scanned the line of buses for the right destination sign or for a familiar face among the disembarking travellers. On a far pavement I saw Bex shuffle into view, dump her rucksack, then squat on it as she pretended to fill in a crossword book.

'Is it all clear?' Paquet asked.

I was about to answer yes when I picked out the first uniformed constable, standing by the information office. He seemed relaxed enough, hands behind his back as he looked idly around the terminal. Not exactly a cop with a mission.

But then I noticed a small knot of men standing slightly to one side of him. Each was dressed in black, or at least very dark colours. Most wore long raincoats and I think nearly all were sporting dark glasses and short or cropped hair. They did not all look the same, but the similarity was sufficient to put me instantly in mind of some cool new rock band.

Unlike the lone constable, they definitely appeared to have a specific purpose for being there. A couple of them were talking to each other, another was on a mobile phone and two others were carefully scrutinizing the bus terminal. When I followed their line of sight, I realized they were watching two more of their number checking passengers boarding a National Express bus headed for Scotland.

Plain-clothes CID, I decided ... Then I immediately changed my mind. No, these weren't typical British detec-

tives. Not even Special Branch. There was a certain arrogance and menace about them and, despite their civilian
clothes, they must have been aware that they looked conspicuous. It clearly didn't bother them. So they weren't MI5
spooks either, because that certainly wasn't their way.

The man with the mobile phone took a couple of steps
out of their circle and exchanged a few words with the
police constable. The officer nodded uncertainly and half
raised his hand as though going to salute before changing
his mind. The man in black rejoined his group and their
collective attention moved on to another coach, this one
leaving for London.

I leaned forward and whispered in Paquet's ear. 'Let's get
out of here. Nice and slow.'

As I reached for her hand, she looked perplexed. 'What
is it, Eddie?'

'A group of guys by the information office. They're
studying the passengers.'

'Police?'

'I'm not sure— No, don't look!'

But it was too late and she turned her head as we were
walking away hand in hand. At least she had the sense to
make her glance seem casual, as though examining the sky
for signs of rain.

She said nothing for a few moments as we drifted clear
of the terminal, but I sensed that something else was trou-
bling her. 'What is it?'

'There is something about those people, Eddie. Seeing them
reminded me what Marcus used to say.' She glanced sideways
at me with a slightly guilty expression. 'When I thought he
was being paranoid about being followed. Or that someone
was out to kill him. He'd make a joke about it *just* being the
men in black. Like the movie. That was the expression he used.
Like they were aliens – in other words, a figment of his imagination. As though he was trying not to get me worried.'

Even as she told me my mind flashed back to the previous night, the group of policemen rushing through New Street station in an attempt to intercept us. There'd been something a little odd about the group, but I'd had other things to worry about at the time. Now, in retrospect, I realized what it had been. Not the uniformed police themselves, but also those I'd assumed were plain-clothes officers. They, too, had been men in black.

At that moment Bex came around the corner in front of us. 'Did you see them?'

'Couldn't miss them,' I replied.

Bex fell into step beside us. 'The shadowmen.'

'What?'

'That's what Marcus told Jude he called them. The blokes who were out to get him.' She smiled without humour. 'A bad joke, as things turned out . . . Anyway, I'm sure they weren't police. I don't think they were even British.'

'I agree,' I said.

'How can you be so sure?' Paquet asked.

'Their manner, their behaviour,' Bex said.

'Reminded me of old Eastern Bloc security police in the days of the Cold War,' I added. 'Soviet or East German.'

Bex agreed. 'As much to do with intimidation of their own people as surveillance. They were virtually above the law – and it showed.'

But Paquet was more concerned with the present. 'How will we get away from here now?'

'We're running out of options,' I admitted reluctantly.

Stealing a car had been the last thing I'd wanted to do, but I no longer had a choice. We had to get out before the net closed.

I'd been away from the game for a long while, so I spent some time hunting for a car that I knew I could break into with ease. Finally I settled on an old Ford Cortina that was in good condition for its age. It was parked near the corner of a quiet suburban street which was not overlooked by CCTV cameras. Bex and I decided on what we used to call the "two-plus-one" technique and I explained it to Paquet as the two of us continued our lovers' stroll along the road beside the line of parked cars.

When we reached the Cortina, Paquet and I halted as I turned and scooped her into a passionate embrace, pushing her back against the car. The taste of her lips and the sensual movement of her mouth against mine was distracting, so much so that I had to force myself to concentrate on the job at hand. The length of clothes-hanger wire had always been kept in one of my bergen side-pockets; it had many uses, one of which was as a hook to slide down between the glass and the rubber surround of the driver's-door window until the lock mechanism could be engaged.

I managed to do this with my hands behind Paquet's back while she ran her fingers through my hair and continued her kisses. I couldn't help thinking that she was taking her play-acting a little seriously – but then, I wasn't complaining. Once I heard the click of the door lock, I slipped the wire hook back into my pocket and prised her arms from around my shoulders.

'Is it done?' she whispered hoarsely. 'Do we stop now?'

I had to grin. 'I suppose we'd better.'

We sauntered on at a leisurely pace until we were out of sight around the next corner. I knew that Bex would be following up, crossing the road straight towards the Cortina with all the confidence of its rightful owner. Door open and in. Then just a couple of moments' fumbling under the dash to hot-wire the ignition.

Sure enough, we'd walked barely thirty yards when we heard the rather unhealthy grumble of a car engine and the Cortina slipped alongside us at the kerb. I bundled Paquet inside and we were off.

At least we knew we were safe for the time being. Dozens

of cars would have been stolen daily from the city and it was not normally a priority concern for the police. Of course, it would have been different if they'd known three murder suspects were in this particular vehicle. But they didn't and therefore, as long as we didn't draw attention to ourselves, the chances of being stopped and caught were minimal.

Nevertheless, the hour's drive was nerve-racking and it was a relief to divert onto the quiet country lanes to the east of Leicester in search of suitable accommodation for Paquet. At last we found a quiet guest house that welcomed a paying visitor in the depths of winter. She went in alone to make arrangements while we waited. Having left her luggage in her room, she rejoined us in the car and we drove on to find an all-day pub that was still serving food.

We ordered some bar meals and settled around a table beside the inglenook fireplace where oak logs burned fitfully. Bex and I had been evading some of Paquet's questions during the journey from Birmingham, so it was hardly surprising when she said suddenly: 'What are you two up to, Eddie? You are hiding something from me.'

'No, no,' I protested, probably too much.

'But you won't say where you are going to stay.'

'Because we don't know yet,' I came back smartly. 'We're going to try and locate Tromain, that's all. It might take a few days.'

'And what will you do if you find him?'

'Try and bring an end to all this nonsense.'

She looked at me and Bex in turn as she sipped at her white wine. After a moment she said: 'That would be good . . . if only you can succeed.'

'We can but try,' Bex said.

'And you want me to stay at the guest house while you are doing this?'

I lit a Gauloise. 'You're the journalist, Fran, and the nearest thing we've got to an expert on all this. We'll leave my part

of Marcus's dossier with you . . . You'll need the time to
study it, draw conclusions . . .'

She nodded solemnly, turning things over in her mind.
'There is a telephone jack in the room – I can use my
laptop . . .'

It was then that I remembered something I had read the
previous evening. 'My section mentioned something called
the Genk Protocol,' I said. 'I got the feeling it was significant, but it was cross-referenced to the last section. The one
you were reading.'

She regarded me with a strange expression for a moment,
then nodded. 'Superstate Security,' she confirmed hoarsely.
'You should have been a journalist, Eddie. You have an eye
for what is important.'

'Not really. It just seemed it might be important to Sir
Marcus. Had you heard of it?'

Paquet pulled a tight smile. 'No. And I doubt that many
have. Marcus says that the Protocol was drawn and signed at
the time of the Maastricht Treaty. Genk is a small town in
Belgium, just a short drive away across the Dutch border. It
must have been quite easy. Anonymous official cars, with their
darkened windows, to spirit key ministers away. Just for a few
hours in the dead of night. No one would be any the wiser.'

Bex's eyes widened. 'That's what happened?'

Paquet reached for my pack of Gauloises and helped herself
to a cigarette. 'According to Marcus,' she answered as I gave
her a light, 'the signing at Maastricht was the crossing of the
Rubicon for the formation of the European superstate. One
parliament, one government, one Court of Justice – and a
single currency. European law becomes supreme law over
all laws of individual member countries.'

It took a moment to sink in. 'A nation state,' I murmured.

'And what is it that any nation state must first address
itself to?' Paquet asked, fixing me with her stare across the
table.

As a soldier, the answer seemed obvious to me. 'Defence,' I answered with barely a moment's thought. 'Defence of the realm.'

Paquet nodded. 'Exactly. But not just tanks and soldiers, although we know that is already happening. No, it is also defence in terms of security.'

'You mean intelligence?' Bex asked.

The journalist drew deeply on her cigarette and exhaled in a long slow stream of smoke, using the moment to choose her words. 'That is what was signed at Genk. The protocol allowed for the setting up of what they call an experimental "research monitoring facility" – I think that was the jargon they used. In secret minutes that Marcus claims to have seen it was to have been called the State Research Office. Then someone points out that the EU is not yet a nation state. So they opt for the Special Research Office. Or the SRO.'

I smiled at that. It must have been the suggestion of a British mandarin. The word 'special' is their gook-speak for secretive or clandestine. Special Branch, Special Air Service, Special Boat Service . . . I asked: 'And what's the function of this Special Research Office exactly?'

Paquet explained: 'The SRO was sold to the EU Commissioners on the basis that – as EU integration continued according to treaty – there would no longer be a role for individual national interests and the agencies that protect them. In Britain, of course, that is your MI5 and MI6.

'Therefore an embryonic superstate security apparatus should be in place to take over gradually as the need arises. Even at the time of Maastricht, security experts in Brussels were identifying targets as *enemies* of the EU. Political as well as criminal or military, inside as well as out. In fact, I am thinking that it is *anyone* who attempts to undermine the great European idea. There is a definition of new crimes within the EU, like xenophobia and seditious libel. These are judged by the criteria of the European Court of Justice. Any individual, journalist or even political party that criticizes the EU can now fall foul of these laws.'

'Then Marcus himself was clearly in the frame,' Bex murmured. 'They must have regarded him as an enemy of the superstate.'

'What powers does the SRO have, exactly?' I asked.

Paquet allowed herself a faint smile. 'None. That is the beauty of it. Very clever. But, as Marcus points out, that is the very danger.'

She'd lost me there. 'I don't follow.'

'Firstly, until this time it has only ever operated in shadow form.' Paquet went to an analogy that was close to her heart. 'Think of a new television news programme preparing to go on air. For weeks beforehand they research, send out reporters, write scripts and run full studio management and anchor teams. They are putting together full live shows – only no one ever presses the transmit button.'

Bex was getting her head around it. 'So it's a dummy operation?'

'Sure,' Paquet said, 'except that the SRO appears to be working as it was designed to – it's just that it won't be able to operate *officially* until the Protocol is finally ratified.'

I said: 'I can believe there'd be a lot of opposition to it.'

Paquet shrugged. 'Some national security agencies have expressed reservations. But I think the protest has been pretty muted because of the way it has been sold. As I said, it has no powers and it has no executive arm – well, not on paper, at least.'

Bex was getting impatient. 'So what *can* it do?'

Paquet stubbed out her cigarette, then flipped out a notebook from her bag and began scribbling a simple diagram. 'This is a fully functioning operation, but so far it is recognized only as a *trial research facility*. And it is placed – technically, at least – under the aegis of Europol. But in fact

European police officers really know nothing about it, let alone have any control of it.

'Yet they, like every other department within the EU, *must* respond to any request that the SRO makes for research data. The SRO has mountains of information about every aspect of the entire Brussels government. It also means that SRO officials have legal Europol accreditation.'

She emphasized one more point. 'Remember that under the Protocol, every national police and security agency is *obliged* to assist them – because, in effect, they answer directly under the Commissioners themselves.'

I was still bemused, still couldn't see the menace that Paquet seemed to be implying. 'So what does the SRO *do* with all this information?'

There was a look of triumph on Paquet's face as though she were about to reveal to us the brilliance of this puzzling proposition. 'The SRO supplies information and analysis – *on request* – direct to the Commissioners for their eyes only. No one else, no other department.'

'So apart from appealing to the Commissioners' egos – having their own sort of private intelligence system at the top – what's all the fuss about?' I demanded.

Paquet's triumphant smile hadn't wavered. 'Just suppose . . . that those running the SRO are crooks, are actually connected to the criminal mafias of Europe . . . They would have access to every deal being contemplated throughout the EU, an insight into every opportunity for fraud, every proposal to counter criminal activity, and whatever lines of inquiry Europol are following. And as for what the SRO show the Commissioners when asked . . . one could imagine how selective that might be!'

Now I understood Paquet's ironic smile. 'Is that what Marcus claims?'

'*J'accuse*,' she replied tightly.

'And who is running it?'

She shook her head. 'I don't know. Marcus has left blank spaces in his report. I think maybe this is what he hoped to find out – or have confirmed on the night he died.'

'From Helmet Frauss?'

'Yes. And something else, I think. Something that very much concerns us today. Maybe the people who killed Marcus are those who killed Jude. And they are the *real* force after us now.'

If she hadn't had it before, Paquet certainly had our attention now. 'Marcus's shadowmen?' I guessed.

'Just that, the men in black,' she confirmed. 'The SRO has no executive arm, but Marcus writes that it has a huge secret budget. It may officially employ only desk officers. But they have Europol accreditation and are free to hire anyone else from private outside agencies. Because of the secrecy, who would know *who* is being used?'

'Thugs?' Bex suggested.

Paquet gave one of her Parisienne shrugs. 'Mostly pretty sophisticated thugs, I should think. Investigators, ex-police experts . . . But yes, maybe criminal thugs to frighten people. Anyway, that is what Marcus claims in his report. And, after the car bomb in Paris, it seems maybe professional assassins, too.'

'So everything is at least once-removed from the SRO,' I observed. 'And the SRO itself is virtually unaccountable because it doesn't officially exist. It doesn't have an executive arm, but it's free to hire-in expertise or muscle that no one ever need know about outside its own walls.'

'So those people at the coach terminal . . . ?' Bex began. 'And with the police at New Street Station last night? They could be SRO – or under SRO control?'

Paquet said: 'I don't know what you think, but to me it seems a safe assumption.'

'That's scary stuff,' Bex said hoarsely. 'A corrupt secret police force that's already out of control.'

Paquet frowned. 'We cannot know that it's out of control.'

'Well, I certainly hope the EU Commissioners *themselves* didn't sanction Marcus's assassination,' Bex retorted. 'Or the killing of Jude . . . Because that prospect is *awesome* – and it's clear that we're next in their sights.'

Paquet stared at her wine. 'Yes, I hope you're right. According to Marcus, the whole point is that the Commissioners themselves *don't* know what's going on.' Then she looked up. There was fear in her eyes. I'd seen that look too many times in the faces of too many people to be mistaken. Her voice rose barely above a whisper. 'But then, would we ever *really* know?'

Of course, given the way the SRO was set up, we wouldn't. Nobody would. No media investigation would get anywhere near unearthing the truth. And given my own experience with such matters in Northern Ireland, it was unlikely that even some future authorized EU inquiry would ever do much better.

It was a distinctly frightening prospect and the air around our table seemed to have noticeably chilled, despite the warmth thrown out by the smouldering logs in the hearth. Our conversation lapsed as we each absorbed the full extent of the odds that were stacking up against us.

So it was a relief when the waitress arrived with our bar meals. But, in truth, even the wholesome comfort food and attempts to change the topic failed to raise our spirits.

It all just served to reinforce to me just how important it was that I got to Tromain before our time ran out.

After dropping Paquet back at her guest house, it was gratifying to be on the road again, speeding through the early-evening darkness into the city of Leicester. And a date with that bastard Mihac. A date with destiny.

Of course, when Paquet wished us luck, she had no concept that an assassination was a necessary part of my plan.

Otherwise, I'd no doubt her reaction would have been very different.

Bex and I decided that it would be less conspicuous for her to drive, and she did so in thoughtful silence. The car owner's taste in music was modern and crass, a deadly combination. So I fiddled with the old radio set until I found Classic FM. The soothing pastoral symphony by Vaughan Williams seemed to ease the air of tension in the car and after a while Bex became more talkative. 'So what's Mihac doing now?'

'Seems to be in the porno business. Another source of embarrassment for HMG.'

'And how safe is your safe house? Your LUP?'

She was using her old army jargon, meaning Lying-Up Position. I said: 'There's no reason to suspect it's been compromised. Tromain doesn't know where it is, except that it overlooks the back of Mihac's house. He's got no reason to go there. And, after what's happened, he's not likely to think that I will.'

'The landlord won't have rented it out to someone new?'

'Landlady,' I corrected. 'I paid up front, told her I was going to London to look for a job, and I left a few things there. So it shouldn't be a problem.'

After that Bex lapsed back into silence until we entered the suburban outskirts of the city. Our first job was to sanitize our vehicle. After ten minutes cruising the back streets, we found a suitable residential area of old housing without garages which provided parked cars aplenty to choose from. This operation would have been best done with an electric screwdriver, but it only took a few minutes longer to remove our old Cortina's number plates manually.

Then, while Bex kept watch, I quickly switched each with the front and rear plates of two other parked cars that had plates of the same dimensions before screwing the stolen ones back onto our vehicle. Now the Cortina's registration number – either of them – wouldn't correlate with the one reported stolen earlier in Birmingham.

With that task completed, we began negotiating the intervening miles of backstreets towards Mihac's detached house. Bex kept to a steady twenty-five as we cruised past the high garden wall and solid timber gates; there was enough ambient light from the surrounding street lamps for her to glimpse the upper storey and roof of the house beyond.

'Looks like it's some pad,' she observed. 'Obviously done well for himself.'

'On taxpayers' money,' I pointed out.

Bex followed my directions, taking a couple of left-hand turns until we were in the street where I had my rented room. I pulled on my iron-grey Serbian toupee and ignored her smirk.

As she parked up, I said: 'Stay here while I check the place out. I don't want anyone to be able to identify you if this goes pear-shaped.'

She nodded, reluctantly accepting the sense of what we'd already discussed and agreed.

I opened the door, saying, 'I'll keep in touch by mobile.'

Then I was out and walking down the street with my bergen over my shoulder until I found the house. At first I thought there was no one at home. I rang the doorbell several times and I had just remembered that the Polish-émigré landlady was hard of hearing when the hall light finally came on.

She seemed both surprised and delighted to see me. 'Did you have any luck in London, young man?'

'I think I've got one of the jobs,' I said as she let me in. 'I could hear in the next day or two, even tonight.'

'I'm so pleased for you,' she said, but she sounded disappointed.

'So I'll have to leave as soon as I hear.'

'And we never did have that cup of tea together.'

'I'm sorry.'

I felt rotten, but frankly I had other more important things on my mind. Once behind the bolted door of my room, I pulled on a pair of latex surgical gloves. Leaving the light off, I made my way to the window. I took my binoculars from the bergen and focused on the conservatory extension to Mihac's house.

Anything could have happened since I'd abandoned the attempted assassination of the man a few days earlier. The government had wanted him dead then, and it was unlikely anything had changed since. He'd served his purpose in an attempted duping of the Real IRA and now he carried a high risk of embarrassing Whitehall as a wanted war criminal. Tromain's ploy with me had back fired, but that wouldn't stop his people coming up with something else. Another assassination attempt, a sudden abduction and disappearance made to look like the action of old enemies from Bosnia . . .

It was a relief as the familiar figure came into focus through the windows of the conservatory. Water was running into the jacuzzi, but he was still dressed in one of his snazzy suits and was pouring out two glasses of Moët from an iced bottle on a side table. He offered one of them to his companion, a rather pretty black girl. She looked demure in a pink skirt and jacket top and accepted the offered glass with an uncertain expression on her face.

My best guess was that she was a new victim, maybe lured by an innocuous ad for models by Mihac's agency. Now the man was filling her with champagne and lies about how much he could do for her career. Luring her into signing a contract and getting her kit off. She obviously had some doubts and I just hoped she had the sense to see through him and get the hell out of there.

I glanced down at my watch. It was just turned six, so he'd probably taken the girl straight home after an interview at the office. If he was still running to form, I could expect him to be soaking in his tub for another hour or so. Longer, if his new recruit was idiot enough to fall for his patter.

There was no time to lose; it could be days before I had another opportunity like this. I put away the binoculars, left the bergen in my room and retraced my footsteps to the door and back to the car where Bex waited.

I could scarcely keep the excitement from my voice. 'He's there, we're on.'

She smiled nervously. 'How d'you want to play this, Ed?'

'Another hot-wire.' I shrugged and gave an apologetic smile. 'When Tromain turns up, we'll need two to tango. Otherwise, Sod's Law we'll lose him.'

Bex saw the sense in that. We didn't hang about and in forty-five minutes had secured our second stolen car, a green Astra, from another neighbourhood and swapped its licence plates with those of two other vehicles.

That done, we split up. Bex parked up in the Cortina some distance away but close enough to eyeball Mihac's front gates, and I took the Astra back to the street where I had my room. I parked and hurriedly returned to the house to take up position by the window. With my recent run of bad luck, I'd convinced myself that the man would no longer be in the conservatory. So it came as quite a pleasant surprise to find that he was.

The squat body, matted with black hair and adorned with a heavy gold medallion, sat on the edge of the jacuzzi with his legs dangling in the water. The young black girl was naked now, splashing around at his feet and trying to keep her champagne glass clear of the bubbling water.

I dumped the binos on the bed and pushed up the sash window, the cool night air a welcome balm as the adrenalin began coursing around my body. Sitting back on the mattress, I forced myself to take the time to look around the room. During my previous stay I'd always worn the latex gloves so there was no chance of there being accidental fingerprints left anywhere.

I pushed that worry to the back of my mind and tipped out the oilskin gun-case onto the bed, before returning the remaining items I'd left behind in my absence to the bergen: alarm clock, portable radio, electric travel kettle and a few essential groceries. That done, I went to the corner by the door, lifted the carpet and prised up the loose floorboard I'd identified during my original stay.

Returning to the bed, I unzipped the gun-case and took out the three parts of the Dragunov sniper rifle. I forced myself to be slow and methodical as I reassembled it to its full four-foot length and snapped in the magazine of rimmed 7.62mm rounds.

I rested the weapon across my knees and took a deep breath, feeling the breeze from the window on the back of my neck while I fitted the non-variable 4x scope. This baby was a real soldier's weapon, like most of the old Soviet stuff. Idiot-proof and weatherproof – unlike a lot of fancy modern arms from the west. Introduced in the mid-1960s, the Dragunov SVD was issued to one squad in every motorized rifle platoon. So any Tom, Dick or Ivan had to be able to pick it up and use it with minimal training.

Once the sights were zeroed you just had to aim through the telescopic sight and squeeze the trigger. Its effective range was around fourteen hundred yards, and Mihac's jacuzzi fell well short of that. So it should be easier than shooting an elephant, which was just as well given my state of nerves and lack of practice in recent years.

'All set,' I murmured to myself, feeling strangely conflicting emotions of relief that I was ready and of trepidation at what I now had to do.

I twisted round and crawled on all fours across the mattress to the window. Then, drawing my knees up into a semi-curl, I rested the barrel on the sill. I fitted the cutaway stock into my shoulder, feeling the comfort pad against my cheek, which also lined me up perfectly with the extension tube of the telescopic sight.

With the thumb and forefinger of my right hand I adjusted the focus, the image of the black girl slowly transforming from a blur into sharper detail. The condensation gathering on the window-pane of the jacuzzi room prevented the perfect picture, but it was good enough.

I shifted my position a fraction, allowing the barrel sight to edge up a millimetre or two, away from the girl until the cross-hairs rested squarely on Mihac's chest. That medallion of his made a perfect target . . . Suddenly I was aware that my pulse had quickened. I could hear the sound of blood rushing in my ears. My heart was like a distant beating tom-tom, low and deep.

Mihac now had a camcorder in his hands, aiming the lens at the girl. He was laughing. I could see the gold fillings. Laughing like I'd seen him laugh on the grainy covert video in Bosnia as he'd danced with his camera around Astrid as she'd died, trying to capture the horror and depravity of it all. I realized in that split second that my own predicament over the past few days had distracted me, had taken the edge off my need to wipe him from the face of the Earth.

Now that he was laughing, now that I finally had him in the sights, that hunger for his annihilation returned with a vengeance.

I filled my lungs, slowed my breathing. Inched my finger around the trigger, ready for the gentlest squeeze. Textbook stuff. I didn't want to miss this moment through one care-less move. I'd waited too long for this. Astrid had waited too long.

Astrid? From somewhere deep inside my brain I was receiving a message. What? Does not compute, does not compute . . . Then it dawned. I was thinking of Astrid, but

I could not see her. I could not conjure her in my mind. That ash-blonde hair, those beautiful, soulful eyes – I knew what they looked like, but I could not see them.

Time and Mihac had taken even that from me.

'Fucking bastard,' I rasped.

Moisture welled suddenly in my eyes. I squeezed the lids tight for a second, but when I opened them again they were stinging and there was a tearful haze over the image of Mihac's chest and that bloody stupid medallion of his.

Sod this! I tightened my finger again. Quick, now. DIE, YOU FUCKING BASTARD! DIE!

Then it was there, staring at me. Astrid's face. Filling the image in the sight. Staring straight at me. Telling me no. Telling me to stop. 'Not now, Astrid! Not fucking *now*!'

I shut my eyes and pulled the trigger.

# Fourteen

Christ!

The butt of the Dragunov slammed back into my shoulder under the recoil. You bloody fool, Coltrane!

I opened my eyes. Astrid had gone. Through the scope I witnessed the scene of mayhem and was filled with disbelief at my own stupidity. I'd shut my eyes at the critical moment, for God's sake! I'd been crying like a bloody emotional cripple, acting like some hormonal teenage girl. And now look at it . . . Peering down the scope was like looking at a magic-lantern show through icy stalactites and stalagmites of shattered glass.

The black girl had become hysterical in the water, her champagne glass thrown away and her hands raised protectively to her breasts as she screamed at the top of her voice. A mute cry, like in a pre-talkie movie. Mihac had thrown himself down to the tiled edge of the jacuzzi and his camcorder to the wind as shards of glass fell around him and my wasted shot whistled silently past into the night beyond.

Windows don't suddenly shatter for no reason. Although he wouldn't have heard the shot, his experiences in war-ravaged Bosnia would have given him a pretty good clue as to what had just happened. The initial shock over, he raised his head, looking around and evaluating the situation. I saw him glance back over his shoulder towards the house.

I knew what he was thinking. The shot had come from

outside. Safety was back inside the main body of his house. I saw his flabby muscles flex to lift himself off the deck, his knee drawn up under him as he prepared to stand and run. There was no thought for the safety of the girl.

Suddenly I was overcome by calm. No, you Poison Dwarf, you're not getting away with this. I shifted the bolt of the Dragunov, to lift a fresh round into the breech.

The girl was wading towards the edge of the pool, in danger of entering my field of fire. I swung the barrel to follow Mihac, the bead in the scope lining up on the furry skin of his back, the faint indentations of his spine. It occurred to me in a moment of slow-motion calm that this might not be the cleanest of kills. He'd either die or be a tetraplegic on life-support for the rest of his days. It was in the lap of the gods. I fired.

This time my eyes were wide open and the trigger pressure was a slightly hurried but gentle squeeze. The impact threw Mihac forward as though he'd been suddenly caught by a demonic wind. I saw the fine spray of blood blast out from the exit wound in his chest, showering the window blinds and bamboo sofa in a trillion vermilion specks. Then he pitched face first into a huge tropical cheese plant. His body was almost lost from sight in the tangle of vegetation. The black girl continued her silent scream.

I'd seen enough. In one fluid movement, I rolled away from the window and across the mattress until I was seated with my feet firmly on the floor. With the rifle across my knees, I began to dismantle it into its three parts and stuffed them into the oilskin case. I zippered it up, crossed the room and dropped the package into the hole in the floor before slotting the loose board back into place. I unrolled the carpet to cover it, shouldered my bergen and left the room.

Thirty seconds later I was in the street. Within the minute I was starting my Astra, pulling out of the row of parked cars and heading out of the immediate vicinity.

I pulled into the kerb a couple of blocks away and killed the engine. It was like I was remembering to breathe for the first time. I blew out my cheeks in relief and rubbed my eyes. God, that was the last time I was ever going to do anything like that.

I pulled out my cigarette pack, lit a Gauloise and punched Bex's number on the mobile.

'How'd it go?' she asked.

'It's done.'

'Clean?'

I smiled grimly to myself. 'Not as clean as it should have been. But done.' I thought of the black girl; I'd probably done her the biggest favour of her life. 'And no collateral damage.'

'Thank God for that.' She thought about it. 'But someone else was there?'

'One of his playthings. A black kid. Scared shitless, but she's okay.'

Bex took that in. 'Okay, I'll call you when something happens.'

I hung up and began the frustrating wait. I wanted to be with Bex, to talk to her. Not about the shoot; in fact, anything but. I wanted to hear her laugh, I needed her warmth and support. And I wanted to be sitting there in the car with her, keeping watch on Mihac's front gates.

I tried not to think about what I had just done. Avoided asking myself how sensible – or, more likely, bloody stupid – it had been. At least I didn't feel as wretched as I had after I'd killed Tex-Mex. I liked to think I was more rational. I'd killed Mihac for me and for gullible girls like the black kid. I'd killed him as part of a strategy to save myself and maybe Bex from twenty years or more behind bars.

Or maybe I was getting to the stage where I just didn't care any more. I was aware that I was starting to feel dangerously fatalistic about the whole thing. I flicked on

Classic FM, relaxed back in my seat and unwrapped a Mars
bar.

I'd barely finished it when Bex came on the mobile.
'Chummy's black girlfriend's appeared at the front gate.
Looks like her coat's thrown over . . . not a lot. Her hair's
still dripping wet. She's one very scared bunny. A couple of
blokes — minder types — are arguing with her . . . to get
back inside, I think. She's having none of it, keeps looking
up and down the street . . .' She paused. 'Ah, d'you hear it?
Police siren.'

I could hear it all right, because it was passing my location to get to Mihac's place.

'Here comes Mr Plod,' Bex intoned a few minutes later.
'Two cars' worth.'

A few minutes later, they'd all gone back inside. Then an
ambulance arrived. When it was still there twenty minutes
later, I knew the answer. It had been a full kill. Mihac was
dead, not struggling to survive. Again I was a killer, but this
time I was right in the frame. And on my own.

I tried not to dwell too much on that aspect and attempted
to concentrate on the music because I'd already assumed
that Tromain would be called up from London and I couldn't
reasonably expect him to show for two or three hours at
the very least.

So it came as a shock when barely ninety minutes later,
Bex was back on the mobile. 'Look's like our boy's just
shown. In a black Merc. Just a glimpse, but I'm sure it's
him.'

Now my heart was starting to race with anticipation. Bex
kept the line open and I turned off the radio. But it was
ten minutes before she had something more to report.
'Tromain's back out. Definitely him. I can see his face clearly
now. Aren't you a clever boy? He's got a face like thunder.
Talking to the cops, waving his arms. Like he's telling them
where to start looking. Maybe to find that place he knew

you had . . . Ooh, he's off now. I'll use the hands-free. Just getting the motor started . .'

And that was it, she was off. I pulled on my own hands-free extension to the mobile, started the car and moved into gear. A couple of minutes later I'd slipped in behind Bex's Cortina as she followed Tromain's Merc.

I'd been convinced that he'd be heading south to pick up the M1, so I was surprised to find us tailing him onto the A47 heading east towards Peterborough. On the outskirts of the town, he picked up the A1 running south. I felt vindicated; it was London, after all. But then he veered off again at Huntingdon, turning east again on the A604 towards Cambridge.

Twice on the journey, Bex and I had switched roles as immediate tails, but to be honest I don't think Tromain had a clue that he was being followed. Of all the things on his mind, clearly that possibility wasn't one of them.

Finally the Merc turned into a business district on the outskirts of Cambridge, where most of the buildings were now in darkness. Tromain pulled up in a private parking bay outside the only modern office block of chrome, glass and marble that was brightly bathed in the glare of floodlights. I parked behind Bex some fifty yards away and watched Tromain's hunched figure scurry from his Merc across the concourse to a set of glass doors beneath the portico. A big gold 73 was etched into the marble columns.

I quickly left my car and walked to Bex's, slipping into the seat beside her. 'So what goes on at Number 73?' she murmured. 'And notice anything?'

I might have smiled if I hadn't been feeling so tense. 'The only building lit up like a Christmas tree round here,' I suggested. 'And more CCTV cameras up there than a television studio.'

She added: 'Punch-code lock on the door.' She indicated her Canon with the telephoto lens on the dash. 'Sorry I couldn't read the numbers, his back was in the way.'

'You can't win 'em all . . .' My words petered away as I scanned the landscaped concourse around the office block. 'But I think I can take a closer look. I'll take the camera.'

As I reached for it Bex touched my arm. 'Be careful.'

I slipped out, closing the passenger door quietly, and moved back down the street until I found elongated shadows to allow me to cross to the far pavement. Then I walked back towards Number 73, across an open area of concourse that was covered with patchy shadow from immature trees planted in a pattern of ornamental raised beds. One of these decorative beds ran for some fifty feet beside the road up to the parking bay outside the office block.

Scrambling up onto the wall of the bed, I crawled through the random pattern of evergreen shrubs until I was no more than thirty feet from the entrance to the office. Even if someone was actively monitoring the CCTV cameras, it was unlikely anyone would be able to detect me.

I smiled to myself. The owners of Number 73 might have been security-conscious, but the local council planning committee obviously had more pressing environmental considerations – like pleasant surroundings in the workplace.

Their decision meant that I could sit unseen under a broad-leafed japonica barely thirty feet from the office entrance. I raised the Canon and peered through the telephoto lens into the lobby. It was the usual soulless marble and chrome foyer of the smart modern office. A uniformed concierge was thumbing through a red-top tabloid rather than studying the bank of CCTV monitors perched to the side of his beechwood desk. I swung the lens across the foyer floor to the lift doors.

Above one of them the light had stopped at the seventh floor. The top.

I shifted position slightly and swung the telephoto lens to focus in on the list of companies etched on the brass plate to one side. The first two floors were occupied by

Personnel Pan-Europa; the next three by Zephyr Investment and Insurance Stategies, Zurich, and the last two by the Asset Assessment Group. So what's in a name? Not a lot, as far as I was concerned.

There was nothing more to be gained, so I took a couple of shots, capped the camera, began wriggling slowly back and eventually retraced my footsteps to the Astra.

'What gives?' Bex asked in my earpiece almost as soon as I'd shut the door.

'He went up to the offices of an outfit called the Asset Assessment Group,' I replied. 'Mean anything to you?'

She thought for a moment. 'No. It could mean anything. Assessing assets . . . ? Accountancy, insurance . . . ?'

'Security?' I suggested.

'Mmm, could be—' Her voice rose in pitch. 'Our friend's on the move, he's coming out of the lift.'

My mind was racing ahead. 'Listen, Bex, he's either heading home to his wife and kids, or maybe a weekday pad somewhere nearby. Either way we need to grab him before he gets to wherever he's going. Otherwise we'll end up following him tomorrow and we'll have lost another day. Maybe even more.'

'I read you, boss.' She was as cool as an ice pond. Like she was sitting in an unmarked car in Northern Ireland, back in 14 Int. 'Want me to take the front end? You can follow up.'

I knew exactly what she was suggesting and this was no time for inflated egos. I may have been one of her original Directing Staff, but the sorcerer's apprentice had gone on to master dark arts at which I was a mere beginner. Aggressive driving and ambush skills had been everyday fare for Bex in Ulster and it was time to give her her head.

We were both watching Tromain climb into his Merc. 'Go ahead,' I said. 'If he goes into town, it may be best to snatch him between his car and his pad . . .'

The Merc's white reversing lights came on and its rear

swung to the right.

'Looks like he's goin' out of town,' Bex observed with relief in her voice.

'Then let's do it.'

'Hokey-smokey, boss.'

Tromain thrust the Merc into forward gear and it surged past us, back the way it had come. Bex let him make some distance, then threw her car in a tight circle, bumping over the opposite pavement and back onto the road before she turned on her lights. I copied, a bit slower and clumsier, then raced to catch her up a few minutes later.

Soon we were heading in a loose convoy out into the open country. It was pitch dark and there was no moon. This was Bex's territory.

She made her move about three miles out of the city precincts. It was a long straight stretch of a narrow road, bordered by high field hedges on both sides. Tromain was already cruising at around fifty and the Merc would have plenty of power in hand to leave Bex's following Cortina in the dust – *if* she allowed him to realize what was happening.

But she had no intention of doing that. Suddenly she killed all her lights in a dangerous move that meant she was driving in an inky void, guided solely by the Merc's tail lights. She changed down and hit the gas. I knew that, if he noticed at all, Tromain would think the car behind had just turned off and he'd missed the moment. If anything he'd feel momentarily more relaxed at believing he had the road to himself.

It was a very short-lived feeling. Suddenly, out of nowhere, the Cortina was alongside him, its lights suddenly back on full beam and already cutting across the Merc's bonnet towards the nearside.

I saw the Merc's tail lights come up as Tromain stood on his brakes. Dust and smoking rubber were emitted from its rear tyres as the wheels locked and began leaving their

twin skidmark scars across the tarmac. He swung the wheel
to avoid the Cortina as Bex completed her manoeuvre,
carving into his lane while keeping just inches ahead of
him.

That was when the front wheel of the Merc hit the
kerb, leapt a couple of feet and landed on the grass verge,
the car fishtailing as it came to a desperate and undigni-
fied halt.

By now I was closing fast and turned the wheel left to
pull my Astra tight behind Tromain before he had a chance
to hit reverse. When Bex reached him, he was already half
out of the driver's door. She threw the full weight of her
shoulder against it, pinning his chest in the gap. Something
dark and heavy fell from his hand and clattered into the
gutter.

I stooped and picked up the Browning automatic. 'You
got a licence for this?'

The expression on Tromain's face was one of absolute,
blood-drained horror. Now he gulped in disbelief. 'Coltrane?
What the hell are you playing at! I thought you were the
bloody IRA or something.'

That annoyed me. 'You'll wish we were when I've finished
with you.' I stuck the barrel of his own gun under his chin.
'Turn round and just don't give me the excuse to blow your
fucking brains out!'

Bex eased up the pressure on the door, enabling Tromain
to struggle out and stand on the grass verge. 'Hands on the
roof and spread your legs,' she snapped.

He turned his head towards me as he reluctantly obeyed
her instructions. 'So it *was* you who shot Mihac tonight. I
couldn't believe you'd be so stupid. I thought it must have
been one of his old enemies.'

I ignored him, so he turned his attention on Bex. 'And
I certainly didn't think *you* were mad enough to get involved
in this sort of thing.'

'Stow it, TT!' she snapped. 'I'd be happy to cut your balls off and stuff them in your gob if you open it again.'

The expression on her face persuaded him that she just might mean it. He shut up while I frisked him and then emptied the contents of his pockets into a carrier bag. I then snapped a set of plasticuff ties around his wrists and frogmarched him to the open boot of the Cortina.

'What are you going to do?' The fear was back in his voice.

'Just get in!' I ordered.

Bex was glancing anxiously back down the road towards Cambridge. A set of headlights had appeared in the distance. She gave Tromain a helping shove and slammed the boot lid shut. We turned round as the approaching car drew close, blinding us with its headlights as it began to slow.

A middle-aged woman's head appeared in the passenger window. 'Has there been an accident? Shall we call the police?'

'It's okay, dear,' Bex said breezily. 'We're all friends. One of our cars got a blow-out.'

'A what?'

'Puncture.'

'Oh, I see.' The woman didn't sound convinced. 'Only two of you? There are three cars.'

I could tell Bex was fighting to suppress her irritation. 'Our friend's gone in the bushes for a pee. Nearly pissed himself when it happened.'

The woman recoiled slightly. 'Oh ... Oh, well ... As long as he hasn't been drinking.'

'Teetotal,' Bex assured her briskly.

Reluctantly the woman wound up her window as her husband decided they'd wasted long enough. They drove slowly off.

As soon as the car disappeared from view, Bex said: 'Let's get out of here, Ed. I know that type. Nosy busybody. If they've got a mobile, she'll be onto the boys in blue – or else she'll wait just long enough to get home and do it.'

I didn't disagree with her assessment and returned to the
Astra, started it up and followed Bex's Cortina, leaving the
Merc abandoned on the verge.

It took twenty minutes before we found a suitable place
to stop, a wooded lay-by beside the metal gate of a farm
track. Passing traffic some thirty feet away was screened by
shrubs and trees. We hauled Tromain out of the boot. He
was shivering with cold or fear, or maybe both, and looked
thankful when we shoved him onto the back seat in the
Cortina's warm interior. I slid in beside him and Bex returned
to the driver's seat.

He didn't give us a chance to start. 'You're a bloody fool,
Edward.'

Oh Christ, I thought, we're already back to Mr Potato
Head . . . ! It didn't take Tromain long to get himself back
into controller's mode. 'I was on my way home to my wife
and kids. There's a protocol, you know. If I'm not home by
a certain time, Andrea will call the office. There'll be a high-
priority police alert . . . This sort of thing will only make
your situation worse.'

'It couldn't exactly be much *worse*, now, could it?' I snarled.
'You set me up over our original plan to kill Mihac.'

He stared back at me accusingly. 'You aborted, as I
remember.'

'The place was swarming with your people.'

'For *your* protection, Edward. In case things went wrong.'

My reply was carefully argued. 'Bollocks! The plan was
to take out me and Mihac together. Nice and clean.'

Tromain's eyes narrowed. 'Not as I know it, old son.'

I pushed on. 'And when I wouldn't play, you had the
bright idea of pinning Jude's murder on me.'

He stared, wide-eyed, as though he genuinely thought I'd
lost my marbles. 'What the fuck are you talking about,
Edward? How the hell did I know you'd got yourself into
some bloody love triangle? All that crap about Jude being

in Paris, killed by the bomb – and all the bloody time she'd come back to London.'

I couldn't believe this. 'It was *you* who told me she was dead!'

Tromain was getting angrier. 'For God's sake, Edward, don't play games with me. The French police and our people in Paris naturally assumed that the woman's body in the wreck was Jude. After all, she was supposed to be minding Sir Marcus. It was only later when they realized it was a street girl, a hooker.' Before I could respond, he went on, 'You never said anything to me when Jude came back to London. No wonder, with your devious little sex triangle or whatever it was. I just couldn't believe it when they said they'd found her body at your place. That you'd murdered her.' He shook his head as he spoke the words.

I was almost convinced that he believed what he was telling me. 'Who's *they*?' I demanded.

'The police.'

'And who told the police? The Met didn't just decide to raid my flat off their own bat. After I aborted the Mihac job, *you* put them onto me.'

'I didn't. I was stuck in fucking Leicester trying to explain to my boss why you'd suddenly gone ape-shit.'

'So who told them to raid my place?'

Tromain shrugged. 'I don't know. Maybe my boss just wanted to find you, find out what was going on. I don't run things, you know that.'

I leaned towards him, so close that I could see the pores in his skin and the fresh stubble that needed a shave. 'Understand this, Tromain, there was no fucking love triangle and I did *not* kill Jude. Bex and I never saw her after Paris.'

He gave me one of his patronizing looks. 'No point in trying to convince me, old son. If you're in denial – fine. It's a judge and jury who you'll have to convince.'

I was almost feeling sorry for him that he'd been so successfully duped. Giving him up as a lost cause, I changed tack. 'And who's pulling your strings, Tromain? Who is your boss? Who *exactly* do you work for?'

He sighed. 'HMG – sort of. Foreign Office.'

'You mean SIS?'

'Not directly, I have this contact . . .'

'And where does this outfit in Cambridge fit in?' I asked. 'Asset Assessment.'

He blinked, realizing at last that we must have been following him for some time. 'A private security company with high-level clearance. My connections with HMG used to be direct – more or less. I was instructed to sign up with Asset a few months ago. It makes my connections with Whitehall even less obvious, more distant still.'

'Who runs Asset?' I asked.

Tromain shook his head. 'Don't know. Its head office is registered in the Cayman Islands and no one's ever mentioned to me who's on the board. I gather they're the usual sort of ex-intelligence people, police chiefs and senior military types. You know, well connected.'

'And they mostly recruit people like you?' Bex suggested.

'Ex-professionals, as far as I can gather. But it's a very compartmentalized and secretive organization. It's got twenty departments – or so-called directorates. Each team only operates with its own members, and sometimes those teams are subdivided for security. There's a strict no-fraternizing rule about after-work drinks. I'm very much an outsider. I'm on the payroll for convenience, but I still get my instructions from my old contacts at the Foreign Office.'

Of course, he meant the Secret Intelligence Service at Vauxhall Cross – or 'Riverside', as they called it – but couldn't bring himself to admit it. Old habits, I guessed.

'Cambridge seems a strange choice of location,' I suggested.

He shrugged. 'Not really. London's increasingly irrelevant politically and I think Asset prefers a quiet backwater. It's close to Luton and Stanstead and under an hour's drive to the Zeebrugge ferry.'

Bex came back in. 'So who hires these people at Asset?'

'I don't know exactly,' Tromain replied, starting to look uncomfortable under the close questioning. 'Christ, I don't bloody well ask, do I? I just know that Whitehall and Brussels are clients, and Europol use them occasionally – you know, the European police force, such as it is. They sometimes want professional help with UK investigations and Asset is highly respected.'

It was somehow falling into place. 'Is this what's happening now? Are these Asset employees involved in trying to find us?' I demanded.

He blinked. 'Sure they are. You got wrapped up with Marcus Whitby and he was a subversive with stolen information. There's a connection and Brussels has got an obvious interest to protect. So I guess Europol called Asset to provide some foot soldiers to assist our police.'

Bex jumped on that. 'Do you *actually* mean Europol?'

Tromain looked perplexed. 'Their people, yes. Accredited. Our Government agencies are obliged to cooperate with them under Treaty law.'

I said: 'The SRO?'

The blood drained suddenly from his face, but he covered his surprise with an almost girlish giggle. 'I see they were right. You got yourselves deeply involved with Whitby. That's very hush-hush stuff.'

'The SRO doesn't have an executive arm,' Bex pointed out. 'They're supposed to be analysts, pen-pushers.'

Tromain clearly didn't understand. Like most people he never read the small print of European treaties and agreements. He said: 'They have case officers who make requests and we're legally obliged to assist. No problem there. I don't know what you're getting at.'

I'd heard more than enough. 'Listen, Tromain, what I'm

getting at is this. You're either a bloody good liar or else you've been suckered along with most politicians, the police and the security services. The simple fact is, I've been set up for Jude's murder. There are people connected with Brussels who want me – in fact, anyone involved with Sir Marcus – out of the way. They're afraid that we've got sufficient information to blow the whistle on them. From what you've said, it seems like the SRO is behind it.'

A sneer curled on Tromain's lips. 'That's ridiculous. They're part of Europol. Highly respectable.'

God, would I ever get through to him? 'The SRO is supposed to be a paperwork and computer-intelligence research office, nothing more. Somehow, by using Asset Assessment, it's managing to field its own bloody secret police – the executive arm that it's not allowed to have. I'm surprised they don't all wear leather macs and trilby hats. They're an embryonic Gestapo. Out of control.'

Tromain shook his head. 'You're fantasizing, Edward. It's not like that.'

I grabbed the lapel of his jacket and jerked his face closer to mine. '*They* are the people who blew up Sir Marcus – not some renegade Irish terrorists. They are the people who must have abducted Jude, then fed you and the Foreign Office with one lie after another. Then they saw their opportunity to ensnare me . . . When I aborted the Mihac killing, they dumped her body in my flat.' I released my grip on him, thinking it through even as I spoke. 'She must have already been dead . . . Maybe kept in a morgue . . . The time of death must have tallied with when I was there . . .'

'Oh, God, Ed,' Bex said suddenly, realizing just how cold-blooded Jude's killers had been about it all.

Tromain sniffed, unimpressed. 'That's for the coroner to decide. No point in your idle speculation. You're fooling yourself if you think this is impressing me.' He fixed me with a stare. 'And what the hell did you go back and take out Mihac for?'

'So you can't ask for your money back,' I said, only half joking. 'You set up the kill, Tromain, so if I go down I'll take you with me.'

'I don't think so, Edward.'

His tone was chillingly confident, but I ignored it. 'And it was the only way to get hold of you, to have this chat.'

The sneer was back. 'And what the hell did you hope to achieve?'

Even as I answered him, I was aware just how naive and lame my words sounded. 'To make you realize what was *really* going on. To get you to call off the dogs.'

Tromain was looking remarkably relaxed. 'Even if I believed you, Edward – which I don't – there's nothing I can do. There was a European arrest warrant out for you and now there's a British one for murder. Common law. The genie's out of the bottle and no one can put it back.'

'Stick your fucking head above the parapet!' Bex interjected suddenly. 'We're on the same bloody side. Ed and I have devoted our lives to this country and people like you, doing your bidding.'

Tromain smirked. 'Happens when you take the Queen's shilling, dear lady. You wanted the job security and the pension, just like me. This thing's out of my humble control, I assure you. Even if I thought one of you wasn't guilty of Jude's murder, I've got Andrea and the kids to think of. My career future and pension. I'd kiss goodbye to all that if I backed a couple of psychopaths like you against the system . . .'

His words trailed away. We all heard it, the wail of the police siren. Our eyes turned towards the road and the flashing blue lights as the police cars slowed at the entrance to the farm track.

'They took their time,' Tromain said.

Bex glared at him. 'What the fuck d'you mean?'

As he spoke I realized why he'd never really appeared frightened after he recovered from our initial pounce. 'Panic button in the Merc, Becky. The car has a built-in GPS system – the wonders of modern science, eh? Just a matter of time before they found us.' He looked very complacent now. 'I do hope you're not planning to keep me hostage. You know you'd probably end up dead. This isn't a game you can win, Edward. I suggest you give yourselves up with good grace . . .'

Bex wasn't listening. As the headlights of the first police car approached tentatively down the farm track towards us, she turned and restarted the Cortina's engine. Her eyes had adjusted to the darkness sufficiently for her to steer the vehicle through the open gate without lights and then up along the track. I looked back as the police car stopped beside the abandoned Astra.

Then the scene was lost from view as we crested the hill. Now Bex switched the headlights on and hit the accelerator. It was a bumpy ride as we careered along the cinder track between the hedgerows at breakneck speed.

Suddenly Tromain didn't seem so confident. 'You're not going to do anything rash, I hope. Nothing you'll regret—'

'Just shut it,' I warned with sufficient menace that he obeyed instantly.

Bex slowed the car as we approached the muddy farm-yard. There were no lights on in the buildings, but then we were aware of a dog barking. She swung round and I watched the illuminated hedges drift past until there was a gap, an open gate and another track beckoning us. Then we were off again.

It took another thirty minutes before we were able to find our way off the farm. A metal gate opened onto a two-lane road. I climbed out and went round to Tromain's side, opening his door and hauling him to his feet.

'Where are we?' he asked.

'No idea,' I answered truthfully as I used some spare rope to tie his bound wrists to the gate. 'But no doubt your police friends will find you at first light. Just a few hours to go.'

'Give yourselves up,' Tromain implored. 'And I'll make sure you get a fair hearing. I'll tell the police what you told me.'

I shook my head. 'Not good enough. That's an empty promise and you know it. You do your duty and contact the right people. Tell the truth for once in your bloody life and we'll get left alone. I'll not stick my head in a noose on your half-baked promises.'

Tromain regarded me for a moment. 'You're a bastard, Edward.'

He obviously now felt safe enough to insult me. I grabbed his lapels and pulled his face to within a couple of inches of mine. 'No, Tromain, *you're* the bastard, you always have been. And a selfish, stupid one. That makes it pretty easy for the SRO people to play you for a sucker. So start asking yourself some questions before you find yourself in some deep shit. Like maybe start accepting that Bex and I are telling the truth. Because if you don't call off the dogs and I go down, I'll take *you* with me.'

'You're wasting your time, Ed,' Bex called from the driver's seat of the Cortina. 'He won't do anything until his own neck's on the line.'

I let go Tromain's collar. 'And believe me,' I said softly, 'it will be.'

That seemed momentarily to take the wind out of his sails. He watched me go in a thoughtful, resentful sort of silence. I slammed the passenger door shut and immediately Bex swung the vehicle onto the empty road and headed back towards Cambridge.

She held up her left hand to reveal a pocket tape recorder. 'Part of Francoise's journo kit.'

'You recorded our conversation?' I was proud of her.

'For what it's worth. TT didn't deny he was involved in the plan to kill Mihac. Mind you, I expect it would be rubbished in court.'

'Still,' I said, 'it's better than nothing.'

But I knew that I was grabbing at straws.

It was three in the morning when Bex found a secluded lay-by. She slept like a baby, wrapped in a car rug found in the Cortina's boot, while I kept watch and shivered. I was bloody thankful when dawn broke and we found a Little Chef for a mainline cholesterol fix of all-day breakfast.

I phoned Paquet mobile-to-mobile as we returned to the car. 'Eddie, did you find your friend?'

'Yes.'

'So soon.' She sounded incredulous. 'And will he help?'

'No. Says he can't – or won't. It hardly matters. But we need to get out of this area. Can you be ready in half an hour?'

'Sure.'

'We'll pick you up.'

Paquet barely had her backside on the rear seat of the Cortina before she was asking questions. 'How did you manage to find him? Did he agree to speak with you, just like that?'

'We didn't give him an option,' Bex replied from the driver's seat.

'And we had an idea where to find him,' I added, being fairly economical with the truth, as they say. 'A firm of – well, I suppose – security consultants.'

'No, really?' She sounded excited and surprised. 'In Cambridge?'

It was my turn to be surprised. I turned back to face her from the passenger's seat. 'You know about them?'

'It's mentioned in what I was reading last night.'

'Asset Assessment?' I asked.

Paquet gave one of those ice-melting French shrugs of hers. 'Marcus says no name. Just that there is a company based in Cambridge that the SRO uses to get around the fact that it is not allowed its own executive arm. That way it can hire investigators, ex-policemen, intelligence people and – he says – criminal elements to do dirty work when necessary.'

'Does he say who runs the company?'

'No. Marcus was always cautious about what he committed to print – but it jogged my memory about something he once said. He was referring to his "whistle-blower". Obviously he meant Helmut Frauss, the German police inspector who got killed in the car bomb with him.'

'What about him?'

'One weekend Marcus and I were at his flat in London. We seemed to have little time to spend together and I was looking forward to it. Then he gets a phone call on Saturday morning and announces that he has to go and meet his whistle-blower. I am really annoyed, thinking Marcus has to go to Brussels or The Hague. It was a surprise when he said, no, just up to Cambridge. In fact, Marcus was back in time for us to go to the theatre that night. I remember, I was so pleased.'

She'd lost me. 'Meaning what?'

'That Helmut Frauss lived in *this* area,' Paquet came back impatiently. 'His wife was English and her family came from here. Last night I used the Internet to find the telephone and address.'

Bex said: 'I'm surprised he wasn't ex-directory.'

Paquet raised an eyebrow. 'Well, he was, but I have access to a website that journalists can use. Strictly speaking it's illegal, but in cyberspace . . .'

'Frauss is dead,' Bex pointed out.

'His wife isn't,' came the slightly irritable reply. 'And Frauss was Marcus's source. He *was* the whistle-blower.'

I stepped in to defuse the argument. 'Well done, Francoise . . . But how much would his wife know?'

'For God's sake, Eddie. What is the matter with you two? Pillow talk. An office at home, a computer . . . I don't know. But the Frauss home is just thirty minutes away.'

I glanced sideways at Bex, who looked just a bit sheepish. I made light of it. 'I guess that's why you're a journalist and we're not.'

Paquet had even managed to pull down an area road map off the Internet and within the hour our Cortina was approaching the Frauss home at a steady thirty miles an hour. It was a detached property, set well back from the main road, which we could only glimpse through the high hedge as Bex drove us past the long drive.

'Oh, shit,' Bex said suddenly. 'Look away! Bods on the gate!'

I barely had time to register what she said and comply. Nevertheless, from the corner of my eye I saw the land-cruiser pulled over on the tarmac drive and two men in dark suits chatting to each other beside it. Paquet was slower on the uptake and had a good look across the lawn at the house. 'I'm sorry,' she said. 'I didn't realize what you said. I don't think they noticed me looking.'

There was no point in arguing the matter. I said: 'Keep going, Bex. Just in case.'

'Junction ahead,' she came back. 'Crossroads. Want me to hang a left?'

'Yeah, do it.' I glanced back and saw the two men now standing in the road, staring after us.

We'd already passed three other properties, so there was no obvious side access to the Frauss garden. Bex took the left turn and kept going. After a couple of hundred yards there was another left turn, which we also took. Another avenue of expensive houses backed onto our target. I'd been hoping there might be access via a field or woodland, but again there was no way in except through occupied properties.

The road ended in a cul-de-sac and as Bex began turning round Paquet said: 'Did you see the removal van?'

'Where ?' I asked.

'Parked outside the Frauss home.'

'I didn't look,' I reminded her unkindly.

'Maybe we are just in time,' she added.

'Only we've got to get past those goons on the gate.' I was already wondering how the hell we could manage to find a way through the high bramble hedge and get across the open lawn in broad daylight without being spotted.

Bex braked suddenly and swung into the kerb. 'Wait a minute. Removals, you said?'

'Yes,' Paquet confirmed. 'A big Pickfords van.'

Bex reached into her jacket and pulled out an overstuffed, man-sized wallet. She took a moment to rifle through its contents, extracting three plastic identity cards.

'British Telecom. Gas or water.'

'What are they?' Paquet asked.

'Indentity cards with my ugly mug,' Bex answered with a grin. 'Jude and me ran some up for our business. Never used them, though.'

Paquet was bemused. 'They are false?'

'Nowadays with computers they're easy enough to create,' I explained. 'In the surveillance game, you have to be able to gain access quickly to any building. It's pretty standard intelligence stuff.'

Bex said: 'Removals are in. We could use any of these. Don't need uniforms nowadays.'

I disagreed. 'Overalls are always more convincing. And we can hardly use this car.'

'Sometimes you're a bloody party-pooper, Ed,' Bex

returned, covering her irritation with a very thin gloss of humour.

'But a great idea,' I added quickly. 'But not gas. It'll be oil or solid fuel out here. BT is better. Let's head back towards Cambridge and find a DIY store. We'll need some props.'

Bex swung the Cortina back on the road with a sense of mission. Twenty minutes later we'd found an out-of-town store and spent fifty quid on overalls, a couple of toolboxes and various bits of telecommunications junk – wire, jacks and cheap handsets.

Within the hour we were back in the cul-de-sac behind the Frauss home and Bex and I were trying on our new blue overalls.

Paquet was looking concerned. 'But you've only got the one ID.'

Bex shrugged. 'How many IDs do people look at?'

We'd passed the driveway to the house twice more now, and I could see how to get over the vehicle problem. The landcruiser and the two gooks in the drive had no room to park on the main road, because there was no pavement to pull up on and just a narrow verge and ditch running outside the property. The hedge prevented them seeing anyone approaching; anyway, they appeared to prefer chatting and smoking to keeping a serious watch. They may have been warned to look out for trouble, but they clearly didn't really expect any.

'You drive,' I said to Paquet. 'Drop us off at the cross-roads and we'll leg it. You get back here and wait. Okay?'

She looked troubled. 'I don't like it, Eddie. You are sticking your head in the lion's mouth. Those men look like they are SRO. Maybe they are armed.'

'It was your idea,' I reminded her.

Paquet smiled nervously. 'Maybe it was not my best.'

I ignored that. Time was running out. 'Let's go.'

## Fifteen

Paquet dropped Bex and me off at the crossroads, leaving us to trudge back down the road, wearing our overalls and carrying toolboxes, to the drive of the Frauss home.

'Morning, gents,' Bex said breezily.

The two men jumped at the sudden sound of her voice and spun round to face us.

Bex flashed her ID, while I went through the motions behind her. 'BT. British Telecom,' she announced.

Both men appeared to be in their early thirties. They shared the same suspicious dark eyes and rather swarthy skins. One of them peered at Bex's pass.

'Not my best picture. Those flashbulbs always make me look like a startled rabbit.'

The first man looked up from the ID, not listening to her chatter. His voice was guttural and did not sound British. 'Your people have been here already. To disconnect the phones.' I put the accent somewhere in mid-Europe – very possibly Slav.

Bex saw her chance. 'We're here to reconnect for the new owners.'

The man frowned. 'They don't have a buyer.'

Bex barely blinked. 'No, sorry. Absolutely right. That's the other house. This is a reported fault on the line.'

'The telephone was fine.'

'The computer link,' she persisted.

The man was becoming irritated. 'No, you leave it. The people who live here are going. It does not matter to them.'

I could see that we were in danger of losing this one. I said quickly: 'Sorry, sir, but it's not your decision, or ours. All lines are BT property and we have a legal obligation to maintain them. It won't take more than a few minutes, I'm sure.'

Bex took her cue and began walking forward towards the house. The second man looked even more unhappy than the first. 'Where's your vehicle?'

'We were dropped off from the team van,' she called back. 'They're picking us up in half an hour, so can't stop to chat.'

I smiled courteously as I hurried past them after Bex. 'Oh, shit,' she whispered as we put some distance between us and them. 'They didn't like that one little bit.'

'They were tooled up,' I said.

'I noticed, Ed. Bit nervy, too. Not coppers, methinks.'

I agreed. 'Our pals from the SRO again.'

As we approached the removals men, who were humping furniture into the open rear of a pantechnicon, I glanced back at the landcruiser. The two men in black were in earnest conversation, one of them punching numbers into his cellphone as he talked. I had a feeling we might not have long.

'Where's the lady of the house?' Bex asked one of the removals men.

'Kitchen, sweetheart. Best place for 'em.'

It was a large hallway with an impressive central staircase and several rooms running off. Through an open doorway on the right I could see down a passageway to a swish terracotta-tiled floor and expensive oak kitchen units. As we approached I could hear a kettle being filled with water.

Jayne Frauss had four mugs lined up on the worktop. She turned as we entered, a slim, striking-looking woman in her early forties. Her facial features had good symmetry with high cheekbones, a full mouth and slightly sad brown eyes. She'd embraced middle age by accepting her greying hair, dyeing it to a rather stunning silver hue and having it cut in a straight classic style that framed her face.

Two girls, aged about ten and twelve and the image of their mother, looked up from the refectory table where they were colouring with crayons.

'British Telecom,' Bex said. 'Sorry to barge in.'

An uncertain smile fluttered around Jayne Frauss's mouth. 'Really? I thought you'd finished.'

I said: 'We need to have a word with you.' I didn't want to talk in front of the kids. 'In private?'

Concern clouded her eyes. 'Is there a problem?'

'Not really.'

'So why not in here?'

Bex intervened. 'Trust us. It really would be best.'

Jayne Frauss's jaw dropped a fraction. 'You're not from BT at all, are you?' Anxiety had crept into her voice. Her eyes darted towards the window that overlooked the front lawn, the landcruiser and the men in black.

'Please,' Bex urged, 'we must talk to you. We were friends of Sir Marcus Whitby . . . he was working with your—'

'My husband, yes.' She looked annoyed now. 'And don't I know it.'

I said: 'Just a few minutes of your time. We desperately need your help.'

She took a sudden involuntary backward step. 'You're the couple who the police are looking for.'

My smile was meant to be reassuring, but under the strain it probably just looked downright menacing. 'You're not in any danger from us, believe me.'

The older of the two girls was staring at us from the kitchen table. 'Who are these people, Mummy?'

Jayne Frauss gave it barely a second's thought. 'Just friends of Daddy.'

'She said she was from British Telecom,' the girl recalled accusingly.

Bex forced a little laugh, 'Sorry, just my silly joke.'

Their mother turned round to face them. 'Look, girls, why don't you finish now? The men will be coming for that table in a minute. Go to your rooms and pack away your crayons. Check you haven't left anything out of your cases.'

'We've already checked.'

'Then check again, dears. Off you go.'

Reluctantly the youngsters collected their books and notepads and left the room.

'Sorry about that.'

I said: 'It's us who're sorry. This obviously isn't a good time.'

Jayne Frauss gave a hesitant smile and gestured towards the men on the drive. 'Not for them. The police said you might come. That's one of the reasons we're moving. Not my idea.'

'Not the police,' I corrected. 'The SRO.'

Her smile deepened. 'Now I *know* you're friends of Sir Marcus.' She inclined her head towards the window. 'Yes, those men are Europol. Or the SRO. I get a bit confused by it all.'

I added: 'And, believe me, Mrs Frauss, Bex and I haven't murdered anyone. But our "friends" in Brussels would very much like it to look that way.'

Her facial muscles stiffened a fraction. 'Look, call me Jayne, but spare me any details. What with my husband and Marcus, I've had enough conspiracy theories to last me a lifetime. And now the Europol boys – or the SRO, as you call them – are telling me a whole different version. Frankly, I've had enough. I'm in the middle of moving house – I just want to get out of here and get my girls settled again.'

'Of course,' Bex said quickly. 'We understand that. The loss of your husband must have been a terrible shock—'

'Yes, we've all suffered.' There was an edge of irritation

to her voice, like she'd had just one insincere condolence too many. Then the kettle began to boil and her expression softened. 'Sorry, I'm being rude. Everything's getting to me a bit. I was making tea for the removal men, but . . .'

'That would be great, Jayne,' Bex said with honest enthusiasm.

'Two sugars, please,' I added. And Jayne Frauss smiled.

'I'll do my best, but I really don't see how I can help you,' she said as she handed over the mugs of best-quality Earl Grey.

I said: 'We're being hounded because people in Brussels are convinced we know things that we don't. The only way we can think of protecting ourselves is to *find out* what we *don't* know. Hope that doesn't sound too Irish?'

Jayne understood exactly. 'You want to know what Helmut and Marcus were discussing?'

Bex said: 'We now know a lot of it, but we were hoping there might be more detail. Maybe your husband had files, computer disks .. ?'

Helmut Frauss's wife gave a sad little smile and shook her head. 'The day after we were told Helmut had died in that awful bomb, those people from Europol came round. The people you call the SRO. Helmut worked with them, you see. They actually had an authorized search warrant and had a local police inspector with them. They cleared Helmut's private office. Took away all his papers, his main computer and his spare laptop. Everything.'

'Nothing was overlooked?' Bex pressed.

Jayne shook her head. 'They were very thorough. Quite ruthless and unfeeling, considering . . .'

'And they suggested that you move home?' I asked.

'No.' She shook her head again. 'That happened just a couple of days ago. Just after your photographs appeared on the TV news about some murder in London. I'm sorry, I don't even remember your names . . .'

'I'm Bex and this is Ed. We both used to be in the armed forces.'

Jayne regarded us carefully, trying to decide if we could be trusted. 'Helmut said Marcus told him he had friends looking after him. Was that you?'

Bex said: 'I'm afraid we failed miserably. But, tell me, why were you asked to move home?'

'Told,' Jayne corrected. 'Ordered, rather. They said you two were on the loose, had killed someone already and were subversives of some sort. Trying to dig up lies about the European Union. That you were involved with Sir Marcus. They said the children and I might be in danger from you . . . I just laughed at them, it was so obviously not the truth. Helmut considered Sir Marcus a very great friend and confidant. Why should I be in danger from friends of his? In danger enough to have us set up with a new identity in Canada?'

'Canada?' I echoed.

'That's where we're headed . . . Ooops!' Jayne gave a genuine laugh. 'Don't think I should have told that you.'

'How ridiculous!' Bex just couldn't believe it. 'The only reason that they'd set you up with a new identity – like some important defector or supergrass – is to ensure you can't give evidence against *them*!'

'I'm not stupid,' Jayne replied. 'I realize that.'

'So why are you complying?' I demanded.

Jayne Frauss glared at me. 'Why d'you think? Because of the girls, their future. If we don't comply with instructions, we will lose everything. My widow's pension, probably the house . . .'

I wasn't following. 'What d'you mean?'

She gave a weary sigh. 'Let me explain. I met Helmut when I was living in Germany with my first husband, Peter. He was a Tornado pilot, flying out of Laarbruch. Frankly, he was a bit of a bastard and our marriage was already on the rocks. I met

Helmut – he was a local police inspector – while I was doing local charity work with deprived youngsters.' She gave me an embarrassed half-smile and averted her eyes. 'We fell in love and there was a divorce. Quite straightforward as there were no kids. We married and started a family.

'Meanwhile Helmut's career took off. He became a high-flyer in the national police, specializing in the European mafias and fraud. Our eldest was five when he was offered a big job in the new Europol set-up in The Hague. It was a fantastic opportunity.'

'So you moved to Holland?' Bex asked.

'Of course. It was wonderful for me and the kids, though Helmut found Europol frustrating as a bit of a paper tiger. But all that changed about three years ago. That was when the Special Research Office became operational and a senior Europol officer was needed in an official liaison role.'

I was curious. 'Why was Helmut interested? Did he know what the SRO was about? That it was a security service for Brussels in the making?'

'No, no.' Jayne was adamant. 'It was never put like that. Just more boring admin – but he was to be based in the UK. Not only that, but in Cambridge.'

Bex was as puzzled as I was. 'What was so special about that?'

Jayne smiled broadly. 'I was born here, brought up here. My late father was a don at the university and many of my family and friends live in this area.'

I said: 'I always assumed the SRO was based in The Hague.'

'As part of Europol?' Her smile was without much humour. 'Helmut later reckoned they wanted to be as far away from Brussels, Strasbourg or The Hague as possible. To avoid all the bureaucratic busybodies. Plus the UK is a very good recruitment ground for the sort of professionals they wanted. Police, intelligence, special forces . . . and criminals.'

'So SRO headquarters is actually here?' Bex sounded as flabbergasted as I was.

Jayne gave a wan smile. 'Helmut took his oath of allegiance and secrecy seriously. He actually believed a united Europe would work. He never told me exactly where his office was, and I never asked.' She saw my disappointment. 'But I did follow him to work once. We were having a troubled patch – or rather, I was. His long, unsociable hours, his secrecy. I suspected . . .'

'An affair?' Bex guessed.

Jayne looked embarrassed. 'Stupid, I know.'

Bex asked, 'Did he know you'd followed him?'

A dry little laugh. 'Not until I told him. Helmut wasn't used to being the bad guy, to being the one who was followed him.'

I was getting impatient. 'Do you have the exact location?' I asked.

Jayne gave another sad smile. 'Not thirty minutes' drive from here. A place called Home Farm, off the Colchester Road. I thought he was having it off with some lonely farmer's lonely wife. He explained that the SRO had built a new high-tech compound on farmland the EU had bought.'

'Hidden somewhere in the flat and innocent wilds of East Anglia,' I murmured thoughtfully, understanding the logic of the SRO's choice of location.

'Punts and picnics on the River Cam,' Jayne corrected. 'And afternoon tea at Trumpington. In the beginning that's what I thought. I was so enthusiatic, dear Helmut could hardly resist. Plus the financial and pension package was fantastic. And I mean fantastic! Only later Helmut realized it was one of the main ways the SRO bought the loyalty of its members. It meant everyone had a hell of a lot to lose personally if they ever thought of rocking the boat.'

I said: 'And that's what you lose if you don't leave now?'

Her face began to crumple. 'I feel such a coward. I feel like I'm betraying Helmut. I mean, I know how he felt about the SRO, about what was really happening inside the EU ... But I'd never read the small print of the financial stuff. If I break the rules, if I refuse to do what I'm told, our family will lose everything ...'

Bex moved forward and hugged her as she began to sob.

I said: 'From what you say, your husband believed in the European ideal. So what went wrong?'

Jayne accepted Bex's offered handkerchief, sniffed and dabbed her nose. 'It began with the hostile reception he got at the SRO. He hadn't been expecting that. Sure, he was given all the trappings, a smart office and glam secretary – but he discovered that she made sure everyone knew about his activities. Of course, that didn't stop Helmut doing what he did best. He was a cop through and through. He could smell a rat where everyone else smelled fuchsias and lavender. Fraud and corruption were his stock in trade.

'He started asking questions. And the more he asked, the more isolated he became. The SRO people started to resent him openly, asked for his removal. I think it was quite a relief when he met Marcus. Another man with the same honesty and values – they shared the same mission.'

'Did the SRO know he was talking to Sir Marcus?' I asked.

Jayne shook her head vehemently. 'No, no, I'm sure. He met Marcus on legitimate business and he told me how cautious Marcus was. Said he used to work in Northern Ireland with some shadowy bloke from the SAS who taught him a lot of security stuff.'

Bex gave me a friendly nudge with her elbow.

'Helmut's big mistake,' Jayne said, 'was contacting Adrian Larby.'

I knew the name, but wasn't sure why. 'The MEP?'

'And leader of the GB-FP,' Jayne confirmed. 'A small anti-EU political party that got in – well, that is, just Larby himself got in – under proportional representation in the last European elections. Like the Green Party. Larby made the most of it, hired one of those tabloid PR gurus and got a lot of media coverage, which is probably why you heard of him.'

'Why did Helmut approach Larby?' Bex pressed.

'Some obscure quote,' Jayne replied. 'To know thine enemy, know thine enemy's enemy. Larby was a QC and an earlier leading light in the Referendum Party. When Sir James Goldsmith died, Larby set up his own GB-FP – the Great Britain Freedom Party. It's never had much of a following and seemed to get itself some unfortunate far-right-connection publicity.'

'So what did Helmut want from him?' I asked.

'He thought that Larby would be interested in what he had to say. That Larby's Party researchers might have political intelligence on the EU that was of interest to him. After all, Larby's party wanted to pull out of the EU altogether. If anyone had the dirt on what was going on, they should have.'

'What went wrong?'

'Larby's people didn't seem to have done much homework and didn't throw up much that Helmut didn't already know. And, although he could never prove it, he was convinced Larby secretly shopped him to the SRO.'

'Why the hell should Larby do that?'

'Helmut and Marcus later realized that all the small anti-EU parties were infiltrated. MI5, MI6, I don't know. Even Lord Tebbit said as much. Some say they were set up to draw off all those with extreme views—'

'Extreme views?' I interrupted.

'Meaning thinking the unthinkable. Leaving the EU. New political parties might actually have been set up to draw off these so-called extreme views from the mainstream establishment parties.'

From what I'd studied in intelligence and para–politics matters, this would make a lot of sense. I'd learned so much in recent weeks about what creating a United States of Europe would actually mean, that I could understand why enthusiasts didn't want it discussed by Joe Public. This way it was kept out of popular political debate, by sidelining hardliners into separate tiny parties who were never given a proper voice.

As if echoing my thoughts, Jayne said: 'D'you remember the last European elections? The BBC was bemoaning the lack of decent debate, yet no minor parties with opposite views, the GB-FP and the like, were ever invited onto their discussion shows. Debate anything except leaving the EU. It was a stitch-up.'

'Helmut had no idea?' I asked.

'Not until he told Marcus that he'd contacted Larby. Marcus was furious. I think he realized then that they were on borrowed time. He pressed Helmut for more and more information. Helmut only hinted at this, of course. But I knew he was stressed. He slept badly, and when he did sleep he woke with night sweats. He began drinking more, getting irritable. And our physical relationship, well, it died away . . . You understand?'

I understood all too well and my heart went out to this woman and her late husband. But I had to focus on the here and now. 'Sir Marcus put a lot of store by his last meeting with Helmut,' I assured her. 'Have you any idea what they were going to talk about?'

Jayne sniffed heavily and drew away from Bex, trying to compose herself. 'Marcus wanted the names of those at the top of the EU scams. But Helmut knew that once he gave them he'd have condemned himself. His liaison job at the SRO really would be over. Although he had to be there because the SRO was officially under Europol control, his presence had been resented from the start. Their people always appeared to play the game, but Helmut was always kept at arm's length. Once Marcus published his report containing the names, Helmut's career would be over and we'd probably face litigation and financial ruin. You might have noticed, the EU is bloody ruthless against whistle-blowers.'

'Do you know those names?' I asked. 'The names Sir Marcus wanted from Helmut?'

'There are many,' Jayne replied, 'as you might imagine. But I only know of two. Helmut never mentioned them, but they stuck in my mind. I saw the names repeatedly. On papers left around the house, or on his laptop screen. Someone called Schmitt. Presumably a German.'

Inwardly, I groaned. The German equivalent of Smith! And no first name.

'And an Italian known as "La Lolla",' Jayne added. 'I think that was some sort of nickname, but I imagine it's one that's well known. Like our own Beast of Bolsover.' She pulled a face. 'Not a lot to go on, is it?'

I tried to sound grateful. 'It's better than nothing.'

Jayne shook her head and bit into her lower lip as though having a mental argument with herself. 'I feel so bad about all this. Especially as you two seem to be in such deep trouble . . . But I have to think of the children's future. I keep asking myself what would Helmut want me to do? But he's not here to ask . . .'

Bex moved in with another hug before Jayne broke down again. She was obviously still in shock, and no doubt would be for a long time to come. She sniffed heavily, thanked Bex and struggled to regain her composure. 'Look, when we get to our destination, wherever that is, I'll break the rules and contact you. If I can help in any way that doesn't jeopardize the girls, then I will.'

'That's most kind,' I said – and meant it. I jotted down my personal mobile number. 'I just hope I don't get your call when I'm sitting in a prison cell.'

Jayne forced a little laugh. 'I don't think they let you keep mobiles inside.'

'Hey-ho,' Bex interrupted suddenly, moving briskly to the window. 'Looks like we've got problems.'

I followed her, pulling back the net curtains. Two other landcruisers had pulled up beside the one on the drive. More men in dark suits were spilling out onto the lawn. Automatic pistols were being pulled out and mags checked.

One man was standing out in front of them, issuing instructions. He seemed to be telling them to keep their weapons out of sight. No doubt not wanting to give the removal men the fright of their lives and so generate a lot of unwanted gossip.

Somehow their leader looked familiar. Maybe it was his stance . . . But he was too far away and had his back to me. Then he turned to face the house. I did a double take. Surely not?

'What is it?' Bex asked.

'Who's the boss man?' I asked. 'D'you recognize him?'

She squinted. 'No . . . Oh, wait a minute. Is it?'

I still couldn't believe it myself. Clearing my throat, I said hoarsely: 'Morgan Dampier.'

'Never!' Bex exclaimed. 'It looks a bit like him, but—'

'He said he'd landed a job with Brussels. Security is his line of work.'

'I still can't believe that Morgan . . .'

The men in black suits were spreading out across the lawn, moving towards the house.

I said: 'Maybe Morgan thinks he's on the side of the angels. We've all fooled ourselves on that one before now.' I turned to Jayne Frauss. 'Play this very cool. Go upstairs and stay with your daughters. Help them pack and pretend nothing's amiss. When those bastards get to you, just plead ignorance. We were BT and you last saw us in Helmut's study. They're professional. You and the girls are in no danger if you just stay calm.'

Through the window we could see the men divide into three distinct groups, the largest heading for the house and two smaller parties flanking to the left and right in a pincer movement to cut off our retreat.

'What are you going to do?' Jayne asked.

'Get out through the back garden,' Bex replied.

Jayne nodded. 'Go to the left. There's a kiddies' play centre and a ladder that you can use. An old couple live over the fence and they're rarely in the garden at this time of year.'

Bex was already moving towards the door.

'One thing,' Jayne added. 'You'll be trying to break into the SRO computer system, won't you?'

I quite literally shook my head in surprise. This was one very sharp cookie. Paquet had already raised this problem with us.

Jayne said: 'Helmut's personal password was "Dorothy".'

'Dorothy?' I echoed.

'From *The Wizard of Oz*. My favourite movie. Maybe that will help, maybe not.'

I really warmed to this woman. She was an old-school middle-class Brit down to her sensible Marks & Spencer knickers, someone to whom values and courage still meant something.

Bex grabbed my arm and yanked me towards the door that led into the spacious lounge with its panoramic picture windows. Then we were through the other side into a utility room and out onto a paved patio. Lawn and fish pond and herbaceous borders beckoned. We ran like crazy, scaring birds from the rustic feeding table, and plunged behind the wicker screen to a child's play area with slides and swings in primary-coloured plastic.

I swiped the ladder from the slide and threw it against the wooden boundary fence.

Now I could hear the slap of shoe leather on the garden path behind us. I glanced over my shoulder at the darker shapes emerging from the wicker screen.

'ARMED POLICE!' The voice was breathless. Armed police, bollocks! I thought savagely. A bunch of jumped-up gangsters out of control.

'STOP OR WE SHOOT!'

Rubbish, I decided. They won't risk using firearms unless they've got a positive ID on us. And as far as they knew we were genuine BT telecom engineers. Bex flew up the ladder and hurled herself over the fence.

I heard the familiar whip-crack sound of a 9mm pistol shot. A hole punctured the fence boards just a few inches from my head. Oh shit!

I spun on my heel and followed Bex up the ladder. A second round splintered the top of the fence just beside my hand. If the bastard shooting had the sense to get his breath and draw a proper bead, I was dead. I swung over onto Bex's crouched shoulders and jerked the ladder over after us, tossing it to the ground. As I landed beside Bex, the fence timbers above my head were peppered with flying rounds.

Jesus Christ! Those bastards were shooting blind into a neighouring garden. Any innocent people could be there and they just didn't care.

'HOLD YOUR FIRE!' bawled a distinctly English voice from beyond the fence. I thought it might be Morgan Dampier, but I couldn't be sure. 'YOU FUCKING MORONS!'

For a moment Bex and I sat together on the damp soil in the neighbour's shrub bed and gasped for breath. Then I was up, with Bex in close pursuit. We raced down the crazy-paved path beside a rough winter lawn, past a line of washing and on towards the neighbours' house. I glimpsed two frail figures and startled white faces staring at us through the rear French windows and hoped that we hadn't given anyone a heart attack. Then we were unbolting the side gate and charging into the front garden, beyond which Francoise

Paquet was waiting in the Cortina. Its engine was turning over, ready as instructed.

Bex waved frantically and yelled:'GET OUT! GET OUT!'

I had a job to keep up, she was now so super-fit. What the hell was she playing at? Paquet, startled, finally got the message, opened the driver's door and climbed out. Then I realized: Bex was taking over the driving, reckoning she'd need all her 14 Int driving skills from Northern Ireland.

'In the back!' Bex snapped at Paquet, throwing herself behind the wheel. I zapped around the front of the Cortina, grabbed the passenger door and threw myself in as Bex hit the gas and the tyres began to smoke. We took off like a rocket from a launch pad, my door slamming closed behind me in the slipstream as we accelerated towards the main road.

Like me, Bex clearly expected our path to be blocked by an SRO landcruiser by the time we got there. It wasn't.

She swung left onto the main road, right in front of an innocent passing motorist, forcing him to brake and blast his horn, and was off. When I glanced back moments later, I saw the landcruiser impatiently trying to pass the car immediately behind us. So did Bex. She took the next right, cutting straight through a line of oncoming vehicles. Her adrenalin was pumping, her judgement terrifyingly split-second accurate.

Cars braked and slewed. Smoke rose from burning tyres. Travelling too close to each other, some shunted, but it looked like nothing too serious. We were away, hurtling down country lanes, using both sides of the road to set ourselves up to clear tight bends. Driving to the max, foot to the floor. On the very edge of a very thin safety margin. Just like Northern Ireland, when 14 Int had more casualties in road accidents than from contact with terrorists. It was a white-knuckle ride that Disney execs would give their kidneys for, but it was worth it. Worth every blessed moment for the freedom and life it meant to us.

At every intersection I expected a dark landcruiser to appear, or even a police patrol car; incredibly, they didn't. I wound down my window, put my face into the slipstream and peered skyward at the scudding clouds. I looked ahead and behind us. No helicopters, an empty sky.

Like him or loathe him, Morgan Dampier had always been good at his job. He was always in control, always had been. It was his trade mark. But today Dampier was slipping. Or maybe he'd lost his cutting edge, rusted through lack of practice in recent months. Or else something as simple as a toothache or a hangover had distracted him. I smiled to myself as we put miles of open countryside behind us. Hangover, no doubt.

Whatever reason, he'd lost vital seconds. And his loss had been our gain. We'd escaped the net, for the moment at least. I've often thought that battles and even wars are not won by great strategies and tactics but by the side that makes the least cock-ups.

Today was Dampier's cock-up and we had a few minutes' jump on them, nothing more. Now I had to make sure I didn't follow with a cock-up of my own. But at least we had that jump and, as the slipstream whistled at the open window, I was suddenly overcome with an immense sense of elation.

'No eagles up?' Bex asked.

'No. We've got a clear run.'

'And where are we running to next?' Paquet asked with an edge of frustration to her voice.

'Nowhere,' I decided suddenly. 'I think it's time to stop running.'

Bex glanced sideways at me. 'The best form of defence?'

She was reading my mind again. 'I think so.'

'And what is that?' Paquet asked wearily.

Bex and I answered together. 'Attack.'

*     *     *

I said: 'I think we've seen enough.'

For two days and two nights Bex and I had been observing the compound from the vantage point of a hill some one and a half miles distant. Our concealed observation post was a foxhole in a rabbit run on the fore-edge of a wood. We'd dug it out in the dead of night, erected a roof of chicken wire and relaid the cut turfs of meadow grass over the top.

It had provided us with a perfect view of the headquarters compound of the Special Research Office.

It had taken a bit of detective work to track the place down. The Ordnance Survey map had no 'Home Farm' marked in the area. Only by chatting in a local pub, passing ourselves off as a couple trying to surprise Bex's long-lost parents with news that they were grandparents, did we glean the information that we needed. That a nearby farm had only two years earlier been renamed "Home Farm" – probably the most common name in the country, as every town and village seemed to have one.

The villagers were a bit cautious of us, you could see it in their eyes. But after buying a few rounds, we got the picture. Something funny about it all, they said. It had been sold unexpectedly a couple of years back and strangers had moved in. No one knew the newcomers, they'd never visited the pub or taken part in village affairs, and no one knew of any local labour employed on the land.

'They bus in illegal immigrants,' said one. 'I've seen 'em. Gypos. A minibus each mornin'.'

'No, East Europeans,' corrected another. 'Maybe Poles or Czechs.'

'Slavs,' added someone else. 'My son was in the army and overheard some of them. Serbs or Croats, he reckoned.'

Dog-walkers from the village had noticed the building work going on beyond the existing farm buildings. A two-storey complex with fences and lots of razor wire. No local contractors had been used. The popular currency of gossip had it that it was a secret government centre for testing GM crops.

An old boy in the corner had muttered something about 'Secret Rural Opportunities – Headquarters . . .' Bex had pounced on him before he passed out after half a dozen pints of Scrumpy Jack. Everyone ignored him as the local village soak, but Bex discovered that while out walking his Jack Russell he had seen a small but official-looking sign hidden in the grass off the main road. It read: SRO – HQ.

Then old George had died, metaphorically speaking, in Bex's arms. And we'd felt duty-bound to get him back to his cottage and dump him on his bed.

The next morning Bex had called round to check that George was all right and had offered to take his dog for a walk. She had taken it down the lane past the entrance to Home Farm and had found the SRO – HQ sign. Old George had been right. It was there and quite official-looking, but its positioning was such that no one would ever see it in the undergrowth.

That had been good enough for me.

Our next move had been to head again for a populated built-up area where we could disappear and avoid any SRO men or regular police still searching for us. We had taken the country-lane route through to Ipswich, some forty miles away. Dumping the Cortina on some waste ground at twilight, we had torched it before slinking away into the city's backstreets.

Again we had booked into three separate guest houses before meeting up in a pub to plan our next move.

I said: 'Bex and I are agreed. We'll get nowhere by running – it'll only be a matter of time before we're caught. SRO Headquarters has to hold the answers that we need for our own defence.'

Francoise Paquet was still smoking, in more ways than one. 'Don't I have a say in all this, Eddie?'

'Not if you still want us to give ourselves up,' Bex had countered quickly.

I had thought she was being a bit harsh. Bex and I had run to the wire before, had been used in the past to living on the edge. Paquet was not.

I'd tried to be reassuring. 'As things stand, the three of us are wanted for suspicion of murder under common law. Despite popular belief, political pressure can be applied in law – and we know that powerful people want us silenced. I'd go down for murder and the two of you . . . ? Conspiracy? It's a distinct possibility. They'd be determined to put you away for at least a few years. Prison is a good way to silence people.'

'So breaking into the SRO won't make it worse,' Bex had added, seeing my logic. 'We in Britain have an expression that you might as well be hung for stealing a sheep as a lamb.'

Paquet's eyes were fierce. 'I know that. Yes, all right. But you two are not back in Northern Ireland, remember that. You are suggesting the sort of things that you did there, but then you had official sanction. And professional back-up.'

I'd had to admit she had a big point. Our plan of action *was* a shade gung-ho, and proposing to act alone felt like the prospect of going into battle just wearing your Y-fronts.

But before I could respond, Paquet had said slowly: 'Then *I* will back you up as best I can. If you do manage to break into the SRO Headquarters, you will need evidence of what you find. Photographs or audio recordings – the sort of thing we use in serious investigative journalism.'

I'd offered a light for her umpteenth cigarette. 'I'm listening.'

'Bugs, miniature camera, radio-wave scanners,' she said. 'I will write a list. At least you can buy this stuff commercially now. I am sorry, Eddie – it will cost you.'

And so it had. We had ordered more drinks, then huddled

over a council of war. I think Sir Marcus and Jude would have been proud of us.

The next morning, Paquet had taken a train to London with a big wad of my fast-diminishing blood money. Bex and I had toured army-surplus and outdoor-pursuits shops in Ipswich to buy the essential gear we'd need: camo fatigues, sleeping bags, entrenching tools, woollen hats.

It was becoming quite routine now for Bex and me to hot-wire cars and swap over number plates. This time we'd planned it more carefully, selecting three nondescript vehicles: two saloons and a small van.

The three of us had a rendezvous at a smart hotel in Bury St Edmunds that night. Paquet had decided that this should be her headquarters: she was more comfortable spending my money on a swanky hotel room and posing as a Spaniard than trying to be inconspicuous in seedy bedsits. I had to concede she had a point.

That night, she had deployed Bex and me by van to a road adjoining woodland that overlooked the headquarters of the SRO. It was like old times in Ulster, but slightly less dramatic. In those days we'd have rolled out of the van at speed as it entered dead ground in case some IRA 'dicker' was on watch. This time Paquet had stopped momentarily for us to leap out the back, slam the doors and dive over a wire stock-fence at the roadside before she drove sedately on.

Then we had been on our own, stealing through the trees under a moonless sky. There may have been no threat from gun-toting terrorists, but it hadn't stopped our pulses from racing. When we'd cleared the far side of the wood, we used the small starscope that Paquet had brought back from London in her bag of tricks. Sure enough, we picked out the lights of the SRO Headquarters compound in the surrounding darkness of the farmland. There's nothing worse than digging an OP and then finding it doesn't quite give you a line of sight to the target. Believe me, that happens!

By the time dawn broke we had been quite snug – and utterly exhausted - in our little bunker under the turf among the rabbit warrens. It was a tight fit, but we could expand it a little on subsequent nights, if we could be bothered. But in the end we hadn't.

Eventually we'd spent two days and two nights there, watching and noting comings and goings, trying to get an idea of what might be happening inside. I'd anticipated a few Portakabins inside a wire compound, but it was a proper modern two-storey office building of bricks and mortar that was clearly expecting to be there for some time. There was a security fence but, apart from the razor-wire topping you'd get at any engineering or building depot nowadays, it was nothing special. In fact, we'd inspected it closely on our first night.

The SRO was clearly relying on anonymity rather than conspicuous security measures for its safety. After all, as an outfit that only existed on paper it wouldn't have anticipated any trouble anyway.

The fence wasn't electrified, but it was overseen by CCTV cameras. Low-key security patrols ran intermittently, usually two low-grade security guards on foot who were sometimes accompanied by a dog. They carried holstered weapons but, frankly, I doubted whether they were very well trained in using them.

On the first morning Tony Tromain had turned up and we got him on long-range telephoto. He hadn't looked very happy. In the same frame we got him talking to Morgan Dampier, who appeared to be his usual urbane and unruffled self.

'One for the album,' I'd muttered with satisfaction as I pressed the button.

'Remind me to cross the little shit off my Christmas-card list,' Bex replied.

More informatively, there was a communications tower at one end of the building which sported a plethora of aerials, including a line-of-sight microwave transmission dish. I guessed these plugged into the national defence system. The variety and complexity of the others suggested that the SRO could speak directly to half the globe, if not more.

Our little radio scanner was of more interest as we were able to intercept transmissions between HQ control and what appeared to be various other SRO surveillance operations. MI5 tends to use 'ambulance-' or 'taxi-speak' to throw off eavesdroppers, but the SRO was not yet so coy or sophisticated. It was more blatant – if you knew what you were listening for – but at least it had code words.

After a morning of listening, we'd decided that we were *Emerald*. Thankfully a missing emerald. What was quite unnerving was that they'd actually traced us to Ipswich, although thankfully there the trail had run cold. We got the feeling that, for some reason, we were expected to try to cross to continental Europe. More disconcerting were the number of reports coming in from around the country. It seemed that at least ten two-man teams had sealed off the whole of East Anglia, backed up by local police in many instances.

The only thing that gave us some slight consolation was that someone called *Opal* was giving the shadowmen a run for their money in Belgium and *Amethyst* had disappeared in Potsdam. Less encouraging was the solemn radio report from Portugal that *Topaz* had been "deleted" following an unfortunate road traffic accident. There was a slightly satisfied and ominous tone to the speaker's voice.

Were these other people similar to ourselves? Considered enemies of the new nation state of Europe? That certainly seemed to be the case.

It made me realize how stupid and naive I had been, along with the rest of the population, in not being aware

what it meant to be part of 'the greatest international political experiment of our times'.

After two days, Bex and I reckoned that we'd learned as
much as we could about the layout of the building and
which part was being used for what. We had called Paquet
on the mobile and arranged for her to meet us in the van
at twelve midnight.

It was ten o'clock when it happened. A set of headlights
appeared at the farm gates and moved up the track to the
headquarters compound. It was a Mercedes, heavy on the
suspension. Armour-plated, I suspected. Bullet-headed goons
jumped out to open the rear passenger door and a rather
tall, thin man in an elegant suit stepped out.

I zoomed in with the camera. I was so busy concentrating
on the focus that I didn't register his face.

'Jesus Christ,' I said suddenly.

'What is it?' Bex asked.

'Not what, who?'

'Who, then, Ed?' Bex demanded impatiently.

The motor-drive whirred. 'Domedzic,' I said, not believing
my own words. 'Fucking Domedzic. Fucking Brigadier Milo
Domedzic.'

'That Serb police chief? The one who ordered your Astrid's
execution?'

'The same one I saw talking to Mihac in the café on the
assassination recce,' I said savagely. 'The one Morgan told me
was dead. There can't be two of the bastards on the planet.'

# Sixteen

Just what the hell was going on? What the hell was that smug bastard Domedzic doing at the headquarters of the EU's Special Research Office?

Questions, questions, questions – and no bloody answers. The uncertainty left me in a foul mood for the rest of the day, until we decided to pull out and called up Francoise Paquet on the cellphone to collect us in the van.

To the second, she arrived, pulling up beside the wood. Bex and I vaulted the stock fence, threw open the rear doors and jumped in.

'How was it?' she asked as we pulled away.

'Good,' I replied testily, still in a bad temper. 'We want to go in tomorrow night as originally planned. Saturday night should be quiet and everyone tends to drop their guard at the weekend.'

'You're mad, both of you.'

Bex glanced sideways at me as we lit up our first ciga-rettes for fifty-four hours. 'Probably,' I said.

'Definitely,' Bex confirmed.

Back at Paquet's hotel, after a soak in the bath and a good meal, we met up at a quiet alcove in the bar. I ran quickly through our proposed plan. As a journalist there was very little that Paquet could say, but her expression suggested we'd finally lost all touch with reality. Indeed, I thought later, maybe that's exactly what happens when you serve in the SAS or 14 Int. But it seems to work.

'What about you?' Bex asked. 'Busy on the Internet?'

'Very,' Paquet answered, perhaps more defensively than she'd intended. 'I attacked various EU websites, utilizing programs that journalists use. Not strictly legal but . . . Helmut Frauss's code word eventually got me into one. No wonder his wife wants to play along with them for the sake of her kids' future – she gets eighty per cent of his salary for twenty-five years. Then it drops to sixty per cent. And that salary was a massive forty per cent hike over what he earned as a regular Europol officer. And his widow's pension deal . . . phenomenal.'

Bex nodded sagely. 'It fits the SRO's recruitment pattern.'

'And those names you gave me,' Paquet added. '"La Lolla"' is the nickname of the Italian tabloids for Giovanni Bestelloli. He's from one of the southern Italian states, a minor aristocrat. Always been involved in local politics and became an MEP. There is much local controversy, accusations of Mafia links. He was charged and taken to trial twice in the 1970s, charged with embezzlement and fraud while in local government office. A judge is murdered mid-trial and a second judge directs the jury to exonerate him.'

'The seventies?' I asked.

Paquet nodded. 'There was another trial. More recent, in the nineties – when he is an MEP. Bigger issues this time – involvement in murder of business rivals connected with EU subsidies. Interestingly, at his trial the prosecution tried to make something of his ties with burgeoning East European mafias, but the evidence was flimsy. The case collapsed. He seems to be untouchable.'

'So what's his involvement with the SRO?' Bex asked.

'An offical website lists him only as Chairman of one of the EU's many oversight committees. I know from Marcus's dossier that this is the one to which the SRO must report. In other words, this committee is the chief conduit between the executive and the EU Commission. But it's all in the small print. I doubt whether anyone knows of its real function and La Lolla is in a perfect position to tell the Commissioners exactly what they want to hear.'

'And Schmitt?' I pressed.

Paquet now looked like the cat that got the cream. 'One Herman J. Schmitt, I think. Very interesting. Listed as Director – top man – of the Special Research Office. Seemingly a German Home Office adviser. But on investigation I find he was a former senior officer within the Stasi – the old East German secret police and espionage service.'

I lit another Gauloise. This was a case of the lunatics running the asylum. 'So we have an MEP with – admittedly unproven – Italian and East European mafia links advising the EU Commission on the activities of an out-of-control security apparatus headed by a former Stasi secret policeman?'

'In a nutshell,' Paquet confirmed. 'But there's more. On finance.'

'Finance?' Bex queried.

Paquet shrugged. 'When I looked at Helmut Frauss's personal financial package using his code word, I saw that in addition to his pension, he had an ongoing financial provision – a regular monthly deduction for immediate investment. And it was remarkably effective! Beat the FTSE and Nasdeq hands down! I only wish my stock-brokers on the *Bourse* were half as good! The profits might not be tax-free, but at those rates who cares . . .'

High finance had always been a mystery to me. 'Meaning what?'

'It must be a fraud,' Paquet said. 'A portion of a fantastic salary is taken monthly for an investment plan of which no details are given. It pays huge dividends. On top of that, the pension benefits are beyond belief.'

'Who runs the investment plans?' I asked.

Again Paquet looked smug. 'Zepyhr Investments looked

after Helmut Frauss's package. Based in the Dutch Antilles in the Caribbean, as it happens the heart of drug-smuggling country. Maybe that bit is coincidence . . . But do I have to spell it out? Be a loyal servant to the SRO and you are incredibly well looked after. It's not an offer many would refuse.' She took a breath. 'And when I checked the personnel files of those people Marcus listed as collaborators – across all the EU departments – almost everyone donates part of his or her salary regularly to a Zepyhr Investment package.'

Now I understood. 'So that's how the SRO controls its empire?'

Paquet stubbed out her cigarette in the ashtray. 'Bribery. Play ball with the SRO and you're invited to invest in Zephyr with spectacular results – and, because of its Dutch Antilles status, the company does not have to explain to anyone how these profits are achieved. Yet, as a Dutch possession, the islands are legally considered as being within the EU.'

'Handy,' I mused.

And, as I thought, a faint bell began to ring in my mind. A few nights ago when we had followed Tromain back to the headquarters of Asset Assessment and Personnel Pan-Europa, one of the other companies listed as having offices in the building had been Zephyr Investment and Insurance Strategies of Zurich.

'Who's behind Zephyr?' I asked.

'That's interesting,' Paquet replied. 'I searched but could find no official company website. Half a dozen references pop up on the search, mostly financial pages just referring to Zephyr's existence, with guarded critical comments. Like how it is secretive, unaccountable, that sort of thing. Then one personal site by what seems like an insider with a grudge. Probably an ex-employee.'

This sounded interesting. 'And?'

'The site not only makes accusations of the investment bank's dubious involvement in various EU funding projects but also lists the directors at the time.' Paquet looked directly at me. 'They include Herman J. Schmitt and Giovanni Bestelloli.'

'What d'you mean?' I asked '*At the time?*'

'The website is obsolete. Its server went bankrupt four years ago. The site is out there, spinning in the ether like a defunct satellite. So much cyberspace junk.'

'And the man who put the site up in the first place?' Bex asked.

'A woman, actually,' Paquet replied. 'At first I thought the story might be relevant to us. That she might be able to help. She was a Belgian national. Once an executive in the EU auditor's office. She'd been sacked for speaking out. It was very, very difficult, but I tried to track her down.'

Bex's eyes widened. 'And?'

'She's dead. She was knocked down by a hit-and-run driver in Bruges four years ago. About the time that the server crashed when its bank unexpectedly withdrew its credit from a supposedly booming young IT company.'

A cold hand seemed to place itself on the nape of my neck. I gave an involuntary shiver. 'This isn't circumstance or happenstance,' I muttered. 'This just confirms what we're up against.'

Paquet stared at me. 'Marcus knew, but none of us really believed him. I know I didn't.'

Bex looked uncomfortable. 'Jude and I joked about it.'

I kept quiet. I'd been no better.

Then Paquet dropped her bombshell. 'Eddie, if we stay in this country *nous sommes dans la merde.* '

'In the shit,' I translated helpfully.

'We are all in deep trouble and we need help.' Paquet hesitated, alternating her glance between Bex and me. 'I've taken steps. I have contacts in Washington. US senators who believe the EU is trying to drive a wedge between America and Europe, Britain in particular. Our politicians in France make little secret of the fact. These US senators are willing to help us.'

My mouth dropped. 'What?'

Paquet came back quickly, defensively. 'We are going to die, Eddie, don't you see that? You, me and Bex. A term in jail will be the best we can hope for. I'm sure these people will prefer to see us dead, if they have half a chance. Marcus warned us and we laughed. Like everyone in Europe, we laughed at the silly EU and its bureaucratic nonsense. Now we know different. It's a power-driven monster that is out of control.'

I could hardly deny that, given our recent experiences. 'But how the hell can a bunch of right-wing American senators help?'

'They are arranging a boat for us,' she said quickly. 'On Monday. To meet us off the shore when you return from the SRO headquarters. A chartered fishing boat. It will take us out of European waters to Norway and they will fly us to the US. The senators will present any evidence we have on an international stage. Media conferences and then publication on a website. Then the public, the politicians, will *have* to listen.'

I glared back at her. 'You're talking CIA.'

She gave one of her sexy shrugs. 'Sure – so what? Britain is the best ally the US has, maybe the only one. They cannot afford to lose you, have your country sucked into a rival and antagonistic superstate. The stakes are high for them, too.'

There was a brief silence, broken by Bex. 'So you haven't just been on the Internet?'

'I had to make some calls.' Paquet gave a patronizing smile. 'Do not worry – I used my pay-as-you-go cellphone.'

Now I saw where Bex was coming from. 'Who exactly did you telephone?'

'A very trusted colleague on *Televu-News*, but I called him at home to be safe. He had e-mail addresses and telephone numbers that I did not have with me. Then I spoke to some of the Americans . . .' Her voice trailed off as she saw the expression on my face. 'I do not understand. What is the matter?'

I said: 'Fran, we are at the top of the SRO's most-wanted list. All three of us. There's no doubt the DST – like our MI5 – will be acting on their behalf to monitor e-mails and phone lines to all our relatives, friends and associates. Calling your colleague at home was probably worse than calling him in a busy office where there is at least a torrent of comms traffic.' I tried to stop myself from sounding too angry. 'I think your virgin cellphone has just had sex on an international scale.'

Paquet frowned, trying to understand my bad pun. 'I did not realize. I'm sorry.'

'I'd be very surprised if your number isn't now compromised,' I added. 'Police and intelligence agencies in this country can get details of all your telephone and e-mail contacts from the server companies without even needing a court order. Then they have other ways of reading the actual contents.'

'But I thought—'

'E-mail was safe?' I shook my head. 'Nor are cellphones. Once they have your number, they can actually pinpoint your location by land transmission and satellite data to within a hundred metres.'

Paquet's face paled. 'I seem to vaguely remember reading that—'

'Today,' I said, 'for people like us, there is no hiding place.'

Bex suddenly reached across the table and touched my arm. 'Time to go to the bar, lover boy.' There was an unmistakable urgency in her voice. She was trying to indicate something with her eyes. I caught the reflection in the dining-room mirror and saw the swarthy individual in the dark suit beyond the door in the hotel foyer.

Oh, shit!

I turned to Paquet. 'You made all these calls from your room?'

'No, from the van.'

'Where in the van?'

'The car park. I did not want to risk being overheard.'

'This car park?'

She now realized that something was wrong, saw the mirror I was watching and gave a shallow gasp. '*Mon Dieu*, Eddie, I am so sorry. They have got a fix on one of the calls.'

I tried to sound calm. 'Have you kept all the equipment kit in the van, like I told you?'

'Yes, yes. Only my case and some clothes are in the room.'

I'd already seen the need that we might have to move on in a hurry, but not quite like this.

'The bar,' Bex repeated. 'It's very busy just now. And there's a fire exit to the car park.'

'Fran, go with Bex. Leave now. I'll join you in a few moments.'

They rose silently and moved towards the far end of the dining room. I tried to stop my hand trembling as I reached for the remaining brandy in my glass and swallowed it. It burned my throat but I hardly noticed. I lit a cigarette and picked up the tab. It was on Paquet's room account. She'd registered as a Mrs Juanita Jones, a Spaniard married to an Englishman, and had paid cash in advance for four days. That raised an eyebrow, but money was money and no impolite questions were asked. It would take the SRO's men in black a while to sort out the link with the cellphone calls and Paquet's room number and true identity.

Another figure appeared reflected in the mirror. Tall and lean. He turned a fraction and I then saw the thin face and

hawklike eyes that would be etched in my mind until the
end of time. Milo Domedzic.

It was definitely time to go.

I swivelled around in my chair until I had my back to
the foyer, then rose to my feet and began walking slowly
towards the entrance to the bar.

From nowhere a wine waiter appeared alongside me. 'Not
more brandy, sir?'

I shook my head. 'No, thank you.' Terse.

'Was everything all right for sir and the ladies?'

'Fine, fine, thank you.' Then I realized. I stopped and
opened my wallet. Typical – nothing smaller than a twenty!
I thrust the note into the waiter's grubby little palm and
moved on.

I stepped into the bar and was immediately swallowed up
in the noise and body heat of the overcrowded room with
its boisterous party of sales reps celebrating the end of a
conference. With the day's work over, the men were interested only in drinking and getting a leg over with the female
colleagues they'd been chatting up all week. And the women
seemed to have a similar determined intent.

Bex and Paquet were nowhere to be seen, but I saw the
gentle tell-tale billowing of the net curtains at the far end
of the panoramic picture windows. I could feel the welcome
rush of cool air. I weaved through the crowd and ducked
out into the night. The two women were already in the
white van, Bex in the driver's seat.

'Where to?' she asked as I climbed in.

'Anywhere,' I replied tersely. 'Let's just get out into the
sticks.'

There were no police cars around the hotel entrance, but
there were a couple of dark-coloured landcruisers that were
typically SRO. That in itself was a little surprising. Did it
mean that now the SRO had the scent it was keen to be
out on its own? Without the legal restraints of the local

constabulary's presence, I had little doubt now how dangerous they could be.

There was another landcruiser parked up by the hotel's driveway entrance, but we boldly drove straight past it on the basis that they couldn't yet know what vehicles they might be looking for. At the moment, they were just hunting for one of us who'd made cellphone calls from the hotel's location.

The two occupants scowled at our van suspiciously but could only see Bex, whose face was shadowed by the peak of a baseball cap.

Once again my impression of the men looking at us was of their dark, Slavic features. I couldn't help the chilling sensation that I was back in Bosnia-Herzegovina.

After driving for half an hour, we pulled into a countryside lay-by, opened the local Ordnance Survey map and discussed our options.

Finally I said: 'Right, there's a small private woodland a couple of miles from here. That's where we'll spend the night. This van's been seen and could be compromised. We'll pick up our two cars, torch this van, and head for the wood. Agreed?'

There were no dissenters. We picked up the Renault estate and Volvo saloon – with their switched plates – from their respective parking places on public streets. Then our three-vehicle convoy returned to the lay-by, where we doused the van with petrol and set it alight. We hightailed away in the two cars and parked up in a village near the wood before setting off on foot with rucksacks to complete our journey.

By two in the morning we'd strung a camouflaged bivvy sheet between the trees and had crashed out in second-hand Israeli army sleeping bags.

It was almost nine before I came to the next morning. If you're warm and dry – and not squeezed into an underground OP – there's nothing more magical and relaxing than sleeping in the open. Bex and Paquet were already up, squatting beside the billycan on the gas burner. Bex looked comfortable and at home, whilst Paquet, wrapped up in scarves and a hat so she was beginning to resemble a bag lady, wore a slightly bewildered expression. It was strange to see that beautiful face smudged with dirt and without make-up. Quite beguiling, I thought.

'Mornin', Rip van Winkle,' Bex greeted. 'Want porridge or porridge?'

I wriggled out of the sleeping bag. 'Better settle for porridge. Any apple flakes?'

'What you think this is, the Ritz?'

I turned to Paquet. 'Never been camping before?'

She recognized the mockery in my eyes and smiled. 'No, Eddie, and I don't intend to ever again. My back is so stiff. I think I slept on a tree root.'

Well, once a townie, always a townie.

After eating, we sat around and planned our operation for that night. Our objective was quite simple: gain entry around midnight, snoop around as best we could and see if there was anywhere suitable to leave a microphone and transmitter or the digital mini-cam that Paquet had brought back from London in her bag of goodies. Then we'd get out before the day shift of security staff arrived. During the week this was at seven, but it might well be later over a weekend.

What we couldn't know yet was what the operational manning levels would be like. From our observations, Bex and I had identified offices in which the lights always seemed to be on, throughout the night. One seemed to be a large operations room, because we could see maps on the wall and various computer workstations. Then there was an office near the front entrance that appeared to be the security staff's restroom. Apart from that an odd light might be on in one or two different offices, suggesting that SRO executives took turns to be duty officer on some sort of rota. Our enlightened guess was that this would be the same pattern over a weekend, although maybe scaled down a little.

In the early afternoon we broke camp and made our way back to our parked cars in the village. Then we split up, Paquet taking the Volvo to look for a new B&B to double as our communications centre while Bex and I took the Renault estate into Cambridge for some shopping at a back-street DIY shop. Our list included heavy-duty bolt-cutters, a hand drill, ropes and a roll-up fire-escape ladder with a fifteen-foot drop.

By five we all met up at a country pub. Paquet had found herself a farmhouse doing bed-and-breakfast before driving many miles away to use her compromised cellphone to finalize arrangements with her friends in the United States. As soon as she'd finished, she hit the road to get away from her transmission location. It seemed to work because she reported she'd had no problems with police or the SRO's men in black.

'My American friend was about to suggest an RV point, but I stopped him,' Paquet said. 'He said it's a beach they've got earmarked for covert landings, if ever . . . I think he was joking.'

That was food for thought. If ever a British resistance movement needed to overthrow the authority of an EU superstate. Suddenly it didn't seem so ridiculous.

'There'll be a boat called the *Kari* out of Fredrikstad stationed a mile offshore. At eight-hour intervals, she'll be in position for one hour, starting at 0600 hours. She must apppear to keep on the move. She won't have her nets down.'

'Meaning?' Bex asked.

'She can't be charged with illegal fishing. If she's asked, she's just recceing waters and fishing possibilities. If they're stopped *after* we turn up, they'll say they just rescued us from a sinking boat in good faith – *if* they're stopped.'

Meaning if we were caught, the US would drop us in it to sink or swim. Nothing new there, then.

Paquet added: 'So I said I'd call on a new virgin cellphone to confirm the RV at the last moment, just like you said.'

Hopefully her American CIA friends would get the picture. There'd be a lot of last-minute telephone number switching so the message couldn't be traced. It was an old but effective method, but then the East Anglian coast wasn't that big and the chances of our escape didn't appear that promising.

But such worries were for the future and the last things on our minds as Paquet drove Bex and me towards the perimeter of Home Farm at nine o'clock that Saturday evening.

It was a rainy night, blustery and as black as evil so you couldn't see more than a few yards ahead. As a result there was virtually no traffic on the roads and we encountered nothing on our run along the perimeter road by the woods. Paquet pulled up smoothly and wished us '*Bon chance*' as we piled out, took our kit from the back of the estate car and jumped the stock fence into the shelter of the trees. We watched for a moment as the tail lights were swallowed up in the grim, wet darkness.

As soon as Bex and I cleared the other side of the wood, overlooking the distant SRO compound, we knew that something was amiss. Every shrub and gorse clump that could offer cover had gone. Charred patches of branch debris suggested that it had been systematically cut and burnt within the past twenty-four hours.

Rainwater was dripping off Bex's face onto her sodden anorak. 'Fran's telephone calls?'

It was a rhetorical question. You didn't have to be a rocket scientist to envisage the sequence of events. The French DST monitors calls to her colleague on *Televu-News Expresse*, following an SRO request that it is obliged to comply with under European law. Paquet's virgin mobile number is checked against geostationary communications satellites to give a fix. It shows that she's still in the area. That means that Eddie Coltrane and Bex Bunnet probably are too. And they could be trouble.

Alarm bells and precautionary measures are urgently put into place. Maybe Morgan Dampier hadn't lost his touch after all.

As it happened, the loss of obvious cover didn't make much difference to us. It just meant that we had to be a bit more careful and take a little longer to get to our abandoned OP, moving more slowly and making better use of dead ground.

We approached it very cautiously, in case it had been compromised or even booby-trapped. But it was just a patch of winter meadow grass, in the middle of open country, not using any shrubs or other more obvious aids to concealment. Once again, the tried and tested SAS methods going back decades had proved their worth.

Slithering uncomfortably into a wet muddy puddle, we grimaced and grinned at each other. It was like going back in a time warp to a world that you thought you'd left behind for ever. Amazingly, it was like we'd never been away. As always the job came first, so we just got on with it.

Of course we were cutting corners. Instead of a couple of days, we were taking the trouble to restudy the target for just a couple of hours and listen in on the scanner until midnight. But it paid dividends.

Bex, examining the compound through our commercial image-intensifying telescope, made the first major discovery. She was mumbling her observations while I scribbled them down on a waterproof pad. 'Opposition deployment at 2330 hours,' she intoned. 'Guards patrolling the perimeter in twos now appears constant, therefore must have doubled. Safe interval for approach down to fifteen minutes – ten to be safe. A dog in evidence, a German Shepherd . . . Looks composed, well trained. Maybe Brit police or military . . . Oh, shit, how did I miss that!'

I glanced up from the tiny pool of illumination from my penlight. 'What?'

She checked herself, kicking back into her half-forgotten military mode. 'Opposition guards now appear to be carrying sub-machine guns.'

I frowned, wondering how these people were able to defend themselves in law? 'Same personnel?'

'Sure, same people as before. Then it was black overalls and leather jacket tops. Tonight it's black or dark blue waterproof smock tops.' Bex slithered back down into the muddy ditch beside me. 'This feels weird, Ed. Like you say, with a heightened state of alert, if anything I'd expect armed cops like at New Scotland Yard or the airports. Not these people. Somehow it doesn't feel like it's this country.'

Various things Sir Marcus had said to me, various dark warnings came flooding back to me. 'Maybe it isn't any more.'

'Do we still go ahead?'

The stakes had just been raised. Instead of a relatively passive target, we were facing an increasingly armed opposition. Of unknown quality and professionalism. An opposition who knew how to kill and get away with it. Who seemed beyond our current laws – or maybe just knew how to manipulate them. Bex and I had both seen enough of that in the dirty wars of Ulster.

I hesitated for a moment. 'I wouldn't ask you to do anything I wouldn't do myself.'

Bex stared at me for a moment, her face wet and streaked with running cam cream. Then she gave a throaty laugh. 'For fuck's sake, Ed. You're not my DS any more. Do we go or not?'

I still didn't want to pressure her. 'What d'you say?'

'For Jude's sake, Ed, I say let's go.'

I couldn't suppress my grin. 'Attagirl.'

We opened up a link between our mobiles, using the hands-off rigs, then I set off down the hill alone while Bex kept watch from the OP. It was slow and uncomfortable work. Leopard-crawling in sodden grass was something I thought I'd left behind when I'd quit the army, and my body agreed – with every throbbing muscle and strained sinew. I inched along, using every available stretch of dead ground and area of shadow thrown out as a result of the compound lights.

Halfway down the slope, Bex called me to a halt while a patrol went past on the inside of the perimeter fence.

There were two men and a dog, although I doubt the animal would have been able to scent much in this downpour. The guards certainly seemed more alert than when we'd been watching them earlier in the week. Suddenly the dog stopped and growled in my direction, although it couldn't actually have been me it had detected. Maybe a fox was slinking by.

But both men paid heed, one shining a powerful torch-beam over the rough meadow grass while the other lifted his sub-machine gun in readiness. The guard was too far away for me to be able to identify the weapon type, but it was a salutary warning that the stakes had now been raised dangerously high.

The dog lost interest and so did the men, moving on down the line and rounding the corner of the building, out of sight. I began wriggling forward again for several minutes until I reached the shallow depression I had targeted from our OP. It was a short distance from the razor-topped fence and offered some minimal cover. I then took over as observer while Bex wormed her way down the slope, following the same line that I had taken.

Halfway down I stopped her, as the other two sentries, this time without a dog, came round the corner of the building from the opposite direction. When they had passed, I gave her the all-clear.

Minutes later she joined me in the depression and we peered through the fringe of tall winter grass at the nearest section of fence. We decided on an area that was in relative shadow. It was barely twenty feet away, so that when the guards came patrolling it was only a short distance to scurry back to the shelter of the depression.

Taking the bolt-cutters, I slid over the rim and crawled to the edge of the fence. To be suddenly exposed like this was nerve-racking and I was out of practice. I could hear the blood rushing in my ears as my heart thudded like the pistons of an old train. Working as fast as I could, I shoved the nose of the cutters into the fence and began snapping a line along the criss-crossed wire.

Bex called me back as I'd almost finished the L-shaped cut. I returned to the cover of the depression just as the dog team came into view. It was a tense few moments as they approached. But, despite my presence moments earlier, this time the animal showed no interest whatsoever. Given the continuing downpour, I wasn't unduly surprised. It was nevertheless a great relief to see them disappear again.

We reckoned we had ten minutes before the next patrol, so there was no time to lose. This time we both went forward, carrying everything we needed in two small back-packs. I peeled back the eighteen-inch wire flap for Bex to slip through, then followed her. Once through, I closed the gap and held it back in place with small twists of thin green garden wire. It was fiddly work with wet, numb fingers in the cold rain, but it was worth it. Short of a close-up examination, no one would spot it in these weather conditions.

But eight of our minutes were already up. Bex sprinted

into the shadowy lee of a flat-roofed annexe that, judging by the outside plumbing, we'd figured housed either lavatories or a shower section. Bex threw her back against the wall and cupped her hands together at crotch height in front of her. As she did so, I reached her, lifting one muddy boot into her cradled foothold and using it to spring up to the first of the down pipes, which provided an easy climb to the top where I struggled to hoist myself up and over onto the flat roof.

There I was in the full face of the squall that blasted down the valley off the North Sea and I found it difficult to balance as I unfurled the fire-escape ladder for Bex to use, carrying both our backpacks of equipment. Once she was up, we sat together on the roof as the wind tried its best to dislodge us.

Barely had we caught our breath when the next patrol rounded the far end of the building.

We pressed ourselves flat against the roof, with the rain pounding relentlessly on our backs. It seemed an age before the crunch of boots on gravel passed by below us and faded away.

Then we were up and across the roof to the main body of the building.

People spend thousands protecting properties, giving attention to doors and windows and then outside fencing, various alarm systems and CCTV cameras. Few ever think of the most vulnerable part of their home – the roof. Lift a tile or two, cut the roofing felt and you're in.

We used these methods extensively in Northern Ireland in dense housing estates against both Provo and Loyalist terrorist suspects. In older terraced houses, an entire row might share the same loft. So you could make your entry in the home of an innocent party at one end of the street to gain access to a terrorist's house at the other. Sometimes this was done to plant monitoring devices on behalf of units of Army Intelligence, or MI5 or the RUC Special Branch, or to mount an OP against a nearby target.

Of course, the method had its shortcomings, especially the need to step only on joists and not put a foot through someone's ceiling. And I know that happened at least once, when an oppo of mine actually did it that and landed in the bath of the naked teenage daughter of a terrorist suspect. He was wearing a blue boiler suit and claimed, unconvincingly, to be a plumber as he made a hasty, limping exit through the bathroom door with the poor bemused girl staring after him.

Luckily for him, her Da was away 'on business' that night. That particular OP was abandoned immediately, of course, but the soldier got constant ribbing during his months off sick with a bad back. When I last saw him, years after the event, he was still known as 'Peeping Tom' Watkins.

But tonight Bex and I were faced with heavy concrete tiles, about eighteen inches square. They were heavier to manoeuvre, but we only needed to clear four to access. Within five minutes we'd slit the waterproof membrane underneath with a Stanley knife and dropped through into the loft area.

The beams from our head-torches scanned across the loft space. It was completely covered in panels of plywood to which polystyrene foam had been glued for insulation. I inspected the nearest of these, prising it up to find that each panel rested in a framework of L-shaped aluminium struts. Beneath was a utility space above the false ceilings on the offices and corridors below. There was a confusing criss-crossed trail of electrical wiring to various power points for lighting and computer operations.

Bex nudged me in the ribs and pointed. Following her gaze I saw that one of the insulated plywood panels had been roughly painted blue. Warily I tested my weight before advancing. They wouldn't have withstood a clog dance, but the aluminium support struts seemed strong enough to walk on gently. This blue panel was fitted with a simple chrome grab-handle to facilitate lifting. I tried it and was rewarded by the sight of a ceiling access hatch immediately below.

I said: 'Let's take a look-see.'

Bex agreed and helped me shift the panel as quietly as possible. We listened intently for any sound from below but the rattle of the rain from the gap we'd left in the roof tiles made that difficult. At last I prised the handle of the hinged hatch up against the spring-loaded catch. It gave way with a faint click. Lying flat with my head pressed against the hatch edge, I was able to get a slanted view into the area below.

In fact the hatch was positioned over the entrance of a very plush men's washroom. That would make sense, of course, because it was above one end of the ablutions annexe that we had just scaled.

There was a gleaming, dark blue tiled floor immediately below and a row of fitted washbasins facing a long wall mirror. We'd already estimated that there were no more than a dozen people on duty. Eight of those were security guards and we were fairly certain that they had their own kitchen and toilet facilities near the building entrance. After all, it figured that in a secretive outfit like the SRO the executives wouldn't want security lowlife wandering through their offices willy-nilly or using their fancy washroom.

'This'll do,' I said. 'Let's go.'

I dropped down through the hatch until my feet landed on the long washbasin cabinet. Bex followed down immediately, straight into my arms, and pulled the hatch shut behind her. I lowered her to the floor and jumped down beside her. It was an eerie, unnerving experience. The two of us alone in the heart of the enemy camp, so to speak.

It was all the more bizarre seeing our own crouched

reflections wearing sodden camouflaged fatigues and balaclavas and staring back at us from the washroom mirrors.

A sudden rush of noise came from the annexe and we
both froze.

It took a moment to realize . . . Stupid. 'Automatic flush,'
I said.

We peered down into the annexe with its long row of
best-china urinals on the left and smart dove-blue cubicles
on the right.

Bex began to chuckle.

'What?' I asked angrily.

'Look at the state of us,' she said, glancing in the mirrors.

I wasn't in the mood to see the funny side. I was on edge,
jumpy.

And it didn't help when I heard the sudden click of the
door handle at the entrance to the washrooms behind me.

Christ, this wasn't happening! But it was.

Even as I twisted on my heel to meet the threat, I saw
the door swing open and the uniformed security guard staring
at us in disbelief. So that was one of our theories rubbished.

It was like the three of us had stepped into a bad dream
and simultaneously woken up to find that it wasn't. It was
real.

His right hand swung to his left. Down across his body
to the holstered automatic pistol.

# Seventeen

As the security guard went for his weapon, Bex and I reacted on trained reflex.

Being lighter and faster Bex got there first, launching herself at him with full force and head-butting him in the stomach. The impact threw him back against the cubicle doorpost. I arrived a split second later, twisting the automatic from his right hand with my left. Simultaneously I scissored his neck inside my right elbow and jerked back, hard. I felt the neck bones at the top of his spine snap. The sound was frighteningly loud.

His body went limp instantly, his eyes rolled up to the whites and he fell away from my grasp to slump onto the tiles like a Guy Fawkes dummy.

Bex stepped back like she'd been burnt. 'Fuck, Ed! You've killed him.'

I stared down at my involuntary handiwork – I'd taken a man's life without even thinking – and felt the sickness and horror of what I'd done. Self-disgust churned my innards like a clenched fist. This wasn't war and this poor fucker was just an innocent security guard doing his job. Probably a retired military or civilian cop with a wife and kids. Well, widow and kids now. And it was all down to me. I'd killed him.

'For Christ's sake, Ed,' Bex was blathering. 'We're supposed to be making our situation better, not worse.'

'Shut the fuck up!' I snapped. I was furious – angry with

myself, not with her. I was trying desperately to think some rationality into this. 'It was him or us. He was armed, we're not.'

She glared at me through the eyeholes of her balaclava.

As a justifying afterthought, I added: 'He's SRO. Now let's not argue and get things sorted.' We had to get a grip on this situation. 'Help me get his body into this cubicle.'

We worked in silent, seething unison and sat the guard's limp body unceremoniously on the toilet seat.

I was angry about something else, too. For not realizing that we couldn't just waltz through the building looking like a couple of terrorists without begging things to go pear-shaped.

'If we're seen dressed like this, we've had it,' I said hoarsely. 'Let's dump the kit and at least look like we could belong here.'

'Like we're ready for a tramps' ball?' Bex replied.

'Dress-down Friday,' I snapped back. 'Or whatever the Yanks call it. It's all the rage over here now. And this is Saturday. Anything has to be—'

'Better than this,' she agreed at last.

We dumped our sodden outer clothes with the corpse in the cubicle. I took his personal radio, a bunch of manual and swipe-card keys and his automatic, a familiar 9mm Browning, which I stuffed into my waistband.

Bex looked fetching in a figure-hugging Royal Marine's navy woolly-pully and olive cargo pants, her hair tied back in a ponytail. I felt under-dressed in black T-shirt, jeans and several days' growth of beard.

'This isn't going to work,' I said.

Magically, Bex produced a comb from nowhere and ran it through my tangled, matted hair, straight back over my scalp so that Jack Nicholson was staring back at me from the mirrors on all sides. Complete with the expression of a restrained maniac.

'Faith in what you are, Ed,' she said. 'That's what you used to teach me. We're here, we're part of the SRO, we belong.'

Christ, I'd taught her well. She was bloody well right. The sorcerer's apprentice was already taking over. 'Well, you don't belong in the gents' lav. Let's get out.'

The sudden bleeping signal on my belt made me start. I snatched up the security guard's radio, sweat breaking out on the back of my neck.

'*Hal, do you copy?*' the voice said in my ear. It had some sort of mid-European accent. '*Rudy here.*'

'I copy, Rudy,' I replied.

'*How you getting on? A bit confusing first time, eh? Where are you?*'

'Gents' washroom. First floor.'

'*Second floor,*' Rudy corrected. '*We use the American reference system. Ground is first, et cetera . . . Anything unusual?*'

My stomach tensed involuntarily. 'No. No one here. Why?'

'*Infra-red sensors on the roof in that area started bleeping . . .*' Oh shit, I thought. '*Guards couldn't see anything. I expect it's the atmospherics from this friggin' weather. Security's too bloody high-tech for its own good. I've over ridden it to stop the bloody noise. We'll get the technicians to check it out in the morning.*'

'Fine,' I muttered non-committally.

'*Do me a favour, Hal, while you're in the area?*'

'What's that?'

'*Open up the main conference facility. Know where that is? Just keep going to the end of the corridor. It's on your left before the Control Room. Guess you were shown it on induction.*'

'Sure,' I said.

'*And sweep the room, will you? The equipment's just behind the door. You can do that, can't you, you being an ex MoD policeman? The sheet's ticked that you were shown on induction.*'

'No problem,' I assured Rudy, not quite believing that I was getting away with this.

'Some unexpected big bananas arriving from Brussels. Private flight. Better get a move on, because they'll be here in twenty minutes or so . . .'

'On my way,' I said, and clicked off.

I told Bex what the security controller, Rudy, had said. She pointed at the dead guard. 'Put his uniform on,' she suggested.

It was a bright idea, except that Hal was a size or two smaller than me. I'd never stripped off a still-warm corpse before and dressed in its clothes. It's not an experience I'd ever want to repeat. I felt quite nauseous by the time I'd finished, with the trousers at half-mast and Hal's hat perched precariously on top of my head.

We'd already lost another five minutes. I replaced the hat on the dead man's head, locked myself in the cubicle with him, then vaulted over the partition to rejoin Bex.

I led the way out of the washroom and into the corridor. As we'd assumed from the outside it ran the entire length of the corridor. There was no hiding place.

To our left, the longest stretch ran all the way back to a utility lift and a stairwell at the front of the building. This was the upper floor and, presumably, the most secure. There were office doors on both sides, each with a secure-code press-pad and swipe-card lock.

But, some thirty yards down, the passageway was blocked by polished teak double doors, which were held fast by more heavy-duty electronic locks.

'That's the Control Room,' I said.

Bex nodded. We'd viewed it from our OP, studied the workstations, computers and radio transmission equipment. It was situated immediately under the building's communications tower with its array of aerials, so it had been easy for us to make such an inspired guess.

'The conference facility must be the door next to it on the left,' I said, moving quickly along the grey carpet of the corridor.

Suddenly one of the double doors in front of me opened. A tall man in his mid-thirties stepped out. I froze in my tracks. He called back to someone in the Control Room. I did a double take. He'd asked his question and been answered by someone inside speaking Serbo-Croat.

Then he laughed without humour and shut the door behind him.

As he turned he noticed us standing there. His black hair had a modern, close-cropped cut and dark mirthless eyes regarded me from a sallow face. The features were distinctly Slavic.

'Haven't seen you before,' he remarked to me in a less than friendly tone.

'First day,' I answered.

He peered at the fuzzy ID picture of security guard Hal Williams pinned to my chest. 'What's happened to your moustache? You don't look anything like your picture.'

I tried making light of it, and took a gamble. 'Like passport photographs,' I replied in Serbo-Croat and could see he was slightly taken aback, 'we all look like serial killers.'

He scowled at that. Maybe that was exactly what he was. So I added: 'A shaving rash.'

He pulled back, a disapproving sneer on his face. Obviously he was someone who liked to have the last word. 'You should always wear a cap.'

I shrugged. 'Didn't have my size in stock. Big head, see.'

He shifted his gaze to Bex, clearly not sure about her military sweater and combat pants. 'And you?'

Oh, shit, I thought. She had no ID tag.

But Bex didn't even blink. She tugged a small wallet from her jeans pocket and flipped it open. 'Jane Rawlings. Security Service.'

I nearly choked at her audacity. This was one of the false identity passes she and Jude had used in their business that she *hadn't* told me about – MI5.

I was proud of her, although the Security Service has one of the least impressive and most easily duplicated IDs, little more than a sealed computer printout with no crests or other ostentation.

But the man's reaction wasn't exactly what I'd expected. 'MI5 has no jurisdiction here, lady, except by invitation. This is an EU facility.'

Bex's eyes blazed. She poked her forefinger in his chest, hard. 'This is my fuckin' country, chum! And *I*'m national security!' Her expression melted as she thought of something else. 'And I *am* invited to attend tonight's meeting – *if* that's all right with you?'

'That's correct, sir,' I added, at risk of sounding like a creep.

His skin paled as he stepped back. The nervous smile sat uncomfortably on the cruel mouth. 'Of course. No offence, I'm just being careful.'

'What's your name?' she demanded savagely.

He was starting to look uneasy, his eyes shifty, like he wanted the ground to swallow him up. 'Er – Galic. "Johnny" Galic.'

'Thank you, Johnny Galic. I'm sure I'll remember you. Now, if you'll allow us to get on . . . ?'

He nodded and skirted round us, anxious to be off.

As he disappeared down the corridor, I said: 'I'm impressed.'

'Piss off, Ed,' she returned affably. 'It's only what you taught us. BBB.'

She was right, of course. Bullshit baffles brains – or how to talk yourself out of tight situations. The Directing Staff of 14 Int had done a better job than I'd realized at the time.

I turned to the left-hand door marked simply 'Conference', and fumbled through the late Hal's ring of security swipecards. At last I found the one we needed and ran it through the lock channel to provide the welcome *clink-clunk* that allowed us entry.

It was a sterile room, I was sure. There was never any daylight in here, no windows and my guess was that the wall panels were specially lined to prevent electronic eavesdropping. A large round table made of pale beech was the centrepiece which, under the circumstances, seemed to make a mockery of the concept of Camelot.

On one wall there were three screens, a large one for an overhead projector and two other monitors which were probably for showing video recordings, perhaps news or surveillance footage. The only decoration in the room was a large blue flag with the circular yellow-star pattern of the European Union, pinned on the opposite wall.

Bex unshouldered her small backpack. 'What d'you reckon? Install Fran's mini-cam in here somewhere?'

I indicated the flag, and a cut-out doorway in the beech wall panelling. 'What's over there?'

It was an equipment cupboard. It stored trolleys for the overhead projector and video players, easels and flip charts for any other type of presentation that might be needed.

I found the light switch and glanced around. 'This'll do. Get me the electric drill.'

While I clambered up onto the side shelves full of clutter, Bex pulled a cordless electric drill from her pack and handed it up to me. I positioned the point and hit the trigger, the teeth-grinding whir giving me apoplexy as I drove a hole through the partitioning. After a few seconds of noise that it seemed could wake the dead, the point broke through. It came out just below the displayed flag of the EU.

We glanced at each other and at the door, expecting someone to investigate the racket.

'Soundproofed room,' Bex said with a smile as she handed up the camera. 'Should have realized.'

I inserted the telescopic lens of the digital mini-cam into the aperture, rested it on the shelf and raised the antennae.

I switched the camera on, then dialled up Paquet on my mobile.

'Eddie?' she gasped after a split second of ringing.

'No names,' I snapped. 'We're in. Safe and sound. So it's on. Any reception?'

'Wait.' Two, three minutes, an eternity, she came back. 'Yes, I have a picture. Not good, but good enough. What about sound levels?'

I turned to Bex. 'Go into the room, on the far side, and speak normally.'

She sprinted past the circular table. As if addressing an assembly of people she began, 'For breakfast I had kippers and poached egg . . .'

'Okay, okay,' Paquet cut in. 'That is reasonable.'

'Fine, sweetheart. We're ready to pull out. Get back in position on the road by the wood for a pick-up. Hopefully within the hour. I'm closing now. Wish us luck.'

There was a small, breathless hesitation. 'I wish you luck.' She sounded like she cared. 'I'll be waiting.'

I snapped off the mobile and dropped it into the pocket of my borrowed uniform. 'Okay,' I said to Bex, 'Let's go.'

But she was suddenly waving her hand frantically, drawing her fingers across her throat. Cut! Cut! Shut up!

Now that I'd got the message she dropped down onto her haunches, peering through the gap in the cupboard door. I leaned over her until I could see what she was watching.

Oh, shit! The brooding young Serb we'd met in the corridor earlier – Johnny Galic – was entering the conference room. There were two other men immediately behind him.

The first one I saw was a lot shorter than Galic and much older. He had a tanned face like slightly burnt and lumpy porridge that had been put in the oven by mistake, with eyes as black and dead as charcoaled raisins. But I could almost be envious of the vigorous grey-white hair that sprouted like florets of cauliflower on the turn. The rest of him, though, was meaty, sturdy and confident in a bespoke three-thousand-dollar suit that evoked one impression only. Power.

The voice was deep, raddled with years of tobacco and alcohol abuse, and distinctly Italian. 'What's the matter?' he asked, noticing that Johnny Galic looked uneasy.

'There's no one here.'

'So?' Giovanni Bestelloli asked. I knew it was Bestelloli. His mug shot had been on the web page that Paquet had printed off. Okay, it had been an air brushed Bestelloli of twenty years ago, looking like a matineé idol, but there was no mistaking the basic features.

'The security guard was here, sweeping the room,' Galic replied darkly. 'Electronically, you understand.'

'So, he's swept the room,' Bestelloli said.

Galic was agitated. 'Then he should be here. He was new, he said. But he shouldn't just go away. He should know that thing.'

The second man stepped forward, looking into the conference room over Bestelloli's shoulder. 'What's the problem?' he asked.

You might take the boy out of Berlin, but you couldn't take Berlin out of the boy.

Herman J. Schmitt – courtesy of the same website.

He reminded me of a fox. He was taller than his Italian companion, with raked-back ginger hair and pointed features. His thin, hooked nose seemed to be sniffing the air as though it was a dubious wine. He seemed alert and highly perceptive.

Galic moved into the room. 'The security man should be here, it's how we do things. But he's new . . . I'll have him sorted out for this. And for bringing that woman in.'

'Woman?' Schmitt picked up on that.

'Yes. I didn't know we were expecting anyone from the Security Service. Liaison, she said.'

Bestelloli and Schmitt became a couple of book ends for a split second, staring at each other with the same horrified expression.

'No!' The Italian spluttered as though fighting his way out of a heart attack. 'This is a Research Office meeting. *Our* personnel only. No one from those bloody MI5 people is allowed in!'

I think Galic saw his authority slipping. 'She's *not* here, sir. Probably the security guard takes her away. That is *why* she is not here.'

Schmitt was ex-Stasi. A former secret policeman and spymaster from East Germany. His cool expression suggested that he could smell bullshit at fifty paces. 'Phone security, Galic. Make *sure* she's off the premises, immediately. She has no jurisdiction here. This is EU sovereign soil. Like any embassy.'

Bloody nerve! I swallowed hard, and watched in silence. I didn't have the option of doing anything else.

Galic led the way into the conference room, Bestelloli and Schmitt behind him, and half a dozen others following. The Slav found a locked drinks cabinet and freed the contents, liberally offering glasses of hooch to the half-dozen people who had followed them in. Their only common denominator was that they all spoke English – of a sort. I'd worked with both NATO and the UN over the years, so I reckoned I was pretty good at matching accents with nationalities.

My quick assessment was: a Frenchman, a Belgian, an Irishman, an uncomfortable-looking Dutchman, a Russian – or maybe Ukrainian – and a Latvian. Well, one of those Baltic states, anyway. None of these people seemed the sort I'd want to invite around for Sunday dinner. Each one, even the Dutchman, had that aura I'd seen so many times in Northern Ireland and Bosnia, and in more than a few other places as well.

Each carried himself with the arrogant air of the Teflon-coated villain. Those who considered themselves above the law, above anything. They were thugs – and pretty successful ones too judging by the expensive sharp suits and half the world's gold reserves on their wrists and fingers. They'd worked the civilized system, screwed it, bent it and even broken it and invariably got away with whatever they'd done. They were reckless and fearless. Virtually untouchable. And didn't they just look like they knew it.

After a few minutes, Schmitt interrupted their impromptu cocktail party. 'I'm sorry to be so formal, gentlemen, but I want to keep this meeting as short as possible for security reasons. Weekends are always best if one wishes such things to go unnoticed, but we shouldn't allow ourselves to become overconfident. So if you'd just take your seats around the table . . .'

These people, who were not used to being bossed around by anyone, reluctantly unglued themselves from their conversation and selected themselves seats around the table in a semicircle facing Schmitt and Giovanni Bestelloli who, I guessed, were the only two official EU representatives in the room.

At that moment a buzzer sounded and a green light flashed at the double entrance doors. Galic moved swiftly to check through the intercom before throwing the security lock to admit the latecomers.

Although I'd seen him back at Jayne Frauss's place, it still came as a mild and unnerving shock to see Morgan Dampier standing there. The same engaging smile and urbane manner, the usual impeccable and expensive Gieves & Hawkes suit. But not this time with some contrived and clever plot to trick rival terrorists into murdering each other. Or to drive a psychological wedge between friendly Bosnian warlords in order to divide and rule. This time he'd left the angels and joined the enemy.

He stepped through the door, then moved deferentially to one side to allow another man to follow him in. It was my personal ghost again, that familiar tall figure with the gaunt and bloodless face and blue eyes so pale that they reminded me of glacial ice.

'Brigadier Domedzic,' Dampier announced.

Schmitt stepped forward eagerly to offer his hand. 'Milo, so nice of you to join us.'

Domedzic wasn't given to smiling. His thin lips twitched a fraction, because it was expected, and his handshake was equally perfunctory, almost contemptuous. And all the time those cold eyes above the thin nose ran back and forth across the semicircle of seated individuals. Assessing, calculating, evaluating, filing away images of the faces in his mind for future reference. Deciding who, one day, might be ally or foe.

Johnny Galic showed him to a seat alongside Giovanni Bestelloli. 'Here, sir, if you please.'

Schmitt turned to Dampier who was lingering by the door. 'Sorry, Morgan, this is a Code One security committee meeting. Invitation only. I'm sure you understand.'

Dampier's smile was as ready as always, but I knew him well enough to see that he wasn't happy. 'Of course, Herman, no problem. I'll be outside.'

Schmitt nodded pleasantly. 'We really won't be long.'

Another smile from Dampier as he backed out of the room, closing the door behind him.

'Well now, gentlemen,' Schmitt began. 'As you are aware, it is three years since we were all able to get together like this. Then I was able to tell you how the Special Research Office had developed since the original Genk Protocol at the time of the Maastricht Treaty. At that time we were developing our operations, starting to glean information regularly from EU departments and building our network of informants within the organization.

'We were doing all this while working out of an anonymous office in The Hague, but we were a little too close to Europol Headquarters under whose general aegis we operate. That meant there was some understandable confusion and we at the SRO have had to fight strongly to maintain and increase our autonomy.'

Not a hint of irony in his voice, I noticed.

Giovanni Bestelloli leaned forward, his rounded face with its heavily shadowed jowls hunched between his shoulders. 'Herr Schmitt makes light of the difficulties we have overcome,' he interjected. 'There have been many individuals who have sought – and even official committees set up –over the years to investigate the way that we operate. None has proven any inappropriate behaviour by the SRO or its staff.'

The man I'd guessed was Ukrainian, almost as vast as the grassy steppes he came from, chortled deeply as he spoke. 'Yes, we've noticed that! Seems most troublemakers meet with a sticky end – one way or another! Congratulations!'

Schmitt looked distinctly irritated. 'Please don't say such things, gentlemen. Even in jest. Walls can have eyes and ears, remember. Besides which, it is nothing to do with us. We have been fortunate, that is all. Bad luck has befallen some of the SRO's more serious enemies, those trying to dig dirt on us that doesn't exist. We are an intelligence research organization for the EU, that is all. As you know – officially – we simply collect information and data, and make reports of our findings to the Commission when requested. That's all. We do not have an executive arm.'

The Ukrainian was chuckling deeply again, glancing at others around the table. 'So is that why you have appointed my old friend Brigadier Domedzic?'

Everyone seemed quietly amused by that.

'That is one of the things I was about to tell you,' Schmitt replied testily. 'Since we moved to this isolated new headquarters here in the UK, Brigadier Domedzic has joined us – officially now – as head of our Field Investigations Unit. His role in the indictment and arrest of the former Serbian president, Slobodan Milosevic, for war crimes means that the EU hierarchy holds him in high regard. His presence lends authority to the reputation of the SRO as an incorruptible arm of Europol.'

The Ukrainian was at it again. 'He *also* brings with him a bunch of ex-Serbian secret police!' His laugh degenerated into a phlegmy smoker's cough. 'Maybe that is why our enemies meet with such bad luck all of a sudden. Excellent! Brilliant idea, my dear Milo!'

Brigadier Domedzic's face was a bloodless mask. When he spoke, he barely raised his voice above a whisper. 'Laughter can be dangerous, gentlemen. There is an old saying in Belgrade: beware the kick of the jackass. My Field Investigations Unit puts men on the ground in all EU countries and sometimes beyond. They are all trained professionals. Former police or security investigators. Yes, some – even most – are hand-picked by me and that is why they are so efficient. But do not, even in jest, ever suggest that they conduct themselves in any way illegally, or outside the sanctioned remit of the SRO. That is how ugly rumours start to spread.'

I had to hand it to them. Neither Schmitt nor Domedzic were dropping their guard. They were consummate professionals, maintaining the façade even when addressing their co-conspirators who knew exactly what was going on.

But I soon realized that the Italian MEP Bestelloli was less cautious. Maybe he'd had one bottle of Chianti too many over dinner.

His voice boomed across the table: 'Our masters in the EU do not ask too many questions of us, because we maintain the status quo. We do not rock the boat and we are efficient – we deliver. We tell them what they want to know. *For Commission eyes only*. That is a big ego-boost.

'Theirs is an organization born of deliberate secrecy and deception: it is used to telling untruths and half-truths, to deceiving their own peoples gently, to turning blind eyes and blocking their ears to criticism. If their critics are silenced, one way or another, this mighty political juggernaut does not tend to ask how or why. They are just quietly thankful. As politicians, they can then just get on with playing their power games and building their personal fortunes. What a perfect world we Europeans are privileged to live in!'

He grinned widely and surveyed his audience as they all laughed quietly together and shared the joke. The joke that was making them all so rich on fraud and deception on a massive scale.

Schmitt smiled uneasily and raised his hand. 'Gentlemen, if I may return to the final business at hand ... That is to inform you that the secret Genk Protocol, which has allowed our prosperity to flourish for so many years, is due to be ratified on Monday. Again this will be done in secret by the heads of government of the European Union.

'Importantly it forms the cornerstone of a pan-European security policy. I – er, I am sorry – *we*,' he nodded respect-fully to Bestelloli, 'have taken longer than we had hoped to persuade everyone that the first thing a nation state must do is to protect its citizens. They had already taken that on board with plans for a European military force, independent of the Americans. Counter-intelligence at the transnational level has been more difficult to sell, especially given the resentment of existing national security agencies. Notably those of Britain and France. But the SRO has quietly and unobtrusively proved its worth. The final persuasion came from an unexpected source on September 11, 2001. Thank you, Osama Bin Laden ...'

Everyone saw the funny side of that.

Schmitt continued: 'With ratification of the Genk Protocol, the SRO in effect becomes recognized as Europe's federal counter-intelligence agency, its albeit humble equivalent of the FBI in the States. I will allow the honourable MEP of the Security Committee, Signor Bestelloli, to explain . . .'

The Italian lumbered to his feet and placed his fist on the table in front of him. 'The SRO will be far more powerful than, as yet, anyone realizes. As always, the politicians have failed to read the small print or understand its true significance. These legally link the Protocol with seemingly innocuous clauses existing in other treaties. The legal wording allows us vast powers of surveillance of citizens, without restraint or any legal political interference from the Commission. And, as now, national security agencies are required to assist us when requested – without question.

'Beyond that, through Europol, we will have powers to initiate arrests. The legal weapons at our disposal against our own and the EU's enemies are already enshrined in related EU laws that have already been passed. Especially useful to us is the blanket definition of "criminal xenophobia" against anyone involved in anti-EU activities. On recommendation from the SRO, the European Court of Justice can proscribe any political party pushing an anti-EU line. In such cases it will be permitted to ban trial by jury and legally to withhold unused prosecution evidence from the defence. In addition it will be permitted to create political detention centres. Again the war against terror has strengthened our hand.'

The Ukrainian was almost beside himself with amusement. 'You almost make the SRO sound like the Gestapo, my Italian friend!'

Schmitt stood up sharply, quick to restamp his authority on the meeting. 'Enough nonsense, if you please!' Smiles vanished from the faces in the audience. 'All that needs to be said is that ratification of the Protocol will lock all EU nations together within an overall security apparatus that will rapidly go from strength to strength. The SRO is at its centre and that position will never be challenged without major political upheaval on an international scale. That, gentlemen, is the measure of our success that we invite you here to celebrate tonight.

'In the words and spirit of the SRO's motto, indeed *Knowledge Is Everything!*'

The applause was slow in starting, but was distinctly appreciative from the men who would make so many billions of euros from the fact that their organized criminal networks were now to be legally infiltrated into the running and policing of the EU at all levels.

Before the clapping stopped, the invasive trilling of a mobile phone diverted everyone's concentration. It was Johnny Galic who pulled the offending machine from his jacket pocket and clamped it to his ear. He listened intently, the furrow deepening on his brow. 'What? . . . Get some people up here now!'

'What is it?' Domedzic demanded.

Johnny Galic snapped shut his phone and turned to the expectant faces. 'That's the front gate. No one from MI5 has been signed in, and no women at all. And there is no response from the security guard in this area. He doesn't answer his radio.'

I knew why that was. I had his radio and it was turned off.

'They've run back video footage of the corridor outside,' Galic added. 'The guard and the woman are seen entering *this* room just before we arrived.'

Bestelloli looked bemused and glanced instinctively around the room. 'What is this? A David Copperfield illusion? A magician's trick?'

The Ukrainian was peering under the conference table.

'Are our security guards on drugs?' Bestelloli added irritably.

But Schmitt wasn't listening. He turned to Galic. 'There are no rooms leading from here?'

'No, sir, just a couple of storage cupboards.'

I heard Bex's sharp intake of breath beside me. Oh, fuck! This was not a decision I wanted to make. What the hell should we do? They'd find us in two seconds flat and then what? I knew what these people were capable of . . . But here, at the heart of the SRO? Would saner voices prevail? I had absolutely no idea.

The only absolute I had was the cold metal of the security guard's 9mm Browning pressed against my spine in the waistband of my trousers. I yanked it out and slid the first round into the chamber.

Bex heard the noise in the dark. 'Christ, Ed, is this wise?'

'I don't know,' I snapped back. 'If you don't like it, stay put and come out with your hands up later. Okay?'

'Fuck that, Ed, I'm with you.'

I raised my right knee and kicked open the storage cupboard door with my foot. The sudden inrush of light was blinding.

All I could see were the ragged blurred shapes of the delegates on their feet. I fired two rounds into the ceiling. The noise was ear-shattering. Instantly all conversation stopped and my eyes began to focus on the white, shocked faces staring at us as we emerged.

'DON'T ANYONE MOVE! ONE *TWITCH* AND YOU'RE DEAD!'

The Ukrainian moved. He was probably drunk – who knew? But he reached rather casually inside his jacket. I squeezed the trigger of the Browning and the round smacked into the centre of his chest, propelling him back over the table edge. A unified gasp of horror rose to be drowned in the sound of the man's demented scream.

'Oh, fuck!' Bex breathed in my ear.

But it had the desired effect. The worst criminal thugs

in Europe were frozen like a tableau at Madame Tussaud's.

'Get in behind me,' I hissed at Bex and began edging around the side of the table towards the door. All gazes followed us. The single black eye of the Browning glared back at them.

Brigadier Domedzic looked like some irritating noise had just disturbed his concentration. He was *that* unfazed. But he was frowning thoughtfully. 'You are Edward Coltrane,' he accused with quiet authority. 'I know your photograph well. And this is the Bunnet woman.'

'SHUT YOUR MOUTH!' Bex shouted. 'SILENCE!'

My eyes shifted to Galic. 'YOU! HANDS UP AND STEP FORWARD!'

His dark eyes smouldered with resentment, like I'd somehow humiliated him, stripped him of his manhood. Reluctantly he obeyed and shuffled forward.

'STOP THERE!' I reached out with my free hand and checked for a shoulder harness. He didn't have one. The holster was fixed to his trouser belt. Very Continental. I jerked out the Beretta automatic and handed it back to Bex. Not the world's best bit of kit, but good enough to kill in the right hands.

'Now move backwards,' I snapped. 'Good. Now – down on the floor, arms out in front of you!'

As he obeyed, I switched my attention to the rest of them. 'Real slow, I want you to place any weapons you have on the table. And all radios and mobile phones. We'll check each of you individually in a moment. Anyone holding out or hiding something gets a bullet between the eyes. No question, no problem!' I tried to sound real cool, like I meant it. Inside I was panicking, desperate to get out of there.

It seemed to work. Perhaps I'd chosen the wrong career and should have joined RADA instead of the army. There was a noisy clatter as an arsenal of automatics and revolvers landed on the table top along with a miscellany of communications gear.

Bex moved fast, stripping the nearby swingbin of its liner and sweeping all the weaponry and cellphones into it. Not quite all: her quick eye spotted an Ingram machine pistol and a Smith & Wesson automatic that took her fancy. She stuck the S&W into her waistband and expertly checked over the Ingram, making sure that it was ready for instant use.

I took a step sideways and ripped out the telephone receiver wire from the wall-set. 'Open the door,' I ordered.

As soon as Bex released the catch, I drove the butt of my Browning automatic into the intercom and electronic code console beside the door. 'Anyone steps outside to follow us, and they're dead!' I threatened with as much menace as I could muster.

Brigadier Domedzic regarded me with disdain. 'You're a fool, Coltrane. What d'you think you can achieve by this?'

I felt the hot flush of anger like an uncontrollable volcanic urge. I could barely control my finger tightening on the trigger. 'Don't fucking tempt me!' I snarled.

Maybe Domedzic realized that he was pushing his luck. I didn't know myself why I didn't blow him away there and then. I'd killed Tex-Mex and Mihac, so why not go for the hat-trick and bury Astrid's ghost once and for all? Maybe all those hostile witnesses had something to do with it.

Anyway, right or wrong, I made a snap decision and turned away.

Bex was in the corridor, Ingram in one hand and black bin-bag of weapons in the other. I followed her through and slammed the door behind me, ensuring that I heard the locks click home. Immediately I smashed the wall-mounted entry system with the butt of the Browning. Now Domedzic, Johnny Galic and the others should be trapped until someone broke down the doors.

'Coast's clear,' Bex breathed. 'Back the way we came?'

I nodded, following as she set off down the deserted corridor. We'd barely moved a dozen paces when the sirens started, an ear-splitting all-around sound from hidden loud-speakers, and bright, disorientating blue lights began pulsing from points along the passage. It was the latest high-tech security, akin to a "flash-bang" or stun grenade and similarly designed to shock an intruder into immobility and indecision.

And, briefly it worked. Of course, we'd half-expected that there'd be some sort of panic button in the conference room or some other elaborate security system.

Nevertheless, it still took precious seconds for us to overcome the immediate phychological effect. I pushed Bex forward, yelling above the din for her to make for the wash-room where we'd come in.

As she reached for the handle, figures burst through the door at the far end of the corridor. Bex instantly let rip with a short burst from the Ingram, hosing the area with 9mm rounds. The figures ducked back behind the swinging doors.

'I'll hold them off,' I said. 'You get out onto the roof. Back the way we came in.'

'I'll need your help to get up through the loft hatch,' Bex gasped.

'What?'

Her eyes were fierce with indignation and hurt pride. 'I'm too fucking *short*, damn you!'

I couldn't even raise a smile. I followed her into the wash-room and gave her the necessary leg-up so that she could push aside the ceiling hatch and scramble up. 'Call Fran on the mobile to pick you up. I'll join you as soon as I can.'

That broad face with its melting smile beamed down at me. 'Make sure you do. And take care, lover boy. I want you in one piece.' The hatch slammed shut.

I turned back to the door and eased it open. I just had time to glimpse figures approaching stealthily down the corridor from the left when a hail of rounds peppered the plasterwork and door frame. I was showered in white powder and wood splinters as I pulled my head back in.

This was one of those moments when you thought that the MoD's latest stupid idea about helmets with head-up displays and guns that shoot round corners might come in handy after all.

I dropped to the floor, poked the Browning outside the door at skirting-board level and let rip half a dozen round, firing blind. Inching forward, I chanced a glance down the corridor. I'd brought down two people, but the others were advancing fast. Not uniformed security men like the unfortunate Hal, but men in dark casual civvies. They were Brigadier Domedzic's former Serb secret police, his men in black.

I chanced taking proper aim. Well, it was bloody fast and furious, scarcely giving myself enough time to draw a bead on each of the three targets. I selected at random. Aim, fire, withdraw. Aim, fire withdraw. Aim, fire – and withdraw *before* a returning round blew my skull open like a ripe pumpkin.

As I pulled my head back for the third time, the world exploded around me in a hail of fire. Plaster fell over me in a cloud. I shook the stuff from my hair and roughly rubbed the dust from my eyes, then inched forward again, poking the snout of the Browning around to the left.

A couple more rounds, I thought, then I'm done. The late Hal hadn't been issued with any spare mags.

Suddenly a foot came out of nowhere and thudded onto my wrist. No, not from nowhere. From my right. The bastard had crept up behind me in the corridor.

As I squealed in pain and involuntarily opened my palm to drop the Browning, I realized that somehow the visitors imprisoned in the conference room had managed to get out.

I stared up at the smirking face of Johnny Galic. And at the revolver in his hand.

# Eighteen

Johnny Galic lifted me up by the scruff of my neck until I was standing. By then the rest of his Serb compatriots had surged forward down the corridor from where I'd been decking them like skittles.

Most of them pushed past us, guns drawn, looking for Bex. They began a systematic search of the cubicles, kicking open the doors.

But one of them had stopped and was staring at me, talking to Galic. 'That bastard's killed one of ours,' he said savagely in Serbo-Croat, his accent Bosnian. 'Another two are wounded. Cut the fucker's throat, Johnny!'

Because I now knew who and what these people were, I felt incredibly angry. My reaction was not heroic, just instinctive and heartfelt – and decidedly stupid.

But I didn't care. They'd killed Astrid, then Marcus and Jude and Helmut Frauss and all the others who'd tried to warn about them.

Unrepentant, I jerked my head back. 'You'll find *another* body in there.'

The men in black began smashing down the locked cubicle door that held the dead security guard. Then some excitable trigger-happy idiot put two rounds into the corpse.

They reported back. 'The woman's vanished.'

Galic looked around. He noticed the muddy footprints on the edge of the basin and looked up at the ceiling hatch. All gazes followed his.

He glared at me. 'Is that how you got in?'

I didn't answer – but then, I didn't really need to.

'Alert all the guards,' Galic ordered, 'and phone those on the emergency roster. Call them all in. She must have got out onto the roof. She'll have to cross the field, so get the dogs out. We'll need road patrols too.'

'Sir!'

Brigadier Domedzic emerged through the scrum of people around me. 'Take him to my office.'

Instantly I was grabbed by two burly Serbs.

'Brigadier, we've got three dead men and two men with serious gunshot wounds,' someone said. 'We'll have to call an ambulance.'

'No,' Domedzic snapped. 'That'll mean the police. Use our own medics.'

'These men will die, Brigadier. Our medics can't cope with that type of injury.'

For the first time passion blazed on Domedzic's usually expressionless face. 'Then they die for a good cause. Call no one. Understand? This must be contained.'

'And the bodies, Brigadier?'

'Get them hidden. We'll lose them at sea later.' Then he focused his cold gaze on me. 'You have a lot to answer for, Coltrane.'

Before I could retort, a familiar voice added calmly: 'My dear Brigadier, I'm afraid your colleagues are right. We've got three corpses and two critically wounded on our hands. You have to call for an ambulance and the police.'

'I don't want the police here,' Domedzic growled. 'Our work is too sensitive. My men can dispose of the bodies. They have plenty of experience.'

But Morgan Dampier persisted: 'Sorry, Brigadier, but this isn't Bosnia. No offence. This is Crown property and the assailants – Coltrane here and the woman – are *already* wanted for murder by the police. We have nothing to hide and you have nothing to fear ... Besides, your European friends are already leaving. They'll be well away before the police arrive.'

Domedzic grunted, not happy. He was clearly used to burying his problems in life under three feet of concrete. 'Maybe you're right.' He looked at me again. 'Get him to my office,' he repeated.

Someone opened the security lock of a door further down the corridor and the two Serbs propelled me into a sumptuously appointed office, all shag-pile carpet and pale wooden Scandinavian furniture. It was the look that I'd been trying – and failing – to get at my flat. As the brigadier sat in his smart swivel armchair behind a vast desk, I was thrust into an uncomfortable hard-backed chrome chair facing him. Johnny Galic and Morgan Dampier followed us in.

I scowled up at my erstwhile friend. 'Exchanged the Queen's shilling for the euro, have we?'

'Be wise for once, Ed,' he returned, smiling icily, 'and keep your lip buttoned.'

'Of course, you know this man,' Domedzic said to Dampier. 'He could say things to the police or in court. Accusations to damage you – damage the SRO.'

Dampier was dismissive. 'Coltrane here's a burnt-out case. He's known to special forces and the British intelligence community. He's murdered once, twice or maybe three times before tonight. Now the Ukrainian and, I'm told, one of our security guards and one of your men. No one's going to believe any wild allegations he might make. Certainly not the police, who are already looking for him. HMG will certainly refute any accusations against the SRO and the Crown Prosecution Service will listen, I assure you.

'Coltrane's fought in secret wars for too long. Bosnia finally blew his mind after his wife died . . .'

I saw just the smallest flicker in Domedzic's eyes, but he wasn't saying anything.

For once I followed Dampier's advice and kept silent as he finished off: 'Coltrane's testimony will be totally discredited. His breaking in here will be seen as just another impulsive offence committed by a paranoid schizophrenic. It'll be a life tariff in a high-security prison or some psychiatric institution. And he's got no family to kick up a fuss.'

Domedzic still wasn't happy. 'You are certain about this? What about your famous British justice?'

Dampier chuckled. 'The Lord Chancellor is a politician – he influences the appointment of judges and can manipulate the actual system when the national interest is at stake. Trust me. After his trial, Coltrane will just disappear from view for ever.' He paused, letting his words sink in. 'The SRO has nothing to fear if it is seen to cooperate openly with the British police. It'll have no problem riding this one out.'

'Very well,' Domedzic decided. 'Then call the police. And you had better be right about this, or—' He added darkly: 'I shall not forgive and forget.'

One of Galic's henchmen appeared at the door. 'Excuse me, but security has just discovered a hidden camera in the conference room!'

Domedzic was on his feet. He scowled at me, then at Morgan Dampier and left the room followed by Galic.

Now that we were left alone, I turned to Dampier. 'You bastard. *They* killed Marcus and Jude, not me or Bex. They did and you know it. I just hope you can live with yourself.'

'Very well, Ed, old son,' he snapped back. 'Be grateful. I've just saved your frigging miserable neck. Domedzic and his sidekick Galic wouldn't hesitate to bury you at sea or chuck you in a limepit like they did their enemies in Bosnia. You'll just have to take your chances in a court of law.' He raised his eyes to the heavens. 'Why the fuck did you have to go and stick your nose in things you don't even begin to understand?'

'Because, Morgan, I didn't feel I had an option,' I retorted. 'Your mate Tony Tromain was trying to stitch me up – and probably Bex – for Jude's murder. And he was making a bloody good fist of it.'

Dampier shook his head. 'Not Tromain, Ed. He's just being played for a patsy. He's a freelance for our security agencies and sometimes for the SRO. A dog with two masters. He just does what he's told and believes what he's told. Sometimes the aims of those masters conflict, sometimes they coincide. There's a bit of a turf war developing between some national security agencies and the SRO. Not surprising given their growing authority. But if there's any plotting going on, my guess is that it's down to Brigadier Domedzic.'

'Your *guess*?' I challenged. 'I thought you were in bed with the bastard.'

'Domedzic doesn't let outsiders into his confidence, Ed.' Dampier gave a half-smile. 'I was provided to him to be the link between his SRO execs and the British police, MI5 and SIS. But I'm regarded as an outsider and always will be. I'm just a humble service provider when asked.'

That sounded like a cheap cop-out. 'But you *know* what's going on!' I accused him.

'I know *some* of what goes on. Or I can make a shrewd guess. That's why I'm saying that any plot to stitch you up is down to Domedzic. And Schmitt, of course. Schmitt is ex-East German Stasi – with a thoroughly unpleasant reputation – and he's apparently known the brigadier for years.

'And I *do* know that they were both determined to stop Sir Marcus's investigation, one way or another. That's their remit, to protect the EU. Jude, Bex and you just got in the way. I'm sure Schmitt and Domedzic would prefer to get you blown away down an alley one dark night. That's the way they've always been used to doing things. But it looks like they'll be satisfied just to get you behind bars for ten years or so.'

I shook my head in disgust. 'You know all this, Morgan, and yet you still work with them. How can you live with yourself? They killed Jude, for God's sake.'

'*You* say,' he pointed out coolly. 'But even if that's true, Ed, I still have to make a living. And I was running out of options. Investigations into my activities back in Ulster were getting uncomfortably hot. The SRO offers powerful protection. I might be supping with the devil, but I use the longest spoon I can find.'

Frankly that didn't impress me, and I was about to say so when the door was flung open and Domedzic strode back in. He was clearly angry and was waving something in his fist. 'What in the hell is this, Coltrane?'

He slammed the digital picture disk on his desk in front of me. I shrugged. 'Sorry, not my department.'

'The woman – Bunnet? This is from the camera you set up. Or did she set it up?'

'Yes, I'm a Luddite.'

'What?'

'I'm no good at technology,' I explained lightly. 'Can't even use text messages on my mobile. She handled all the technical side.'

'My security people say this camera can transmit. Has it transmitted the images on this disk?'

'Transmitted them to who?'

Blood finally coloured Domedzic's sallow face. 'Don't fuck with me, Coltrane! You of all people should know how stupid that is.' He meant Astrid and we both knew it. No pretences now. 'The French journalist, Francoise Paquet. Is she still with you?'

'Hell, no,' I said, trying to sound indignant. 'Your people scared her. She went off on her own. Bex and I were trying to film you—'

'Why?' he demanded. 'You're wanted for murder. Are you a fool? You should be on the run, seeking an escape.

Why break in here, try and film an innocent committee meeting . . . ?'

This guy was incredible, on guard like he was always being taped or videoed. I looked him squarely in the eyes. 'Tell yourself the lie enough times and you believe it yourself, is that it? We had nowhere to run, Domedzic, and you know it. That's why we came here. To get proof of what you're up to. It's the only defence we've got.'

His expression relaxed a little. 'Then it is not a very good one.'

I ignored that. 'Tell me, Domedzic, do you still deny to *yourself* that you ordered my wife's execution?' I knew he was married from the old files, knew he was supposed to be devoutly religious. 'Did you tell *your* wife and kids that you had Astrid sliced in half like a side of beef? Confess that to your priest, did you?'

There was a second's silence that froze the air like an Arctic wind coming in through the open door. It was as though a patina of ice crystal was forming over those pale eyes. The brigadier said nothing to me, but eventually turned to Galic. 'Get him out of my sight. Take him down to security until the police arrive for him.'

I was grabbed roughly and dragged out of the room, Dampier walking by my side. When we were in the corridor, he said quietly: 'Don't keep pushing your luck, old son.'

I turned my head and met his gaze. 'Go fuck yourself, Morgan. You're judged by the company you keep, remember? In my book that makes you no better than him.'

Dampier's stride slowed to a halt and I was aware that he was watching me go. There was nothing left between us now; what had been, was dead.

Then it was all surprisingly civilized. I was escorted to a regular waiting room near the reception foyer with rows of imitation leather seats set against the walls and a low table covered with out-of-date magazines. Rather like waiting to get your teeth fixed. One of the Serbs even offered me a plastic glass of water from the cooler. I declined and pulled out my cigarette pack. He shook his head and pointed to the No Smoking sign. Quite bizarre.

I picked up an old copy of *Horse & Hound* and had barely begun turning the pages when the ambulances and local police turned up. Uniformed officers went past the door to the waiting room, no doubt to inspect the carnage that I'd caused and to take initial statements and measurements. Finally a sergeant entered and removed his cap. 'Mr Coltrane? Our officers are inspecting the scene of the incident, but a senior detective from Special Branch is on his way to talk to you. Are you okay waiting here?'

It was like I'd been involved in a major traffic accident. 'Do I have an option, Sergeant?'

He gave me an old-fashioned look. 'Ex-SAS, aren't you?'

'Sure.'

'Then you'll know the drill. I'm sure this gentleman will make sure you're comfortable until the detective arrives.' My big Serb minder grinned, his gold tooth glinting under the fluorescent light.

Some time later, after the ambulances had departed, I saw a couple more unmarked cars pull up outside. Plain-clothes policemen emerged and spent some twenty minutes outside in the foyer. I could see them talking to Morgan Dampier and Johnny Galic. Schmitt and Domedzic, I noted, were keeping well out of sight. In fact, I wondered if they'd already left the building before the first police had arrived.

At last the Special Branch officer came in to see me. He was tall and hunch-shouldered with prematurely white curly hair and a face more lined than it should be for a man in his early forties. He walked like he carried a physical burden on his back and he looked worried. In fact, he looked like the sort of man who'd been born looking worried.

His sidekick, keeping three feet behind in the shadow

of his boss, said nothing as the senior cop introduced himself: 'Mr Coltrane, I'm Superintendent Waverley of Special Branch.' Despite the attempt to sound cultured, his accent was fairly uncut south Thames. 'Sorry to keep you, but I've been the one in charge of trying to find you and Miss Bunnet – and Miss Paquet, of course. Thought I should see you personally . . . I think it would be best if you came with me to the local police station to conduct an interview.'

No histrionics, no telly or Hollywood drama. I said: 'Am I being arrested?'

'No, Mr Coltrane. But I want to interview you formally.'

'And if I refuse?'

He sighed. I'd probably interrupted his one night off in the week. 'Then I might well arrest you. But I think it better all round if we go to the local police station.'

I saw it then, something in those tired seen-it-all-before eyes. 'Might it be complicated to arrest me here?'

The face screwed up in irritation. 'What? No, we can arrest you anywhere, Mr Coltrane. You must know that.'

'Does this place have embassy status?'

I'd got him slightly flustered, but he hid it well. 'Maybe, we're not sure . . . Anyway, we're interviewing you about crimes committed under British common law.'

'But it would be simpler to arrest me at the police station. Less complicated, less chance of embarrassing publicity . . . ?' I suggested. Seing that my words had hit home, I gave in. 'Okay, fine. I'm all yours.'

The unmarked car was waiting outside on the floodlit forecourt, the engine running. A hand went over my head to protect it as I ducked into the rear seat, followed closely by Superintendent Waverley. His sidekick climbed in beside the driver, who took off immediately. The high mesh fence and razor wire flashed past and then the big gates were rolled back by two uniformed security guards.

Then we were out, our headlamps piercing into the close country darkness as we bumped down the track to the old farm buildings.

I said: 'It was self-defence back there.'

Waverley grunted. 'Keep it for the station.'

But I wanted to get him thinking for himself. 'Why are armed foreigners allowed on British soil?'

'I said stow it, Coltrane.'

The driver negotiated the old farmyard, hesitated for a moment and then found the right track that would lead him to the main road.

'They killed Jude, I didn't. Not Bex or Fran Paquet. *They* killed her.'

Waverley stirred in his seat, becoming irritated. 'Keep it for the interview. We agreed that.'

'Just putting you in the picture,' I replied. 'They murdered Sir Marcus Whitby too, in that Paris car bomb.'

'I'm not listening,' Waverley growled.

'Then perhaps you ought to start.' As I spoke his henchman, probably a detective sergeant, glanced back over his shoulder and I caught his eye. 'You'd better listen to what I'm saying too, chum. You may have to testify to it in court.'

'One more word,' Waverley warned, 'and I'll have to charge and caution you now.'

I said: 'The SRO has been hijacked by international criminals. Its so-called head of executive operations is a man called Domedzic. Brigadier Domedzic.'

'Coltrane—'

I raised my hand. 'Just bear with me. Did you know that Domedzic is a former Serb secret policeman?'

Lights from the dash faintly illuminated Waverley's face. Enough for me to see that he wasn't a happy man. 'A Yugoslav, yes. Police officer, yes. No more than that.'

I saw my opportunity. 'Not that he was wanted for war crimes, but the charges were mysteriously dropped? Not

that he gave the order to execute my wife, a UN interpreter? To butcher her with a chainsaw?'

Waverley looked at me strangely and opened his mouth
to speak. Then, simultaneously, several things happened.

Our car was passing between high field hedges on each
side of the track. Suddenly a bright white wall of gleaming
steel lurched out in front of us, dazzling back the reflection
of our headlamps. I was so taken aback that it took me a
second to realize it was a white van that must have been
waiting in a field gateway.

Our driver hit the brakes. I felt the rear of our car start
to slide, heard the spray of stones and mud in our wake.

The side of the van loomed, filling the windscreen. I shut
my eyes. Our car shuddered, throwing us all forward against
our seat belts. Then back, hard. There was a faint sound of
crumpling metal.

I opened my eyes again. We'd stopped half an inch too
late, the nose of our car just starting to bury itself in the
dented side of the van.

Bright light abruptly stabbed into our car's interior from
the left, blinding and momentarily disorientating. Then the
front passenger door flew open. I barely registered the automatic pistol or the eyes in the balaclava before I was deaf-
ened by the muzzle blast.

Someone screamed. Either the detective sergeant or the
driver thought he was a dead man. I think we all did. It was
a shocking moment of surprise and I too screamed or shouted
or made some other incoherent animal noise as I instinctively ducked down.

Oh Christ, I thought, this is Domedzic or Galic doing
things their way. The Balkan way. I'm the one they want
silenced . . .

Then there was a brief, stunning sort of quiet as each
of us realized that our attacker had only put a round
through the driver's-side window, shattering it to

smithereens. Now the figure in the balaclava had our undivided attention, waving the smoking snout of the automatic at us.

'OUT! ALL OF YOU!' It was a harsh, barked order, almost a yell.

Everyone scrambled to obey, including me. The detective sergeant was out of the passenger seat first. 'HANDS ON HEAD!' yelled our attacker, pushing him face first against the hedge.

That voice . . . ? Then it was me. I was shoved roughly to one side, to allow Superintendent Waverley to climb out behind me. 'HANDS ON HEAD!' the voice ordered again, pushing him alongside the detective sergeant.

I was just left standing, slowly realizing that the voice screaming at us wasn't male. I watched, lowering my hands, as Bex ordered the driver to join the other two men facing the hedge with their hands on their heads.

She glanced over her shoulder at me. 'Get in the driver's seat, Ed. Then follow us!'

I just can't tell you how wide the grin on my face was. 'Yes, boss.'

As I raced around the bonnet and into the police car, I waved at the second figure at the wheel of the white van. Paquet's eyes even managed to look beautiful through the slits in a balaclava.

Bex had stripped the hapless Special Branch officers of one automatic pistol, three personal radios and two cellphones between them. She threw the items onto the passenger seat beside me.

Then she was off, rushing towards the van as Paquet swung round onto the track. A filthy cloud of diesel exhaust belched from the back of the vehicle as Bex jumped up and disappeared into the passenger door. I gunned up and let out the clutch, glimpsing the three forlorn Special Branch officers in the red glimmer of my rear lights. Then they melted into the blackness as I followed the van fast towards the main road.

I followed the tail lights of the van for some twenty minutes, heading east through the fens towards the coast. It had started raining again, a new front coming in from the North Sea with a vanguard of vicious squalls. No wonder there was so little traffic on the roads.

As I drove, I picked up one of the Special Branch radios and listened to the signals traffic. Some ten minutes after we'd left the scene, it appeared that Superintendent Waverley and his friends were found by a passing SRO vehicle. About seven minutes later an all-cars police alert for us was out. Again we appeared to be the suspected killers of Jude on the run. There was an ominous additional message: '*All units are advised that officers from a criminal intelligence department within Europol, known as the Special Research Office and located in the area, have offered assistance in tracking the suspects, who are well known to them. Constabulary officers should offer every assistance to and copy any new information to SRO operatives if requested to do so.*'

A little later, the van signalled left, turning off on a narrow counry lane that meandered for several miles, passing only the occasional farm. At last the vehicle pulled over into a muddy lay-by and doused its lights. I switched off the car engine and splashed through the puddles towards the back of the van. As I approached the rear doors were thrown open. It was a welcoming sight, Bex and Paquet waving at me from inside the small steel cave.

'You scared the hell out of me back there,' I said as I scrambled in and shut the doors behind me.

'It's called using our initiative,' Bex answered, pouring a tin mug of steaming coffee from a thermos. 'So stop whingeing and wrap your kissing gear round that.'

As I gulped the stuff down thankfully, Paquet said: 'I've

never been so terrified either. I've never had to drive in front of another vehicle like that.'

'Tosh,' Bex answered, pouring another coffee for herself. 'Daily routine for Parisienne drivers, innit?'

'Who were the other people in the car?' Paquet asked. 'SRO?'

'Special Branch. I was being taken in for questioning. Jude's murder.'

'Ooops,' Bex said. 'Still, never mind. We nearly didn't get you back at all. I was peering through the hedge at every car that left and it's difficult to see who's inside them. I was sure I'd already missed you. By chance you were seated on my side and turned your head in my direction. I only had a split second to alert Fran here.'

'About time the gods smiled on us,' I replied dryly.

'So what happened to you?' Paquet asked.

'I expect Bex explained that I was holding them off while she escaped. I slotted one of their gunmen and wounded a couple of others. Then my luck ran out. Domedzic wanted to shoot me and feed me to the pigs or bury me in quicklime or something else equally Balkan and barbaric. But Morgan Dampier talked him out of it.'

'That's the man who used to be a friend of yours and Bex's?' Paquet asked.

I nodded. '"Friend"' is putting it a bit strong. A colleague. Anyway, now he does liaison work between the SRO and the British authorities. He recommended calling in the police on the basis that I was already being hunted for murder. It was touch and go, I think, but Domedzic relented.'

'Thank God for that,' Bex breathed.

I turned to Paquet. 'They found our camera, I'm afraid—'

She raised her eyebrows and gave a triumphant little smile. 'It does not matter, Eddie.' She patted the pocket of her jacket. 'It transmitted the entire meeting . . . well, almost. It all came through onto my laptop. Mostly the picture was good. Some of the sound was a little difficult to follow, but that can be digitally enhanced.'

'So mission accomplished,' Bex added. She sounded just a little smug.

She was sitting on a toolbox in her filthy wet waterproofs, with her balaclava turned up into an unbecoming woollen hat. She had no make-up on, but her blue eyes were twinkling with mischief. Somehow I'd never seen her look so utterly beguiling in all my life.

I tried to concentrate on our situation. 'I don't know about accomplished—'

Paquet broke in. 'It's exactly the evidence that the Americans will need, Eddie. I've contacted them again and confirmed the rendezvous with the Norwegian fishing boat. Bex told me the best place. At dawn on Monday.'

'Not night-time?' I complained.

'American thinking,' Bex said.

'Will we need a boat of some sort?'

'No,' Paquet replied. 'They will send a motor launch in and we get aboard. Norway within two days and then a flight to Washington. The senators I speak to say there will be a new website up and running within a week, exploding the whole SRO myth and featuring Marcus's report published in full.'

I didn't want to puncture her balloon, but that didn't exactly get rid of the trumped-up murder charges against us. Well, me especially. And I hadn't been helping myself by adding three more to my tally at SRO headquarters, as well as Mihac and Tex-Mex. Unless I had a guardian angel in Her Majesty's Government, I could see me being extradited from the United States in pretty short order.

Right there and then, I made up my mind to disappear. Somewhere remote and obscure where I'd have to build a new life under a new identity. Not that I really cared about that . . . Except, of course, I'd never be able to see my son Timmy again. Ever.

I swallowed hard, choking back the emotional lump in my throat. But that was in the future. First we had to get to the Norwegian boat.

'How far are we from the RV?' I asked.

Bex reached back into the driving cab and retrieved an Ordnance Survey map that she'd obviously been studying. 'From this precise point, Ed, just a smidge over twelve miles.'

I looked down at her grubby fingernail on the map. 'A few small woods,' I observed, 'but mostly open fen country. No towns or villages. Low, isolated coast.'

She must have picked up the disappointment in my voice. 'I thought that would be ideal, Ed.'

Suddenly, it was as if the years had been rolled back. Again I was Directing Staff, training up the novices. 'It would be, Bex, if we weren't compromised and half the British police force, the spooks and the SRO weren't after us.'

'We can make our move tomorrow night,' she came back.

'Night movement is what they'd anticipate. Think helos and thermal-imaging cameras. We'll stick out like a dog's what-its-names in this sort of open country.'

Bex looked irritated. 'Okay, smart-arse, any better ideas?'

As it was, I thought I had. 'Remember the Escape and Evasion stuff? Behind enemy lines? Getting to an RV in daylight?'

She nodded. 'Look like you're going nowhere . . . Carry a ladder . . . a bucket . . .'

'Your options are wider in a more built-up area. That's why here . . . I was thinking that you and Francoise could push a pram, maybe. But there's no village, no church, nowhere for Sunday school.'

'It'll have to be rural,' Bex thought aloud. 'Okay, Ed, I see what you mean.'

'I want us to separate,' I added. 'I think you two stand a

better chance together. Maybe I could get hold of a wheel-barrow. That way I can carry some basic kit. But a pram . . . ?' It was also what we'd used many times as cover in Northern Ireland, but it sure as hell wasn't going to fool anyone out here in the remote fens.

'A cow,' Francoise said suddenly. 'The French comedian Fernandel once made a movie called *The Cow and I*. He escaped the Germans in the Second World War by walking hundreds of miles with a cow. I think it may even have been based on a true story. No one thinks a farmer with a cow is going anywhere far.'

It was inspired. 'Brilliant!' I said and impulsively reached out, cupped her face in my hands and kissed her full on the lips. She looked startled and pulled gently away, glancing nervously at Bex who wore a distinctly disapproving expression.

'We English are clearly more impulsive than you French give us credit for,' Bex observed and gave a tight little smile.

'But can we catch a cow?' I asked quickly, trying to defuse the antagonism between the women.

'You've got rope,' Bex said. 'We make a lasso like in the cowboy movies. Fran and I have welly boots, headscarves and dirty outdoor clothes. We can look like a couple of old farmers' wives, I'm sure. Probably without trying.'

'Right,' I said, coming to a decision. 'Let's look at the map and plan our routes. Dawn will be up before we know it and I want to be well away from here by then.'

Twenty minutes of frantic deliberation followed. While we talked, we drank coffee and ate sandwiches that Paquet had acquired for us the previous day as part of her back-up role.

We discussed whether or not to torch the two vehicles, but decided against it. While it would help to reduce any forensic evidence that might be used against us, fire would also draw attention to our whereabouts. And the one thing we needed was time to get well away.

It was already four o'clock and sunrise would be around seven-thirty. Three and a half hours. Across cultivated country in the dark, avoiding roads and stumbling across fields, trying to find gates and a passable route we'd be lucky to make seven miles. Very lucky. If we hit four, I'd consider it a good hack under the circumstances.

We gathered up everything we needed, including our cell-phones, two automatic pistols and an Ingram, stuffed Bex's and my rucksacks with what we considered essential and set off together into the ink-black night. The rain was still lancing down under a stiff and ice-cold north-easterly blow.

The journey was even worse and even slower than I'd anticipated. There were few features on the map to guide us, so our navigation was done mostly by dead reckoning with the compass. Thick, scudding black cloud obscured any ambient moon- or starlight and the rain seemed to march towards us, wave after wave like an army determined to stop us at all costs. Visibility was zero, the ground was a quag-mire and the three of us were cold and sodden.

Time and again we had to change course as we met with an impenetrable bramble hedge or swampy ground that sucked us in up to our thighs. Francoise even had a hiking boot sucked from her foot by the mud and it was sheer good fortune that we managed to retrieve it after floun-dering around like hippos for fifteen minutes.

After revising our dawn target destination several times, I finally got us to a narrow country lane as the first shimmer of daylight seeped up into the eastern sky. The cloud cover had thinned and the rain had reduced to a spasmodic drizzle. We sank to the ground in a semicircle, just hidden from the lane by a field hedge. The portable hexi-stove was lit for a quick and much-needed brew.

Funny stuff, tea. Its properties are almost mythical, but

only one nation has really ever recognized them and seriously absorbed the whole ritual into its collective psyche in the same way that Britain has. We have survived and won wars on tea, run the world's biggest empire, conquered enemies and crossed mountains, jungle and desert fortified by that strange and humble infusion of hot water and vegetable leaf.

As always, after just ten minutes spent huddled together, clutching hot mugs with cold fingers, we all felt reinvigorated and ready to go again.

The surrounding landscape was lightening fast, colouring-in the long meadow grass on which we were crouched.

Bex prodded at the clear plastic front of the map case. 'So we're here. About three and a half miles from where we dumped the vehicles. About two miles down the road towards the sea there's a hamlet. Well, a collection of houses. Maybe just outbuildings.'

'I'll make for them. Try and find something to use for cover. Ladder, bucket, wheelbarrow . . .' I said with more hope than genuine optimism.

The sudden noise right behind us was deep, mournful and very loud. Paquet jumped and splashed her tea into her lap as Bex and I instinctively rolled away from . . . From what, exactly?

Hardly enemy fire. Feeling slightly foolish, we both blinked back at the row of big, moist and inquisitive eyes watching our every move. Steam rose from the flared nostrils like stage smoke . . . Two Friesians and a Hereford.

'*Mon Dieu*!' Paquet gasped, clasping her chest. 'I thought this field was empty.'

'Don't make a move!' Bex hissed. 'This is our chance. Ed, have you got some rope handy?' As I slowly reached for my bergen so not to alarm the cows, she added: 'Give them something to eat. Some hard-tack biscuits?'

'We want them friendly,' I replied acidly.

'Oh, sod it, sugar lumps, then. What the hell do cows like?'

Paquet ripped up some grass. 'This stuff. It's always greener in another field, or if someone gives it to you.'

'Not a farm girl, are you?' I asked, unravelling some rope and trying to fashion a running bowline to make a lasso. Knots never were my strong point.

'*Non*, Eddie,' Paquet replied. 'But I ride with a hunt in France. I know horses and the rural life.' She proffered the clump of thick winter grass. One of the Friesians backed away, but the Hereford looked slightly interested. 'Bread, too.'

Bex chuckled. 'I can manage a grass sandwich.' She pulled the last one of a pack from her sodden parka. 'Best take the beef out. Might offend.'

Moments later, the Hereford was edging forward, sniffing at Bex's proffered grass sandwich. I made a mental note to write to the SAS one day to advise the instructors there of a tip that I felt they'd overlooked in their manuals. Meanwhile, Paquet took my rope, holding the loop in her right hand and coiling the rest in her left. As the cow tentatively nibbled at the sandwich, she edged back and around, coming in towards it from behind the animal's line of sight.

Suddenly it realized she was there and jolted its head up as it took a nervous backward step. Paquet moved decisively, stepping forward to cast a perfect circle of rope that slipped effortlessly over the creature's head. The rope loop snapped tight. The two Friesians bolted away in alarm. The ensnared Hereford snorted in disgust.

Bex grinned. 'Well done, that girl.'

Ten minutes later we were ready. Bex had dumped her rucksack and all surplus kit in the hedge and hacked a reasonable-looking headscarf from an old blouse with her penknife. She took one of the pistols and stuffed it into the waistband of her mud-splattered jeans.

Paquet rolled up one of our balaclavas to use as a woollen hat and rubbed her very expensive sweater on the ground until it resembled something that could walk by itself. When I offered her one of the automatics, she hesitated.

'Take it,' I said. 'You don't ever *have* to use it. But at least you then have an option.'

She seemed to see the sense of that and took the weapon from me with obvious reluctance.

I discarded most of my kit, lightening the bergen until it held little more than Sir Marcus's dossier, a sleeping bag, waterproofs and my Argentinian automatic. Then I stuffed the Ingram machine-pistol in the cargo pocket of my parka – just in case.

For a few moments I waited and watched at the field gate as Bex pulled the reluctant cow through onto the road, Paquet tapping the animal encouragingly on its rump with a long, thin branch. They looked almost convincing as they sauntered along the muddy lane that would eventually take them to the coast.

Then I heard an ominous sound and pulled back into the hedge beside the gate. Seconds later the dark landcruiser appeared from the west, moving slowly down the lane. Eerily, I could see nothing and no one behind its smoked-glass windows as it passed my position and crept up behind the two girls and the cow.

Bex turned, smiled and waved for the car to pass. The driver seemed in no hurry. My heart fluttered and I found myself holding my breath. The landcruiser edged past them before accelerating gently and finally disappearing around the next bend.

I exhaled with deep relief. I really couldn't see that we going to get away with this . . .

But then, this was no time for doubt or hesitation. I crossed the lane, jumped the low fence into the opposite field and headed off towards the next parallel lane that would be my route to the destination. I'd scarcely been going five minutes when I became aware of the low distant beat of a helicopter engine.

There is nothing more unnerving than being hunted from the sky. I was haunted by the sound of that aero engine, sometimes distant, sometimes sounding suddenly and frighteningly close, depending on distance and wind direction. Then it would vanish as quickly as it had come.

But, just as my shredded nerves began to settle, the noise would spring up again from nowhere, on a different bearing. And always tantalizingly, tauntingly just out of sight, behind some hill or tree line.

Yet I knew that at any moment it could burst into my line of sight and I'd be done for.

Thankfully I made the next parallel lane before that happened. I began striding along the tarmac, ready at any instant to hurl myself into the roadside ditch if a car approached or the helicopter suddenly flew overhead.

After ten minutes I slowed, the unidentified buildings shown on the Ordnance Survey map coming into view. My hopes were dashed when I saw it was a three-sided yard of farm outbuildings opening onto the lane. They were extremely derelict and there was no sign of life.

I began hunting around. There was a rusty old tractor that raised my hopes for a moment. That would have been a way to travel in style. I continued rummaging, but could find nothing. One building and then another. Outside, the helicopter came in again, hovered, and then faded away.

Just as I was about to give up, I saw it. Well, I saw the handles poking up out of a mass of rotted straw. I pulled it clear. A wheelbarrow, of sorts. Probably pre-war, which was why it had lasted despite the huge hole in the cargo pan. The wheel axle was jammed with gunk and rust, but the solid rubber tyre was serviceable.

I spent just ten minutes getting the wheel to spin free

and felt elated at the result. I dumped my half-empty bergen on board, squashing in all the free material, and covered it with handfuls of mouldy hay. On top I perched a broken-handled pitchfork for effect. After a final check that I looked suitably rustic, I set off down the lane with an air of bravado.

Walking with a heavy wheelbarrow is hard work and I found my progress was disappointingly slow. Every fifteen minutes or so I had to stop and stretch my back. Then I moved on.

Every so often my heart skipped as I heard an approaching car. A farmer in a Land Rover observed me oddly as he passed. But others simply failed to take any notice at all: a couple of churchgoers, two men off to do a spot of fishing, and someone coming back from a DIY store, judging by the sheets of MVF strapped to the roof-rack.

Then, just as I was getting complacent, a dark landcruiser appeared. It came straight at me, up the lane from the coast. I'm sure my heart literally stopped for several beats and I felt the adrenalin rush. I dropped the handles of the wheelbarrow and went through the motion of stretching my back, giving me the chance to get a hand on the butt of the automatic in my waistband.

I forced myself to smile at the black mirrored windscreen, wipe a hand across my brow and then wave briefly at them.

The landcruiser slid unhesitatingly by, its exhaust burbling softly.

Christ, I thought, was it the SRO? Or was it a wealthy farmer or a posh landlord with a liking for landcruisers with darkened windows? It could even be some media celebrity – more than a few enjoyed the anonymity of the remote East Anglian coast. Everything could be exactly what it seemed, or everything could be the exact opposite of what it appeared to be. And I would never know – until it was too late.

I plodded on, round countless bends, up inclines and

down slopes in a seemingly endless journey towards the sea. A dozen vehicles passed, this way and that, each giving me a near heart attack as my apprehension soared. The drivers seemed to be mostly younger men, probably on their way to a pub for a Sunday lunchtime drink. That was a thought that kept me going! My parched throat cried out for a pint of best and I'd have killed right then for some pork scratchings or a packet of dry roast peanuts. I swear to God that I was starting to hallucinate.

Then the cop car turned up, all gleaming white and harlequin livery.

A window wound down and an officer stuck his head out. 'Afternoon, sir.'

I grunted.

'You got a licence for that wheelbarrow?' He grinned. His funniest joke of the week. 'Local, are we?'

I forced my lips into a smile, despite the knot tightening in my gut and managed another non-committal grunt.

'Haven't seen any unusual characters around, have you? One bloke and two women. Maybe together or separate. Women in their thirties, man quite a bit older.'

'Ain't seen no one,' I said. 'Just a couple of badgers and an old dog fox.' Christ knows what the accent sounded like. A mix of Yorkshire and Dorset, I thought. For all I knew that's what the local East Anglian pronunciation was like anyway.

But thankfully the young cop was none the wiser. 'But if you do see anyone answering the descriptions, sir, call the local station, won't you?'

I grunted for the third time and nodded. Then I watched with a feeling of relief as the car pulled away off inland.

I'd barely walked another hundred yards when the landcruiser came along the same way. It slowed and I could sense the occupants staring hard at me, although I could see nothing through the smoked glass. It was an unnerving couple of moments, but again they continued to glide by and disappear into the gathering dusk.

In the utter silence that followed I heard it for the first time. The distant sound of breaking surf. And then the forlorn screech of a gull.

I shuffled to a halt beside a field gate. A cold, misty twilight was coming down fast. Within twenty minutes or so it would be dark. I reckoned I was close enough now. Under the cover of darkness, if Bex and Paquet had stayed lucky, we should meet at the RV. So I opened the gate and pushed the barrow in behind the hedge. I threw off the straw, shouldered my bergen and took out the Ingram. A quick glance at the map and a compass bearing was all I needed before setting off diagonally across the field.

Then I heard it. But it was too soon, too quick. It had approached upwind and was suddenly above the tree line in front of me before I knew it. Just a menacing inky shape in the dark and misty sky, its safety light pulsing like a heartbeat.

# Nineteen

I threw myself to the ground and lay motionless.

The pilot or observer would have to have been on the ball to see me. As the aircraft's rotor clattered a hundred feet above my head, I squinted up. There should have been enough ambient light for me to see the usual bright livery or markings of a police or rescue service helicopter, even if I couldn't distinguish them exactly. But I saw none.

Then it moved on, reaching the lane I had left ten minutes earlier. I exhaled gently into the damp grass in front of my face. You lucky bastard, I told myself.

But I was not quite lucky enough. The damn thing began pivoting, canting over in a wide turn to bring it back onto its original course, returning the other way. It was heading straight for me again.

A thermal imager or an image-intensifier – of course. It could be either, but it didn't matter because someone up there obviously *knew* I was down here.

I froze every muscle, squeezing my breathing to a stop. The noise of the aero engine was overwhelming. Then the pitch of the sound became constant.

Deafening, it was hovering directly over me and it wasn't moving on. I felt the icy down draught of its rotor blades blasting against my back and flattening out the meadow grass in a rippling circle. That circle widenened and the rush of cold air intensified as the helicopter began to descend.

'COLTRANE!' The boom of the amplified voice was like

the wrath of God and I involuntarily jerked with surprise as I heard my name. 'COLTRANE!' It repeated. 'STAND UP AND THROW DOWN ANY WEAPONS YOU HAVE!'

Still I didn't move. I think I was clinging to some idiotic notion that they weren't sure they had something in their viewfinder, that it was a bluff. It's called clutching at straws.

For a long moment there was just the helicopter's racket filling my head. Then a Nitesun lamp was turned on, throwing a huge spotlight around me, and the voice resumed: 'DON'T MOVE. WE'RE COMING DOWN TO LAND. DON'T DO ANYTHING STUPID – WE'RE NOT GOING TO HARM YOU!'

Harm me? No, they certainly weren't going to do *that*.

Suddenly I rolled over onto my back with the Ingram clutched in both hands. The helicopter was coming down no more than thirty yards away. I aimed as near as I could to the core of the blinding light-source and squeezed the trigger. The machine pistol came alive in my hands, its vicious kick throwing off my aim instantly, but the sound was magic to my ears. I'd missed the lamp, maybe missed the entire helicopter, but it had the desired effect. The machine bucked backwards like a startled beast, the pilot backing and climbing as fast as he could. Seconds later the light went out, so as not to provide a target.

I crawled up onto all fours, panting, watching the shape melt into the night, mesmerized by its safety light. Then someone thought of that, too. It went out and there was nothing. Darkness. Darkness and then utter silence crushing in around me. Almost velvet, but too cold and abrasive to be velvet. Then that other faint sound again, somewhere distant. Surf on shingle.

Scrambling to my feet, I set off with renewed vigour, determined to put as much distance behind me as I could before the helicopter returned or directed other land units to the scene. Soon I was sweating with exertion and fear despite the icy cutting edge of the wind coming in off the North Sea. Every few minutes I thought I could hear the distant sound of car engines or the menacing *thwack-thwack* of rotor blades. Maybe I could, or maybe it was just my frayed nerves and my imagination.

So it was actually a relief when the new weather front swept in, driving a band of rain before it, coming down like spiteful little spears that stung my exposed flesh. And the noise of it beating against my clothes and the trees and the bushes swamped all other alien sound. It blissfully deadened the audible traces of anything that could be my pursuers.

I pushed on. In my mind I was back on the Brecon Beacons, crossing Pen-y-fan in the dead of winter on the most arduous military training exercises in the world. I gritted my teeth and slitted my eyes against the torrent, the small voice in my head screaming: *'On, on, on, you can do it! You're invincible, no one can stop you!'*

The rain finally stopped around four in the morning. A half-moon even made a brief appearance between the breaking cloud. By five I was approaching our RV.

This was a derelict boathouse beside a track that cut through the sand dunes to the beach. I edged forward until I was within a couple of hundred yards, hiding behind a clump of long grass on the embankment. It overlooked the track, which had been reduced to an ochre-coloured quagmire of mud and sand by the rain. I spent twenty minutes watching through my mini-binos, first the boathouse and then the surrounds. In all that time there was not a movement, not a sound.

The area certainly didn't appear compromised, but then you could never be a hundred per cent sure. Of course, it was possible that Bex and Paquet hadn't even reached it yet, although they'd had a shorter and more direct route than I had. But then again, with Bex's fieldcraft training and experience, I didn't really expect any tell-tale signs of their presence.

I pulled out my mobile and switched it on. The signal was good, but the battery was almost flat. I punched in Bex's number.

After what seemed an interminable ringing time, the familiar voice answered. '*Yes.*' Terse.

'Scotch here,' I said.

'*Mine's a gin and tonic,*' she responded. I gave a sigh of relief. "And tonic" meant she wasn't being held against her will and was free to speak.

'You there?'

'*Ninety minutes ago. Come round the back. Loose window boards.*'

'Roger,' I replied and snapped off the phone.

I buried my bergen in the sand, just in case I was wrong and we had been somehow compromised. Marcus's dossier would be buried and retrievable at some time in the future. If we weren't compromised, I'd return and collect it before our dawn departure on the Norwegian fishing boat.

Then I crossed the track and proceeded along the far embankment of dunes until I arrived at the rear of the boathouse. It was an ancient tar-timbered affair with an asphalt roof. The white paint had long since weathered away around the windows, which had been boarded up. Some of the planking hung down, retained by a single nail. I imagined this to be the work of local vandals.

Suddenly Bex's face appeared in the dark aperture. 'Welcome to our new home, lover boy.' She grimaced. 'Just remember to hold your nose.'

She wasn't joking. As I clambered through the window into the interior, I took in the stench of mildewed wood and vague lingering essences of urine and human faeces.

'I think this is a favourite haunt of local junkies and God knows who in the summer,' Bex said. 'Thankfully too cold this time of year.'

She shone a small flashlight, picking out Paquet perched uncomfortably on an old fish crate, hugging herself as if in protection against the sea of rubbish around her. Old beer bottles and cans, takeaway cartons and condom packets. They'd swept a pile of debris into the corner and I could see the light glinting on hypodermic needles.

'Careful where you stand,' Bex warned. 'I think I've cleared them away but you certainly don't want one of those in your foot.'

'I'm cold,' Paquet complained balefully. 'Soaking wet and cold.'

I slung down my bergen. 'Make sure the windows are sealed, then light the hexi. A drop of soup won't go amiss and it'll warm the place up a bit.'

'Is that wise, Ed?' Bex asked.

'Probably not, but what the hell . . .'

Bex said: 'Is this my old DS talking? You'd have had me shot for even thinking such a thing once.'

I felt suddenly very, very tired. 'Yeah, well, my standards have slipped.'

Standards or not, we were ultra-careful and in twenty minutes the hot tomato soup, some stale bread and the gentlest of warmth seemed to have raised everyone's morale a vital couple of points.

'Any trouble getting here?' I asked.

Bex shook her head. 'Not really. We had a couple of scares when a landcruiser came by. It was SRO all right, because they wound the window down to have a good look at us but then asked if we'd seen a strange man acting suspiciously. You, we presumed. I said no and asked who they were. He said CID, but I'm sure his accent was Serbian.'

'Then a real police car stopped and asked us the same

question,' Paquet added. 'Then it was all right until the helicopter came over.'

'Helicopter?' I repeated. 'Unmarked?'

'Came out of nowhere,' Bex replied. 'Startled poor old Daisy and she stampeded off down the road. We followed for a while, but then let her go. We headed overland after that. We didn't see the helicopter again.'

'It nearly caught me at dusk,' I confessed. 'Called me by name on a loud hailer. But I put a few rounds its way and it took off. Nothing since.'

Bex stared at me. 'That was close. Real scary.'

I turned to Paquet. 'What about your American friends? Are they going to confirm this pick-up?'

She shook her head. 'No, Eddie, it is already confirmed. I just have to call my contact number half an hour before – at seven – to confirm that we are here. They'll send a launch.' She gave a nervous smile. 'But they warned that we may have to get our feet wet, wading out to them.'

'I can't believe this is nearly over,' Bex said.

'I'm not sure it will be. Even if Fran's senator friends can make a big noise on the international media front, will it persuade our government to look into these trumped-up charges? If so, they'd have to own up to some big errors of judgement.'

Bex nodded grimly. 'Not something politicians and civil servants are renowned for . . . So it could *still* be a life on the run. Bonnie and Clyde, eh?'

'Just Clyde,' I said. 'It'll be me they'll want. But I'll give them a run for their money.'

Bex's eyes glistened and I could see the moisture gathering in their corners. 'Sure, I know you'll do that, Ed. I just wish . . .' She let the sentence fade, unable to finish it as she turned her head away.

In the remaining time before dawn, I retrieved my stashed bergen, cleaned and checked over my automatic pistol and the Ingram – just in case – then hunkered down at one of the holes in the woodwork that would give me a good view of the beach when the sun came up.

The time went remarkably quickly and before I knew it, it was time for Paquet to call her American friends. There was a bit of a scare, because her mobile battery too was running low. But then she was gabbling away in French for a few moments, so fast I found it hard to follow.

Bex glanced at me and frowned, then looked back at Paquet.

Suddenly the Frenchwoman looked relieved, smiled and snapped off the phone.

'Problem?' I asked.

'No, just some confusion. Everything is all set. The launch should be here in thirty minutes.'

And not a moment too soon, I thought.

Outside, Monday was dawning cold and bleak. Appropriate for the day when the country's politicians were going to sign over the future security of Europe into the hands of the very people that they should have been protecting it against. Appropriate for the day I'd probably be leaving my homeland for the very last time.

A cold Monday, in every sense. Despite the warmth of my parka, I felt an involuntary shiver that raised the small hairs on the back of my neck. It was a strange sort of sensation.

The wind had dropped a little but the cloud was low and brooding. The sea was the colour of dull pewter before it spread out over the flat wet expanse of sand in long, crisscrossing lines of rippling surf. The awakening sun created a muted aurora on the murky North Sea horizon and sent a gleam of light across the beach. Seagulls were up now, as soon as there was enough visibility to fly, hunting over the turning tide for anything edible left amidst the pungent detritus of seaweed and driftwood.

'Any time now,' Bex murmured, 'there'll be dog-walkers.'

She was echoing my very thoughts. This was all too late; it should have been done a couple of hours earlier. But then, we were hardly calling the shots. We were in the hands of some redneck senators in the US.

I scanned my binoculars over the sea, sweeping slowly and steadily from left to right. My only find was a distant oil tanker heading down towards the Dover Straits. Nothing else. I swept back the other way – and almost missed it, hidden between the swells. I pulled up the focus to max. An ungainly silhouette with that seemingly top-heavy look that fishing boats have. It was too far away to say if it was a trawler or another type. But it was there, on station, on time. It had to be ours.

'I think she's there,' I muttered.

'She,' Bex said. 'Why are ships always female?'

I allowed myself a smile. 'Because . . . they're unreliable, unpredictable – and decidedly dangerous.'

As I felt the elbow in my ribs, Paquet said: 'What about the launch?'

'It would be too small for me to pick out at this range,' I replied. 'The tide's out a good five hundred yards.'

'Think we should start walking?' Bex asked.

She had a point. It was twenty past seven – just ten minutes to the pick-up time. The closer we were to the shoreline the less chance there was of any compromise.

I said: 'I'll take my bergen. Leave anything else that isn't absolutely essential.'

Moments later we emerged cautiously from the rear of the boathouse. Bex had her automatic out and I had the Ingram as inconspicuously as possible at the ready. We checked inland, up the track cutting through the dunes for any sign of life. Nothing. Then we advanced slowly towards the beach. There was nothing to the left, but to the far distant right there were minuscule outline figures. The predicted couple and their dog. But they would take a long time to reach us. Our luck seemed to be holding.

'Right, let's go,' I said.

The previous night's rain served to firm up the usually dry sand on the upper slope of the beach so at first we made fast and fairly easy progress. While I pressed ahead in the lead, Bex hung back slightly to check our rear every few minutes, her eyes scanning along the dunes.

I pushed on, my soles now slapping on the wet sand beyond the tideline of kelp, seashells and marine detritus. The surf was still several hundred yards away, shrugging onto the shore in a restrained but powerful rhythm. Around me the air was beginning to fill with the salty spume carried by the chill and blustering offshore breeze. I gazed out at the grey-green rollers, their white-frothed tops hiding the gap between foreshore and horizon. Then suddenly I glimpsed it, bobbing momentarily between swells. The launch. It was substantial, with inboards I guessed, and half a dozen crew on board. It was nudging its way towards the shore. Of course, the tide was on the turn at this moment and I was aware that their progress could suddenly become swifter. The swifter the better, I prayed.

'ED, BEHIND US!'

I turned as Bex's warning eddied on the breeze. She'd stopped and was looking back at the dunes.

There they were. A line of silhouettes against the pale grey skyline. Hard targets, in army jargon. Easy pickings, if you had a long-range 'jimpy' – or general-purpose machine gun – in your hands. Sadly, we did not. So instead of being badly deployed targets, they represented menace. And they were walking steadily forward, down off the dunes and onto the beach. Closing slowly.

I turned back towards the sea. The launch seemed to have made hardly any progress, struggling through the breakers. I just hoped it would get there in time.

'We'll make it,' I said with more assurance than I felt.

'We must!' Paquet gasped, splashing forward through a wide sea-water pool left behind on the sodden sand. Her movements were untidy and unco-ordinated. She clearly wasn't used to physical exertion – and nothing drains your energy more than fear.

'Don't panic, Fran,' I advised. 'Keep calm and walk steady. They're a long way behind us.'

Bex was striding alongside me. 'They're not rushing, Ed. I don't get it. Why aren't they using that bloody helicopter of theirs . . . ?'

I'd missed the beat. It was somehow muffled by the rolling surf breaking like an artillery barrage along the tideline. Maybe Bex's words had got my antenna twitching. But then I'd heard that sound too many times, was too attuned to it, not to pick up on the faintest vibration. Too many times it had represented my salvation – although, just occasionally, like that time in the Russian–Afghan War, it had presaged the likely arrival of the grim reaper. This one was no Hind gunship, but its threat to us now was no less dangerous.

'You and your mouth!' I hissed at Bex.

She glanced back at me, perplexed. Then she too picked it up. 'Oh, shit!'

The blurred speck was coming at us from the north, its urgent beat carried now on the ragged edge of the wind. It was low, flying nap-of-the-earth, almost hidden by the dunes and the misty spume drifting in from the breakers.

'What the hell do we do now?' Bex gasped.

'Keep going!' I snapped back, my face contorted by the blast of icy wind, salt and sand particles whipping in over the surf. 'Look after Fran!' I added, yanking out the Ingram from the cargo pocket of my parka.

Bex understood. 'But don't get left behind, Ed! You've got the dossier!' Then she turned away, threw an encouraging arm around Paquet's shoulders and urged her on.

Now the sound of the helicopter was swelling rapidly until the noise seemed to fill my head and the landscape itself, drowning out the crashing of the waves and the howl of the wind. It was dark and bore no markings that I could distinguish. I didn't know what make it was – it wasn't any military variant with which I was familiar. But civilian or armed forces, it made no difference, I just knew it was the one that had been after me last night.

Then it abruptly left the dunes on a dead-reckoning course straight for me, a black and all-devouring bird of prey. The pulse of the landing light was a blinking eye. With me in its sights.

I swung up the snout of the Ingram in a double-handed grip and dropped to one knee to steady my aim.

The two three-round bursts peppered the air around the cockpit, and the pilot pulled back harshly. The machine rose violently like a bucking bronco as it passed above my head, gathering height.

I glanced back towards the dunes. The men in black might have been walking slowly, but they were also advancing inexorably like zombies in a horror movie.

Already they were on the edge of the wet sand. And they were close enough now for me to make out the weapons hanging loosely in their hands. Some short-, some long-barrelled. Shotguns, carbines or sniper rifles, it was impossible to tell at that distance. But whatever they were carrying, it didn't look good.

Turning round, I decided to put some distance between us and them. I was surprised how much progress Bex and Paquet had made. They were some hundred yards away already and maybe only another two hundred from the edge of the breakers. I jerked the bergen higher onto my back, put my head down and started running. But it was like running through wet porridge. At each heavy footfall, my boots either skidded on the sodden sand or were sucked under. It was as if the bloody ragworms were in a conspiracy against me!

The faster I tried to run, the slower my progress seemed to be. My thigh muscles were starting to feel like they'd been stretched on a medieval rack. Despite the bite of the wind, I was in a sauna-sweat. So hot, I felt I could hardly breathe.

Now the helicopter was circling around me like an irritating and aggravated fly. I tried to follow it with the Ingram's muzzle as I ran, but it kept on the move, hovering, round and round, never giving me a second to take a snatched shot. I'd have to stop and aim again, and maybe then they'd shoot me first next time. They clearly weren't playing games . . . Or then again, perhaps that was exactly what they were doing.

But at least I was now catching up with Bex and Paquet. They were only some thirty yards ahead of me and the surf another hundred beyond them. Fuck only knew where the bloody launch was! The sweat was running into my eyes and combining with the salt in the air to damn near blind me.

Then the helicopter was directly overhead again, the pilot getting bolder. The down draught of the rotor was like an extra gravitational pull, trying to crush me into the soggy wet sand like some helpless insect. I cursed as I was forced to stop, turn my face up into the core of the maelstrom and lift the Ingram again. This time I'd blast the bastard's fuel tanks . . .

But my finger froze on the trigger. No, not so clever when I was standing directly beneath a potential fireball.

'ED, STOP FOR GOD'S SAKE!' The loud-hailer voice reverberated around me. 'DON'T SHOOT AGAIN! IT'S ME – MORGAN! TRUST ME! YOU'RE WALKING INTO A TRAP!'

I glared up at the swirling vortex above my head.

'BOLLOCKS!' I shouted back, and pulled the trigger. The three-round burst was deliberately well wide, but it served its purpose. Momentarily I was released from the typhoon's grip as the helicopter backed away, taking its awesome down draught with it.

*'WE'RE LANDING, ED!'* the voice started again. *'I'VE GOT TO TALK! I'M UNARMED!'*

Oh, sod you, I cursed, pushing on towards the receding figures of Bex and Paquet. I was aware of the helicopter swooping around in a wide loop to my left, slowing to a hover close to the two girls. I raced forward as the landing-skids came jerkily down to rest.

I half-expected Bex to shoot, but she didn't. Then I realized that the women, too, would have heard Morgan's loud-hailer message. I just hoped to God that Bex wouldn't fall for it.

But as I closed the gap, I realized that she had. She'd stopped and waited as Morgan Dampier dropped down from the helicopter cabin in his smart suit trousers, only to disappear up to his calves in silt.

'Don't listen to him, Bex!' I yelled into the wind.

Paquet looked nervous, still backing towards the surf. I could now see the launch struggling to make the last fifty yards to the beach.

Dampier squelched his way forward onto firmer sand. 'I'm sorry, Bex!' I could just hear him say. 'You weren't to know that I've been working to get evidence *against* the SRO! Now I think *you*'ve got what I need.'

'Liar!' I screamed as I came to within yards of him.

He turned towards me. 'It's true, Ed! And that launch isn't coming from some Norwegian fishing boat organized by the CIA. It's from a Yarmouth trawler hired by the SRO!'

Paquet's face had turned ashen. 'Don't listen, Eddie. You *know* he's with the SRO – why believe his lies? *He's* probably the one who had Marcus and Jude killed. The SRO want to stop us at all costs! Please, the launch is nearly here! Please come!'

Suddenly I knew what had been wrong about the events of the past fifteen minutes. What had been wrong from the moment that the men in black had appeared over the line of dunes. They hadn't run out to stop us, to cut us off. They'd moved forward with slow, steady menace. They hadn't been trying to stop us, they'd been closing the trap, pushing us towards our rendezvous with the launch. Like beaters on a pheasant shoot.

I was almost beginning to believe Dampier as he said: 'Hurry, Ed. Those SRO bastards don't know who the hell we are in this helicopter. Let's get out of here before they recognize me!'

'NO, EDDIE!' Paquet shouted. 'Why do you listen to this? You know what they're like!' Behind her I could see the launch wallowing just yards off shore, darkly dressed occupants dropping over the side.

Dampier gave an awkward smile. 'I hate to tell you this, Ed, but there's a traitor in your gang. We've been monitoring Miss Paquet's mobile since she made calls to France.'

My heart sank. I just couldn't bring myself to believe it. Not Marcus's lover, not after all we'd been through together.

'Seems like she lost her bottle,' Dampier added.

I turned on her. 'Is this true?'

Paquet managed to look beautiful and dishevelled, defiant and defensive all at the same time. 'It was the only thing to do, Eddie. You were getting us deeper and deeper into trouble. I could see no escape for any of us . . . Going to prison or being killed by those thugs. So I did the only thing I could. I called my old contact in the DST. Through him I got assurances from your British intelligence services that no charges would be brought against us . . .'

Dampier gave one of his irritating little smiles. 'Your friend at the DST wasn't talking with British intelligence, he was talking with Domedzic. Your DST man is in the loop.'

Paquet shook her head. 'I'm certain that's not true.'

Dampier ignored her denial. 'And no charges are needed when you play Brigadier Domedzic's way. Drowned people don't stand trial.'

'No, no,' Paquet protested. 'I was promised we will all be safe. Come on, we can still go. The launch is here.'

I was suddenly aware of voices raised from inland. The zombies were closing in fast now. One had a cellphone clamped to his ear and was shouting out orders to the others in Serbian, clearly having sought instructions from Brigadier Domedzic on what to do about the surprise arrival of the unmarked helicopter.

'Decision time,' I said, translating what was being shouted. 'He's ordering them to close in regardless. Get us on the launch – dead or alive. And destroy the helicopter and witnesses as necessary.'

Bex stared at me. 'Domedzic's mad.'

Dampier glanced at the nearing line of SRO gunmen. 'He knows he'll probably get away with it. With no witnesses to worry about, the EU will hush it all up. Much too embarrassing.' He turned to me. 'You've got the dossier?'

'In my bergen.'

'And the video recording?'

'Fran's got it.'

Paquet backed away, wide-eyed. 'No, no! You are fools, this is idiocy.' Dampier took a step towards her, but only one. Suddenly there was a gun in her hand. 'Keep back! I know how to use this and I won't hesitate—'

She never finished her sentence. Bex fired from the hip, double-tapping her cleanly in the heart. The force of the two rounds threw her hard onto her back in the wet sand like an elegant and discarded rag doll.

'Selfish, double-crossing bitch,' Bex hissed beneath her

breath as she rushed forward to the corpse and began checking the coat pockets. She held up the cassette sealed in a plastic bag. 'Bingo!'

I stared in disbelief. Paquet was dead and all I could see in my mind was the beautiful white body twisting and writhing with such abandon as we'd made love just days earlier . . . Then the image went blank as if a camera shutter had closed and I was back to the cold, bleak reality.

Dampier was yelling: 'Bex, give me that gun!' He snatched the automatic from her, wiped it with his handkerchief, then tossed it onto the sand. 'Right, now let's get the hell out of here. Go, GO!'

The first rounds were barely audible above the breakers and the noise of the thrashing helicopter rotor, but there was no mistaking the fountains of silt and sea water suddenly erupting all around us. Bex began running after Dampier, crouching low as she approached the down draught. The men in black were spreading out now in a pincer movement, running and shouting to each other as they encircled us.

I lifted the Ingram and let rip a full hosing ripple of fire that sent many of them flying for non-existent cover in the wet sand . . . and then I got the dead man's click. Out of ammo.

The noise of the helicopter engine gathered momentum as the machine began to rise, sucking the skids free from the gluey grip of the silt. I threw away the Ingram and raced the remaining twenty yards to the aircraft as it pulled away. A trail of rounds snapped at my heels all the way across until I threw myself at the cockpit. Willing hands grabbed the neck of my parka and my arms as the helicopter peeled away, low and fast out over the pounding surf and the wallowing launch to a safe range above the cold grey-green swell of the North Sea.

Dampier grinned but waved me to silence as he pulled

on his radio headset and spoke into the mouthpiece: 'X-ray to Tango Five. Blue Fox and She-Wolf are okay. Red Cockerel is down. Killed by hostile fire . . .'

Bex glanced in my direction, bewildered. 'She-Wolf? Is that me?'

'Sounds like it.'

'Wow . . . And Red Cockerel is Francoise?'

'Symbol of France.'

'Of course.'

Dampier was saying: 'Repeat, killed by *hostile* fire. Therefore authority given for police handover to military command and control. Over.'

Seconds later he was listening intently to the reply, before allowing himself a satisfied smile and nod of the head. While this was going on, the co-pilot handed Bex and me bone-domes with radio rigs. The crew were wearing camo trousers, but the rest of their uniform was a bit casual. There was something sort of familiar about it all.

Dampier's voice came over my intercom. 'That's right, Ed. This is your old mob. You won't recognize any of them. Jesus, aren't they young nowadays? Bum-fluff cheeks, never seen a razor. Just like our coppers . . . This is one of their liaison helos. Virtually got their own air force these days.' He tapped on the perspex. 'Take a look. The boyos are going in now.'

The pilot had wisely climbed to several thousand feet, out of range of any fire from the men in black. It was strange, looking down on the strip of coast through the layer of mist and spume. This wasn't reality – it was like watching tiny metal war-game figures on a sand-table in ops planning. A semi-circle of men formed around a single body on the vast expanse of sand that disappeared into murk and infinity in each direction. Other figures from the launch coming ashore.

But what really caught my eye was the movement, coming from the dunes. White Range Rovers, by the look of them.

Half a dozen. Coming down behind the men in black, and fanning out to their left and right.

'Counter-Rev Wing,' Dampier explained. 'Some people have really stuck their necks out on this one. Let's hope those bloody Serb rednecks don't put up a fight.'

They didn't. Maybe it was the nature of the beast. Bullies are always cowards and all that. But the sight of the black combat-clad anti-terrorist SAS troops in assault gas masks and bristling with weaponry surrounding them seemed to be enough. As we pulled away, hands were going up and firearms were going down. It was all over.

I turned to Dampier. 'Just what the hell is going on, Morgan?'

He looked at me directly. 'More than you could ever imagine, Ed. I've been on the case against the SRO – on the orders of a faction inside SIS, who believe this is all wrong.' He saw the incredulity on my face. 'Yes, Ed, the Secret Intelligence Service at war with itself. My people have been forced to operate in secret from most of their superiors who are blindly following the line from Number Ten. Some high-rankers have put their careers on the line by briefing senior Cabinet ministers, but they just didn't want to hear.'

'I don't understand that,' Bex interjected.

Dampier shrugged. 'They and their political egos are too plugged in to the European power game. There's a big party going on and they want to go. All those motorcades and big banquets. What politician wants to stay at home with Buttons?'

I said: 'And that's the task you took on when you left me after the Tex-Mex business?'

'Yep, Ed, and I sure as hell didn't expect you to pop up on the scene to damn near ruin everything.'

I was indignant. 'How the hell did I do that?'

'Because after the SRO killed Marcus, everyone wanted the copies of his dossier. They wanted to destroy them, we wanted just one for the evidence. Trouble was, you'd gone and hidden them and my small group, operating covertly within MI6, didn't have the resources and manpower that the SRO had. They had the authority to call in MI5 under the Genk Protocol – and they did.'

'But you were based at SRO headquarters,' Bex reminded him. 'Surely *you* were at the heart of things.'

Dampier gave one of those charming little smiles of his that got women damp between the legs. 'Oh, if only! Schmitt and Domedzic are nothing if not consummate professionals. And Johnny Galic ruled his men with a rod of iron. Maybe if we could have got MI5 involved professionally we could have cracked it, but their hierarchy have been even more in the EU camp than ours at Riverside. They're convinced that one day they'll run Europe's security. So we were on our own. My faction had very little grounds to authorize anything.'

'But someone's authorized something pretty big now,' I pointed out. 'A major anti-terrorist deployment.'

Dampier nodded. 'My boss is a department head due for retirement. Not that he expects a pension now. But he's made provisions, I gather. Salted funds away in the Caymans. Old school, you see. Got the Foreign Office to sanction this thing on the belief that we're tackling a gang of Serbian gun-running racketeers who are trying to supply arms to the Real IRA.'

I shook my head in disbelief. 'Christ, Morgan, you haven't changed.'

'Not sure that was a compliment, old son.'

I had to laugh. 'I'm not sure, either.'

'Point is, Ed, we're very much at the Last-Chance Saloon. That's why we needed a copy of the dossier. Your contin-uing involvement with my old department after I left proved a bloody nuisance. Nightmare, in fact. My successor Tony Tromain has always been a toadie and ended up with flippers in all camps. Not an original thinker, exactly. SIS and the SRO were both trying to use you for their own ends. When you went in to kill Mihac the idea was that you'd both end up dead in a major triumph for UK security operations.'

It was a relief to have my paranoia confirmed. 'You know?'

'Tromain told me himself. What threw him after that was the police finding Jude's body at your place. Johnny Galic told me it was Domedzic's bright idea to get her body out of the fridge at the morgue – originally she was to have died in a holiday accident. Tromain didn't know anything about that, of course. In fact, before that he knew as much or as little as you did.'

'Wait a minute,' I interrupted. 'How the hell was Jude killed? Not in the bombing?'

'No, Ed.' Dampier seemed to be searching for the gentlest way to put things. 'To the best of my understanding, she was snatched off the street by the SRO just hours before Sir Marcus had been due to meet his whistle-blower, Helmut Frauss. Stupid, really. She'd just popped out to buy some nicotine patches because she'd decided to quit smoking as a New Year resolution. We think Marcus waited for her as long as he could in the hotel foyer, then had to leave—'

'And what happened to Jude?'

His face looked suddenly drained. 'She was held by the SRO while they planted the bomb in the car.'

'Then killed,' I reminded him.

He nodded. 'I'm afraid so. Suffocation with a plastic bag is my best guess. Her body secretly returned to London . . .'

'Oh Christ,' Bex said.

I felt the bile rising in my stomach. 'And the third person in the car? The hooker?'

Dampier raised his hands. 'The result of panic to concoct a plausible cover story by Whitehall, French security and the SRO. That was after the Paris police found that Marcus's mystery companion – Jude – had also disappeared from the hotel. In fact, there was no third bomb victim.'

'And the Paris bomb itself?' I asked.

'That was pure SRO. Schmitt and Domedzic reckoned that they'd get the three of you on the run and let the British police and legal system do their work for them – although they'd have been happy to get to you first. They tried, believe me.'

'I know that,' I said with feeling.

'If they'd succeeded,' Dampier added, 'they reckoned they'd privately get big plaudits for the SRO as an example of what the EU's new security apparatus could achieve. But then you confounded their plans and went on the run. They were stuffed, until—'

'Fran broke ranks?' Bex guessed.

'My faction had friends in Paris running taps on her close friends,' Dampier confirmed. 'Once we had her mobile number it was easy. I gather she'd been used by the EU – in fact, an SRO operation – from the start as soon as she got cosy with Sir Marcus. They put pressure on her.'

I felt rather bad now. 'She admitted that to me.'

Dampier saw the look in my eyes. 'Don't feel too bad about it, Ed. I'm sure she was genuinely with you for a while, but got bloody frightened by the turn of events. She's admitted as much on the tapes of her calls. Of course, she got looped back to Schmitt and the SRO. He came up with this coastal pick-up scam and the US-CIA angle.

'Her contact in French intelligence told her that we Brits had promised her immunity from arrest in return for the delivery of you two. She thought she was dealing with MI6, but in fact it was the SRO itself. Some of these journos like

Paquet think they know it all, but in truth they know diddly-fuck.'

He sighed. 'Anyway, Schmitt and Domedzic thought they had the three of you in the bag. You'd walk onto their boat . . . and be erased from their files. Just vanish from the face of the Earth. Weighted corpses over the side, I should think . . . What they hadn't counted on was your raid on their own headquarters!'

Bex didn't follow. 'Fran didn't tell them?'

Dampier raised his eyebrows. 'I'm sorry, Ed. I didn't explain it very well. Francoise Paquet only half-shafted you. She thought she'd got a good deal with the British Government. She was told what she wanted to hear. So she believed it.'

It took a moment for the implication of that to sink in. Although Paquet had believed that she'd won immunity for herself from Whitehall, in her mind the SRO was still the real enemy. The more evidence against it, the better for Bex and me if and when we were ever to face a trial.

That's why Paquet had kept her mouth shut about our plan. Sure, in panic she'd saved her own skin, but she'd also done her best for us.

The vision of that beautiful body sprawled inelegantly on the pale sand flashed into my brain. I could see the black cloud of blood spreading into the sea-water pool beneath her and could almost smell the burning in my nostrils as the image was acid-etched into my memory. I knew at that moment that it would be there for all time.

Bex said bleakly: 'Oh, fuck. And I killed her.'

I turned my head away, feeling a most awful knot of guilt tightening in my stomach. I'd damned near come to love that woman. Fran had enchanted me, fired me up even more than I wanted to admit to myself . . .

But, despite her brave, tough and professional façade, she'd been out of her depth. A frightened animal. She'd had no training or experience of the dangerous and secret world that Bex and I had inhabited for so long, yet we'd expected her to cope with it as we did. I realized now that that had been totally unfair.

Although it had been Bex who'd shot her, it could so easily have been me. I felt totally wretched.

I was staring, unseeing, out of the cockpit at the landscape sweeping by below. A country road, a muddy track leading off, a deserted farmyard.

Fear rose in my chest. 'Morgan, what the hell—?'

'Ed?' All innocence.

'Where the fuck are you taking us? This is the bloody SRO headquarters!'

# Twenty

'Quite so,' Dampier answered evenly as the momentum of the helicopter started to slow. 'You two wanted so desperately to expose the truth about the Special Research Office – now's your chance.'

He tapped on the perspex of the cockpit door. 'Look down there at the compound. In the parking lot you can see half a dozen black Range Rovers with smoked-glass windows. They're Ministry of Defence VIP wagons. Just brought in a contingent of all the Prime Ministers whose countries were signatories to the Genk Protocol. Secretly flown into RAF Mildenhall before first light this morning.'

'What are you saying, Morgan?' I asked.

'The politicians are here for a tour of the SRO Headquarters facility and grandiose little speeches by Giovanni Bestelloli and Herman Schmitt, assuring the great and the good of Europe how safe the security of the EU will be in their hands. Then, before a little light lunch and a glass of Chardonnay, the Genk Protocol will be secretly ratified. Set in stone for all time.'

Although Dampier was smiling, the light behind his eyes was thin and bleak. 'In fact, this quaint little ceremony will legally lock security and fraud into the EU infrastructure in a way that'll make it impossible to demolish for years to come.'

The helicopter had slowed to hover above the landing pad at the rear of the compound and now began its descent.

I knew Dampier was playing games with us. 'So what the hell d'you hope to do about it?' I asked angrily.

'Not so much me, old son, but you and Bex,' he replied blandly.

This was madness. 'Christ, Morgan, if we step off this bloody chopper in the SRO compound, we'll get crucified.'

'Not with all of Europe's chief ministers watching, you won't.' At that moment the helicopter's skids touched down on the pad. Dampier leaned towards us earnestly. 'Listen, you two. I'd have picked you up yesterday and gone through all this if Ed hadn't been so trigger-happy and taken pot-shots at us. My boss in SIS has jumped off the burning tower on this one, Ed. He got special permission through the PM's office to get me into today's shindig with chosen colleagues. You and Bex.'

Bex looked astounded. 'The PM knows we're coming?'

Dampier's laugh was genuine. 'Don't be daft, Bexy. The PM doesn't know me, you or Ed from Adam. All he knows is that he's received an urgent request from a senior officer in the Secret Intelligence Service for an urgent briefing from an advisory team prior to today's ratification ceremony.'

I was incredulous. 'And we are that team?'

'I can't think of anyone better to give a full and accurate rundown of what the SRO is really about and what ratification will mean.'

Bex and I looked at each other. I don't know exactly what she was thinking, but I know what I was. Apart from acknowledging that Morgan Dampier was every bit the maverick genius he had always liked to give the impression he was, I was petrified. Not of encountering the SRO and its thugs, but at the thought of standing in front of the Prime Minister of Great Britain and trying to explain the truth behind the organization. Where the hell would I start? Panic had already blanked my mind.

I took a deep breath. Jesus, this couldn't be worse than

some of the briefings I'd given back in my early Regiment days. I reached for my bergen. 'Okay, Morgan, let's do it.'

'No, Ed. Not the dossier.'

'What?'

'It's the only one that we have in friendly hands. As soon as we step out, this helo will fly with it back to Hereford. Copies will be made and secretly dispatched to different locations for safe keeping.'

My eyes narrowed. 'This had better not be a con, Morgan.'

'No con, Ed.'

I quickly detached the side pouch that contained all my few very personal belongings, including my souvenir Argentinian pistol from the Falklands.

At that very moment a commotion began outside on the pad. The uniformed security guards were standing around, looking nonplussed by our unexpected arrival. Someone had been on the radio for advice. That advice materialized in the shape of Johnny Galic and a bunch of men in black. He strode towards the helicopter.

Dampier threw open the cockpit door and stepped out. While he did so, I surreptitiously transferred the Argentinian pistol from my side pouch to the waistband of my trousers. I still didn't fully trust the man.

'What the hell are you doing?' Galic demanded, glaring at Dampier. Then, without waiting for a reply, he ranted on: 'This is an unauthorized landing on restricted government property. You are to leave immediately.'

Weapons surreptitiously appeared in the hands of Galic's men in black as they stood back, menacing but restrained, just awaiting orders.

Dampier flashed his security pass in the man's face. 'Sorry, Johnny, but as you know I'm a representative of the *British* intelligence service and our arrival is authorized by the Prime Minister himself. We have a meeting scheduled with him.'

Galic's face reddened at the challenge to his authority. 'There *is* no meeting. There is no time. I know nothing about such a meeting.'

I could only see the back of Dampier's head, but I just knew he was smiling. 'Of course you don't, Johnny, this is a private British meeting. Nothing to do with you.'

But Galic was hardly listening, instead he tried to push past Dampier to get a look at who else was in the helicopter. Instinctively Bex and I shrank back in our seats.

'You!' the Serb gasped as he recognized me.

That was it for Dampier. He turned back to us. 'Right, out – NOW!'

He pushed Galic roughly away to give us space to scramble out. I was just aware of the rasp of cocking handles on weapons and sensed the emotional temperature soar.

'STAND ASIDE! STAND ASIDE!'

It was a loud and gloriously British military voice.

As I climbed out of the copter I could see the short column of twelve men in casual civilian dress enter the helipad area. They appeared to be unarmed, but looked mean and intimidating and had no hesitation in elbowing the Serb gunmen aside. Different heights, burly and most of them lightly tanned and sporting moustaches, I immediately knew who the new arrivals were.

Dampier leaned towards me and whispered. 'We had them escort the VIPs in. Bit of a Trojan-horse job. Your old mob.'

Of course. I almost wanted to laugh – or even cry with relief – as I saw the SAS men casually form themselves in a protective semicircle around the three of us, facing out. Two more, I noticed, held back behind the bemused and aggrieved SRO gunmen.

A harsh sergeant-majorly voice announced loudly and crisply. 'Escort present for party to British Prime Minister. Stand away!'

I did a double take. The last time I'd seen little Geordie

Fenwick, he'd been a shy and weedy recruit who'd scraped through Selection to the Regiment by the skin of his snaggle-teeth. But it must have been some seven years since I'd last seen him on that fateful tour of Bosnia. He'd been as nervous as hell. He'd filled out somewhat since then to become something resembling a one-man tank and now he carried himself with confidence and a mighty air of authority.

As Bex, Dampier and I allowed ourselves to be surrounded by our escort, I was aware of the helicopter winding up for take-off. We ambled forward in a phalanx, brushing the Serbs aside. Johnny Galic followed up behind us, still protesting loudly.

I found myself walking next to Fenwick. 'Hi, boss, how y'doing?' he asked.

'Fine, Geordie. And yourself?'

'Never better.' He looked up and gave me a confident wink. 'And don't you worry about a thing, boss. Just stick with me. I'll look after you.'

Cheeky little sod!

Then, with the roar of the helicopter taking off rever-berating in our ears, we entered the headquarters building. Security doors slammed shut behind us and we were suddenly engulfed in an air-conditioned hush. The sound of marching feet was deadened by the thick pile carpet.

The leader of the SAS squad turned back to Dampier. In a quiet Scots accent, he said: 'The PM's waiting for you upstairs in one of the offices.'

It was then that I recognized that tall, grey-haired figure, too. Dave McVicar was something of a legend in the Regiment and a year or so back had been involved in a major operation in mainland China. A staff sergeant now, he must be very close to the retirement age for active service. No offence to Geordie, but I was very pleased to see an old friend and such a seasoned professional in charge.

We dutifully followed him up the stairs to the next floor.

When we reached it, I was aware of SRO staff just standing on either side of the corridor and looking at us. None of them seemed too pleased to see us.

McVicar stopped at one of the office doors and rapped smartly on it with his knuckles. The door opened a fraction and I saw a vaguely familiar face in the gap. I recognized him from the newspapers and TV footage as the Prime Minister's Press Secretary. The PM's spin-doctor-in-chief. Or his Svengali, some said – or, even more unkindly, his Rasputin. The power behind the power.

'McVicar, sir. I have Mr Dampier and party for the PM.'

The Press Secretary glared warily and stepped back a pace. 'Very well. Come in.' His tone didn't suggest that we were exactly being welcomed with open arms.

As Dampier stepped forward, McVicar said: 'I'll keep a couple of men on the door.'

'Wise move,' came the murmured reply as the SIS man strode in to meet our nation's leader.

Bex followed and I was next.

McVicar nodded at me. 'Good to see you, Ed.'

'And you, Dave.'

He gave me a roguish grin. 'Never could keep yourself out of trouble, could you?'

I gave him a playful thump on the arm as I passed him and stepped into the office. Someone closed the door behind me. It felt like being trapped in a cage.

It was a smart, ultra-modern high-tech office decorated in shades of grey, white and black, with sleek Swedish-looking office furniture. The Prime Minister half-sat on the edge of a huge ashwood desk, the Press Secretary and someone whom I took to be his Private Secretary hovered uncertainly by the smoked-glass coffee table and charcoal leather armchairs next to it.

'Good morning, Prime Minister, I'm Morgan Dampier of MI6.'

The politican rose off his perch to shake hands. I thought the slightly elfin face looked lined and weary, his pallor and his fluffy but thinning hair greyer than I'd realized from the TV news. His eyes were glittery, wary and seemed to be avoiding looking at any of us directly for more than a moment.

Dampier continued: 'These are my colleagues—'

But the PM cut him short: 'Yes, Mr Dampier, your advisory team. Look, I have a dozen heads of state waiting for me in the conference hall. I am holding up proceedings, which is exceedingly embarrassing for a host. I've absolutely no idea what this is about, or why on earth my Private Secretary agreed to this most inappropriate timing . . .' He stopped himself there and gave a forced little smile as he saw his PS frowning in his direction.

'Well, yes, of course I *do* know why he agreed. An urgent request from a very senior SIS officer has to be taken most seriously.' At last the flitting eyes reluctantly settled on Dampier for a moment. 'But not a request from the *most* senior SIS officer. That is more to be expected in such circumstances, is it not?'

Dampier's smile was more nervous than normal. 'Er – that's true, Prime Minister. But this is of a very dangerous and delicate nature. And I really need to talk to you in private with my colleagues.'

The Press Secretary had been standing in silence, thoughtfully rubbing his chin with his hand as he glowered at us from under his eyebrows. Now he decided to speak: 'Spit it out, man. The PM's in the devil of a hurry. You can say anything to him in front of the two of us. He'll only tell us as soon as you've gone, anyway.'

That irritated the Prime Minister, who flashed him an annoyed sideways glance. 'Thank you, but I am capable of talking for myself, you know – when you let me.' It looked like cracks were starting to show in their relationship.

Dampier stood his ground. 'Prime Minister, this is very much for your ears only. I'm sorry, but that's the way it is.'

The PM grimaced uncomfortably. The Press Secretary and PS looked at each other, unsure.

'It's a matter of national security,' Dampier added dramatically.

The Prime Minister took a deep breath and, wringing his hands together, looked up. 'All right. But just five minutes.'

Before I could stop myself, I blurted out: 'Sir, it might take a little longer than that.'

The PM seemed to notice Bex and me for the first time. I could see him taking in the rough state of our dress and our dishevelled appearance. He looked at his two colleagues. 'Apologize to our guests for the delay, will you? Give them some excuse. And a drink, give them drinks. I'll call you as soon as I can.'

The Press Secretary glowered at us once more and started moving reluctantly towards the door. 'If you're sure . . .'

It seemed an age before we were alone together in the room with the Prime Minister. He indicated the charcoal leather sofa and armchairs. 'Make yourselves comfortable – and this had better be good.'

As Bex and I sat down, Morgan Dampier stood in front of the PM. 'Sir, my departmental director took this decision to ask for an interview independently of the head of SIS because he realized that the ratification of the Genk Protocol would be an absolute disaster for Britain and, indeed, the entire EU community.'

'Oh really,' the Prime Minister protested. 'I've heard all these sorts of rantings before . . .'

'Not rantings, sir,' Dampier came back forcefully. 'This is Ed Coltrane, formerly SAS. And Rebecca Bunnet, formerly 14 Int. They've been investigating the SRO for my people – okay, a minority group within SIS—'

'Working for you?'

'Alongsiders, Prime Minister. I'm sure you're aware of the term. Acting unpaid agents. Friends.'

Bex and I stared at each other open-mouthed. Morgan Dampier was actually claiming responsibility for all of our actions. On behalf of MI6. I just could not believe it.

The Prime Minister blinked, then frowned. 'Wait a minute. Ed Coltrane and – er – and Rebecca Bunnet . . . The Judith Sinclair murder . . . Hey, wait a minute! I've seen the TV coverage. The police are actively seeking to arrest these two . . . And you've brought them to me!'

'But, Prime Minister!' Dampier protested.

The PM wasn't listening. 'Call my PS and Press Secretary here immediately. This interview is at an end—'

I was suddenly filled with immense anger, engulfed in a blinding rage. This was about Astrid, about Marcus and Jude, about Fran.

The Argentinian pistol was out of my waistband and pointing at the Prime Minister before I'd even had a chance to think about it. 'You're elected by the people to listen to the people,' I snarled. 'I'm one of the people. So fuckin' start listening!'

Dampier moved in. 'Ed, this isn't helping.'

The blood had drained from the PM's face. 'No, no,' he said in a wheedling sort of voice. 'Mr Coltrane obviously feels strongly that he must tell me something.' He struggled to regain his composure and tried to straighten his tie, but his hands were trembling too much. He gave a tight little smile, as if having a gun pointed at his head was the most natural thing in the world. 'All right, Mr Coltrane, what do you have to tell me?'

So I put the gun away and began.

The words just tumbled out. They didn't come in any particularly logical order. I told him about Sir Marcus and his research, the mysterious and untimely end of so many who had helped him in any way. I explained how Bex and

I had got involved, about the Paris bomb and the subsequent SRO efforts to snap up all copies of the dossier. And, of course, the disappearance of Jude Sinclair.

I skipped the stuff about the attempt to set me up over Mihac's assassination. The PM wouldn't have known anything about that anyway, and he certainly would not *want* me to tell him now! I was already overloading him with enough to ruin his day.

Instead I went straight to the return to my flat where Bex and I found Jude's body. That seemed to really shake the PM. He glanced up at Dampier and got the nod of confirmation that I guess he didn't really want. He chewed on his bottom lip and from then on seemed to listen a lot more intently.

After a brief account of our being forced on the run and the SRO thugs using our own police to help give chase, I got to our break-in to this very building two nights earlier.

Dampier said: 'Of course, Ed and Bex were helping us, but not under tight or formal control by any means. When they found Jude's body they realized they'd be wanted for murder under common law . . . they had no option but to go on the run and my people didn't know what was happening. They still face a great difficulty if the real culprits cannot be charged.'

The PM nodded his understanding. 'And you knew nothing about their break-in to these premises?'

Dampier smiled proudly. 'Their initiative, entirely.'

'Who Dares Wins,' the PM muttered under his breath. It didn't sound like it was his favourite catchphrase at this moment.

'I'd already been attached here as a liaison officer,' Dampier went on. 'It was an attempt for me to penetrate what was going on. But Schmitt and Domedzic were old pros at keeping their dark secrets. I couldn't call on MI5 technicians, because the Security Service suffers under the illusion that it'll get control of the SRO eventually. And, as we're overseas intelligence, I couldn't use our own because this is the UK and, anyway, this was – essentially – an unauthorized operation. Inadvertently, Ed and Bex pulled off what we needed to achieve.' He lifted a leather Gladstone bag onto the table. 'If you'll permit me, Prime Minister.'

'What's this?'

'A recording of who met and what was said on Saturday morning in the very conference room where you and the other EU ministers are about to ratify the Genk Protocol.' Dampier extracted the miniature video player from his case, placed it on the table and plucked the mini-cam cassette from his pocket. 'Ed and Bex filmed this meeting. You will possibly recognize Schmitt, Bestelloli and Brigadier Domedzic. I can tell you the others are pan-European mafia godfathers. From Italy, the Ukraine, France, the old East Germany and Belgium. They are all on our files. We can name and identify them. I think they're all untouchables. SIS holds information, but it would not stand up in court . . .' He hit the play button.

The display of blatant arrogance and self-congratulation that followed in the formal speeches and informal replies was staggering when seen afresh in the tiny television monitor.

Judiciously, Dampier stopped the tape before the moment when Bex and I were discovered and I was shown killing the Ukrainian. Nevertheless, it was enough to leave the Prime Minister looking pale and shaken.

Dampier said: 'This morning, members of the SRO executive arm did something which is expressly *not* allowed under its secret constitution – they ambushed our friends here and the French television journalist Francoise Paquet on a beach nearby. We had an authorized SAS team intervene, but not before the SRO shot dead Paquet.'

The PM gulped. 'God, really? That's just too terrible.'

I was momentarily fazed by Dampier's quick rewriting of history to get Bex off the hook. No doubt she was even more relieved than I was.

I hesitated in picking up my cue: 'Sir, this is why you must not ratify the Protocol. Give any reason – a delay, more consideration . . . anything. Just do not ratify it.'

'It does, of course, require *unanimous* agreement,' the Prime Minister was mumbling to himself. He stared then at the floor, his feet, us and at his wringing hands for what seemed like several minutes. In fact, it can have been only seconds. Then he glanced up sharply. 'Look, all this evidence can be properly presented. I need to consult with legal experts within my government. The SRO cannot be beyond the law. Hey, I know, I'm a lawyer. There's no need to stop the ratification – we can deal with this later, if what you say is true.'

'No, sir,' Dampier cut in. 'Ed and Bex here are wanted for murder. Unless others in the SRO are arrested now on suspicion of that crime, they will be held responsible and probably convicted.'

The PM was wobbling. I realized then that he didn't give a sod about the SRO, let alone Bex or me. All he wanted was no trouble and to stay in office.

I said: 'Sir, there's something else I want you to see.' There was a TV and video recorder beside the desk. 'Let me show you this from one of my recce patrols in Bosnia.'

It was a punch below the belt, I knew. But I took the cassette from my side pouch and pushed it into the machine.

And instantly the image was back, the camera footage from the rear of the laundry van, the misty mountain road, the café on the bend. And the woman hung upside down from the tree, her skirt covering her torso and face. The plain white pants and the straining muscles of her abdomen, the sweet beauty of her navel. And the bringing down of the chainsaw between her legs.

'Oh, for God's sake!' the PM gasped and turned his head away.

I said coldly: 'That killing of my wife, a UN interpreter, was ordered by Brigadier Domedzic.'

The silence that followed was stunning. The PM leaned forward, his head between his hands. He was clearly upset; he could even have been sobbing. Eventually he sniffed and looked up: 'Okay, what do you want me to do?'

Dampier stepped forward. 'Sir, don't ratify the Protocol – any reason you like. Sanction Special Branch to arrest and detain those whom the SAS are already holding at the beach on suspicion of the murder of Francoise Paquet. And have all leading executives of the SRO arrested under the Prevention of Terrorism Act. With immediate effect.

'I've already taken the liberty of putting local Special Branch officers on standby to act. My department can furnish all the details that you and they need.'

The PM had regained his composure. 'You're asking me to act against advice from MI5 and from the head and most of the rest of MI6. Do you really think I could do that?'

Bex spoke for the first time. 'Sir, I've put my life on the line many times on the say-so of you and your predecessors. No question. I think this is payback time. As someone – probably John Wayne – once said, "A man's gotta do what a man's gotta do."'

I don't think the PM really appreciated her black humour. He looked hunted, a man desperately seeking a way out. 'I really don't think you understand the political repercussions of all this. And I honestly can't have Bestelloli arrested – he's a respected veteran MEP, for heaven's sake!'

'And he's been tried for fraud in his own country,' I snapped back.

But the PM was sharp. 'And found not guilty . . . And then there's Schmitt, a highly placed civil servant and former police officer.'

'A spymaster, sir,' I retorted, 'who barely more than a decade ago was directing Soviet Bloc dirty-tricks operations against us.'

'History,' the PM said bluntly.

Of course, I was forgetting that our PM didn't do history. 'And Brigadier Domedzic? He was wanted for war crimes until all that was quietly dropped because he turned Queen's evidence against President Milosevic. That original evidence must still exist.'

'It was officially destroyed,' Dampier chimed in. 'But SIS has copies.'

The PM shook his head. 'What sort of signal would it send to the world if these people were arrested?'

I bit my tongue and cast my initial knee-jerk response in slightly more measured terms. 'What sort of signal would it send if they're not? And the story will get out, sir, believe me. Francoise Paquet had powerful journalist friends who knew what she was investigating . . .' I let that one hang for a moment. 'And we're only asking that these people should be arrested on suspicion – I expect – of conspiracy to murder.'

'On what *evidence*, man?' the PM came back irritably.

'I'm sure you'll find most of the evidence you need in this very building. Everything seems to have been controlled from here. And if there is no evidence, the innocent will walk free.' I added: 'As they always do.'

But the PM missed the irony in my voice. He had his head buried in his hands again and was scratching his hair. At last he said: 'Look, look. I just can't make a decision on this. I have to consult – my Press Secretary, some of my senior Cabinet colleagues . . . My inclination, however – and I probably shouldn't say this – is to arrest Brigadier Domedzic . . . having seen that film.' He suddenly looked alarmed, as though he'd walked into a trap. 'I never said that, by the way. You'll have to make your own decision with your own agency's legal powers and remit.'

Was that a result? I wasn't sure. 'And the Protocol, sir?'

It was as though a portcullis had come down over his eyes. 'That's it, gentlemen. The meeting is over.' He turned to me, his eyes narrowing. 'Unless, Mr Coltrane, you intend to get it going again at the point of a gun?'

I wish, I thought savagely. I turned abruptly and left the room with Morgan Dampier and Bex close on my heels. The PM's Press Secretary and PS seemed to sense there was a crisis and almost pushed us out of the way in their rush to get back in. The door crashed shut behind us and I heard the bolts closing.

'Where the hell does that leave us?' I asked Dampier and lit a cigarette. Christ, I'd never needed a smoke so much in all my life.

'Well, Ed, the PM's obviously not going to make a decision. So I guess it's going to be down to me. If we don't act now, nothing will happen. Nothing satisfactory, anyway.' Dampier helped himself to one of my cigarettes. 'Sod it, I've only just managed to give up.'

As he inhaled hungrily, he added: 'Look, I've called in the local Special Branch and my boss has informed Special Branch in London that he believes he can supply sufficient evidence for a conviction in multiple acts of murder and terrorism against members of the SRO. Unless they're specifically stopped beforehand, the police have a duty to act. No one is above the law.'

'That *was* a joke, wasn't it, Morgan?' I asked.

Dave McVicar suddenly came rushing up the stairs. 'Looks like some gents have just arrived from Special Branch. Seemed to be some reluctance from the SRO to let them into the compound, but my chaps are sorting it out . . . So, how'd it go?'

Dampier said: 'I want everyone in the SRO arrested and taken in for questioning and the entire building searched from top to bottom for evidence.'

McVicar gave a wan smile. 'Don't believe in givin' tall orders, then, sonny? I'll let *you* tell that to the SB plods.'

'Fine. Send them up. Just make sure your guys are ready to back them up. I think some of those young Serb thugs might not like the idea.'

'Sure.' McVicar hesitated. 'By the way, a private car's turned up. Driver says he's here to pick up Johnny Galic and someone called Mr Bertram.'

'Who the hell's Bertram?'

McVicar shrugged. 'I've no idea. And no one else here seems to either.'

'And where's Galic now?'

'Haven't seen him for a bit.'

Dampier frowned. 'No one – but *no one* – leaves this place, Dave.'

'That's what I thought.'

I said: 'Galic is Domedzic's Number One. I smell someone's about to do a runner.'

Dampier threw down his cigarette and stamped it out on the plush carpet. 'And could be destroying evidence . . .' he thought aloud. He turned back to McVicar. 'Bring those SB detectives up to see me, Dave. There's a spare office down the corridor. I'm just going to make sure that slippery bastard Domedzic is safe and sound.'

'I'll come with you,' I said.

Dampier didn't bother answering – he'd already begun striding down the corridor.

I knew the door; it was the office to which I'd been dragged when we'd been caught on the previous Saturday night. Then I realized that the electronic switch had been thrown.

Dampier saw my frown. 'Don't worry, Ed, my efforts haven't been entirely useless. I have managed to get the codes for most doors.'

He proceeded to tap a number quickly into the keypad,

then glanced at me and put a finger to his lips before gently edging the door open. The smart, ultra-modern office seemed to be in a certain amount of chaos. Three or four big attaché cases were open on the desk amid a sea of papers and photographs. Johnny Galic was frantically sifting through them, tossing them on the floor or allocating them to one of the cases. Vertical venetian blinds jiggled at the window door which opened onto an outside fire-escape staircase.

'Packing to go somewhere, are we, Johnny?' Dampier asked.

It was as though Galic had been bitten by a snake. He spun round, mouth agape.

'Who's that?' an angry voice came from somewhere beyond the Serb. Brigadier Domedzic's voice.

Then I saw that the tall beech bookcase had been slid to one side on brass rails. The doorway beyond flickered with the blue light of televison monitors.

Of course – I should have expected as much from a former Stasi officer. I strode fast across the office before Galic could respond and stood at the entrance to the secret room.

There was a bank of CCTV monitors and tape recorders all along the wall of the long, narrow room where Domedzic stood at the control table stuffing tapes into another attaché-case. He had hidden cameras in most if not all the rooms in the SRO establishment. A quick glance showed me the conference room where heads of state were milling together with earlier than expected cocktails.

Another looked down like an out-of-body experience on the Prime Minister of Great Britain in earnest conversation with his Press and Private Secretaries. Yet another viewed the front courtyard. The bastard had seen and heard everything we'd been talking about.

'Game's up, chum,' I said, leaning against the door jamb.

The eyes widened in the gaunt, grey face for a second as he recognized me. But only for a second. Then he was again as calm and cold and calculating as ever. 'Don't be a fool, Coltrane,' he said softly. 'I'm answerable to the European Commission, no one else. As you can see, I've watched and heard the nonsense you've been bleating to your Prime Minister. You've got it all wrong, but I'll not explain that to you or a British court. This is a European matter.'

He had no compunction in pushing past me, clutching his attaché case, and striding into the office.

'I'm s–sorry, Brigadier,' Galic spluttered, still overtaken by the speed of our arrival. 'I locked the door – I swear it!'

Morgan Dampier smiled gently. 'There's no escape from justice this time, gentlemen.'

Domedzic ignored him. 'Close the cases and let's go.'

I watched, bemused, as Galic frantically snapped the cases closed and tried to work out how he was going to carry them all. 'If you didn't have so much you wanted to hide,' I said, 'you might have got away with it.'

'We have diplomatic immunity, Coltrane,' Domedzic snapped back. 'We're leaving and you cannot stop us.'

'On the contrary, old son,' Dampier said laconically. 'SAS troops have been ordered not to let anyone leave. Special Branch police are now on the premises to arrest all SRO members.'

'We have diplomatic immunity,' Domedzic repeated. 'Just look at the Genk Protocol.'

I smiled at that. 'Trouble with secret protocols, Brigadier, is that no one can read anything. By their very nature, they don't exist.'

My answer was smarter than I realized. I think it brought home to Domedzic for the first time that he really couldn't just walk and then talk his way out of this one. In one swift movement he grabbed at Dampier's collar and yanked the man towards him. I don't know where the gun came from but the snout of the automatic was suddenly jammed under Dampier's throat.

'You want to play hardball?' Domedzic hissed. 'I think that's what our American friends say . . . So just stay back and let us go. No one gets hurt. This is a matter for diplomats and international law, not you or your SAS hoodlum friends.'

Dampier must have been as tired and slow as I was to have let this happen. It was clearly time that we were both put out to grass to let younger blood take over. I kicked myself. And the SAS Directing Staff would have kicked us both even harder.

Domedzic motioned to Galic. 'Grab the cases and come with us.'

He started dragging Dampier back towards the open fire-escape door.

I hadn't even seen Dave McVicar's approach. He'd slipped up the outside steel staircase like a wraith and now stood nonchalantly outside the window. There was a 9mm Browning in his hand.

Domedzic must have sensed his presence and half-turned, dragging the hapless Dampier with him. 'Throw that gun down,' he ordered McVicar, 'or I'll blow this bastard's brains out!'

McVicar's own gun didn't waver. 'You're assuming he has any to blow out. Pull that trigger, Brigadier, and there's only one place you'll be for the next twenty years.'

Realizing that his boss's bluff wasn't going to work, Johnny Galic decided to take matters into his own hands. He reached inside his jacket towards his shoulder holster. The gun had barely cleared his lapel when McVicar's double-tap thudded into the centre of his chest and blew him halfway across the room. He skidded to an untidy halt on his back, blood pumping out onto the carpet. For several seconds his limbs twitched in involuntary spasm before he lay still.

Domedzic suddenly pushed Dampier away from him. In retrospect he might have been going to put his hands up.

But I didn't know that. He could have been using the abrupt movement to distract McVicar for a second to get his own shot in. It all happened so fast.

But then all speculation was irrelevant because my hand had already been inching behind my back to within reach of the automatic in my waistband. My fingers were already closing around the butt when Domedzic made his move.

It was the last move he ever made. I fired from the hip. It was a faith shot, directed by my anger and my sheer hatred of the man. Of course, I should have gone for the centre of the body, but all I could focus on was that cold, grey face.

The two rounds arrived almost simultaneously, the first creasing his cheek and ear, causing his head to turn away. So the second round smashed straight through his cheek and into his mouth. It must have severed the spinal cord at the nape of the neck where it joined the brain, because he just went straight down like a collapsing tower block. He was dead before he hit the floor.

One outflung arm knocked over the attaché case he'd hurriedly dumped by his side. It toppled over and the lid, left unfastened in his haste, fell open. An eddy of breeze from the fire escape set papers and photographs tumbling over the carpet in all directions.

Dampier, McVicar and I didn't speak. I think we were all too stunned at what had happened and at the suddenness of it all. We just looked at each other and at the carnage around the place.

When I glanced down at the floor, it came as a jolt to see what was staring up at me. It was Astrid's face.

I reached slowly down and picked up the photograph. I'd burnt all her pictures some time ago, but I'd never seen this one. It looked like it was a surveillance shot, grainy black-and-white, taken with a long-range telephoto. And it was beautiful. A classic snapshot, or moment in time. A full head shot, catching her as she turned her face towards something. Those eyes alert, slightly worried. A crease of a frown between her finely etched eyebrows. A glimpse of white teeth between the slightly parted lips. And the blurred whip of her pale hair as her head moved.

I stared at it for a long moment. This captured the essence of Astrid. It was simple and mind-stunningly beautiful. I wondered why Domedzic had kept it. Maybe he just liked looking at it.

Then the awful cold thought occurred to me. It had almost certainly been taken by that dwarf war pornographer. So even Zoran Mihac could capture pure beauty when he wanted to. Or was it just a fluke?

I shoved it carefully inside my parka, to lie flat against my chest.

Dampier said: 'This is all evidence, Ed. Don't take anything that isn't yours.'

'I haven't.'

It wasn't pictures of Astrid's face that a court would be interested in. I had no doubt that there would be plenty of filth in the file. Murder, rape and the sort of sick stuff that some weirdos get off on.

'I think we should get you out of here,' Dampier said, 'and far away. You're in quite enough trouble as it is. Give me the gun.'

I handed him the automatic. 'Who's taking the rap for this one?'

Dampier gave a wan smile. 'Mind if I claim the credit for your kill?'

McVicar nodded silently.

'It'll look better,' Dampier added. 'I'll leave Dave to look after things here. I'll call down our chopper and have you and Bex spirited away. Don't want the two of you around after I've briefed Special Branch.'

I followed him out into the corridor. A few yards farther

down the double doors of the conference room were open. There was quite a lot of noise going on. Before Dampier could restrain me, I stepped forward to the back of the crowd of European ministers and their most trusted advisers.

Above the heads of the onlookers, I could see the Prime Minister standing on the rostrum. He had his usual fixed smile, which looked distinctly nervous as his gaze darted around the room. As always he seemed not to look anyone in the eye.

'Gentlemen, gentlemen.' A little self-conscious giggle of a laugh. 'And the few ladies present, of course . . . I must first of all apologize hugely for the delay in keeping you waiting here at this Special Research Office facility in the UK. But the fact is that there have been some very serious and unexpected developments in the last few days . . . Which means that for practical reasons we are unable to go ahead today with the ratification–signing ceremony. Er – if, indeed, 'ceremony' is really the right word.'

A ripple of gasps and whispers ran through the gathering.

To defuse the situation, the Prime Minister added quickly. 'Please bear with me. In the next few days my ministers and civil servants will be in touch to explain the whys and wherefors of this unexpected postponement . . .'

I'd heard enough and turned away.

Bex was standing behind Morgan Dampier. She gave a crumpled little smile. I could see she was struggling to hold back her tears. 'Jude's last case, Ed. She got a result.'

'Sure, hon,' I said and put a comforting arm around her shoulder. I turned us away so that no one could see our tears. 'We got a result.'

Morgan Dampier had been talking on his radio. He looked uneasy. 'Your helo's coming in. Time the two of you weren't here. Follow me.'

With arms around each other's waists, we pushed our way through the bewildered throng of SRO staff, civil servants, plain–clothes SAS men, and now uniformed police from the Cambridgeshire Constabulary.

Moments later the three of us were outside. It was cold and refreshing as I looked up at the helicopter circling overhead.

All of a sudden I felt like I was walking on air. As though some great burden had been lifted from my shoulders. For the first time in seven years I felt like a free man again.

# Epilogue

I leaned on the balcony rail of the old timber beach house and stared out at the wide sweep of the bay. It seemed to stretch to infinity. Out there I could see the explosions of white in the azure swells as the dolphins broke surface in magnificent leaps.

The shadows were lengthening but the sun still hadn't lost its strength as it dipped towards the Atlantic horizon off the Namibian coast. I looked down at the photograph in my hands and wondered for the millionth time what I should do with it.

Bex's voice carried up to me in the aromatic smoke from the barbecue on the beach. 'Sun's over the yardarm, Ed. Supper in fifteen minutes.'

'I'll get some beers,' I replied absently, but I was still absorbed with the picture of Astrid. Well, I suppose it was Astrid. The more I looked at it the less it seemed like the woman I remembered, the woman I'd loved so dearly. It was as if the image was gradually, day by day, metamorphosing into someone else.

At last I looked away from it and down at Bex cooking giant *crevettes* on the oil drum beside the wooden steps. She'd lost weight in the two months we'd been here – all the fresh seafood bought from the beach fishermen, hard manual work and the clean air. Her statuesque figure was now honed and lightly tanned and she looked mouth-watering in the thin cotton bikini and casually draped sarong.

I think at that moment I knew why the photograph was changing.

Carefully I folded the print in half, and then quartered it and stuffed it into the back pocket of my denim shorts. Then I pushed aside the mosquito net and went inside to the kitchen area. I took four cans of Lion beer from the huge and ancient American refrigerator and returned to the wooden terrace.

It was then that I heard the old open-topped Land Rover labouring along the beach. Our top farm boy Isaac was at the wheel, smiling as always and waving energetically. Someone was sitting beside him. A battered straw fedora hid the passenger's face from view.

Bex stopped cooking, shielding her eyes against the sun, as the vehicle bounced over the last few flattened sand humps to the beach house.

'Boss! Miss Bex! You gotta visitor!' Isaac called out excitedly, killing the engine. 'He got to the farmhouse just half an hour ago!'

There was something distinctively suave about the newcomer as he stepped onto the sand. He was slim, had on canvas deck shoes without socks, but incongruously wore his white linen trousers rolled up to the knees. And his striped blue shirt with white collar just had to have come from Pink's in London.

'Sorry to intrude without warning,' the man said, removing his fedora, 'but no one was answering your phone.'

'Morgan!' Bex cried. 'What a lovely surprise!' She dropped the barbecue fork and rushed towards him. After giving him an enthusiastic kiss on the cheek, she added: 'We've been down here all day. Our first break in eight weeks.'

I clattered down the wooden steps, shook Dampier's hand and gave him one of the chilled cans. 'Christ, Ed, you certainly get your priorities right. I'm parched.' He ripped off the ring-pull and took a long and grateful swig, wiping his mouth with the back of his hand. 'So you bought the place, then?'

I grinned at him. 'Fell in love with it. Ten thousand acres with a small vineyard and olive grove with existing UK supply contracts. All for ninety thousand sterling. It was too good to miss.'

Dampier gave an uneasy smile. 'And I guess you didn't have too many options.'

Bex and I knew what he meant. After the events at the SRO headquarters we'd been whisked away 'for safe keeping' until everything could be 'sorted out'. And they could hardly have put us farther out of harm's way than this beach house in south-west Africa.

Locals called it Bluestone Bay, after the unusual colour of the rock formations on the headlands, although there was no actual name on the map. But it was also the brand they used on the farm's wine-bottle label, so it was good enough for us.

The farm had belonged to an Englishman who was a friend of the British ambassador. Fortuitously, the farmer was in the process of selling up, anxious to return to Europe for medical treatment.

We'd been in the happy position to hand him a cheque on the spot. Part of our "resettlement" money, as the government had called it. One hundred thousand pounds for each of us.

'Our hush money,' had been Bex's view at the time.

Two hundred grand between us was hardly a queen's ransom, but it perhaps showed the value that HM Government put on our risking our lives to expose the evil and corruption that we did.

'That money wouldn't have gone far in the UK,' I agreed. 'But you hinted there would be more to come.'

Dampier took another swig before replying. 'Ah, well, that's what I was told *then and there*, when the politicians were faced with a major crisis. Now that you've vanished from immediate sight, they seem to have developed amnesia. No one can remember saying anything of the sort.'

'It's getting dark,' Bex said, 'and the Land Rover's lights don't work. You must join us for supper and sleep over. I've got some gorgeous shark steaks in the kitchen.'

'You're most kind,' Dampier replied and watched her scamper up the stairs, Isaac following to help. Then my old colleague turned to me: 'So – not planning to return to the sunny UK, then, Ed?'

I lit a cigarette. 'Not immediately. To be honest, we haven't had a chance to think about it. We'd barely been here a week when the money came through and we were able to make our offer. After restocking – we're looking at specialist cattle breeds and ostrich – we'll have about sixty grand to invest. Income from abroad will be useful, living here.'

Dampier stared out at the sinking blood-red sun that had set the sky ablaze like a living Canaletto. 'Then that's just as well.'

I frowned. 'What d'you mean?'

'Just before I left London it was confirmed.'

'What was confirmed?'

'The murder charges still stand. If you or Bex set foot in Britain again – or anywhere within EU jurisdiction, for that matter – you'll be arrested on suspicion of the murder of Jude Sinclair.'

I stared at him. 'What sort of sick joke is that?'

Dampier grimaced. 'A politician's joke, Ed. I was informed personally by a junior government minister – and without a trace of irony – that they were unable and unwilling to influence the impartiality of the judicial system in any way. That's the way they put it. The police still have you and Bex down as the prime suspects and therefore the law must be allowed to take its natural course.'

Was I really that surprised? Perhaps I shouldn't have been, but I was. I felt totally betrayed.

'I heard that,' Bex said, climbing down the steps, carrying a plate of shark steaks. 'What about the evidence from the SRO headquarters?'

Dampier shook his head. 'What evidence? Talk about political impartiality . . . Virtually as soon as you two were flown out by helicopter, the PM told me that the Security Service was taking over the initial investigation on the grounds of national interest. The boys from MI5 moved in immediately and took over. That was the result of the PM's huddle with that bastard Press Secretary of his. The Special Branch plods stood around like spare pricks at a wedding.'

'And?' I asked.

'A complete news blackout for the best part of a week,' Dampier said. 'Internally to us and to the media. Then suddenly there's a report in *The Guardian* about the deportation of a gang of Serbian criminals for running an illegal immigration network.'

Bex could hardly believe it either. 'What about Fran?'

'The same day there's a small piece in *The Times* about French TV journalist Francoise Paquet having shot herself while on the run from the believed love-triangle murder of Jude Sinclair.'

'I shot her twice, Morgan,' Bex said emphatically. 'In the chest.'

Isaac had been busy opening more beers and handed another to Dampier. He accepted it and looked steadily at Bex. 'I recommend you never say that again, anywhere or to anyone. According to the story, Paquet's body was washed up after a week at sea. It was badly battered and decomposed. The weapon used was never found.'

I wondered if we'd achieved anything at all. 'And the SRO?'

The African twilight was closing in fast now and Dampier's

features were fading, highlighted only from the glow of the barbecue embers. 'Well, inasmuch as it barely existed at all officially, the building in Cambridgeshire has been razed to the ground and the farm sold on to a wheat-baron contributor to New Labour.'

'But the operation?' I pressed.

'The Special Research Office is being renamed – no decision yet. And the Genk Protocol definition of its functions is apparently being carefully reconsidered for a redraft.'

'For Christ's sake,' I said. 'Haven't those stupid idiots learned anything?'

'Not a lot,' Dampier answered. 'But it's the old established EU response to whistle-blowers. Destroy their credibility and careers . . . It happened to all of them. They like to get rid of the messengers.'

'So what next?' Bex asked. 'Have those bastards Bestelloli and Schmitt been arrested?'

Dampier allowed himself a hollow laugh. 'Not with Brigadier Domedzic dead! Everything was blamed on him . . . Well, dead men can't tell tales, can they? No, Bestelloli and Schmitt retired honourably and, having the *confidence* of the EU Commissioners, have since had an input into the reconstruction of the SRO.'

I stared up at the purple velvet of the sky as the first stars struggled to appear. 'So we've achieved nothing.'

'I wouldn't say that exactly.' He seemed to be searching desperately for some good news. 'The Serbs have gone and the criminal mafias will have taken a knock-back for a bit. And the Genk Protocol still isn't ratified. There'll perhaps be a few stronger safeguards . . . I wouldn't say *nothing.*'

'Next to,' I murmured, lighting another cigarette.

'What about Marcus's dossier?' Bex asked, opening another beer. 'The one you took away.'

Dampier cut into his shark steak, took off a succulent slice and almost groaned with ecstasy as he ate it. 'God, I have never tasted the like . . .' He wiped the running juices from his chin. 'The dossier? Well, of course, everyone knew you had it and MI5 pounced on Hereford almost as soon as the helo landed. The SAS isn't a law unto itself – despite what the public might think.'

For some reason my shark wasn't tasting so good. 'So another total waste.'

Dampier shrugged. 'I made sure that a lot of people in the Regiment and elsewhere knew the true story, Ed. Who knows, in ten years maybe this will all be the subject of an award-winning Channel Four documentary that no one will watch.'

'About sums it up,' I responded moodily. I knew I was looking for a target. 'Still, you can console yourself with that, Morgan, when you're retired on HMG's pension and cruising round the world.'

He'd demolished his steak already and belched lightly as he reached for the new beer that Isaac had offered him. 'You and Bex aren't the only ones who put your heads on the block, Ed. My boss was pensioned off with a severe financial loss – and so was I. I'm out, finished. That's what happens when you step in the way of the mighty European juggernaut.'

Bex and I both stared at him. The slippery Morgan Dampier finally caught out. It took a moment before he realized that we were looking at him. He seemed momentarily embarrassed and gave a little shrug. 'Well, certain people won't let some of the army's past Northern Ireland activities alone, keep prodding a stick into the hornets' nest. And now this. Someone decided it was time for me to reinvent myself elsewhere.'

'Where?' I asked.

He shrugged. 'Here? . . . On the way I saw a smallholding up for sale. Very reasonable.'

Bex frowned. 'So you might become a neighbour?'

Dampier's smile looked just a little drunk. 'I'm told this country could be going the same way as Zimbabwe. The government forcing white farmers to hand over to blacks and all that.'

I felt suddenly angry. 'So why even think about it?'

'Maybe one day they'll need help. You'll need help.'

Your sort of help, Morgan, I wondered? Christ, I hoped not.

Bex recognized that Dampier had had a can or two too many. 'Come with me, Morgan. Isaac will help sort out the spare hammock.'

Dampier struggled to his feet. I'd never, ever seen him this drunk. Something told me he was demob happy. Glad to be out of the sewers of intelligence work after so many years. He swayed slightly and tried to pat me on the back, but missed. I steadied him. 'Great to see you again, old son,' he slurred. 'Hope I haven't spoiled your evening.'

'C'mon,' Bex coaxed and supported him on one side while Isaac rushed to assist on the other and half-carry him up the steps.

I poured another beer and stared out towards the bay. Now that the talking had stopped the constant noise of the cicadas, broken only by the distant beat of the surf, seemed to swell up and cocoon me. The night was as warm and black and soft as velvet. Above me the stars were so bright and close that you really could believe you just had to reach up to touch them. It was many years since I'd sat under a sky like this.

For a moment I thought about Morgan Dampier's arrival and the news that he'd brought. Initially, I'd felt a huge sense of anger and betrayal – but then, what had I really expected?

Now the sad truth was, I didn't really care. Having spent many years of my life risking death and injury to defend its interests, I now found I wasn't sure that I loved my country any more.

What had happened to those sunlit uplands and the land fit for heroes that the hundreds of thousands of our fathers and grandfathers had fought and died for in two world wars? All that promise had been squandered by self-serving politicians and fat-cat civil servants while the people – the likes of me – had never really stopped to think for ourselves. We were too busy getting on with our lives, never asking questions, while trusting like children that our leaders would make the right, selfless and wise decisions . . .

No, I was relieved to be out of it. From now on I'd run my life, no one else. For good or ill, I'd be the master of my own destiny.

And my first act? I grinned bleakly to myself, lit a cigarette and pulled the crumpled photograph of Astrid from my pocket. I moved towards the barbecue and tossed it onto the dying embers. I watched it, mesmerized, for a second before it curled and then suddenly flared.

'Ed?'

I turned. Bex was on the steps. 'Morgan crashed?'

'Flat out in the hammock. What are you doing?'

'Astrid's photo. Her funeral pyre.'

She joined me, linked her arm in mine and watched the little spiral of blue smoke curl up towards the heavens. 'I think it was time, Ed.'

A spray of shooting stars darted across the sky like fiery arrows.

I handed her my can of beer. She put it to her lips, drank and looked at me. 'To a new beginning?'

I reached forward and kissed her lips, slowly.

When she eventually drew back, smiling, I said: 'A new beginning.'

# Author's Note

Readers may be interested to know that the fictional events described in this book are considered frighteningly plausible by experts whom I have consulted on the past and likely future development of the European Union.

We cannot know if there is a real-life equivalent of the secret Genk Protocol. But if there is, we will not be allowed to know until it is too late. If an internal security apparatus is in the making, the portents (given the EU's track record of secrecy and bad management) that it will be properly controlled and accountable are not good. The nations of Europe should beware.

If anyone still doubts where all this is heading, it should be remembered that over two years ago a pan-European intelligence unit called MI9 (yes, after the department responsible for operating Allied escape networks in wartime Europe) was established in Brussels. The British contingent comprises 'Foreign Office personnel attached to NATO as liaison officers'. It has access to the Echelon computer system. The United States, Ireland and Austria are not participants.

In June 2003 British troops were deployed to operations in the Congo under the European Union flag and command for the first time in history.

Anyone wanting to have a better idea of what is *really* happening on the big European issues – as Britain enters one of the potentially most dangerous periods of its history, with the whole world order in a state of flux — can find out more by visiting *www.eufactsfigures.com.*

(Sadly, events described at Snake Pass were not my invention but, like other stories in the Bosnian conflict, news of them was considered too horrendous to be broadcast to the general public at large.)

*Terence Strong*
*London 2003*

**POCKET
BOOKS**

This book and other **Pocket** titles are available from your bookshop or can be ordered direct from the publisher.

| | | | |
|---|---|---|---|
| 0 7434 2895 1 | **Last Man Standing** | David Baldacci | £6.99 |
| 0 7434 5005 1 | **Absolute Power** | David Baldacci | £6.99 |
| 0 7434 1555 8 | **Chosen Prey** | John Sandford | £6.99 |
| 0 7434 1556 6 | **Mortal Prey** | John Sandford | £6.99 |
| 0 7434 6823 6 | **The Third Option** | Vince Flynn | £6.99 |
| 0 7434 6825 2 | **Transfer of Power** | Vince Flynn | £6.99 |

Please send cheque or postal order for the value of the book, free postage and packing within the UK; OVERSEAS including Republic of Ireland £1 per book.

**OR: Please debit this amount from my**

VISA/ACCESS/MASTERCARD..............................................

CARD NO:.....................................................................

EXPIRY DATE.................................................................

AMOUNT £.....................................................................

NAME...........................................................................

ADDRESS......................................................................

...................................................................................

SIGNATURE...................................................................

Please send cheque or postal order for the value of the book,
**free postage and packing within the UK,** to
SIMON & SCHUSTER CASH SALES
PO Box 29, Douglas Isle of Man, IM99 1BQ
Tel: 01624 677237, Fax: 01624 670923
Email: bookshop@enterprise.net
www.bookpost.co.uk

Please allow 14 days for delivery. Prices and availability
subject to change without notice